The Farce News

Morgan E. Hughes

# The Farce News

2006

© Copyright 2006 Morgan E. Hughes
All rights reserved. No part of this publication may be reproduced, stored in a retrieval system, or transmitted, in any form or by any means, electronic, mechanical, photocopying, recording, or otherwise, without the written prior permission of the author.

Note for Librarians: A cataloguing record for this book is available from Library and Archives Canada at www.collectionscanada.ca/amicus/index-e.html
ISBN 1-4120-7975-6

*Printed in Victoria, BC, Canada. Printed on paper with minimum 30% recycled fibre.*
*Trafford's print shop runs on "green energy" from solar, wind and other environmentally-friendly power sources.*

## TRAFFORD PUBLISHING

*Offices in Canada, USA, Ireland and UK*

**Book sales for North America and international:**
Trafford Publishing, 6E–2333 Government St.,
Victoria, BC V8T 4P4 CANADA
phone 250 383 6864 (toll-free 1 888 232 4444)
fax 250 383 6804; email to orders@trafford.com

**Book sales in Europe:**
Trafford Publishing (UK) Limited, 9 Park End Street, 2nd Floor
Oxford, UK OX1 1HH UNITED KINGDOM
phone 44 (0)1865 722 113 (local rate 0845 230 9601)
facsimile 44 (0)1865 722 868; info.uk@trafford.com

**Order online at:**
trafford.com/05-2873

10 9 8 7 6 5 4 3 2 1

*The Farce News*

*For my kids,
Gwyn and Jack
with all my love;*


*For my friends,
Jim and Diana,
without whose love and support
this adventure would not have
come full circle;*


*For the memory of
Raymond Chandler,
whose stories made me want to read,
whose characters made me want to write.*

*The Farce News*

I think a man ought to get drunk at least twice a year
just on principle, so he won't let himself
get snotty about it.

*-- Raymond Chandler*

# The Farce News

*The Farce News*

## Chapter 1

Sometimes you just gotta ask yourself, "What the hell am I doing here?" It's not so much a geographical question as it is a kind of philosophical riddle, one that has more to do with personal experience than with momentary global positioning. "What the hell am I doing here?" Goes hand in hand with questions like, "What the hell do I know about extortion and blackmail, lying and cheating, murder and mayhem?" Other than what I see on the nightly news, that is.

Sometimes you just gotta ask yourself.

This was one of those times. So I asked the questions. Not out loud. I'm not insane, after all. But I did wonder, as I climbed out of my car and walked up the ritzy driveway to the house, if I was heading into some kind of twisted Laurel and Hardy tragicomedy. What the hell was I doing here? What kind of mess had I gotten myself into?

It wasn't just any old house I found myself approaching. It was one of those old money Prospect Avenue mansions, designed and built to make visitors feel poor just by looking at it. Set up on a hill, it had an expensive rear view facing West Hartford. Tudor in style (a popular architectural choice in the area), it had a roomy circular driveway behind a tall stone wall, done up in carefully selected beige and black gravel. Neatly trimmed hedge rows bordered the approach to the front entryway. The front door was heavy, perhaps oak, and ornately carved. The doorbell was brass and highly polished.

I left a thumb print on it when I gave it a push. Lovely chimes like distant church bells sounded. Without a blueprint to crib, there was no way of telling how many rooms the house contained. Could be a dozen. Could be forty. I wasn't even sure how many wings the place had. More than a Boeing 707, I'd guess, but fewer than a flock of gulls. It belonged to family, distant relations, but if I'd ever met any of them before, I couldn't recall. Would have to have been when I was only a small boy. I'd been living in town for several years now and had never been invited over. I suppose that's what comes of growing up on the wrong side of the tribal tracks. Now, I was perceived as useful, so now I was called upon to serve.

There are worse things than being estranged from remote relations. Like cold shoulders from friends. Or house pets who won't talk to you.

If I still smoked, I'd have lit up a cigarette while I waited for someone to answer the door, just so I could toss the butt on the front step and grind it underfoot when admittance was finally conceded. A little gratuitous? Perhaps, but you gotta find your fun where you can.

It took less than half-an-hour for someone to respond to my ringing. The woman who opened the door was a short, wiry Hispanic. She wore the traditional uniform of a housekeeper, her pale blue uniform cinched a little tight at the waist, the skirt stiff with starch. On her mocha face she wore the expression of one who harbors some deep suspicions, although whether her dubieties were specifically for me or directed at the world in general I couldn't say. What *was* clear was her palpable reluctance to grant me entrance. She guarded the hallowed halls behind her as if they were her very own, and looked upon my presence as she would if I were some kind of homicidal sex fiend. Or worse, a salesman.

I smiled and told her who I was and whom I'd come to see. She squinted at me and made a face. Clearly she wasn't buying.

"Choo got song identifikayching?"

Identification? Was she kidding?

"*Senora*, I'm not here to hawk Fuller brushes," I said, charming and witty as usual. I tried a smile I'd seen in a Mel Brooks film, but it had no effect whatsoever on her leery demeanor. "I was invited," I said. "Swear to God." I crossed my heart and held up two fingers, Boy Scout style. It was one more finger than she had coming, but I was willing to play it cool.

She remained steadfast, clearly not happy with me for taking her lord's name in vain. "How I know choo who choo say choo are?"

I wondered if she played this game with everyone who rang the doorbell. Maybe it was her version of civil disobedience. Maybe she just didn't like my face.

I produced my Connecticut drivers license and held it up for her inspection. It showed me with short hair and a mustache, features which had changed significantly since the photo was taken.

She studied it, did some calculations in her head, helped along by the fingers of one hand. Then she looked at me with renewed disdain. "Choo thirty-fy and still got a ponytail?"

"Thirty-eight, actually."

"Thirty-fy? Ain't choo a li'l ol' for dat?"

"Let's just say I'm still very much in touch with my inner child."

She snickered as if she were considering the merits of slamming the door on me. I would hardly have blamed her.

Only when I was able to correctly spell the name of the party I sought (or who sought me, if you want to get picky), did she relent. Still, it was with great hesitation that she ultimately stepped aside to let me in. And to demonstrate what little regard she held for the fact of my arrival or its purpose, she raised one castigating eyebrow at me and promptly turned on her heels and strode away. Her white rubber-soled shoes squeaked on the great marble floor like angry mice.

"Thanks," I said to her back. "I'll just get the door ..." But she was going, going, damn near gone.

The foyer in which she left me standing was only slightly smaller than the main lobby at the Metropolitan Museum of Art.

"Good thing I don't suffer from agoraphobia," I said, "or any real pangs of personal inadequacy." Too late. She was already out of earshot. I yelled: "Even when environmental cues -- such as these -- bring my socioeconomic shortcomings into such sharp relief." The maid paused, turned and scowled at me from a distance. Now that I had her attention, I lowered my voice, the relaxed college professor delivering the well-worn lecture, "This place may be bigger than my three-room apartment, but I'll bet my vacuuming doesn't take nearly as many hours as yours does."

She stood with her arms folded across her chest and peered at me with an expression of tweaked impatience. The punch line had better be worth the telling of the joke or she'd go away royally pissed. "So?"

"If only I owned a vacuum cleaner."

Her arms dropped to her side, her jaw dropped, and she gawked at me. "Hol' on a minute," she said. "Choo tellin' me choo don' hab a vachoon?" She stalked off, shaking her head, gesticulating somewhat madly, muttering in Spanish. I understood a couple of words. *Loco* was one. *Porco* was another. *Dios mio* was in there, too. The rest I could only guess at.

I had arrived fully girded to the possibility that the matron of the manse would, if only out of a lifetime of habit, treat me like the poor relation I was. However, I wasn't prepared for the domestic help to give me the bum's rush. Oh, well. It was Monday, after all, when indignities tend to pile up like crumpled cars in a bad highway wreck. Another week off to an inauspicious start.

Abandoned to cope with my shame in solitude, I wandered into a large empty sitting room and spent a couple of minutes checking out the furniture, gaping at the artwork on the walls and gathering material to bolster my position when it came time to pass judgment on the whole shebang, as is my basic custom. The overly stuffed couches and chairs had that rare quality of appearing to be both obscenely expensive as well as extremely uncomfortable, a combination which implicitly discouraged their practical use and all but guaranteed they would last forever, or at least well into the next millennium. Credit where it was at least moderately due, I noted that at least the paintings didn't appear to have been selected solely for their ability to complement the furniture.

I wondered if it was the principal occupant of this vast dwelling who'd done the decorating. I knew her alternately by the peculiar nickname *Ice Queen* as well as by the somewhat more traditional moniker *Auntie Peg.* She was a distant great-great aunt, several times removed by several convenient layers of familial hierarchy which had spared me from participation in much along the lines of personal interaction, and thus saved me from the constant reminder that my branch of the family was the one which suffered from comparative tree rot.

Auntie Peg was, for all intents and purposes, a total stranger, and one glance at the paintings confirmed that *strange* was the operative word. As I scanned the room, I concluded that the old bat had what could only be described as sociopathic tastes. Like an emotionally disturbed gourmand turned loose at the Saturday night all-you-can-eat buffet in some nondescript suburban shopping mall food-court.

On one wall, one could hardly fail to recognize the stunning beauty of a Van Gogh masterpiece, its swirling brush strokes and vivid colors. For all I knew, it was an outright fake, but it was no less sublime. Opposite the Van Gogh, however, I was startled to encounter a massive portrait, at least the size of a pool table, of Elvis Presley done on black velvet and set in a garish frame.

I blinked several times and actually rubbed my eyes to make sure I wasn't hallucinating. But it was the King. Decked out in his sequined Vegas jumpsuit with the ten-inch collars. Well into his last-gasp fatboy stage. The artist (which is to say, the miscreant individual responsible for committing this startling image to canvas) had successfully captured the essence of Elvis, from the suggested swagger in his hips right down to the beading sweat on his plump jowls, glistening in his pork chop sideburns. The only thing missing was a tray of peanut butter and banana sandwiches and the portable medicine chest.

A little out of breath, I wandered over to a pair of double doors that led out onto an enormous flagstone patio. The expanse of grass beyond the terrace was extraordinary, at least the size of a couple of football fields but without the white chalk yardage markers and bright yellow goal posts. I would hardly have been surprised to find the New England Patriots conducting practice in full swing, except that it was Monday and I figured they probably had the day off.

I was admiring the vast acreage behind the house when I spotted a dark-skinned kid in denim work clothes trudging across the endless lawn about a hundred yards away from where I stood. I watched him slip into a tool shed large enough to house a midsize family. Brief motion at one of the windows caught my eye and I suddenly had the feeling I was being watched. The guy had borne the same mocha complexion as the Puerto Rican maid who'd abandoned me in the foyer. He seemed to have her manners as well. When I waved casually toward the shed, he ducked away from the window.

As he did, the quiet was interrupted by footsteps behind me. I turned, assuming the maid had come to apologize for her inhospitable behavior. Instead it was a young woman, pale as death, blonde on blonde. Bleached out or naturally faded to near invisibility. I couldn't tell which. She had a wraithlike quality and I suddenly had the very tangible (if not very courageous) urge to hide behind something. From my inside jacket pocket, I retrieved my brand new prescription Ray Bans and slipped them on, effectively cutting the glare of the girl.

She approached with the swaggering grace of a bronze medal gymnast who hasn't quite mastered the balance beam, sashaying like an emaciated runway supermodel. She mixed it with the subtlety of a locomotive barreling through a small town at midnight. Her dead-straight hair wafted slightly in the breeze. Her shoulders jerked back and forth as she strode my way. I didn't hear music coming from anywhere, but this girl was definitely strutting to a tune. I guess it was playing only in the private recesses of her gray matter.

She wore the kind of peekaboo outfit teenagers seemed to favor: a tee shirt two sizes too small, baring a little too much midriff skin, and low-riding hip hugger bell-bottom jeans. If she was shooting for sex kitten she was coming up about eight lives short. I had the feeling she could turn around, bend over and show me the crack of her ass and she'd remind me more of a refrigerator repairman than any kind of legitimate temptress. And she looked seriously vitamin-deprived. Too much Britney. Not enough broccoli. As she edged closer, she smiled like a hungry piraña. Too much eye makeup and not enough clothing. A typical adolescent. But her eyes were older. She was no kid.

I smiled casually and waited for her to shatter the ice.

"Who let you in, cream puff?" she said. Being pretty intuitive, I was able to detect right away that this was meant as a challenge, a strategy to keep me off balance. "And what's with the hair? What is this, 1972?"

"Excuse me, 1972?"

"Answer the question. What's the matter? Don't you hear so good?"

"I hear just fine, thanks," I said.

"Good, then answer."

"Which question? You asked several. And I've already answered one of

them. Check the transcript if you don't believe me."
"Listen, I don't what your game is," she said.
"It isn't Monopoly," I said. "That's for sure."
"I'm guessing two can play."
"Actually, my game's solitaire, so you'd be wrong."
She studied me. "You're the world's prettiest gargoyle, aren't you?"
"Meaning?"
"Nuthin'."
"You don't find me pleasing? Is that what you're saying?"
"I haven't made up my mind yet. Are you a very tall midget?"

I stand six-two in socks and weigh 175 soaking wet. At the moment, I was wearing a pair of Tony Lama black-on-brown boots, the heels of which elevated me to a relative altitude of about six-four, making me taller than the City of New Orleans.

"I don't follow," I said.
"You're short."
"Short on patience, maybe" I said.
"Oh, really?" She put her hands on her hips and rolled her fingertips nervously. "You don't look much like a doctor. Maybe a vet. You're not a veterinarian, are you?"
"Nope."
"Then why'd you say you were a doctor?"
"Did I?."
"I believe so."
"Well, don't believe everything you hear."
"I rarely do."
"Me neither," I said. In fact, I was having a hard time believing I was actually having this *non compos mentis* conversation with this odd young woman. If someone offered me a straight jacket, I'd gladly put it on.
"So, we've established that you're not a doctor. Or a vet."
"I can't afford the insurance," I said. "Plus I hate elephants."

As she stared at me I began to be concerned at her lack of a natural blinking mechanism. Could she be on some medication? "Let me guess," she went on. "I'll bet you think those shades make you look cool or something."

I took the glasses off and looked them over. "They're brand new. Just got 'em this morning."

"Congratulations. When is the ticker-tape parade?"

"Don't you like them?" I rather liked them, although admittedly they were tinted perhaps a bit too close to pitch black. I had asked for something extra dark to keep the sun's harsh glare off my eyes. Like a lot of blue-eyed night

*The Farce News*

crawlers, I'm sensitive to daylight. But in all fairness, what I ended up with should have come with a white cane, a dented tin cup, and a ratty piece of cardboard with *Help the needy* scrawled in black magic marker. Not one to complain, I had accepted the new glasses and filled out the appropriate insurance forms -- even though like forty million other 21st century Americans I can't afford health insurance. And even if I could, it was doubtful the shades would have qualified for reimbursement.

That was only a couple of hours earlier. The *first* indignity of the new week. Later, as I wandered up and down Asylum Avenue hunting for my car, I realized that the glasses, spiffy as they were, had a fundamental problem. The dark lenses tended to make all the parked cars look strikingly similar, particularly the dark ones. For example, my key didn't work on a certain black BMW 325i that vaguely resembled my 1987 VW Jetta, but it did get the Beemer's anti-theft alarm going loud enough to wake the dead. It was an honest mistake and I did my best not to look like some petty car thief as I sprinted blindly from the scene. After that, I had pocketed the Ray Bans and made my way squinting like a newborn mole.

"They're prescription," I said to the girl, apropos of nothing.

My day, clearly, was not improving much with the sluggish passage of time. But, Mondays can be that way. Tuesdays, too. Wednesdays? Why do you think it's called "hump" day?

She looked me over with new skepticism. "What's with the jacket?"

"How do you mean?"

"The flowers," she said, as if it were obvious. "Kinda faggy, don't you think? In a faggy sort of way?"

Honestly, I had been so encouraged at the prospect of a paying gig that didn't take place in a bar, I had even dressed up for the occasion. Instead of my usual uniform of blue jeans and a sweatshirt, I had put on my favorite black suit. It most closely resembles the color of charcoal. It's not only my favorite suit but also my *only* suit. It's a snappy Western get-up, the kind Hank Williams, Sr., himself would have been proud to wear. Or so I like to think. With it I wore a button down shirt, unbuttoned at the collar. My tie (my *only* tie), which features silver Stanley Cups on a navy blue field, was loosely knotted in what might be described as a rakish manner, and hanging on a hook on the inside of the door of my bedroom closet. I hate ties (even that one) and wear it only to funerals, weddings and other somber occasions characterized by widespread grieving and excessive drinking. My suit pants were neatly creased. My socks were clean. My two-tone Tony Lama shitkickers were shined and my hair was combed back into a neat ponytail and gathered in a slim brown leather strap.

*The Farce News*

Cleaned up and neatly coifed, I was feeling pretty good about myself. I hadn't taken a drink in anger since Shrub & Chicanery and that band of lawless pirates had done a reverse Robin Hood on the 2000 presidential election. I had quit drinking and switched to Afghanistan black heroin to blunt the pain. But Afghani smack is pricey and those Taliban shitheads weren't offering discounts. I'd gone back to booze as finances and bouts of depression dictated, and once in a while I indulged in a weekend bender just for the sheer fun of it. But never in anger. At the moment I was sober and clear-eyed, steely in my determination to complete a meaningful task. And put some money in the bank, if only for novelty's sake.

All I needed was a focus for all this ironclad resolve. Instead I was faced with a smart-ass cock-tease to whom I was, sadly, related, if only remotely. Hell if I was about to take the bait when she began to chide me about my prized jacket. "It's traditional Western garb." If I'd worn a cowboy hat for the occasion, this would have been the perfect moment to tip it in one of those hokey "Howdy, ma'am" gestures.

She stared at me. "Yeah, whatever. I know a guy who wears a big yellow straw cowboy hat with pinstripe suits. He's kinda spooky."

"That's nice," I said.

"So, what's your name, wise guy? You have a name, don't you? Or are you traveling incognito? Hieronymus the Anonymous?"

I gave her question some thought. My choices were simple. I could give it to her straight and be done with the topic. Or I could feed her a line of bullshit, string her along like a fish at the end of the line, toy with her, play some petty, meaningless mind games.

For the record, my name is Robert Vaughn. Which doesn't thrill me as it once did. I share the name with a moderately famous, sharp-featured actor best known for his role as Napoleon Solo in the 1960s television series *The Man From U.N.C.L.E.* and, more recently, for hawking the services of a local Hartford law firm on late night TV ads. My friends call me Robby. My enemies call me other things, sometimes to my face depending on how much they dislike me or how brave they're feeling at the time.

"It's Carter," I said. "Jimmy Carter."

"So, Jiminy," she said. "You don't mind if I call you Jiminy, do you? Like the cricket?" It wasn't a question so much as a reiteration of a fact she had already opted to take for granted. "I'm a Cancer. *Please* don't tell me you're a Sagittarius."

"Tropic of Emphysema," I said.

She didn't smile. Neither did she frown. She simply stared at me as if I were one of the paintings hanging on the wall in the big sitting room. Again I was struck by the lack of brightness in her eyes.

She looked at me without a spark of anything resembling real curiosity, as if she'd stared at me a thousand times before and didn't see the details anymore. I have this effect on people. Girlfriends mostly. Wives once in a while. Not my own wives, of course, never having been married. Usually it takes a little longer to induce the 10,000-yard gaze in the opposite sex. This one came in under than five minutes. A new personal record. Maybe if I'd said Sagittarius, things would have worked out differently. Probably not.

She reached into the back pocket of her hip huggers and brought out what looked like a half-eaten bar of salt water taffy. Without taking her eyes of me, she peeled back the wrapper and stuck the exposed end of it between her teeth. They were very beautiful, white and perfectly straight. Looking blandly into my eyes, she pulled slowly on the taffy. It wasn't immediately clear what emotion she was attempting to affect.

I yawned.

Watching her work the taffy, I was transported back to my childhood in New York City and family outings we took to Coney Island. The poor man's seaside holiday. The subway ride from Manhattan took hours, which added to the sense of getting away. But it was worth it for the foot-long hot dogs at Nathan's, even though they invariably made me sick to my stomach. And the roller coaster rides, even though they, too, often made me want to puke. Hell, I even loved the filthy beach and its garbage strewn sand. I had no qualms about splashing around in the polluted Atlantic Ocean. So many interesting souvenirs washed ashore. Some of them you could even pick up without first pulling on thick rubber Haz-Mat gloves. And if you accidentally swallowed a mouthful of Atlantic Ocean tidal wash, it was no big deal, since this particular stretch of ocean water was famous for its capacity to induce spontaneous vomiting. *Ipecac Beach*.

I loved everything about Coney Island but the taffy. To my mind, taffy was stupid and pointless, totally flavorless (apparently by design) and dangerous -- capable of ripping your teeth out by the roots if you weren't careful. Where was the fun in that? It was as idiotic as cotton candy, just not as sticky.

As I watched my petulant distant cousin pull her taffy and yank my chain, my teeth began to ache. I solemnly wished she would retreat to her room and resume instant messaging her friends or whatever she did when she was pretending to be a teenybopper. Just so long as she left me off her dance card.

"How old are you?" I said. "If you don't mind me asking."

"Twenty-six," she said. "Why?"

"Just curious," I said. "You seem to be shooting for seventeen."
She pouted. "I'm twenty-six. Swear to God and hope to die."
"I'd have said eighteen, nineteen at the most."
"My drivers license says twenty-six. Wanna see it?"
"No, not really."
She stared at me and took another bite of taffy.
"So, do you like candy?"
I shrugged. "Four out of five dentists recommend I steer clear of temptation. Sugarless gum seems to be okay -- in moderation."
"Moderation? I hate moderation. I'm just an old fashioned girl."
"Whenever I chew gum, I seem to bite my tongue. Hurts like hell."
"Clumsy," she said.
"You have quite the sweet tooth, don't you?"
"Oh," she said, nodding. "You don't know the half of it."
"I'll bet I can guess the rest."
She smirked. It was a whole new expression. Kind of cute. I wish she'd shown it to me sooner. "Yeah, well, don't lose any sleep over it."

She reached into her mouth and removed the wad of taffy, pulpy and pink. She kneaded it into a ball, then turned and hurled it into the distance. I tracked its trajectory for a moment, then lost sight as its arc took it toward a stand of pine trees. She had a hell of an arm.

"Play any baseball?" I asked. "I think the Red Sox are looking for starting pitching."

She smirked some more. "The Red Sox," she said, "are *always* looking for starting pitching."

"Good point."

She turned and stared into the distance, as if searching for the spot where her wad of taffy had disappeared. "Gee, I hope some poor little squirrel doesn't choke to death on that," she said. Then she giggled. "So, Jiminy, what are you doing here anyway?"

"I was invited."

"Oh, really? By whom? If you don't mind me asking?"

"Margaret Waddley-Wordstone."

"No shit?" she said, surprised. "What could someone like *her* possibly want with someone like *you?* What it is you do, anyway? Rustle horses? We don't have any horses. Are you part of some gay rodeo?"

More jokes about my jacket. Real funny.

"As a matter of fact, I'm a musician by trade."

"What does that mean, *by trade?*"

I considered telling her it was just an expression, a form of speech. But,

*Oh, hell.* "I started out as an engineering student, years ago. But I kept misplacing my slide rule and forgetting to carry the decimal point. I took it as a sign and asked to be moved."

"I don't get it."

"The musicians' union needed steel workers, so they arranged a swap. They picked me up for two minor league draftsmen and an architect to be named later."

She stared at me. "You're making fun of me, aren't you?"

"It's possible," I said. "I'll have to check the transcript."

"So, you're some kind of musician?"

"Yeah, some kind."

"What do you play, the violin?"

"Now who's making fun?"

"So, what then? What kind of music?"

"Kind of a honky tonk thing, mostly."

"Yeah? So, what's your thing? The mandolin? The *dobro*?"

"Steel guitar."

"You mean the *pedal* steel guitar?"

"Yeah."

She shook her head. "Never heard of it," she said flatly.

"Very funny."

"J.K. Have a sense of humor. I know all about it. Pedal steel. That's the whiny, irritating thing that sounds like a couple of alley cats having sex in a centrifuge."

"Nice," I said. "No wonder you have so many friends."

She looked at me funny. "What's *that* supposed to mean?"

"Forget it. J.F.K."

At that moment, the maid reappeared, clearing her throat. Without another word the blonde girl turned and sprinted toward the house, waving over her shoulder. "Bye, Jiminy!"

"Chee a wil' one," the housekeeper said, shaking her head in what I judged to be rather poorly disguised loathing. "*Puta.* Don't nobody can't control her no more."

"And that was ..."

"Lita Wordstone, of course," the maid said.

"Of course," I agreed.

"Chee one of the granddaughters."

One of the heiresses to the Wordstone frozen yogurt fortune. A girl with millions in her future and nothing but boredom in her present.

"Choo know son'thing?" the Puerto Rican maid said. "Yust between choo an' me? If chee was my kid, I slap the chit out of her. Then, no more *puta*. But tha's yust me."

I couldn't help but wonder why the maid was so hostile. And why she was confessing to me, a virtual stranger, that she wanted to slap the *chit* out of her wealthy employer's granddaughter. Didn't seem right.

"Don't get me wrong," I said, "I'm no Henry David Thoreau. And nobody's ever going to mistake me for Mohandas Gandhi ..."

"Jess, for one thing, choo way too tall," the maid said. "And pale."

"The point is, I'm not necessarily a pacifist."

"Like the ocean?"

"On the other hand, I don't advocate corporal punishment, either. It's a major problem, granted, but in general I believe it is best handled in private. In any case, I've been around a little bit and have not yet seen definitive proof that slapping the *chit* out of anyone ever accomplishes anything. At least not anything positive."

"Chore, that's easy for choo to say. Choo don' know her like I do."

"True," I said. "Irrelevant, but true."

"Once choo get to know her, bam!" The maid slapped her hands together. "Choo gonna wanna slap the chit out of her yust like me."

I decided that arguing with the help, particularly when I was on the verge of hiring on and thus joining her ranks, might not be such a smart idea. So I let it drop.

"Anyway, choo follow me now," the maid said. "Tine to see the boss. Chee waiting for choo in the lib'ary."

"With the wrench?" I asked.

The maid turned and stared at me. "What choo say?"

"Nothing."

## Chapter 2

In fairly short order, I had overcome the recalcitrant Puerto Rican housekeeper's attempt to bar me, and successfully traded pithy quips with the candy-coated granddaughter, Lita. With my confidence renewed and my rapier wits sharpened to a veritable razor's edge, I was fully braced for my meet-and-greet with the fabled matriarch of the manor, the Ice Queen herself, my dear old Auntie Peg, known in formal circles as Mrs. Margaret Waddley-Wordstone.

I damn near slipped my Ray Bans back on, but thought better of it at the last moment. The last thing I needed was some kind of Three Blind Mice routine with the Puerto Rican maid introducing me to the old lady, and me saying, "Keep talking, I hear you. Oh, there you are, a little to the left ..."

We marched down a series of long hallways and finally arrived at a set of heavy wooden doors. I assumed the library was on the other side. The maid slowed her pace and spoke over her shoulder. It was a hissing conspiratorial whisper. "Whatever choo do, don' laugh."

"Excuse me?" I said, shrewd as ever.

"I said, *don' laugh.* At hare, I mean. Chee don' like nobody not to laugh at hare." Her tone betrayed a growing impatience with me.

"What do you mean, *don't laugh?* Why would I laugh?"

The maid put up a dark, meaty little hand, the fingers like a row of ballpark franks. Our conversation was officially over.

"I get it," I said, going along with the charade. "We haven't spoken?"

She shook her head at me. And with that, stepped to the ornately carved wooden doors. She turned both knobs and pulled the doors open. A gust of arctic air swept over us. Then the housekeeper stepped to one side so I might enter.

"Goo' luck," she hissed, not looking at me. "Choo gonna need it."

I turned around, took a couple of steps into the library and immediately slammed on the brakes. Swear to God, If I'd been wearing rubber soled shoes like the Puerto Rican housekeeper instead of my leather bottom boots, I'd probably have left tread marks on the carpet. Such was my initial response to this shocking Brobdingnagian chamber of horrors. It was so cold I could see my breath (which usually only happens following a long night with a bottle of Tennessee bourbon). It was also intensely damp and gloomy and had the ghastly odor of artificial air freshener one expects to find in bus station restrooms. It was a huge dank cavern, missing only the dripping stalactites and bats hanging from the ceiling. I could only guess the room's dimensions. But if it were less than 1,500 total square feet, I'd have been surprised (and disappointed in my hitherto inestimable powers of estimation).

I've been around, traveled here and there, spoken bits and pieces of two or three languages and seen the extremes of the human condition at its best and worst, but nothing could prepare me for this room. This was like some scholarly death chamber where books -- be they good, bad or merely mediocre -- came to die. I was willing to wager that at least one copy of every book published was in here somewhere, crammed into shelves, stacked on tables, shoved under chairs.

Suddenly, my side of the tracks seemed rather tame, the grass not so brown after all. I couldn't wait to learn if Auntie Peg was responsible for this pandemonium, and whether it was a purposeful expression or the byproduct of steadily deteriorating mental acuity. I'd heard she was nuts. I was starting to think at least some of the family gossip was true.

A fire place with a complete set of living room furniture dominated one end of the room, and several smaller clusters of chairs and tables with reading lamps on them were set about the rest of the vast space. The ceiling had to be sixteen feet. An elaborate chandelier dangled from its center. Every inch of wall space not interrupted by a door or a heavily curtained window was covered in floor-to-ceiling shelves. Two rolling ladders were attached to railings fastened to brackets along the two longer walls, and an oversized rolling step ladder sat idle. It was big enough to be used by passengers boarding a midsize private jet. At present it was landlocked by stacks of books. Its rolling days were over.

Elsewhere about the room, every flat surface -- every tabletop, every seat cushion, every window sill -- was piled high with books of all size and shape and category. Hardcovers, paperbacks, coffee table tableaus. What looked like two dozen or so copies of Douglas Adams' *Long Dark Tea Time of the Soul* were stacked on the same table beside a collection of unauthorized investigative exposes which promised to reveal the behind-the-scenes secrets of cast members on the TV hit, "Friends." There were volumes of French philosophy and stacks of Greek pornography. Shelves of Native American mysticism and basketloads of radical Lesbian manifesto stuff. All piled one on top of another in a kind of literary orgy. I didn't see any sign of Truman Capote, but I was willing to bet ten bucks he was in there somewhere trying to scratch and claw his way to the top of the pile.

A low-level hum attracted my attention and I looked over at a huge industrial air conditioning unit that had been placed under one of the tall windows.

The venting had been expertly hidden. At least I knew why it was so damned cold.

In the center of this maze of old paper, cardboard and leather, there sat a woman in a very large stuffed chair. At least I thought it was a very large stuffed chair. On closer inspection it turned out to be a very large stuffed woman seated in a comparatively small chair. The chair seemed to be struggling for its very survival under the burden of its occupant's prodigious weight. For a moment I thought I heard it groan.

So this was my fabled dear old Auntie Peg, the eminent Mrs. Margaret Waddley-Wordstone. It was about time we'd met. All of the stories I'd heard growing up had hardly done her justice. Seems justice is in fact, at least in some cases, blind, and has a shoddy memory.

She was quite a specimen, although I'm not sure any established branch of organized modern science has yet conceived (to say nothing of constructed) a test tube or Petri dish capable of hosting her elephantine proportions. I couldn't help but feel that even the most crass and unfeeling of carney barkers would probably resist the temptation to give public utterance to this matron's grand obesity.

Her head was quite large and haloed in a crown of golden ringlets. A wig perhaps? Her face, while quite bloated, was oddly dwarfed by the surrounding mass of unruly curls. Her eyes were dark and beady, imbedded in puffy flesh and traced in unsteadily applied mascara. Though her cheeks were heavily rouged, the crimson splotches could not completely conceal the pale skin that lay beneath what looked like a veneer of pancake make-up. It could have been waffle mix. Or spackle. Her mouth was painted a peculiar shade of maroon, like the lips of a corpse. She had several chins which closely resembled a stack of flesh colored automobile tires on which sat her large cranium. She wore a gilded robe with loose fitting sleeves. I'm not a religious man but I stopped to thank whatever God is in charge of such things that the robe reached well down past her knees and covered her all the way down to the ankles, leaving only a glimpse of black satin slippers in which two disproportionately miniscule feet were snugly cocooned.

I advanced cautiously, unsure of how best to proceed. What little confidence I had reconstituted prior to entering this room was now shot to hell. My mental clutch had gone mushy. Not only was I no longer braced for this encounter, I would have given my eye teeth for the use of a back brace to help me maintain my posture, which was beginning to sag. Questions of etiquette sprinted across my mind like streakers at a tennis match. (I tried to ignore them but they kept waving and laughing, enjoying the spectacle they made of themselves.) Should I offer this woman -- who was, after all, a distant relation -- my hand in greeting? I could feel the maid's eyes staring at me from the doorway where she stood silently watching, and no doubt shivering.

"Meesta Vaughn!" my great aunt said, looking up at me from her chair, smiling and bearing her pearly teeth. Her voice was as brittle as roof slate, harsh as the winter wind. In it one could hear the shriek of a predatory arctic bird, as well as the scream of a dentist's final victim.

"Mrs. Wordstone," I said, bowing my head slightly.

"Oh, caw me Onty Peg, won't you?" she said, or howled.

"Okay, sure," I said. "Auntie Peg."

"I am so vewwy sawee about the tempoo-a-tooa in this wooom," she said. Her manner was surprisingly regal, in contrast to her unfortunate oral handicap. Nobody ever mentioned a speech impediment. I tried to discern the presence of a harelip, but saw no sign of one. You know the rich. All the inbreeding.

"There are pahkahs avaiwaboo, if you pweefooa..."

I did a quick mental Google search and came up with a rough Gibberish-to-English translation: There are parkas available, if you prefer. Or words to that effect.

"I'm fine for the moment," I said. My first lie.

"Vewwy good," she said. "May I offer you anyfing?"

"No, really, I'm fine," I said, again. My second lie.

"Maybe a wuvwee dish of delicious ice queen?"

"Excuse me?" I said.

"Ice queen. We have evwee fwavah. Name you pwehzuh."

The maid had taken up position at Mrs. Margaret Waddley-Wordstone's elbow. She was indeed shivering against the cold, but steadily giving me the eye, and having a hell of a good time, too. Daring me to laugh out loud. I bit the inside of my cheek. Hard. I tasted the salty warmth of my own blood. Now *there's* a flavor I'll bet Auntie Peg didn't have in the freezer. Although you never could tell.

"Wosa," Mrs. Margaret Waddley-Wordstone said, turning to the maid, whose name I now registered as Rosa. "Pweeze pweepah ouah guest a nice dish of peppahmint pistachio ice queen, with whipped queen and a chewwy on top."

"Si, senora," said the maid, rather too obsequiously.

"No, really," I said, but I could see it was no use.

Mrs. Margaret Waddley-Wordstone shrieked again. "Ice queen! Bwing the ice queen."

And with that, Rosa, one hand held tightly to her mouth, gave me another look and ran from the room.

*The Farce News*

Auntie Peg pointed a fat hand and directed me to find a chair and pull it closer. She told me in her high-pitched howl how she hated to have to raise her voice. I removed a stack of Tony Hillerman mysteries from a high-backed Windsor chair and placed them carefully on the floor. I smiled at the old lady and rubbed my hands briskly together. They were starting to get the same shade of blue Mrs. Wordstone wore from head to toe. I smiled at her again, then cupped my hands and blew into them. Vapor trials escaped through my fingers.

"Meesta Vaughn," she said, peering expectantly at me. "May I speak stwait wiff you?"

"Please," I said.

Auntie Peg let out a lungful of air. "Oh, thank God," she said, dropping the pretense of a speech defect. "Honestly, sometimes I get so tired of putting on that ridiculous show. It's just for the help, you know. They're so easily amused. I know it's wrong, but I'm afraid I just can't help myself. Before Rosa came to me, I had a girl from a little town near Montreal who was utterly convinced I had a harelip and a clef pallet. *Brioche* was her name. How she would regale me with stories about someone called Rocket Richard, a professional ice hockey player of some distinction if I recall correctly. She even had a tattoo of this Rocket person on her ankle. In return I'd give her my full harelip gag. What a funny girl she was. Brioche. I believe she thought I was mildly retarded. Poor thing. It was probably wrong of me to lead her on. She moved to Raleigh when the Hartford Whalers left town. She took that game entirely too seriously, if you ask me."

I stared silently at her. I was thinking about regaling her with a story of my own, the one about the invited guest who runs screaming from the library, holding his head in both hands, hoping it's all just a bad dream and that he hasn't in fact lost his mind.

"Now, Robby," she said, smirking at me in a way that reminded me somewhat of Rosa, but even more mischievously. "Please close your mouth unless you have something cogent to add to our conversation."

I clamped my jaw shut. "Sorry."

"Why don't you help yourself to one of the parkas?" she said, pointing at a coat tree near the heavy wood doors. "You'll feel better."

What the hell, I thought. No use freezing to death before I found out what this was all about. I got up again and crossed the room, trying not to knock anything over along the way. What a nut house. Someone should move this place and all its occupants over to Asylum Avenue. I found a red, white and blue ski jacket with *Patriots* emblazoned across the shoulders. It looked to be about my size, 40 Long. I slipped it on and found a pair of gloves in the pocket. I pulled them on. They were already warm, which gave me the creeps.

Mrs. Margaret Waddley-Wordstone -- who, it suddenly occurred to me, wasn't quite far enough removed for comfort -- addressed me in a tone that in no way resembled the raptor's screech I'd first heard, but was instead throaty and rough, and very possibly just as phony as the two previous voices. Now she was the mafia don who's smoked one too many truckloads of highjacked cigarettes. She explained that she kept the room at twenty-two degrees Fahrenheit because, in her words, she tended "to overheat rather easily." I smiled. In her condition, it probably took a Herculean effort to raise a fuss, let alone a limb. "You see," she said, leaning over, suggesting that she was about to impart a great hidden secret to me, "I'm rather fat."

What could I say? If she was waiting for me to dispute the fact, we were both going to grow old in silence.

"I've lived a long, long time. That's how I got to be this old. To say nothing of this fat."

I nodded, wondering if I should write any of this down. "I see."

"Now, I'm tired. Exhausted, really. All I ever want to do is sleep."

I thought of another possible explanation. *Hypothermia.*

At this moment, Rosa the Puerto Rican housekeeper returned. I never heard the door open. She was damn good at this business of coming and going in sneaky silence. I wondered if there was some school of stealth from which modern domestics were required to graduate before hiring on. I'd have to watch my back.

Rosa carried a silver tray. On it was a blue and white ceramic bowl filled with green ice cream topped with fluffy white whipped cream and a bright red cherry. The tray also held a cut glass bottle and a crystal highball glass. The glass was empty. The bottle was three quarters full. The liquid within was amber. I hoped it was bourbon and that I'd get some. Rosa put the ice cream in front of me. Then she poured an unhealthy shot of liquor into the highball glass and presented it to the old lady. I wasn't offered any. Rosa shrugged and slipped away.

I looked back and forth from my dish of green ice cream to the old woman's glass, poorly concealing my displeasure. She seemed to read my mood. But I quickly learned that the her interpretive skills left a lot to be desired.

"Don't feel too badly for me," she said. "It is a small tragedy that I may no longer indulge my favorite vice -- ice cream. And it is but a small consolation that I take any pleasure at all from a rather expensive reserve of malt whiskey. This one is from Scotland, I believe. Twenty-six years old if I remember correctly."

"Did you say *twenty-six*?" I wiped spittle from the side of my mouth.

In a somewhat shaky hand, she tipped back the heavy glass and drained its contents in a single swallow.

I watched jealously. Part of me hoped the old bat would choke. It would serve her right for being so selfish. Of course, she didn't choke. She didn't gag. She didn't even swallow hard. This was a boozer. She was a drinker's drinker, just not a particularly generous one.

"Ah," she said, putting down the empty glass. "That's a little better." She smiled and displayed her slightly maroon teeth. "But you're not eating your ice cream. What's the matter? Don't you like pistachio? I thought *everyone* loved pistachio."

I looked down at the ice cream and weighed my options. None of them, alone or collectively, provided me the kind of leverage I needed to hold this 800-pound gorilla at bay. If I passed on the pistachio, she'd no doubt insist on some other flavor. On the other hand, I could play the gracious guest and simply eat the pistachio, despite the arctic climate of the room. But this strategy fell under the general heading of "adding insult to injury" and chipped away at my peeling self-respect in a way I found untenable. I could always get up and walk out, but that would mean no paycheck, and I wasn't particularly enthusiastic about rejoining the ranks of the unemployed so soon after landing this new (albeit increasingly peculiar and unappealing) opportunity.

"What is it you wanted to see me about?" I asked.

"Do you like books?" she said, studying me.

"Sure," I said, glancing about the room. "I'm not what you'd call a collector or anything. I leave that sort of thing to the professionals. You know. Librarians. Bookstore owners. Literary aficionados. Intellectual posers."

She ignored my commentary much the way I was ignoring my ice cream. "I believe the smell of dust and decay which emanates from these millions upon millions of pages is representative of a life lived to its fullest. Wouldn't you agree?"

I might have agreed if I knew what she was talking about. Since I wasn't at all sure and didn't want to say the wrong thing, I merely shrugged -- the international symbol for indifference. "I guess," I said.

She raised one eyebrow at me. That or she suffered from a facial tic I hadn't noticed before.

"Brilliantly annunciated," she said. "Simply marvelous how you're able to boil it down to the essence so seamlessly."

Great, now she was mocking me. First the girl, then the maid, now the old coot! I reached for the goddamn dish of green ice cream with the cherry on top and tried to manipulate the spoon gracefully despite the insulated ski gloves on my hands.

She watched me eat for a moment. In her face I saw the same kind of feverish envy I'd probably exhibited while she was knocking back the malt whiskey.

"I don't suppose you brought a resume with you?" she said.

I shook my head in the negative. I don't even have a resume. With a mouthful of pistachio ice cream, I told her as much. She suggested that, in lieu of a *curriculum vitae,* I fill her in on some of the *salient* details of my life experience to date. All she knew was that I was the son of a distant cousin several times removed -- the New York side of the family as opposed to the Connecticut side. For the first three and a half decades of my life, that morsel of data had been plenty, but now, now that she needed some help of some kind, she wanted to know more about me. Such as, would I steal the silver if left unattended? I wasn't exactly flattered. But at least it gave me an excuse to stop eating the ice cream. I pondered the meaning of "salient" and how she was using it Was it the same as "interesting" or more along the lines of "relevant"?

There wasn't that much to tell, but I gave her the shortest version I knew. Dropped out of college after two years to pursue a career in music, and was now only semi-regularly employed. There just weren't enough gigs these days, at least not like the old days.

"Gigs," she said. "What an odd expression. Please, go on. This is all most fascinating."

Did she say *almost* fascinating?

I told her I shared a small apartment in Hartford with a medium sized mutt named Rufus and two teenaged cats, Buddy and J.D., and that much to my chagrin none of them ever kicked in so much as a dime toward food or rent. I admitted that my latest girlfriend, Bonnie, had not returned any of my calls nor been in touch for three weeks now (or was it four?) and I was beginning to think it might be over.

"Children, young Robby? Any children?"

"Not that I know of."

"Excuse me?"

I told her I'd never been married.

"By choice?" she asked.

"As a matter of fact, yes," I said. "Just not mine."

There'd been a couple of keepers who got away. Who, in fact, walked away. Okay, who ran away.

"And your professional career, young Robby? In addition to your foray into the capricious world of *music*, what legitimate areas of commerce have you pursued?"

My ill-conceived attempts to land employment included a stint framing houses and hanging drywall in Avon, driving a hack in Springfield, baking bread at three in the morning for a crazy one-armed Italian named Luigi Francischetti in Enfield, and delivering car parts to mechanics around the county on behalf of an auto parts distributor in Farmington. Those didn't work out so well. Now I tried to limit myself to playing in the band with Artie and the boys, although making ends meet was an ongoing concern. I offered one or two extraneous details just to flesh out the story. But I needn't have bothered.

Auntie Peg said she'd never heard of anything called a "steel pedal" guitar (I think she got it wrong on purpose) and asked what was wrong with the bassoon. As far as I knew, there was nothing wrong with the bassoon, short of it sounding somewhat like a large duck with laryngitis. I saw the window shades go down behind her eyes when I used the phrase "Bakersfield honky tonk" to describe our music.

"Well, if you'd gone to Yale, young man, perhaps you wouldn't find yourself floundering this way. And at your age ..."

Yale? Clearly, she had forgotten which side of the family I came from. "Maybe if alligators could dance, they wouldn't live in swamps."

"Excuse me?"

She peered at me, then cleared her throat. "In any event, I need somebody for a little assignment," she said. "It's rather sensitive and unorthodox. Do you suppose you'd be up to such a challenge?"

I put the ice cream dish back on the silver tray. "Is it legal?"

"Of course!"

"Just checking."

"It's entirely legal," she said. "You were selected on the basis of, how shall I put it, serendipitous circumstances. Not only because of your ... experience on the streets."

"There it is. My experience on the streets."

"And serendipitous circumstances!"

"Whatever those are."

"You know a man named Ernie Newman, don't you?"

"Sure."

"Just out of curiosity, do you know *many* policemen?"

"A few."

"I see."

"Ernie's a good guy."

*The Farce News*

    I knew a few cops because a few cops -- not many -- hung out in some of the bars where we played. We played all kinds of joints. Cop bars. Cowboy bars. Dance halls and meat markets where off duty cops went trolling for female companionship. We'd even played a couple of gay bars, back during the line dancing craze of the nineties. Late into the evening, when the lucky ones (with lives) had all gone home, the rest of us (without lives) would meditate and self-medicate and pretend we preferred a life of solitude. One such lost soul was Ernie Newman, a former vice cop who'd moved over to homicide before retiring after twenty-five years on the job. He currently ran a security company in town. Auntie Peg said she had used his organization once or twice to update the home security system here at the manse. I reminded her it was Newman who had tipped me that she wanted to hire a private investigator and that it was Ernie who'd recommended me for the gig, despite my lack of private eye credentials. The fact that we, Auntie Peg and I, turned out to be relations was, well, the *serendipitous* part.

    "And what exactly do you know about me?" she asked.

    "Only what my parents told me," I said, which wasn't strictly true. I may not have been the best student in class, but I did my homework. I knew the Wordstones were as filthy rich as we were filthy poor. I knew Auntie Peg was a widow with a couple of grown-up granddaughters. I knew that she'd inherited them as children when their parents where killed in a skiing accident in Aspen. Sooner or later the granddaughters would inherit quite a fortune. I knew I was far enough from the main trunk of the family tree not to expect anything in the will. The granddaughters were going to get it all. That much was a *fait accompli.*

    "I made the acquaintance of Lita, already," I said.

    "Charming, isn't she?"

    Without giving up Ernie Newman as my source, I told her what I knew about the older sister, Lillian. She was a few years younger than me, a two-time loser at the marriage game, ex-wife of a guy named Blackie Buenavista and another named Jarkko-Jussi Tuomalainen. According to Ernie, Blackie Buenavista had sold himself as some kind of Central American freedom fighter on the lamb from one of those banana republics. One of the good guys, apparently, but those messy little wars leave so many dead bodies scattered about it's difficult to know who's who without a scorecard. And what with all the shooting and bombing, it's a wonder if anyone can keep from spilling their beer and peanuts. The marriage between Lillian and Blackie had lasted less than a year, which was longer than her first jaunt down the primrose path of holy matrimony. Husband number one was a hockey player, an uncharacteristically belligerent left winger from Helsinki who spent more time in the penalty box than he did in the sack with Lillian. Problems with anger management and performance anxiety. A vicious cycle if ever there was one. J-J was currently in Ft. Worth, Texas, playing in some semipro beer league, hanging on for dear life to the dying dream that he could still fight and brawl his way to the National Hockey League. At five-foot-two and 130 pounds, his chances of success were probably about as slim as he was, which only made him madder than hell, and made him fight all the more. He was a huge hit in Ft. Worth.

"That's about it," I said.

"I miss him terribly, you know."

"Who? J-J or Blackie?"

"*Benizio*," she said. "And please don't call him Blackie. I absolutely detest that deplorable nickname."

I shrugged.

Mrs. Margaret Waddley-Wordstone sighed, then yawned. Maybe it was time for her nap. I found myself thinking once more about the deadly effects of hypothermia.

"Benizio could really put away the ice cream," she said, somewhat wistfully. "And I don't mean back in the freezer. We have Rosa for that. Benizio used to sit here with me and eat dish after dish after dish. He never seemed to get full. I don't know how he did it. Oh, he was marvelous. And he liked all flavors, too. He showed absolutely no favoritism when it came to ice cream and frozen yogurt. He was what I like to call an equal opportunity connoisseur. Any flavor, any time. Mint chocolate chip, toasted almond, fudge swirl, marshmallow twist. It didn't matter one little bit to my Benizio. Strawberry, vanilla bean, chocolate crunch. He was the closest thing I've ever seen to a bottomless pit. Rocky road, butter pecan, peach parfait. I have never seen a man hold his ice cream like my Benizio. It was an art form with him. Oh! He was so young, so strong and he absolutely had the constitution of an ox. He never, ever got sick. He was truly remarkable. One of a kind."

I looked at my half-eaten dish of green ice cream. It looked sad and unappealing. Maybe someday I'd be one-of-a-kind at something. But it wasn't going to be ice cream consumption.

"Oh, and the toppings! He ate so many toppings, sometimes *I* wanted to vomit. I don't know how he held it all down."

I jumped in before she could launch into another grocery list. "You say you miss him terribly?"

"Oh, yes."

"Why is that, Auntie Peg? Did he move away?"

She sighed again. At least I think it was a sigh. She might just have been breathing heavily after all the sentimental talk of ice cream. "He vanished," she said. "Poof! Like the proverbial rabbit scurrying back up the magician's sleeve."

"He just skipped town?"

"I really couldn't say. He never said he was leaving. He certainly never bothered to say goodbye. He just disappeared. No post card. No phone call. No flowers. No *Thank You* note from Hallmark. No mention of all the ice cream."

"Maybe he checked himself into some kind of dairy detox program."

Auntie Peg suddenly seemed very disheartened. I don't think she heard me. "Of course, I knew it could never last. It was only a matter of time once he and Lilly signed the papers. I suppose I was lucky he stayed around as long as he did." She sat silently for a moment, perhaps reliving some past visit with her beloved Benizio Buenavista.

"I said ..."

She stared at me with her beady little eyes.

"I heard what you said. It's an absurd notion. Dairy detox indeed! But that isn't why I asked you here. We're getting woefully off topic."

"Sorry." I said.

"You see," she said, "somebody is attempting to extract money from me through means of intimidation and the threat of physical harm."

"Really? I hate when that happens."

"Blackmail, young Robby. There's no other word for it. How many times will I have to endure this?"

"This isn't the first time?"

"No," she said. "I'm afraid it isn't."

"When was the last time?"

"Several months ago. I thought we were done with this business."

"Why don't you tell me about it?"

Auntie Peg took a moment to arrange herself and her thoughts. It took considerably less time to arrange her *thoughts*. "An individual by the name of Brashear became, how shall I say, *entangled* with my granddaughter, Lita. She has a certain, how shall I put it, *vulnerability,* and this Brashear individual exploited her weakness. In any event, I thought it prudent at the time to make, how may I best express this, a *contribution* to Mr. Brashear's modest operating budget in exchange for, let's call them *assurances* that he would have no more to do with Lita."

"And did he, for lack of a better word, *comply?*" What the hell, I wasn't going to let her have all the fun.

"Yes."
"Yes?"
"Well, more or less."
"More or less?"
"To some degree."
"To some degree?"

I was determined to see if Auntie Peg could withstand the kind of savage interrogation only a hardened private eye can administer, although I was neither a private eye nor particularly hardened if you discounted the fact that I was stiff from head to toe from the twenty-two degree climate in which we sat. So far, she was holding her own. But, once again, that might have been because it was so damn cold. I know that's why I was holding my own.

She gave me (what else?) a frosty look. "I'm not sure I like where this is going."

"Just for the record, I don't like where it's going, either."

She gave me another look, even frostier. I zipped the parka another several inches and blew on my gloved hands.

"In any event, I presented Mr. Brashear with a twenty thousand dollar benefaction. Cash, of course. And he went away."

"And you think he's back for more money?"

"No. Unless he's taken on a partner. This latest communiqué comes from a different source."

I nodded. Word on the street must be that dear old Auntie Peg, the stately Mrs. Margaret Waddley-Wordstone, is a soft touch.

"I received a telephone call the other day," she said. "Honestly, people are so stupid. The things they say on the phone, forgetting that modern technology enables us to record and preserve every word, should we so choose."

From somewhere within her voluminous folds of cloth, the large woman extracted a microcassette recorder, silver, with a few buttons. She pushed the PLAY button and we listened to a pair of tinny voices, one clearly belonging to Mrs. Margaret Waddley-Wordstone, the other to her would be blackmailer. It was a woman's voice and I was willing to go out on a limb and say it was an African American (although African Canadian quickly became a viable choice).

"Yo, dis Mizzis Werstow?" the voice asked.

"The name is Wordstone," my aunt answered, rather snobbishly, if truth be told.

"Yeah, whatever. Listen up, grannie. Dat little ho chil' a yours, Lita? She owe me some money, eh? I best see dat shit 'fo long, else I'mo come cut it out yo ass. You hearin' me, playa?"

"Perfectly."

"Dat's good, yo. 'Cause I don't want they to be no misunderstandin' 'tween us."

"And to whom am I speaking?"

"Don't worry none about dat, eh? I tell you to whom you speakin' when I feel like tellin' you to whom you speakin'. LaTwanda Jefferson don't answer to nobody. You ax around about me, you find out I ain't nobody you wants to mess with, eh?. You feel me, playa?"

"And what exactly is the nature of the debt you claim is owed to you by my granddaughter?"

"Say, what? Damn, grannie. Speak English an' shit."

"You say Lita owes you money?"

"Damn straight."

"What for?"

"Don't you worry about what for, eh? Dat's between her and me."

"And, pray tell, Ms. Jefferson ..."

"How you know my name?"

"... what is the outstanding sum?"

"Some? Hell, I don't want some. I wants it all. Eighty large, eh?"

"Excuse me?"

"Eighty thousand Got-damn dollars, eh? U.S. dollars, that is."

"That's absurd."

"Yeah, whatever. You just get a boy to bring me my cash."

"Does it have to be a boy?"

"Make it a kangaroo if it makes you feel better. Just get the cash."

"And what's to stop me from calling the authorities?"

"Oh, no you didn't! I *know* you didn't just say you gonna call no po-po."

"And why shouldn't I?"

"'Cause I know where you live, eh? That's why. Now you get me my bling and everything be cool. You start callin' the Five-O and I'm a get all mad an' shit. You ain't want no piece of that. Trust me."

Mrs. Margaret Waddley-Wordstone pushed the STOP button and the tape quit. She sighed deeply and returned the tape recorder from whence it came, out of sight within the folds of her robe. "Well, young Robby? What do you think of *that?*"

"Who is LaTwanda Jefferson?" I asked.

"I haven't the foggiest."

"You don't know her, then?"

"Certainly not," she said.

*The Farce News*

"And what does Lita have to say about all this?"

"We haven't discussed the matter."

"Why not?"

"She and I are not currently on speaking terms. We're on what one might more accurately call screaming terms. It's very exhausting, as you can imagine. Me at my age."

"Okay, let's change the subject for a minute. Tell me what you think I can do about this?"

"Advise me, Robert. How should I handle this awful woman?"

"What do I know? I'm not a policeman."

"Exactly. She said no police."

"But I have no experience with extortionists," I said. "Not counting the phone company."

"But you grew up in that ... how shall I put it? ... *environment*."

"What environment are you talking about?"

"You know. New York City. With those people."

"Which people, Auntie Peg?"

"You know," she sighed. "Oh, don't be difficult."

"You mean black people?"

Auntie Peg blushed slightly. The red offset the blue and white of her complexion to give her a truly American countenance. "You make me sound like some kind of bigot. Are you going to help me, or are you going to add to my misery with this cruel persecution?"

I didn't burst out laughing, but I wanted to. "Do you have any idea what the deal was that LaTwanda Jefferson referred to on the tape?"

"I haven't the vaguest. My worst fears, of course ..."

"Save those for the time being," I said. "No point leaping off the diving board before we know if there's any water in the pool."

She looked at me strangely. "Excuse me?"

"Look, I don't know what you think I can do. But if it's all the same to you, I'm going to suggest you go ahead and pay the money and put this behind you. It's not like you can't afford it, after all. It may be a shakedown, but the aggravation factor ..."

"Meaning?"

"You can't put a price on stamping out aggravation at its source."

She was shaking her head in a very small motion, as if fighting the urge to listen to reason. "Oh, no, no. Don't you see? It's not just the money. It's the principle of the thing. I won't shed blood money to every scoundrel who sticks out a hand and says, 'Gimme, or else.' I don't wish to spend the rest of my life -- what little of it I may have left -- like some kind of cash spigot."

*The Farce News*

"What do you want me to do, Auntie Peg? You want me to go see LaTwanda Jefferson? Get her to back off? If her deal with Lita is illegal, then she has nothing on you but the threat of retribution if you don't pay up. That could be anything from a physical assault ..."

"Oh, my!"

"... to an anonymous phone tip to the cops. If their deal is legit, you should have one of your lawyers handle it. Not me."

"I'm fairly confident this is no job for my attorney," she said.

"I thought lawyers would do just about anything for money."

"Oh, please ..."

I shrugged. "It's your ball game. I guess I can pay her a little visit."

Auntie Peg smiled for a moment, then spoke. "And how much will this cost me? If I might be so bold."

That's what I figured. It really was the money. I thought about telling her eighty-one thousand. "How much? That's a good question. If only I had a good answer." Playing in the band, I could make a hundred bucks in a night at a decent gig, or work the whole weekend for seventy-five. It all depended on the venue. I knew Auntie Peg had more money than God, and more money than common sense, but that didn't necessarily give me the right to hold her up like Jesse James taking down a mail train. "I suppose you should give me some kind of daily rate, say a hundred dollars. For my time. Plus whatever expenses I run into. And it might not be a bad idea to budget for a 'gift,' so to speak, to offer this Jefferson woman as a kind of going away present. This way she saves a little face and doesn't go away mad, or think about payback. Of course, that's totally up to you."

"Now, that's very sensible. You see? I knew it! You do know how these things work. May I leave it to your discretion to determine a suitable sum for this 'going away' present?"

"After I meet LaTwanda, I'll try to figure out what it'll take for her to leave you alone. Don't be surprised if it's several thousand."

"Oh, thank you, Robert," she said. "I knew I could count on you."

Yeah, right. "Sure," I said.

"And we'll agree to keep this business between us?"

Despite her own sense of self-importance, I didn't think this was something the Hartford *Courant* would put on page one. "Certainly," I said.

"Excellent." She clapped her chubby little hands together. "Then if there's nothing else at the moment, I'm afraid I must leave you now. I'm rather fatigued. Anyway it's time for my sitz bath."

I stood and began to unzip my borrowed parka, madly riffling through a pack of mental images from my nearly forty years of life for something to chase away the image of Auntie Peg having her sitz bath. But it kept creeping back, slithering, wet and hideous like some kind of monstrous afterbirth. I shivered.

"And please accept my apologies about the cold, Robert."

"No, it's not that," I said.

"Oh," she said. "Well, then. It's been lovely to finally meet you. Please give my regards to your parents when you speak to them next."

I smiled at her. I'd be willing to bet everything in my wallet that she didn't know my parents' names. Okay, that was only about seventeen bucks, but, hey, it's everything I had at the moment. "I'll make a point of it," I said and hung the winter jacket back on the coat tree.

## Chapter 3

I was halfway down the hall and out of the Wordstone nut house when I became aware of the Puerto Rican housekeeper, Rosa, suddenly lurking in the vicinity of my back pocket. I stopped short and turned. She was standing not two feet away, grinning like the Cheshire Cat.

"Proud of yourself?" I said.

"Mrs. Buenavista, chee like to see choo before choo leab."

Now I stopped. "Lillian Buenavista?"

Rosa raised one eyebrow at me. "I chore don' mean Blackie's mamma." Inexplicably, Rosa vigorously crossed herself. I should have run while I still had the chance. "Follow me."

The longer I stayed in this grandiose manse, the larger it seemed to grow. Or maybe that was just me feeling increasingly small, to put it somewhat oxymoronically. (I've been accused of worse.)

Unlike the meat locker library I'd just left, Lillian Buenavista's inner sanctum, though expansive, was comparatively cozy. The chairs came in all shapes and sizes, and were quite inviting. Couches of varied colors had been arranged neatly, none cluttered with anything more offensive than a satin pillow or two. Tall windows with immaculately polished panes of flawless leaded glass allowed plenty of midday sunlight to bathe the room, infusing it with a warmth my frigid bones welcomed. It had all the charm of a G-rated boudoir. I wasn't foolish enough to be drawn in. Looks can be deceiving.

The room also featured several doors, including the one through which I'd entered. I had a moment to wonder what lay beyond them and I didn't waste it. Closets, perhaps? Always a safe guess. Maybe a bedroom or two? Perhaps. Bathrooms? Why not? When you gotta go, it's nice to have somewhere handy to do it. In a house like this, you wouldn't wanna be caught more than a half-mile or so from the closest indoor plumbing.

Then, from behind me there came a woman's voice: "Mr. Vaughn?"

Women were forever sneaking up on me in this house -- with the exception of Auntie Peg, of course, who couldn't sneak up on a graveyard without scaring the corpses back to death. I turned. A woman in her early thirties stood before me. She had dazzling red curls, sparkling green eyes, and the kind of statuesque physique you might find on a sculpted goddess in a large urban museum. She wore the traditional black and white uniform of a French maid. The cliché was just a little too flagrant to be taken seriously. I remained silent while I mulled things over. (It never occurred to me that Rosa the Puerto Rican maid might be part of a domestic service coterie. Frankly, she didn't strike me as much of a team player. Certainly not a squad leader. Except for the outfit, this dazzling redhead didn't seem any more like a French maid than Rosa seemed like a friendly, cooperative "people" person.) She was spectacular and refined and in no way looked like a person who did much in the way of house cleaning. I couldn't help but wonder what she was doing in this unequivocal nut house. She ought to be in pictures. I wondered if she felt the same way.

"That's me," I said, reaching for my wallet and my drivers license, just in case. "I was told Mrs. Buenavista wanted to see me."

"Of course. Won't you have a seat?" She put out a hand to indicate a love seat near one of the tall windows. It was a lovely hand, not one that looked like it scrubbed many dishes. I followed obediently and sat where I was told. "May I get you anything?" she asked. "Coffee, perhaps? Or a cup of tea? Something cold?"

"No, thank you," I said. If she offered me a dish of ice cream -- of *any* flavor -- I was outa there. "I'm fine. I'll just wait for Mrs. Buenavista."

The woman smiled, then turned and disappeared through one of the doors. Call me a pig, but it was a pleasure to watch her walk away.

And then I was alone again.

I must have drifted into a daydream because I didn't notice when one of the other doors opened and I was thus taken somewhat by surprise when the lovely redhead returned from a different side of the room. At least I thought it was the lovely redheaded woman. It was certainly the same face, the same eyes. But the French maid had been replaced and now I feasted my eyes on a rather provocatively dressed Egyptian temptress in a decidedly revealing Cleopatra outfit, complete with a single-strap toga-style robe and resultant exposed shoulder. My eyes immediately went to the bare skin. The shoulder was slender without being skeletal and featured a delightful smattering of light brown freckles. I wished I had a felt tip pen on me so I could play connect-the-dots (provided the good queen didn't violently object).

On her feet she wore a pair of fine leather sandals. Starting around her ankles, two thin strips of leather snaked up her legs in sexy, intimate coils before they disappeared under the hem of her robe at about the knee line. My mind wandered off for a moment to consider where the sandal straps might conclude their bawdy adventure, but I let out a shrill interior whistle and it scampered back like a well-trained dog. I did what could only be accurately described as a Three Stooges double take, although I stopped short of poking myself in the eyes or clocking myself in the forehead with a wooden mallet.

"So, you're Robby," she said, smiling beautifully. "It's a pleasure to meet you. I'm Lillian. We're practically cousins, aren't we?"

In accordance with Miss Manners' official rules of engagement, I climbed to my feet and stepped forward to offer my hand. The blood which until that moment had been happily circulating in my brain took the opportunity to catch the DOWN elevator, rushing immediately to my feet to see what was going on down there. With what little mental acuity I had left I wondered for about the the eighteenth time in the last hour, *What the hell am I doing here?* In my dizzy state, I only got to, *"What the hell ...?"*

"Thirsty, Robby? May I call you that?"

"No," I said, as stasis gradually returned. "That is, yes."

"Around this time I usually have juice. Won't you join me?"

"No, thanks," I said. "I just had, er, ice cream."

"Oh, yes," she said, smiling demurely. Her voice was soaked in sympathy. A little too much of a good thing, really. "Of course you did. Well, I hope you don't mind if I go ahead."

"Of course not."

"I won't be a minute," she said.

And with that she turned and exited through the same door through which she had just made her second entrance, but who's counting?

Alone again, I had only my growing confusion and apprehension to keep me company. It wasn't much company. I shook my head, if only to clear it and sat back down. My brain, refueled with a fresh supply of blood, leap-frogged back to a notion I'd entertained not long ago while hunkered down in the sub-arctic book repository with Auntie Peg, the Ice Queen: *Run, man, run. Get up. Go. Don't think twice. Don't look back.*

But I had successfully pushed those thoughts down once, so now I pushed them down again.

I didn't have to wait very long by myself this time. Soon, a new door opened. Instead of the scantily clad Cleopatra returning with the nectar of the gods (or whatever it was Cleopatra quaffed at this hour of the day), a completely different person emerged. A construction worker, complete with dirty blue jeans, heavy black work boots, a red checkered shirt with the sleeves turned up to the elbow, a thick leather tool belt around the waist and a bright yellow hard hat. But the face, those eyes, that hair ... Oh, it was her all right. She smiled at me. She carried two glasses. One contained orange juice. The other was filled with tomato juice, except it was too dark and not nearly thick enough to be tomato juice. Cranberry juice? Perhaps blood?

"I took the liberty of bringing you ..."

I put a hand up to stop her. "Wait a second."

"Yes?" she asked, innocent as a newborn vampire. "What is it?"
"What's the gag?"
"Excuse me?"
"This wardrobe thing. It's charming as hell, but c'mon ..."
"Oh, that," she said, dismissively. Even laughing a little. As if it were nothing at all and I were grossly overreacting. "It's part of my therapy."

I looked at her anew. Therapy? More *doctor's orders?* I said nothing and she didn't elaborate. As a rule, one's course of psychoanalysis tends to be a very personal thing. At this point I wasn't sure I wanted to hear any more about it. If this was the treatment, I didn't want to know what the problem was.

Besides, the sooner we got off the topic, the less likely it was that she'd think to ask me if I'd ever been in therapy. I'm not a very good liar. I have no poker face to speak of, or so I'm told by card players who've paid their rent with my money. Next thing you know, Lillian Buenavista and I would be into one of those weird I'll-show-you-mine-if-you-show-me-yours scenarios that tend to end badly, with embarrassment and law suits for all concerned.

She handed me the glass with the orange juice. I took it. The little voice on my left shoulder (the bad news kibitzer) insisted that I not refuse anything this gorgeous woman wanted to foist upon me. Hopefully, the little voice claimed, she'd eventually get around to foisting something on us that we actually wanted. I didn't mention to the little voice on my left shoulder that Lillian Buenavista was a relative, however distant. And while I was at it I didn't mention to Lillian Buenavista that I hate orange juice or that I sometimes hear little voices.

"Come, cousin Robby," she said, sweetly, her voice like velvet. "Join me on the davenport, won't you? Let's relax and have a little chat."

I followed her to a larger couch under a different window and sat down, leaving the middle section of the couch between us as a kind of social DMZ. She took a sip from her glass and wiped her mouth on the sleeve of her red checked shirt. It was a manly gesture, but she made it sexy and feminine. She doffed the helmet and shook her head to let the red curls bounce free. "Ah, that's better," she said. "Tell me, what did you make of Nana?"

"I assume you mean Mrs. Wordstone," I said, setting the orange juice glass on a side table. "She's a very ... er, *interesting* woman."

"You mean *weird,* don't you?" Lillian Buenavista said. "An *oddball.* A *piece of work.*"

"I wouldn't go nearly that far."

"Why the hell not? You'd be perfectly correct if you did. She's all that and more. Just because we all adore her doesn't make her any less ... er, *inter-*

*esting*. Honestly, Robby, don't feel you have to uses euphemisms. We're all adults here. She may be my grandmother, but I'm a big girl. I can *handle* the truth." She winked at me. "Jack Nicholson."

Huh? "I'm sure you can." Now I was confused.

"Most people think Nana's peculiar. Comes with the territory. When you're as rich as she is, the tendency is to look for fault, to soften the blow. I'm sure there are people who even find *me* a little *different*. But I'm comfortable in my skin."

"She was very cordial, very generous." Except with her liquor.

"But still you think she's a quack, don't you? You think she's barking mad. Be honest."

I thought I *was* being honest. Maybe she wanted me to ratchet my assessments to a level of *brutal* honesty. "Okay," I said. "So she's a bit flaky. Who among us isn't?"

Lillian Buenavista smiled a little and looked at me cockeyed, sipping from her glass. "You mean who among us *in this room?* Should I take offense at your insinuation?"

I took a quick peek at her steel-toed boots. They seemed to fit just fine. *Brutally honest* apparently wasn't going to work out after all.

"Some people thought my ex-husband was pretty interesting."

"Which one?" I said. "The fighting Finn or the revolutionary."

"Why, Blackie, of course. Nana was entranced. Didn't she tell you?"

I decided not to say, one way or the other.

She took another sip from her drink, then stood up. "I'm just going to freshen this up a bit. Is your O.J. okay?"

I hadn't touched it. "Perfect," I said. "Just the way I like it."

"I won't be a minute," she said. I'd heard that before. She wouldn't be a minute, and odds were she wouldn't be a construction worker the next time I saw her.

I sat back and ran through a catalog of costumes Lillian Buenavista might change into. It was too much to hope for something in the way of a middle Eastern belly dancer or maybe a Dallas Cowboys cheerleader. The Cleopatra thing had worked on a certain level, but only if you could block from your mind the disconcerting image of a bloated Elizabeth Taylor and all that hideous blue mascara. I couldn't. But that's just me.

Although Lillian Buenavista was turning out to be quite the entertainment value, her act was making me a little edgy. On one hand I felt as if I could easily sit here all day and watch her peculiar fashion show unfold before me. On the other hand I was troubled by a growing sense of the day getting away from me. I was supposed to be "on the job" hunting down a profane extortionist named LaTwanda Jefferson who was threatening my dear old batty Auntie Peg with a beat down if she didn't fork over the somewhat odd sum of eighty thousand dollars. Instead I was sitting here playing at some odd psychological guessing game with my distant cousin Lillian.

(Was it really possible that I was related to these people? I'd have to do some genealogical research and see if there was *any* chance in hell that I was actually adopted.)

Another door opened and, in near monastic silence, cousin Lillian reentered, garbed this time in the black and white penguin suit of a Roman Catholic nun, complete with the tight fitting head gear and a giant silver cross hanging from a heavy pewter chain across her breast. What now? Would she attempt to extract a confession from me? I thought that was the purview of priests and homicide detectives.

"Don't tell me," I said. "You wanted to slip into something a little less comfortable."

She smiled placidly. Her green eyes seemed a bit duller.

I started to climb out of the deeply cushioned sofa.

"Oh, no," she said, serenely. "Don't go."

I made a point of looking at my watch. "Really, I'd love to hang around and continue this little ... *whatever* it is. But I've got errands I need to run before winter sets in."

"Don't be absurd, it's only the first week of October."

"It's a long list."

"Oh, humor me, won't you? All I want is a little conversation. That's not too much to ask, is it, cousin Robby?"

"Okay," I said. "Pick a topic. Anything but comparative religions."

"Nana spoke to you about my ex-husband, didn't she?"

"The hockey player?"

"No." She folded her hands, very nun-like.

"Ah, you mean Benizio."

"Did she tell you how he disappeared."

"She didn't say how. Only that he did."

Lillian took a moment to consider this. In the silence, she reached into one large sleeve and extracted a packet of unfiltered Camel cigarettes and a gold lighter. She shook one loose, placed it between her lovely lips and struck fire to the end of it. She blew smoke at the ceiling, then spit a morsel of loose tobacco at the floor. She was quickly becoming my kind of nun. If she pulled out a whiskey flask, I'd give careful consideration to converting. Atheism doesn't have nearly enough national holidays. "Will it take you long to find him?"

*The Farce News*

"Find him? I wasn't planning to look for him."

"Really? Why not, if I might inquire?"

"For one thing, nobody's asked me to. For another, I wouldn't know how to go about it. That would be a job for the Hartford PD. Or the FBI if he crossed state lines."

She puffed her cigarette and blew smoke out of her nose and mouth. Very sexy, for a nun. "But if Nana doesn't want you to find him, then ..."

She stopped and stared at me, her head turned a little to one side. We let the silence hang in the air between us like a ping pong ball nobody wanted to take a swing at. She waited. I waited. She waited some more. I started to get bored. I don't like ping pong that much. And I don't find much inspiration in suspended animation.

"Look, sister," I said, playing along with her for a minute, "I'm doing your grandmother a favor. She thinks I have the requisite skill set for this particular chore. Usually I don't make a habit of hiring out ..."

"That's very funny! Really it is. Actually, it isn't that funny. You're just making fun of me, aren't you? There's no call for that. You wouldn't make fun of me if I were in a wheelchair, would you? Or if I were dyslexic? Or suffered from dwarfism? You know, the more I think about it, the more I think you owe me an apology."

"Sorry. Was there anything else you wanted to talk about?" I started to get up again. "Otherwise, I'll just climb on my horse and ride on out of Dodge, so to speak."

Her eyes suddenly brightened. "Oh, that's a wonderful idea! I have a simply fantastic Dale Evans ensemble. I got it last spring on Rodeo Drive. You'll love it. It'll only take me a minute to change."

"Don't bother." I stood up -- slowly this time, hoping the blood in my brain would stay put. "I have to go."

"It's no bother at all."

"Perhaps another time."

"Don't be silly. I have all the time in the world."

"Yes, but I don't."

"You must *make* the time. *Always make the time.* That's my motto."

"I guess I don't really have time for mottos," I said. "Really, I need to get going."

"Oh, stay. Don't be a spoiled sport. You don't have to tell me anything if you don't want to. Just stay and play. Don't be a fuddy duddy. We can do improv. We'll have so much fun. I promise."

I couldn't help but smile. "It sounds intriguing."

Even as a nun, she was a knockout. Good thing I'm not Catholic or one of those ex-Catholics with a bunch of sex-and-authority baggage to lug around. Hers was a habit I could easily break, or tear to pieces, or rip to shreds. But only if the stars aligned *just so.* The real sticking point was the apparent bloodline we shared. I'm as liberated as the next guy, but I did grow up north of the Mason-Dixon line after all, and I still like to draw the line at incest. At the moment it was all I could do to tear myself away from this perplexing engagement, and all we'd done so far was chat a bit and share a little fruit juice. The voices on my shoulders were carrying on like warring countries at a United Nations Security Council meeting. Lefty was lobbying strongly for an hour or so of quality adult play time. Meanwhile, Righty shook a bony finger and spoke with an accent straight out of some Salt Lake City tabernacle: "Get thyself to work, young man, and cease thy tomfoolery."

Lillian Buenavista looked me over like a tailor measuring a rich customer for a new suit of silk. "I could put together a rather terrific cowboy ensemble for you in no time. What do you think about chaps? A little too gay? How about a holster and a pair of six-shooters?"

"Sounds a little violent," I said. I really did have to get going. Auntie Peg was rather generously paying me more than the engagement probably deserved to perform a fairly specific and mundane task, and I was pretty sure this wasn't part of the general job description.

"Oh, well," Lillian said, expertly feigning disappointment. Expertly, that is, if you're a cheesy soap opera hack who learned to act through a correspondence course. The smile on her face was a bit too devilish to belong to a truly disheartened soul. "You don't know what you're missing." Something in her tone was flat out suggestive, but the nun outfit went a long way toward spoiling the effect. Of course, it's also possible I was reading more into it than was actually there. Wishful thinking can be like that, raising expectations where they don't belong. It wouldn't be the first time I'd misjudged a woman's sexual signals. Not even the first time today.

"Goodbye, Mrs. Buenavista."

"You *must* call me Lillian. I insist!"

"Okay, Lillian," I said. "It's been very interesting."

She smiled. "You mean *weird,* don't you?"

I decided to go for brutal honesty. "Actually, yes."

"I thought so." She pouted. Then smiled, happy with herself.

I stopped. "It's not right, you know."

"What's that, cousin?"

"You insisting on honesty, then putting on this act. Where's the justice?"

"Oh, so now you're cutting to the chase, huh?"

"Don't take it personally," I said, not that I thought she would.

"Listen, do you have a business card or something?"

I patted myself down and found one tucked away in a jacket pocket. I handed it to her. She read it over slowly, then looked up at me. She smiled in the way women smile when they want to put the whammy on you. I froze in my tracks.

"What on earth does this mean?"

"What do you mean?"

She read from the card. "Elvis Jihad."

"That's the name of the group."

"What group? Are you part of some terrorist organization?"

"No, it's a band."

"A band of brothers? What are you, an anarchist?"

"It's the name of a band I play in."

"Oh! Really? Is this another joke?"

"No."

"You're a musician?"

I confessed I was.

"But I thought you were a private investigator."

"Nope. And if your little sister asks, I don't play one on TV."

She looked at the card again. "What's this address and phone number?"

"That's our rehearsal studio on Farmington Avenue. There's an answering machine. Agents and bar owners call there to book us for gigs."

"How interesting," she said, tucking the card away. "I'll be in touch."

I almost said "I can hardly wait," but that would have been a lie. And as far as I know, you're not supposed to lie to nuns.

"I look forward to it," I said, wondering if that was like telling a doctor you looked forward to your next checkup. There was the truth, and then there were lies, fear, and loathing all mixed up like a fruit cocktail with a little too much syrup. Sometimes you can't separate what's good for you from what has the potential to kill you.

As I crossed the room, I felt her eyes on me. I guess I had it coming after all the ogling I'd done. As I got to the door, she spoke, as if she simply had to have the last word. More therapy?

"By the way, I simply adore your jacket. It's incredibly sexy. You just don't care what anyone thinks, do you? And the detail. Especially the thorns on the stems of the roses. Promise me one thing, Robby. If you ever decide to get rid of it, let me have first dibs. I could make you a very generous offer for it. Or we could work out some kind of barter."

Okay, so I'm not a Catholic. Still I was a little uncomfortable having a nun come on to me this way, particularly a nun who's related. It just didn't seem right. If only I could figure out why not. But that was a philosophical question for another day, preferably not a Sunday. Maybe the lovely and peculiar Lillian Buenavista -- in any other outfit but this one -- could help me sort it all out. Maybe I could even work up the nerve to accept her help. Then we might have the beginnings of a truly wonderful (if twisted) relationship. So long as we both remained dressed, or I could prove I *was* in fact adopted. For now, I could think of no better tactic than to bid her a fond adieu. She had threatened to be in touch, so at least I had that to look forward to.

Without any further help from Rosa the Puerto Rican housekeeper, I made my way out of the big house and across the circular gravel driveway where I'd left my piece of shit Jetta. It was sitting there in the sun, looking lonely and disheveled, covered in dust and dents, missing three of its four hubcaps, the radio antenna bent. It has better (or worse) than 189,000 miles on it, the brakes are nearly gone and the clutch is dangerously mushy. The small dings and dents that cover its body are among the car's finest features at this point. But it's paid for, and it runs, albeit with a slight limp.

I climbed into the driver's seat and sat for a minute. Instead of saying the little prayer I usually recite just before turning the ignition key, I thought of other things, other people. Margaret Waddley-Wordstone, my fruity Auntie Peg. *The Ice Queen.* And LaTwanda Jefferson the mystery extortionist. And quirky Lillian Buenavista and her odd little sister Lita. My cousins! How many times removed would it take for me to feel safe around them? I didn't know what I was getting myself into with this crew. To say I was skeptical about the whole thing would have been an overstatement of the painfully obvious. But at least it was *something,* and that fact alone was in fairly stark contrast to the whole bunch of nothing I'd been getting myself into lately. This wacko Wordstone clan had already demonstrated the capacity to be pretty damned entertaining, but it might not be the worst thing in the world to watch from a distance. Just to be on the safe side, I'd look into the possibility of borrowing a set of extra long arms from the first chimpanzee who crossed my path. The way my day was going, I didn't think I'd have to wait long before such an opportunity presented itself.

And what was I up against here? Would this be a straight forward family favor worth a couple of day's time and pay -- provided I could concoct some reasonably effective method for repelling the advances of LaTwanda Jefferson? Or would it become a weedy morass of twisted garden paths leading from one dead end to another, as family business so often tends to do? At the moment, there was just no way to predict. All I could do was start at the top and work my way down, or start at the bottom and work my way up. Hell, I didn't even know which it would be, or if it was only a matter of semantics, or perspective.

All I knew for sure was that old lady Wordstone wanted me to scare off a scam artist who apparently had her hooks into Lita, the pale rider from hell. I didn't know anything about this Jefferson woman other than what I'd heard from the audio tape of her phone conversation with Auntie Peg. She certainly had a way with words. But I wouldn't hold that against her. The whole thing might have been an act. It sure sounded like one. Until she got in my face and started calling *me* names I'd give her the benefit of the doubt. Beyond her bawdy vocabulary and debatable claim to compensation in the amount of eighty thousand dollars, I didn't know very much about her.

I didn't even know where to look for her. But I knew who would.

Sully.

*The Farce News*

## Chapter 4

Kareem Abdul Sullivan claims to know everything going down in Hartford. The players and the games they play. Which items of gossip contain kernels of truth and which are so much bullshit. Which politicians are truly crooked and which ones are just a little bent out of shape.

Sully is a first-generation American, an Iraqi orphan who came to the U.S. as an infant, the adopted son of a large-hearted reinsurance mogul named T. McIlhargy Sullivan and his equally large-hearted but barren wife, June. Sully, who adheres to Islamic doctrines and speaks without any trace of a Middle Eastern accent, is New England prep-school trained and a graduate of Yale where he earned a Ph.D. in the novels of Mark Twain. He currently serves as the sole proprietor of a 10-page community newspaper he puts out every Friday. He publishes it himself and pays the bills with money left to him by his wealthy father, to whom he affectionately refers as T-Mac. The paper's a tabloid he calls *The Farce News.* He uses it to poke his editorial finger in the eye of everything he deems to be pretentious and fraudulent in Hartford, from its hypocritical renaissance approach to urban renewal to its phony claims to a legitimate night life to its humorous attempt at civic politics. Under the banner, Sully runs an italicized subtitle: *Hartford: Established 1623. Elected first Mayor 2001. You do the math.*

Sully, who dropped his American name (Michael Francis) in high school, insists Hartford provides an inexhaustible supply of grist for his editorial mill. To his credit a preponderance of what he prints turns out to be factually dead-on. Consequently, like major league pitchers pussyfooting around Barry Bonds, savvy Hartford politicos don't mess with Sully too much -- for fear he'll turn his attention their way, which could be bad for one's reelection aspirations.

Sully keeps a combined office-and-living space on Albany Avenue in the same building that houses the local branch of Planned Parenthood. He complains that the rent is a little steep, but otherwise he likes the location as he's found it's as good a place as any to meet *experienced* chicks, and it's cheaper than the local bar scene. Since he rarely leaves his command post, it's that much more convenient. Sully stopped going out on the streets sometime in the winter of 1991, right about the time the United States started bombing Iraq for the first time. He said he didn't feel safe showing what he called his "desert nigger" face in public. In the weeks and months that fol-

*The Farce News*

lowed, he got used to his indoor seclusion, made necessary adjustments to his various information pipelines, and put a more or less permanent embargo on going outdoors, unless absolutely necessary. One night, on a beer run of vital importance, he was crossing Albany Avenue when a cabbie eleven hours into his 12-hour shift ran a red light and nailed Sully, breaking both of his legs and fracturing his pelvis in five places. He's been sitting in a wheelchair ever since, although his injuries have long since healed. I'm of the opinion that Sully is full-tilt bozo, but I don't tell him so. Like everyone else, I don't particularly want to get on his shit list. Besides, what's wrong with full-tilt bozo? Some of my best friends ...

I decided to pay Sully a visit and tell him about the daffy ducks with whom I'd spent the early afternoon, including the curious quick change artist Lillian Buenavista. I couldn't help but wonder if he'd be jealous or just feel sorry for me (as he usually does). I could hear him now. "These people are your family? God help you."

Yeah, right, Sully. Praise Allah and pass the dynamite.

"I'm no private eye," I told Sully.

"And yet here you are playing Puddin'head Wilson to the hilt."

"I need to track down this LaTwanda Jefferson. See what we're up against. She sounds kind of low stakes and high profile."

"Large pig in a Mickey Mouse sty, to mix bestial metaphors."

I shrugged. "I've never met the woman."

"So, for all you know, LaTwanda Jefferson might be elegance and grace personified."

"From what I heard, I wouldn't use the word *elegant.*"

"So, she's no Coretta Scott King."

"More like Moms Mabley after too many bowls of Cap'n Crunch."

"Okay."

"So, can you help?"

"Of course, Huckleberry," he said, stroking his beardless chin. "That's why you came to me, isn't it?"

Sully wheeled himself to a roll-top desk, pulled out drawer and riffled through a batch of a manila folders before finding the one he wanted. He opened it and leafed through a thick sheaf of papers, then stabbed at one of the pages with a narrow brown finger. "Here we go. LaTwanda Jefferson owns a sports collector's shop on Park Street near Sisson Avenue. You know the area?"

"Over in the North End."

Sully snapped the folder shut. "Rumor has it the place is a front."

*The Farce News*

\*

LaTwanda Jefferson's shop was one of those places where sports memorabilia goes to collect dust. Everything from baseball cards, football cards, hockey cards, to wall posters, plastic action figures, felt pennants, autographed game-worn jerseys, and assorted other wall hangings and colorful tin garbage cans with team logos on them.

The last time I'd plunked down any money on trading cards was going on thirty years ago. I was a kid on a weekly allowance and the cards had set me back something in the neighborhood of twenty-five cents for a pack of ten. From what I could gather, the same cards had since moved to a significantly more high-rent district, commanding upwards of a buck and a half for that same pack of ten.

After stopping off at my apartment to doff my Hank Sr. suit in favor of jeans, sweatshirt, sneakers and a blue New York Rangers ball cap, I headed for Park Street, thinking about how the card collecting industry had changed over the years. This was what happened when misguided adults interjected themselves into childrens' innocent activities: the fun went out of it like helium from a punctured mylar balloon, and all that was left was the bitching and moaning.

I thought about all the guys -- the ex-jocks who were washed up at 30 or 40 -- who made their way hawking signatures at card shows all over the country. Seated at folding tables for hours on end, charging money to scrawl their has-been name on somebody's card. Even sadder was the image of the long lines of cynical middle-aged adults (who'd replaced the uncorrupted wide-eyed kids as customers), stockpiling materiel with the singular purpose of reselling it at whatever mark-up they could manage. The vision of some 50-year-old schmuck dropping ten or twenty bucks for some other 50-year-old schmuck's autograph was as laughable as it was disturbing.

As a kid, I'd forged hundreds of autographs on hundreds of baseball and hockey cards, no doubt ruining a couple of thousand dollars worth of "product" along the way, but I'd had fun doing it, pretending to be Brooks Robinson, or Catfish Hunter, or Johnny Roseboro, or Jacques Laperierre, or Marcel Pronovost, or Orland Kurtenbach. Afterwards, I'd moved on to other things. Bully for me.

I found Jefferson's place where Sully said it would be, at the end of a block cluttered with small businesses run by hard working entrepreneurs: barbers and travel agents, convenience store owners and tobacconists.

I pulled open the glass door and walked inside. The place smelled of dust, bubble gum and, for some inexplicable reason, airplane glue. I looked around but saw no sign of any aircraft models being sold or built. No biplanes hanging from the ceiling. No F-14 fighters perched on clear plastic stands. Maybe the glue was for recreational purposes other than bonding. Overhead fluorescent lighting bleached the color out of the place and gave it the antiseptic feel of a hospital waiting room. It wasn't an atmosphere that encouraged one to spend a lazy afternoon browsing. I wondered if it was intentional.

Waist-high glass display cases were situated against all four walls and through the middle of the store forming several narrow aisles. Instead of containing jewels, they held carefully arranged sets of cards. Ice hockey here. Baseball there. Football and basketball, each grouped neatly segregated. One cabinet had nothing but single cards, each one in a clear plastic sleeve and marked for sale with a small red sticker on which a dollar amount had been neatly inscribed.

LaTwanda Jefferson was either a dreamer or there was actually a sucker out there who'd eventually walk in and drop $23.95 for a Tim Thomas basketball card. I'd never even heard of the guy, but I didn't hold that against Thomas. I watch two basketball games a year: the NCAA Final Four championship game, and the deciding contest of the NBA playoff finals. The other thousand or so games comprising the NBA and college basketball seasons held no special drama for me.

I also found a Dave Semenko hockey card selling for $17.95. At least I knew who this guy was, but I couldn't believe the old Edmonton Oilers winger had a card worth that much. Semenko (a.k.a. Cement Head) was a Cold War nuke, a cheerful bully who'd been kept around as a deterrent to anybody who thought about taking liberties with Wayne Gretzky, the greatest player ever -- and, of course, to pound the living crap out of anyone foolish enough actually to do so.

Behind the front counter on which there a sat a midsize green and black cash register, a collection of large white cardboard boxes were piled nearly to the ceiling. Someone had written on the fronts of the boxes with a thick, black marker. It was a very simple and efficient filing system. Name of the sport (baseball, basketball, etc.), issuing card company (Topps, Fleer, Upper Deck, etc.), and year of the set. Basic stuff. Nothing sexy or provocative. Factory warehouse fodder. Judging by the number of boxes, LaTwanda Jefferson was sitting on quite a backlog of inventory. I wondered how she'd ever move this much merchandise -- other than with an industrial forklift. Perhaps it was more lucrative to hold it and take a loss at the end of the tax year. Lots of folks were in business with precisely this economic strategy in mind. They were also the ones who often ended up hiring professional arsonists to help them make ends meet.

A small desk had been placed in one corner of the room and behind it sat

*The Farce News*

a pretty brunette in faded blue jeans and a peekaboo silk blouse. She was reading a paperback, or at least staring at one. I hitched my pants up a little too high and turned my hat around so the bill pointed backwards, then walked over and stood in her light, swallowing her up in my shadow.

After a moment she reluctantly looked up. I smiled. She didn't smile back. The look of boredom on her face shifted slightly to an expression more closely reflecting the long suffering tolerance of one who spends their days administering to the mentally impaired. If I were a soothsayer, I would have predicted that her first words to me would be something along the lines of, "Yeah, pal? What do *you* want?"

"Hey, lady," I said in my best Nutty Professor voice.

"Can I help you?" she said, no doubt hoping I'd say, "No," so she could go back to not caring about me one way or the other.

It wasn't so much the words as the tone, the attitude.

I pulled a piece of crumpled paper from my hip pocket and sniffled hard, like a guy with a bad cold, which I didn't have at the moment. I pretended to read from the paper as I barked at her through me nose.

"Maybe you can help me, but I doubt it." My winning smile was losing this round, but I didn't get discouraged. "I'm looking for a Wayne Gretzky Rookie of the Year card. Topps or Upper Deck. It don't make me no never mind which it is so long as you have one or the other. If you have both, maybe we can work a package deal. That would be vintage 1979-80. You got either one a them? I won't pay no more'n eleven-fifty for the Topps and seventeen for the Upper Deck, so don't try to pull a fast one. I'd didn't just fall off no turnip truck."

She looked at me as if I were something awful that had perhaps been used to fertilize the turnip patch to which I referred.

"No," she said. "I don't believe we have that one."

"*Which* one?" I said, taking off my cap and wiping imaginary sweat from my brow. "The Topps or the Upper Deck? Which one don't you have?"

"Either one, I'm afraid."

I cocked my head sideways, like I didn't believe her. "I'll go to twelve-fifty for the Topps, no more. Eighteen-fifty for the Upper Deck."

"I'm sorry," she said. "We simply don't ..."

"Okay, okay. How about a Gordie Howe Norris Trophy card? The Fleer set. Issued in 1969. I'll go twenty-one for it."

"I'm afraid not."

I dragged one sleeve under my nose. "Ain't you got nothing good?"

"Well, sir ..."

"You even know who Gordie Howe is?"

*The Farce News*

"Sir, we have thousands of ..."

"Save it. I don't need no speech. Or bubble gum. Say, whatya got back there, a bubble gum factory? Whew! And who's been sniffin' glue? Man, that stuff'll kill yer brain cells. I musta built about a million model airplanes when I was a kid. I *think* I know what I'm sayin'."

To my surprise, that got a bit of a rise out of her. She glanced over her left shoulder toward a door framed in the wall behind her, then immediately righted herself. "No, of course not."

I made a face back at her, stuck out my lips as she had done. "You don't object if I browse a little?"

"Help yourself," she said, smiling just a little bit, as if she could see the light at the end of the tunnel and it was a locomotive about to run me down. Maybe she was looking forward to a time in the very near future when I'd leave the store and walk out of her life forever.

I felt a little bad, actually. I'm a pretty nice guy, once you get to know me. I'm even a pretty nice guy before you get to know me, it's just harder for strangers to tell. This girl and I could really be throwing away a golden opportunity to find true love, and the fault was mostly mine what with all this foolish role playing. All I really wanted was to get a line on LaTwanda Jefferson's whereabouts. But in so doing, I could be unwittingly blowing it with the future mother of my children.

"By the way," I said, readjusting my hat and fussing at the waist band of my jeans, "this is a very nice joint you got here. In case I didn't mention it."

"Thank you," she said, negligibly warmer now.

"You had it long?"

"Oh, I'm not ..."

"Oh," I said.

"Twannie Jefferson is the owner," she said. "I just help out."

I nodded and looked around, as if I was giving the place a whole new appraisal based on this important news update. "This Tommy Jefferson ... he around?"

"Twannie, not Tommy," she said, and spelled it.

"Twannie?" I said, feigning incredulity. "That a man or a woman? Nowadays you can't necessarily tell just by the name. I know this guy, he's an accountant at Cigna, his name is Leslie. You believe that? And there was that actor Carroll O'Connor. That was a dude, too. What kind of mother names a baby boy *Carroll?*"

"I don't know. An Irish one?"

"It was a rhetorical question," I said.

She bristled. "For your information, *LaTwanda* Jefferson is a woman."

"Yeah? LaTwanda, huh? Nice. She around by any chance? Maybe she could help me with my list." I held up my crumpled paper. "Or maybe I could make an appointment." I was starting to feel sorry for *myself.* I hoped the pretty brunette was, too.

She hesitated. "I wouldn't be able to arrange anything like that."

"No?"

"I just help out around the store. I'm not her secretary. She has an executive assistant."

"An executive assistant? Well, well. She must be *real* important."

"Well, I couldn't say ..."

"It was a rhetorical statement."

"Oh."

"Is he here? This executive assistant, I mean?"

"It's a she."

"Sorry?"

"Miss Jefferson's assistant is a woman."

"No shit." I let it hang in the air. "Is it *all* women running the place?"

"You have a problem with that?"

"No, it's cool," I said, sniffling.

"Well, I don't know how cool it is ..."

"Anyway, is she here, then? This woman assistant?"

"Miss Jefferson and her assistant come and go constantly."

I shrugged. "Oh, well, Guess I'll just poke around. Who knows, maybe I'll get lucky."

"Help yourself," she said. I smiled as if I believed I'd made some points with her, and she smiled as if I was the saddest creature she'd ever encountered. I went back to pretending to scour the glass display cases in search of hidden treasure and she went back to pretending to scour the pages of her paperback for words she could pronounce. Pretty girls just don't go for guys who go out of their way to act like total schmucks.

I wandered around the store for a few minutes trying to decide what to do next. If the pretty brunette was going to stonewall me, and clearly that was part of her mandate, I'd have no alternative but to stake the place out and hope Twannie Jefferson showed up or emerged from the back room, if that's where she was currently hiding out.

A few minutes later, the front door opened and a very short, very round woman in a very ugly orange Miami Dolphins jumpsuit with teal trim waddled into the store. The jumpsuit fit her very poorly, tight where it needed a little extra room, loose where it didn't need to sag quite so much. She walked with the limp of one suffering from gout, or who perhaps has a collection of sharp rocks in her shoes. It was painful to watch. I did my best to dissolve into the scenery and eyeball her without being obvious. She went directly to the desk where the pretty brunette was pretending to read. They spoke in hushed tones, which I thought was pretty rude in view of the considerable tact with which I was brazenly attempting to eavesdrop on them.

After a moment or two, the badly dressed visitor hobbled around the desk and disappeared through the door in the back wall. I continued to pretend I'd seen nothing. I feigned a careful study of an array of baseball cards featuring the famous Alou brothers (Filippe, Matty, and Jesus) and watched the door out of the corner of my eye.

There was no activity for a few minutes and I shifted to another part of the store, where football cards were displayed, and from which vantage point I could easily watch the door.

I spent a few minutes trying to figure out how a future Hall of Famer like Deion Sanders, whose nicknames included "Neon" and "Prime Time," demanded only $4.00 for his 1997 Dallas Cowboys All-Pro card while Sebastian Janikowski, a brawling, boozer -- and a place kicker, not even a real player, for God's sake! -- whose nicknames included but were not limited to "Sea Bass," "Jane," "Fatso" and "Jailbird," could get $7.50 for his 1999 Florida State University championship card.

As I mused pointlessly, the round woman reappeared carrying a package under her arm. It was flat and rectangular, about the size of a large hardcover book, perhaps a dictionary or a thesaurus. I doubted it was either a dictionary *or* a thesaurus. Maybe a cookbook? Or a fad diet book? Much more likely. Package firmly nestled under one arm, she left the store without taking any notice of me. It's possible she might not have noticed me if my shirt was on fire. I slipped out in her wake, my departure unnoticed by the pretty brunette.

Thanks to her unfortunate wardrobe choice, she wasn't hard to tail from a safe distance. She shuffled east along Park Street, then crossed the wide motorway against the light, hung a left and headed north on Sisson Avenue, moving slowly. After a block or two I actually began to feel sorry for her. I had to work at reducing my pace to match hers. With my comparatively long legs, it wasn't easy to walk so slowly and not look like some kind of recalcitrant loiterer. At Capitol Avenue she had to stop for the heavy traffic which angled for the entrance ramps to east and westbound Interstate 84.

Casually as I could, I strolled up and stood beside her and waited for the light to change. It seemed like a good time to shake her up a little, get this show on the proverbial road. I cleared my throat as conspicuously as possible, then spit loudly into the gutter. It was a gesture my mother would likely have found revolting. It sure got the attention of the dumpling Dolphins fan. Maybe she had ill-mannered kids of her own. She glanced over at me, then frowned, as if she wasn't quite sure if she knew me from somewhere. I saw the nerves crawl around in her face, looking for a way out. Her jaw tightened.

The light turned green and she took off. Rocks in her shoes or not, she could move when she was motivated. I guess I'd given her just the right kind of prod. Whether it was the spitting or my general appearance I'll never know. One can't stop to hand out questionnaires in the middle of an amateur tail job and ask, "Which aspect of my shadowing technique do you find most -- or least -- effective?"

She strutted purposefully across West Boulevard and continued north. I let her have a little distance, but not too much. She crossed a few streets without once checking for traffic or looking back to see if she was being followed. I didn't want her to think I was some kind of psycho stalker, so I stayed back. At Farmington Avenue she hooked a left, and although she tried to be cagey about it, I saw her take a quick peek over her shoulder as she made her turn, to see if I was still dogging her. Once she disappeared around the corner, I ran to catch up. Good thing, too. As I made the turn on Farmington, I saw her at the next street, turning back south on Evergreen Avenue. Now it was going to get a little tricky. Evergreen is more or less a dead end with a small escape alley and an assisted living facility at the far end. And no other way out.

The harsh glint of sunlight reflecting on a windshield blinded me for a moment, but when I stopped seeing stars, I spotted the woman hiding behind a large maple tree in the center of the nursing home parking lot. She was trying to stand perfectly still, but I could see the backside of her jumpsuit bobbing up and down as if she were trying to catch her breath. I found a doorway and slipped into its shadows. From here I could watch and wait without being seen.

After a few minutes, there was movement behind the maple tree and the squat woman emerged. She looked both ways, bending slightly at the waist like a child about to dart into traffic from between parked cars. It was almost comical. Then she scurried back the way she'd come, limping badly under the weight of her guilty conscience. She was empty handed. I let her go by. She never saw me in the doorway. I gave her time to get back to Farmington Avenue and watched her turn right and disappear eastbound.

I stepped out from my hiding place and walked to the maple tree. Unless she'd been delivering the package to a family of squirrels, it had to be here somewhere. I planned to give the area a thorough frisking.

Fifteen minutes later I was thoroughly pissed off, my hands were thoroughly filthy from rooting around among the roots and branches, and I'd found absolutely nothing. No package tucked neatly into some clever hiding place. No clever squirrels stockpiling nuts for the coming winter. Nothing but dirt and grime. I used a handkerchief to wipe the damp muck from my hands. Then I balled up the cloth and looked for somewhere to ditch it. There was a city garbage can a few feet from the tree. Disgusted, I went over to it. I was about to drop the handkerchief into the trash bin when I discovered the package I'd just spent the last quarter of an hour hunting for in the stupid maple tree.

I lifted it out. It was wrapped in brown paper and sealed in clear plastic packing tape. It weighed about a pound. Didn't have the heft of a book, not even an oversize paperback. It had no markings on it whatsoever. No name or address for either the recipient or the sender. Well, I knew who the sender was, or at least I thought I did. But where had the package been headed when the dumpling lady panicked and ditched it? Was she, herself, the recipient, or just a courier? For the time being, these questions would remain unanswered.

And I was no closer to making contact with LaTwanda Jefferson.

I hoped there'd be something in this package that would lessen my nagging sense of futility. Failing that, I hoped it contained something good to eat.

*The Farce News*

## Chapter 5

I headed back to my stakeout on Park Street, the new treasure tucked securely under my arm. I felt like a world class bully, scaring off the limping Dolphins fan that way, but what choice did I have? The affable Grand Inquisitor? "Excuse me, good madame, but kindly explain what you've got there, would you?" That wasn't going to get the job done. And manually wrestling the parcel from her might well have resulted in my arrest for assault and battery. Not to mention petty theft.

On the way back to Park Street, I stopped in at a shop where they specialized in shipping supplies and services and asked to see a copy of the Hartford county white pages. A town-by-town search revealed that LaTwanda Jefferson had a home on Duncaster Road in Bloomfield, a predominantly working class bedroom community just north of the Hartford city line. I copied down the address and phone number on my crumpled piece of paper and shoved it back in my hip pocket for future reference. As I legged it back south on Sisson Avenue I was pretty sure Sully was right about the store being a front. But for what?

A couple of blocks south of Park Street on New Park Avenue, I found a hobby shop similar to Jefferson's, but quite a bit older and more homey and comfortable. It was called "Wally's House of Cards." I liked the self-mocking double entendre and hoped it was intentional. I went in. The interior was dustier, mustier and generally speaking, quite a bit little less cared for than Jefferson's sterile shop. In other words, my kind of place, reminiscent of the places where I'd bought baseball cards as a kid, the kind of shop that made you want to sneeze, the kind of place that made you want to stay all day, because you just knew that somewhere in all this chaos was a treasure, a Mickey Mantle rookie card, or a Willie Mays, or a Leo Durocher. Okay, maybe not a Durocher.

There were no chimes, no sleigh bells attached to the door frame, no frills. I slipped in virtually (no, make that completely) undetected. And unlike Jefferson's place, Wally's had several customers, all of whom were bent over thick reference books or peering down into the glass display cases in various states of impenetrable concentration. None bothered to look up when I walked in. If I weren't so thick skinned, I might have been offended.

I looked around for someone who might fit the general description of proprietor but nobody seemed to be in charge. Plenty of buyers contemplating their next life-affirming purchase, but nowhere a seller aggressively hawking his wares.

I strolled about, taking it in. The shop was small and cramped, with the air of a great big toy chest full of promise if one has the patience to do some digging. Large glass bulbs hung from the stamped tin ceiling on dusty black chains, giving the room a warm orange glow.

Near the back, I found an open door over which there hung a sign that said *OFFICE*. On the door was a square sheet of cardboard that looked like it came from a folded shirt that had been laundered at some neighborhood Asian dry cleaners. It was scotch taped in place. The tape was yellowed and peeling. On the cardboard someone had written a curious message: *KINDLY KNOCK BEFORE ENTERING -- OR DON'T*. Another double entendre?

I poked my head in and glimpsed a man of about thirty-five, slightly balding and sorely in need of a shave. He was dressed for comfort in baggy brown corduroy trousers and a bright orange Baltimore Orioles warm-up jersey.

He sat behind a beat-up desk eating a hero sandwich off a sheet of wax paper. For just a moment I felt bad about interrupting the guy's lunch. But it was going on three o'clock and the traditional lunch hour had long since passed. I tapped lightly on the door frame. He looked up at me and nodded his head like a big horse. His eyes were clear and sharp. His mouth was full, but that didn't stop him from greeting me in a naturally friendly manner.

"C'mon in," he mumbled, directing me with another nod. "What can I do for you?"

I stepped into the windowless room and glanced around. On a shelf against the opposite wall I spotted a silver and black executive name plate bearing the legend: *MacArthur J. Eastgate, Proprietor*. The guy was clearly a huge baseball fan, but not one of those stereotypical Yankees or Red Sox fanatics who comprised the majority of baseball fans in the Nutmeg State. This guy's passion was inexplicably directed toward the Minnesota Twins. The walls of his office were covered with enormous posters of his favorite Twinkies, including Kirby Puckett at the plate and Bert Blyleven on the mound, and a jersey -- number three -- pinned in place and handsomely displayed in a large glass frame. I stared at it. The thing looked huge.

"That's my Harmon Killebrew," he said.

"Nice," I said. If memory served, Killebrew was a burly power hitter who was about as wide as he was tall.

He finished chewing and swallowed. "What can I do for you?"

I told him my name and said, "Sorry to bother you while you're eating, Mr. Eastgate ..."

*The Farce News*

"Call me Wally," he said, wiping his mouth with a paper napkin. "Everyone calls me Wally."

I looked back at the name plate on the shelf that said MacArthur J. Eastgate. "Okay." Made no sense, but who was I to say so?

"The 'J' stands for John."

I nodded. "Well, sure. That explains everything."

He grinned. "Nobody in his right mind names a kid MacArthur and calls him that to his face, am I right?"

"I suppose. Unless they're just plain mean. Or a war freak."

"Bingo! How'd you know?"

"How'd I know what?"

"My dad was a huge World War II guy? Korea, too. Served in both. Loved MacArthur. I mean, almost in an unhealthy way. Used to run to the cigar shop down the street and tell everyone in the house, 'I shall return.' As if 'Be right back' wasn't good enough."

"They could have called you Mac."

"And expose me to a life of cruel hamburger jokes?"

"True."

"In any event, they went with the middle name. John."

"Right," I said.

"The conventional nickname for which is Jack. Jack Kennedy. Jack Kerouack."

"Jack the Ripper."

"Jack of all trades. Most people don't know the original phrase was 'John of all trades.'"

"Bullshit. Next you'll gimme some story about the John of Hearts."

He grinned. "It was a slippery slope after that. Jack became Jackson. Next thing I know, I'm Stonewall Jackson."

"Like the General?"

"And from Stonewall to Wally?"

"Could have been worse, they could have called you 'Stone.'"

"Yeah, that would have been worse."

"Anyway, my name's Robby."

"And what's your story, Robby? You don't look like a collector."

"I wonder what you know about a dealer in the area by the name of LaTwanda Jefferson? Has a place over on Park Street."

His eyes narrowed but he didn't say right away if he knew her.

I leaned against the door frame, *tres* casual. "I think you have common business interests."

He smiled broadly. I don't know what amused him. I was momentarily

distracted by a morsel of lettuce stuck to one of his front teeth.
"That's a good one," he said. "Common business interests."
"But you do know her?"
"Sure. I know Twannie." He became aware of the lettuce on his tooth and let his tongue do some work to set it free. "Excuse me."
"So, obviously you'd know her on sight?"
Now he let his features drop into a small frown. "Of course."
"Great. Would mind describing her to me?"
"You want to tell me what it's all about first?"
"Just research," I said. "I'm after basics. What she looks like ..."
Wally Eastgate leaned back in his wooden swivel chair and gave me a hard look for the first time. "You a cop, are you? I haven't seen any I.D."
I went to my hip pocket and took out my wallet and pretended to look through it. Then I flipped it shut again. "Nah, I'm not a cop. Do you want to see my drivers license?"
He chuckled and then snorted, like maybe he was amused. "No, thanks."
"Look, I didn't come here to give you any trouble."
"That's good to know."
"Suppose we start over? Let me ask you a different question. Nothing to do with Jefferson. Something business related."
"Fire away," he said. "I always like to talk about business."
"What you know about the National Hockey League?"
"I've a passing interest. Why?"
"What would you say if I walked in here and told you I was looking for a Wayne Gretzky Rookie of the Year card? Topps or Upper Deck. Vintage 1980. And that I'd only pay up to eleven-fifty for it?"
He rocked back and forth in his chair and stared at me. I could only assume he was giving my question his full attention. I smiled a little bit and he joined me. "I'd tell you to get your facts straight."
"Yeah, huh?"
"First of all, Gretzky didn't win the Rookie of the Year award. It's just about the only award he didn't win. Anybody in New England knows Ray Bourque was rookie of the year with the Bruins that year. What you're looking for doesn't exist."
"Exactly. You know it and I know it, but the pretty brunette who works over at LaTwanda Jefferson's shop didn't know it. She didn't bat an eye when I asked, either. She didn't think it over. She didn't take a minute look it up. She said they didn't have that particular card."
Wally leaned over his desk again and took another bite of his sandwich. He chewed for a while, a guy who clearly enjoyed his food. He swallowed

and shrugged. "Who knows? Maybe trading cards aren't their strength."

I shared his outlook and thought about Sully's comment.

"Maybe the same reason you see people in my shop looking at cards all day long, six days a week. You'd be lucky to catch a dozen people in Twannie's place in a month."

"So, help me out here. Let's say, for the sake of the argument, that I have a pretty good reason to believe LaTwanda Jefferson is into something other than sports memorabilia. Thing of it is, I'd like a chance to find out what she might be up to without ringing every alarm bell on the north end of town. If I could watch from a distance, it sure would help. But first I gotta know what to watch for. You follow?"

"Sure, I guess so."

"So, what's she look like? Tall? Short? Skinny? Fat?"

He ran his tongue around the inside of his mouth, cleaning food bits from the corners. He licked his lips, then made the exact same tooth sucking sound my father always made after eating -- principally to drive my mother up the dining room wall. "You could probably meet her just by walking into the store."

"I tried that," I said. "All I got was the pretty brunette."

"Ah. Jennifer."

I shrugged. "She didn't formally introduce herself. And it would be better if I could observe discreetly. 'Til I get the lay of the land."

"The lay of the land?" Wally burst into laughter. "That's a good one. Christ Almighty, I hope you're making a joke."

I gave him a look. "What did I say?"

"A mouthful." He chuckled.

"You care to elaborate?"

"C'mon," he said. "You're the guy playing detective here. Everyone knows which way Twannie and her crowd swing."

I thought about it for a minute but offered no comment.

He must have decided I didn't get it. "From the Isle, man. And I don't mean the center aisle. Although, come to think of it, that's not a bad analogy either."

"Analogy for what?"

"The Isles of Lesbos," he said.

"Oh," I said, wondering if he'd add, "Not that there's anything wrong with that." He didn't.

"They're a bunch of major league dikes."

"As opposed to Triple A dikes."

Wally snorted. "Twannie's a big, tough-looking broad. From what I hear, she's just as tough as she looks. You can hardly miss her. She's about your height, but quite a bit heavier. I'm guessing she outweighs you by a hundred pounds. Face and hair like James Brown."

"James Brown?" I said. "The king of soul?"

"And let me tell you, it isn't the greatest a face I've ever seen on a woman. That's just my opinion. Wait'll you eyeball her for yourself and see if you don't agree. Also she wears a lot of purple. And travels with a bodyguard. Cute little mocha *latte*, name of Billie something. Billie does the driving and holds the doors. If there's more to it, I wouldn't know. I've heard rumors that Twannie did time once for receiving stolen goods. They say she spent a couple of years on The Farm down in Niantic and got an early parole."

"So she's a fence?"

"More like a brick wall."

"How come the local police don't shut her down?"

"Far as the anyone's concerned, Twannie's legit. She's got the store, the employees, the payroll and everything. Even pays taxes. It's all women, of course. But that's her choice. Some of 'em make pretty sweet eye candy, but I'll bet dollars to doughnut holes they're all butch. Some folks say Twannie runs a halfway house for wayward broads who can't figure out which buffet they wanna eat at."

It occurred to me that Wally, now so forthcoming, might just be a bored guy who loved to shoot the shit, a guy who, in the final analysis, was pretty much full of crap.

After I thanked him for his time, I left him to finish his meal. As I took my leave, I spotted thin strips of magnetic alarm tape on the glass door as well as on the front window. I made him for a street smart businessman who knew the neighborhood. I wondered how much value to put on his line of Twannie gossip.

My piece of shit Jetta was parked on South Whitney Street. I climbed in and rolled down the window. It was time to open the package I'd scared off the Dolphins fan. I used a pocketknife to cut the plastic packing tape at one end, then peeled back the paper just far enough to allow me to extract the contents. My original assessment had proven correct. It was not a dictionary, nor a thesaurus for that matter, nor any other name for a book with lots of words in it. It wasn't a book at all. Instead, it was an ornately decorated cardboard box, shrink wrapped in pink translucent cellophane.

I didn't recognize any of the words printed on it. They were printed in some exotic foreign language I had neglected to study during my abbreviated college career, one of many exotic foreign languages I had neglected to study in college. I'd have to get someone to translate the lettering for me, but it could wait. For now there were plenty of clues pointing to the box's origin and contents. I held it to my nose and gave it a good sniff. Even through the cellophane there seemed to be little doubt but that it contained chocolate. Not quite truffles. Not that sweet. The picture on the box provided additional hints: a hand painted illustration featured several chunks of chocolate piled in triangular mounds. In the background was a field of pyramids against a desert landscape. And for some unknown reason, a pair of surly looking camels loitered in the sand, waiting, no doubt, for the chance to hock phlegm at some unsuspecting passerby.

Egypt seemed like a hell of a long way to go for a box of chocolates. Maybe it was worth the airfare. I wondered if you had to fly through Atlanta to get there.

I rewrapped the package and tossed it in the back seat. Oh, well.

After several false starts, I got the piece of shit Jetta running, popped the clutch and lurched into the flow of traffic, in search of a parking space closer to Twannie's place. I found one just down the street. If the limping dumpling returned, I'd see her.

Right about the time I killed the engine and pulled the key, my stomach let out a growl and I realized I hadn't eaten since breakfast, save half-a-dish of pistachio ice cream at Auntie Peg's. Watching Wally Eastgate gobble his hero sandwich had no doubt planted the idea that I was hungry. Sniffing at the rich dark chocolate had no doubt sealed my fate. Unfortunately, I'd spent enough time doodling around the neighborhood. I couldn't risk missing a Twannie sighting while I chased down lunch. Instead, I rummaged around in the glove box, hoping for something at least nominally edible. Among the Jiffy Lube receipts, unpaid parking tickets and folded road maps, I found an apple cinnamon Powerbar that looked like it dated back to the late 1990s. Fortunately the things have a shelf life of about six hundred years. I peeled the wrapper off one corner and bit into of it. It was like solid molasses and I found myself thinking of Lita Wordstone pulling on her taffy and giving me the business. And the nagging question: What kind of trouble was she in that Twannie Jefferson needed eighty large to put things right?

Was it true that Jefferson was some kind of Svengali power dike with a stable of young lesbians under her control. And if so, did it have any bearing on her relationship with Lita Wordstone or the business that had gone sour between them?

An hour later, I was still sitting there thinking things over.

My teeth ached from chewing the Powerbar. I hadn't come up with any

*The Farce News*

new ideas and Twannie Jefferson still hadn't put in an appearance. I had no clue what I'd say to convince her to leave dear old Auntie Peg alone, much less forget about the eighty grand. Twannie Jefferson didn't sound like someone who scared easily.

## Chapter 6

Waiting is something I do pretty well. Some might consider it a gift. Not me. I view it as an acquired skill, like wielding a hammer without mashing your thumbnails to hell. I mastered the craft as a child when my father traveled a lot. We lived in an apartment overlooking Greenwich Avenue, where there was always something interesting to watch, from the hippies and homosexuals to the real freaks who came in from New Jersey on weekends to shop on Eighth Street and cruise for fights on Christopher Street, home of the nation's first gay bars.

I must have spent about a million hours sitting at that front window, watching the world go by in a parade of irrepressible social change, waiting for the yellow cab that would deliver my father home from his latest assignment. Sometimes the wait was longer and thus more difficult by degrees. When he was due home on a Saturday afternoon and didn't arrive until Saturday night, I'd kill half the day waiting and watching. If he was expected on a Monday and didn't get back until Wednesday, it meant a couple of days glued to the window while I might easily have been doing something else, like playing baseball or doing my homework. Once I waited four days and as a result earned an F on my chemistry test at the end of the week. It got worse as the years ticked by.

The last time I waited, it took him eight years to turn up.

My mother had more or less kicked him out for failing to live up to any of his responsibilities (or perhaps any of her expectations). He'd moved a few blocks north to a studio apartment in Chelsea. Just before Christmas the year I was twelve, he stopped by to tell me he was going out of town for a couple of weeks and would call when he got back. I accepted the assurance on face value. I had no reason yet to doubt him. I hadn't yet learned that adults lie to kids all the time. Particularly to mask their shame. The greater the shame, the bigger the lie.

Then January came and he stayed away. January stepped aside for February. Then February ebbed gradually into March. Still he didn't return. The seasons continued to shift. Nothing I could do to hold them back. Summer drifted by. Fall came, a new school year and my thirteenth birthday. But the phone call never came, nor a yellow taxi transporting my yellow father.

Then, before I knew it, Christmas came and a year had gone by. Day by day, week upon week, month after month. At some point I stopped waiting and turned to other things. Not baseball, however, and certainly not homework.

Next time I looked up I was fifteen and footloose, chasing girls and dabbling in whatever mechanisms of diversion I could find. Adolescent bravado took over and I asked (rhetorically, of course), *Who the hell needs a father anyway when all they do is complicate things with their pathetic versions of their own father's authoritarian tyranny?* I saw my friends fight it out with their parents on a daily basis. Quietly I thanked my lucky stars. I didn't know yet that teenagers lie to themselves all the time. To mask their shame. The greater the shame, the bigger the lie.

I wasn't thinking about my father or my teenage angst as I sat on Park Street in my piece of shit Jetta, waiting for Twannie Jefferson to put in an appearance. I was thinking about Indian Summer, which had arrived in Hartford in all its glory. I was marveling at the October sun and how it beat down mercilessly, making if very hard for me to keep my eyes open. My brain felt swollen. My eyelids wanted to glue themselves together and stay that way for about a month. A rivulet of sweat trickled down the right side of my rib cage and I was glad I'd gone home to change into more comfortable clothes. All I wanted was to stretch out my legs and snooze away the afternoon. Instead, I propped my chin in my hand and watched the traffic go by. The vehicle traffic wasn't nearly as interesting as the pedestrian parade. It never is.

I keyed the radio to an AM talk station. The late afternoon liberals who followed the early afternoon conservatives were ripping the governor a new asshole, which was only moderately entertaining. (Every time I saw the guy on TV, I paused to wonder how much he must spend to have his shirts professionally stuffed.)

I kept an eye on the door to Twannie's emporium. There was a moderate flow of customers, none of whom left empty handed. Wally Eastgate had apparently been blowing a little smoke when he claimed to outclass Twannie Jefferson in terms of regular clientele. I had no way of knowing what Jefferson's consumers actually purchased, but judging by the excessive skulking on display I was willing to bet the merchandise could be catalogued under the general heading of Contraband. In two hours, not a single kid under thirty walked in. I guess the youth of America isn't into baseball cards anymore. Or maybe they just can't afford 'em. Life's a bastard that way.

The five o'clock news report was crackling (more "astonishing disclosures" about our crooked governor) when a pastel purple Lexus SUV pulled to the curb in front of the storefront. I sat up a little straighter in my matte black piece of shit Jetta. The Lexus had barely rolled to a full stop when the driver's side door swung open and a petite, athletic woman with richly tan skin jumped out. She wore a sleeveless, black leather biker's jacket. A couple of chains were draped through the epaulets and looped under her sinewy arms. She also sported shiny leather pants that looked like fresh black body paint. The jacket was unzipped to a spot just below her sternum and I saw no evidence of a shirt beneath it. Her face was almond shaped and gorgeous. High cheekbones dominated the mocha landscape while a perfectly shaped nose and large eyes demanded a standing ovation in their own right. Her black hair was done in neat corn rows with shoulder length extensions decorated with colorful beads. In the few seconds it took me to catalog her many charms, I fell completely in love. (In six months or so I'd probably forget all about her.)

As I watched, she gracefully circled around the front of the Lexus and pulled open the door on the passenger side. A large, somewhat regal figure emerged: the entirely purple-clad LaTwanda Jefferson. She was everything Wally Eastgate had promised. My height if not taller, and heavier by a couple sacks of concrete mix. She wore the purple well and moved with surprising grace. Nothing out of breath or sweaty about her. She comported herself in the manner of the empress of the realm, and I struggled to square her image with the voice I'd heard on Auntie Peg's tape recording.

My attention was drawn back to the girl in black leather. Call it a wild guess, but I decided this was probably Billie Something. She fit the description. I wondered what her last name might be. She floated deftly to open the door of the shop. She moved with Fred Astaire style. When she held the door for Twannie it was without overt deference. She was no lackey trying to score points with the boss. She was no ass kisser. She was a working girl doing the job for which she was paid. The big woman in the flowing purple never broke stride as she passed through the doorway. This was a coordinated dance they'd done many, many times.

And just that quickly, it was over.

I'd been sitting there a couple hours, practically killing myself to avoid nodding off. My quarry had finally turned up, and now she was gone again. And I had no way of knowing if and when she might reappear. Ten minutes? Three hours? And what was my best move? Go back into the card store and demand to see the owner? That didn't feel right. So, what then? Play another five rounds of the waiting game?

What choice did I have? (I could hear my third grade teacher, Agnes Grossman: "This is what comes of hiring an amateur to do the job of a professional.")

The sun went down while I sat there trying to come up with a next move.

*The Farce News*

The six o'clock news came on and, though it was hyped as "the latest in breaking news," I could swear it was a tape recording of the five o'clock report, complete with the same bad grammar and illiterate mispronunciations of key names and places.

"Less people than expected showed up at the courthouse today for the beginning of deliberations in the racketeering case of local builder ..."

"Fewer, you moron!" I yelled at the radio. "Fewer people."

I considered bagging it for the day and heading home to grab some dinner. My dog, Rufus, would need to get out. But there was no hurry. If I didn't show up by seven and knock on my neighbor Jolie's door, she'd let herself in with the key I'd given her. She'd feed and walk the hound, pull his ears for a while, and give J.D. and Buddy some tuna. It's good to have a neighbor you can count on. The world is currently in short supply of reliable souls; you have to hold on tight to the ones who present themselves. That's what I'd done with Jolie, at least metaphysically. If it wasn't that I was half-heartedly (make that one-eighthheartedly) waiting for Bonnie to come to her senses and beg forgiveness for her wrongdoing, I might have pushed things along a little more aggressively with Jolie. But we were getting on well enough and isn't *well enough* what we're supposed to leave the hell alone? Anyway, chances were I'd just screw up a really good friendship if I started chasing Jolie *that* way. I don't have that many good friendships, particularly with women, that I can risks with the ones who haven't yet written me off as hopeless.

I was thinking about beer and Jolie when Twannie Jefferson pushed open the door of the card shop and stepped out onto the sidewalk. She crossed the sidewalk like she owned it, and went to the parked Lexus, which I'm guessing she actually did own. She was alone this time. Billie Something, the mulatto angel in black leather, was nowhere to be seen. Twannie went to the driver's side and climbed in behind the wheel. Never so much as glanced my way. I couldn't hear her start the Lexus, but the lights came on at all four corners. I fired up the Jetta, mashing the clutch and pounding the gas. It wheezed emphysemically but the engine caught and held. I spun the steering wheel and hooked a serious U-turn into the middle of the wide avenue. I didn't worry about Twannie taking notice of all the car horns that joined together to honk at me. Her windows were up when she passed me heading east, and I doubted she was going to roll them down and subject herself to the grime and noise of Hartford's North End. She looked like a woman who preferred a controlled climate, and when possible to keep it heavily filtered. Probably in there listening to Melissa Etheridge or k.d.lang on her Blaupunkt sixteen-speaker system. I could just be a pig, however. The possibility exists.

I stayed a few car lengths back and kept some traffic between the front of my piece of shit Jetta and the back of Twannie Jefferson's high-end Lexus. Even in the growing darkness of evening, it wasn't hard to keep her in sight. She didn't seem to be in much of a hurry (good thing, considering traffic), and I determined after a couple of turns that she was tacking north by northwest, heading for Bloomfield and, presumably, home, the address of which was written on a crumpled piece of paper in my back pocket. Just in case I lost her in the rush hour traffic.

She navigated with the skill and polish of a seasoned veteran, using comparatively empty back streets instead of clogged major thoroughfares to reach the city limits: Kenyon north to Asylum, then left and right onto Scarborough, past all the really big houses. At Route 44, she swung left and veered west. The next right turn was Bloomfield Avenue, or Route 189. She hooked the right as I expected her to and we picked up speed as we passed the Watkinson School, then the University of Hartford, called "Yooha" by some of the yahoos enrolled there. I glimpsed the sign for the Museum of American Political Life and made a mental note to spend a Sunday afternoon there sometime, perhaps when my fully motorized wheelchair arrived from the Medi-Care folks on my 90th birthday.

Twannie Jefferson signaled a right turn as we came to the split at Simsbury Road. We continued north on 189. Single-family houses lined both sides of the street. A neatly maintained community. Comfortable as an old pair of sneakers. Dull as the mud caked in the treads of those sneakers. Traffic thinned and I dropped back some more.

She split off the main road and took a shortcut along Terry Plains Road. Half a mile east of Penwood State Park, we intersected Duncaster Road and she signaled right again.

Throughout our journey, she never exceeded the speed limit or ran a single traffic light, nor failed to signal any of her turns. She might be a scumbag extortionist and two-bit hustler trying to get rich on illegal imports and exports, but Twannie Jefferson was a fine driver. Conscientious and considerate. In a world where inconsiderate schmucks sat behind 80% of all steering wheels, I had to give her credit for that much. She pulled up to a four-way stop sign at Adams Street and I dropped back even farther.

Watching the house numbers, I knew we were getting close to her place. I didn't want to attract Twannie's attention now, not after such a brilliant job of tailing her. (Okay, so it wasn't that hard. Maybe any idiot could have pulled it off. And for all I knew she'd been watching me in her rear view mirror since leaving Park Street. I had to put the thought out of my mind.) Just before we reached Duncaster Hollow, Jefferson lit up her brake lights and blinked a left turn. From a couple of hundred yards back, I marked the yellow glow of incandescent light spilling from her garage onto her blacktop driveway as the electric door lifted. She pulled smoothly into her driveway and disappeared into a side-by-side car port that looked larger than my Summit Street apartment. It was attached to the main house by means of a glassed-in breezeway. The house itself was a clapboard structure surrounded by trees and thick hedges, two stories tall with a brick chimney and rear dormer windows on the upper floor. I cruised by slowly and passed her driveway as the garage door began to descend on its rails.

I continued along another hundred feet or so and pulled over. It was one of those neighborhoods where every house has a garage and a driveway, and there were no other cars parked on the road. It might draw attention sitting here, but I didn't have much choice. It was a case of watch-and-perhaps-be-watched or go home and devise some other strategy. I killed the engine and doused the lights. The Jetta creaked and popped as it cooled.

In the growing darkness, I climbed out to stretch. I popped the front hood and slid the support bar in place to hold it open, like a baby grand piano (but somehow different). Then I climbed back into the car and turned on the four-way flashers. For the next little while I just sat there. With the sun gone below the western horizon, the temperature dropped quickly. A few cars, thankfully none of them containing police officers, rolled by. Nobody stopped to offer help or even to inquire if I needed any. New Englanders can be a reserved bunch.

At around seven-fifteen, new headlights shone in my side mirror and from my slunk-down position watched them approach from the south. The car slowed, then pulled into the driveway of Twannie Jefferson's home. A silver Camry, this year's model. Very sedate except for its rather ostentatious chrome rims. Spinners. It looked like something out of a catalog specializing in "pimping the rides" of certified public accountants. The driver's door opened and someone climbed out. The dome light didn't come on and I didn't get a look at the driver. I'd have said it was a woman judging by the way she ran to the house. A woman, or a guy who was about to piss in his pants.

After she disappeared, I walked over and copied down the license plate off the back of the Camry. In the morning I'd get Ernie Newman to run the tag past one of his pals on the Hartford PD and maybe learn a little more about Twannie Jefferson's friends and acquaintances.

Half an hour later, another car approached from the south and slowed as it rolled past the house. Then it sped by me without stopping. A Chevy Monte Carlo SS, black with silver trim. Definitely not this year's model. Jacked up in the rear. It broke hard and turned into Duncaster Hollow, tires squealing.

Then nothing. For the next ninety minutes cars rolled by only sporadically, mostly Volvo wagons, Chevy Suburbans, and about a thousand maroon Subaru Outbacks. None stopped on my account, but no cops came cruising for trouble makers in broken down piece of shit Jettas, either. Call it a wash. As boredom set in, my stomach began to growl again and I gave further consideration to heading back to Hartford.

Then some juvenile delinquent set off what sounded like an M-80.

Growing up in New York City, you learn a few things -- among them the ability to differentiate between firecrackers and gunshots. One you shake your head, the other you hit the deck. And this was no firecracker. It was a gun. Something not too big. A pistol of the genus *Saturday Night Special.* And unless I was nuts, it had come from Twannie Jefferson's house. Without thinking twice, I ricocheted out of the Jetta and sprinted toward the driveway where the Camry was parked.

Staying in the shadow of the bushes alongside the north side of the driveway, I edged up close to the front windows. They were covered with curtains, but the fabric was sheer and light came through them. I couldn't make out any movement inside, but I could hear muffled yells. Doors slammed. More shouts. I tried the front door knob and was not surprised to find it locked. Ringing the doorbell was not an option so I circled around to the side of the house, looking for a kitchen door or some other means of entry. That's when I heard two more shots, in rapid succession, then a third several seconds later. I reached the back of the house and a large deck with two glass doors.

I saw movement, a backlit silhouette. One of the doors slid open and the dark figure emerged. It turned my way and pointed.

Instinctively, I hit the deck and rolled hard to my right, toward the house and the deeper shadows. There came a flash of light and another loud bang and I knew I was being shot at.

I yelled, "Hey, asshole, knock it off!"

Footsteps beat the rhythm of retreat on the deck. My assailant was hauling ass. Typical. It's a scientific fact that most guys will run away if you call them an asshole. *Cocksucker* remains an unfailing invitation to fight.

Leaping to my feet, I gave chase, forgetting momentarily that I don't carry a gun or wear a bulletproof vest or have Kevlar-quality skin. (Or, apparently, have half a brain in my head. Must have been the adrenaline talking.) I didn't recognize the guy sprinting away, but the same bias I'd practiced earlier told me it was a guy, all right. Or Jackie Joyner Kersey with a heater.

My sneakers slipped in the damp grass as I chased the guy around to the front of the house. Predictably, I failed to gain much ground. He could have been wearing soccer cleats, but I didn't think so, particularly when he hit the solid pavement of the driveway and picked up speed. At the top of the driveway, he turned left and sprinted down the road, past my car, and then around the corner into Duncaster Hollow.

"Got you now, dumb ass," I said to myself. Duncaster Hollow is a cul-de-sac with no way out but the way my attacker had just run in. I arrived at the intersection just in time to have a blast of headlights blind me. Without thinking about it I did the dive-and-roll thing again.

The car behind the headlights roared at me full speed, growling menacingly, kicking up gravel and sand. I was well off to the side of the road and out of any immediate danger. As it went by I noticed, much to my disgust, that it was the same black Monte Carlo Sport I'd seen earlier. So, how had the driver managed to slip past me? Had I dozed off after all? I don't think so. I think the guy was just a naturally shifty sonofabitch. A skulking, lurking, pistol-toting asshole without a shred of common decency, shooting at me for no good reason other than I just happened to arrive at what for him was perhaps an inconvenient moment. The Chevy didn't hesitate at the turn, nor come to a complete stop at the octagonal STOP sign. It swerved left onto Duncaster Road and sped south, fishtailing as it went.

I dusted myself off and started back for Twannie Jefferson's house. It occurred to me that none of this commotion seemed to have aroused the least curiosity among the immediate neighbors. Maybe they were already cuddled up around the family TV watching programs so much louder and more violent, they didn't take notice of a little genuine gun play in their own backyards. Or maybe they just didn't want to get involved.

I let myself into Twannie Jefferson's house through the deck doors. All was quiet now. A little too much so. I listened for any sounds of life, or even for sounds of life slipping away. I heard nothing, no moaning, no groaning, no last gasps, no death rattles. I moved silently along floors carpeted wall-to-wall in a thick pile. The front of the house contained a comfortable living room featuring a fake fireplace with an electric log aglow in the hearth. Everywhere I looked, there were signs of a party. A full wet bar on a low black lacquered cabinet, silver ice bucket, glasses, and various bottles. A couple of cushy sofas. A huge plasma screen TV on the wall grabbed my attention.

A videotape played silently on the screen. The production quality was pretty poor but it nevertheless captured my imagination. A beach party of some kind was going on, but wait a minute ... I stopped to watch. I'd never seen anything quite like this before. This was no Frankie Avalon summer bash with bad singing and phony surfers. It was all women. And all of them were naked. And blond -- although I'm guessing a few were bleached that way. More bizarre still, they were playing volleyball. Playing very badly, as if they were drunk or even physically handicapped (excuse me, *challenged*). Or perhaps just amazingly clumsy. I'd never seen the game played quite this way before. Point after point ended with somebody sprawled in the sand, moaning. In honor of the late and over-the-hill Siskel & Ebert (respectively), I wanted to give two thumbs up, if for nothing else to show my appreciation of their fascinating and provocative use of injury time-outs. They did seem genuinely concerned with each other's well-being, constantly administering direct hands-on care in the form of massages and assorted other intimate expressions of TLC. Call me a pig but before I knew it I was scanning the room for popcorn.

I dragged myself away from the TV screen and turned what was left of my considerably redirected focus to a different section of the room. Near a bay window that faced the front of the house, I saw two people. One was sitting in an ordinary dining room chair. I recognized her from our meeting earlier in the day. The glazed expression she now wore suggested it was doubtful she'd recognize me, even if I bothered to introduce myself again.

The other one wasn't sitting in a chair, she was laying on the floor. I'd been chasing her for half the afternoon and evening. And now I'd finally caught up with her. She was on her back, arms outstretched, a loving mother waiting for her favorite child to run into her warm embrace. Spread out like a giant purple star (a four-pointed star) she lay in a pool of blood that blended strangely with the purple diaphanous gown she wore over her large body. I knelt at her side and felt her wrist for a pulse. She was still warm, but the life was gone from her. Up close, I could see the peculiar facial similarity between LaTwanda Jefferson, the queen of Park Street, and James Brown, the king of soul. Wally Eastgate was right. It didn't look that good on a woman. Particularly a dead woman.

Twannie Jefferson may have looked like James Brown, but it didn't look as if she was ever going to sing me any rhythm and blues.

*The Farce News*

## Chapter 7

So, what had I gotten myself into? That's what I wondered (yet again). And a damn good question it was. Cogent, to the point, and timely.

The answer: *Another fine mess, Ollie.* That's what.

Standing there in the middle of a fresh crime scene where gunshots had recently been fired (recklessly but with devastating results), it crossed my mind that I should really do the smart thing and hightail it out of there. Instead, I stopped to gaze down at the large and freshly expired form of LaTwanda Jefferson, and in so doing couldn't avoid taking a moment to ruminate philosophically on the existential fragility of life, that here-today-gone-by-noon sense one gets upon realization of the fact that, in the final analysis, we're all just marking time.

While I was at it, I further paused to contemplate the inexplicable fact that someone somewhere had apparently thought it would be a pretty good idea to shoot a soft-core porn video in which nude volleyball played by a squad of peroxide blondes was the main attraction, and that this individual also believed such a commercial enterprise would be viable to undertake.

And speaking of undertakers, Jefferson was going to need one.

How my mind wandered. And still I didn't do the smart thing and get the hell out of there. Or at least pick up the phone and dial 911.

Staring down at Twannie Jefferson as she lay in her state of permanent slumber I thought about the ill-fated flight of Icarus, which featured the mother of all meltdowns. Had LaTwanda soared out of her comfort zone, only to be shot down like a clay pigeon at some cracker barrel back country gun club? Who'd want LaTwanda dead? Who'd have the balls to pull a trigger and take a life?

A poet once wrote, "Some are born to sweet delight, some are born to endless night." Another suggested, "Tis better to be lowly born, and range with humble livers in content, than to be perked up in a glist'ning grief and wear a golden sorrow." Not to be outdone, a third scribbled, "Solomon Grundy, born on Monday, christened on Tuesday, married on Wednesday, took ill on Thursday, worse on Friday, died on Saturday, buried on Sunday. This is the end of Solomon Grundy." It was only Monday but Twannie Jefferson had definitely gone the way of Sol.

I wanted to call a time-out and search the house; get a better line on Jefferson, her life, what she was into, and what hold she may have had on

Margaret Waddley-Wordstone's granddaughter, Lita. But I knew it was a bad idea to hang around the house much longer. Just because none of the neighbors had come running to see what all the shooting was about didn't mean there wasn't one of them hiding behind a curtain, watching and waiting for the right moment to pick up the phone and summon the cops. I forced myself to operate under the assumption that time was playing for the other team. I'd have to do a cursory once-over and be satisfied.

Unlike the ostentatious Wordstone palace, Jefferson's house was modest, the rooms comfortable but not large, the trimmings and trappings thoughtfully chosen. Most of it was done up in various shades of purple. The wall-to-wall carpet was cream colored, which didn't blend too well with the blood that had leaked from LaTwanda Jefferson's perforated carcass.

Abstract art hung on the walls in simple frames, mostly patterns and studies in color rather than portraits or still life exercises. I didn't see any photographs of friends or family. On a pedestal beside one of the sofas sat a bust of someone I didn't recognize. It sure wasn't James Brown. I looked closer. On the back of the statuette, a small gold-plated plaque had a name and date: *A. Walker, 1997.*

In the midst of this information gathering, I realized I was ignoring LaTwanda Jefferson's guest.

At a small dining room table near the swinging door which led to the kitchen, in the soft glow of a hanging light fixture that contained about a thousand chips of colored glass, sat a dazed and confused Lita Wordstone. Since my arrival, she had not moved nor made a sound of any kind. By all indications, she had taken no notice of my heroic entrance. Glassy-eyed and subdued, her features were slack, her mouth smeared with something brown. If she smiled at me now it would be the classic shit-eating grin. She didn't smile. Aside from her near comatose blank stare, she seemed none the worse for wear and tear. At least she wasn't bleeding. Without conducting an invasive body search, I satisfied myself that she was not injured, other than perhaps between the ears (but I'd thought that about her almost right from the very beginning). If you asked me, this was a girl who'd been dropped a few times, and not just by disillusioned boyfriends.

She was sitting in a simple padded ladder back chair, one of four just like it situated around the table. Her chair was neatly tucked in, like that of a child who has spilled too many crumbs and now pays the price by sitting as close to the table as is humanly possible without cracking any ribs. Lita Wordstone's mouth was covered in chocolate.

Then I noticed her outfit.

My eyes went wide and my head did one of those backward jerking neck cranes, as if my brain wanted a different vantage point, perhaps with the hope of putting a manageable spin on possible ramifications. Alas, it didn't. My brain threw up its hands and said, "What the hell ..?"

Lita was dressed in the uniform of a boarding school student. Not American style, however. She had on the kind of garb you might see at one of those English "public" academies. Navy blue wool blazer and knickers in dark brown tweed. Starched white shirt with a necktie that featured diagonal stripes of gold and maroon. She even wore beige knee socks and heavy black shoes. The caricature was nearly flawless. All that was missing was a leather satchel and the psychological scars; at least I didn't see any satchel. I wondered if she had a Latin text book somewhere nearby. Or something thick as a Manhattan telephone book detailing every fact (relevant and otherwise) relating to such a "today" topic as Geopolitical Repercussions of the Peloponnesian War.

Women in this family were certainly into kinky masquerade.

"Hey," I said gently, shaking her shoulder. "Lita?"

She looked up at me. Rather, she looked up through me. "Hello?"

"Anybody home?" I said.

She tilted her head back a little more and gazed up at the stars, as if I weren't standing there in front of her, blocking the view; as if there were no roof on the house making a quick peek at the stars physically impossible. She had a disturbingly vacant smile on her face, made more troublesome by the smear of chocolate on her lips and chin.

"Have you been eating your own shit again?" I said, cheerfully. She made no sign that she heard me, understood, or took offense. She was mushroom stoned. Traipsing in another time zone.

I left her there, figuring she was unlikely to stray. Meanwhile I could have a quick look around the place. I moved briskly through the downstairs. There were trays of hors d'oeuvres on several low tables. Among them, canapés, which I hate. Something else that looked frighteningly like caviar. I gave it a wide berth. I had no desire to perform an impromptu taste test, just in case it was caviar. Last thing I needed was some forensic team finding DNA evidence of my vomit on the premises. There was a tray of neatly cut cucumber sandwiches. I skirted them, too. There was no popcorn anywhere. This realization made me stop and wonder, Who the hell watches cheap, tawdry porno with fancy hors d'oeuvres? Skin flicks go best with cheap beer and popcorn. Everyone knows that. I fleetingly considered the contents of the video and almost succumbed to the temptation to take another brief glimpse.

I went back through the living room and found another hallway which took me toward the back of the house. There were two rooms off this hallway. The first was clearly the master bedroom, as it was completely decorated in shades of purple.

Over the course of my lifetime to date, I'd slept in my share of beds, in spacious homes, in cramped apartments, in metropolitan hotels, in roadside motels, in park trailers, from singles and twins all the way up to a king or two. But I'd never seen anything like this. LaTwanda Jefferson's bed was, like its deceased owner, a step or two beyond huge. You could sleep in this thing with a pack of total strangers and never run into them once, never be forced to introduce yourself and make small talk, let alone share the covers. On the wall over the bed was a very large print resembling some of Andy Warhol's work with colored negatives. It was done in pinks and purples. Of course. The face was that of 1960s militant activist Angela Davis. I stared at it and lamented the violent passing of LaTwanda Jefferson. In her own peculiar way, she was becoming more interesting to me by the minute and I wished I'd had a chance to meet her and hear her side of the story.

The room, like the others I'd seen, was scrupulously neat. Even the louvered closet doors were perfectly aligned. How often does that happen? I went over and pulled them open. On the left side was a collection of gowns, dresses, pants suits, muumuus, and caftans. All in variations on the purple theme.

On the right side of the closet was the cold weather gear. Not your standard snow bunny wear, however. Unless they were fakes (which was always a possibility), these were big ticket items. Exotic animal skins. Furs. Wraps. Jackets. Full length coats. Quite an expensive collection indeed. I checked a couple of tags. Some were written in what looked like Cyrillic, suggesting Russian, which could mean sable or mink. Several other tags had *Product of Norway* stitched into them. Seal skins? Highly illegal (if there are incremental degrees of illegality).

I didn't have the expertise necessary to conduct the kind of inventory that would do me any good. Nor did I have any guarantee that the doors to Twannie Jefferson's house weren't about to be kicked in by Bloomfield's finest. Then, like Lucy Ricardo, I'd have some explaining to do. A lot, in fact.

Across the hall, the second bedroom was done up like an office, complete with wood shelves on the walls, metal filing cabinets, an oak desk large enough to lie down on, and an executive office chair. On the desk, there sat a green glass lamp with a tasseled pull chain. A purple area rug lay on the floor beside the desk, and a fold-out couch was positioned under a pair of windows along another wall.

Next to the large oak desk, a smaller satellite table was positioned perpendicular to the mother ship. A purple *iMac* desktop computer sat waiting for someone to pay it some attention. I pressed the circular button on the front panel below the screen. The button lit up green as the computer came on. I double-clicked the mouse on the Current Files folder and it opened. A subdirectory appeared consisting principally of single names. None were along the order of Bob or Dave or Jim. They were all last names. I scanned them quickly. Near the bottom I found a familiar one.

Wordstone.

I opened the file and it got a little tricky. Twannie Jefferson wasn't into passwords and other diabolical computer gibberish. But she damn sure wasn't into sharing valuable information with just any old schmuck who happened along and had a nose like a prevaricating Pinnochio. The Wordstone file opened and I found myself staring at several lines of numbers and symbols, upper and lower case alpha codes, with incongruously positioned punctuation marks. None of it made the least bit of sense to me. But that was no surprise. I closed all the files and used the Shut Down prompt to turn off the monitor. One of the best features of this particular *iMac* is its built-in handle and single-piece design. I unplugged a few cords, wrapped them into coils, then hauled the monitor, the keyboard, and the mouse out of the office.

Lita was still sitting where I'd left her, still staring at the night sky through the living room ceiling, the upper floor, and the shingled roof. I thought of a joke about the midget astrologist "gazing up at Uranus," but decided Lita probably wouldn't appreciate it.

I noticed the stairs to the upper floor and bounded up them two at a time. Time was of the essence and I wanted to get out of there, but I didn't want to overlook something obvious through sheer chickenshit, cowardly haste. I found two more doors. One led to a spare bedroom that looked completely unused. Not a hint of purple in the place. The closets were empty, ditto the bureau drawers. The other door was locked. I jiggled the knob and leaned my weight against it, but it didn't budge. I didn't feel like injuring myself trying to be macho. Breaking and entering is bad enough. Breaking and bruising is unnecessary and totally avoidable.

With a little time, I could gain entry to the locked room in Twannie Jefferson's house without breaking a sweat, let alone any bones. At the moment, I had neither the time nor the requisite tools for the job.

Back downstairs, I picked up the *iMac* like a bulky suitcase in one hand and draped Lita's overcoat around her shoulders. I took her by the arm and led her toward the sliding doors and the back deck. She came along quietly. When we passed the prone carcass of Twannie Jefferson, she paused for a moment, then spoke for the first time. "Hey," she said in an airy voice. "What's a matter with Big Jeff?"

I gave her a little more of the tavern bouncer routine, shoving her out of the house faster and rougher than she was probably used to. Whatever interest she had in "Big Jeff" was rapidly replaced by a new and infinitely more pressing mystery.

"Who're you?" she said, looking at me over her shoulder.

"Sammy Sosa," I said.

"Hi, Sammy," she said. Then: "You got any candy? I like candy."

"I'm sure," I said, guiding her around the back of the house, along the dark edge of the driveway to the silver Camry. I found a set of keys in the pocket of her overcoat and unlocked the car using the remote keyless entry fob. The Camry's headlights flashed and the doors unlocked. Across the street my piece of shit Jetta sat flashing its emergency lights at the world like some bus depot pervert without an audience to horrify. I tucked Lita into the passenger seat. She stared out the window at the night sky. I looked around in the glove box for something to wipe her face, but found nothing and quickly gave up on the idea. Hopefully we wouldn't be pulled over.

After shutting the door on Lita, I hurried over to my Jetta and opened the trunk. I stashed the computer among the old blankets and tire changing tools, then re-locked it. There was no activity in the street. I went around to the front of the car and put the hood down and killed the four-way flashers. I went back to the Camry and climbed in beside Lita. It was well appointed. Heated leather seats, very nice. Electric moon roof, how classy. Automatic transmission, oh well.

I cranked the key in the ignition and backed out of the driveway, then cut the wheels hard and pointed us south, toward Hartford and the Wordstone compound on Prospect Avenue.

"Where are you taking me, Sammy?" Lita asked.

"Home."

"Oh, goody. I hide candy in my room. Peppermint Panties. I'll show you if you want."

"No, thanks."

She giggled. "Did I say 'panties'? I meant Patties."

I groaned.

Thankfully, we didn't encounter much traffic until we were back on Route 189 in West Hartford, and even then nobody took any special notice of us. Just another middle class couple in a middle class car, coming home from a middle class date in a middle class neighborhood. Except Lita wasn't my date. She was way too young for that, plus we were supposedly related, which added a whole other strangely Appalachian component to it.

At one point, Lita Wordstone turned to me and said, "Sammy, do you like volleyball?" When I didn't answer, she said: "I like volleyball. Sort of. I don't play very well yet. I keep straining my groin."

I kept my eyes on the road and a firm grip on the wheel. I began to count down from one hundred. She quieted down and returned her gaze to the stars. I was at seventeen before she spoke again.

"Where are we going, Danny?"

"Who's Danny?"

"Aren't you Danny?"

"Sammy," I said.

"Oh, right. So, where are you were taking me, Danny?"

"Home." I said.

"Your place or mine?"

"Shh," I said. "Let's have some quiet time, shall we?"

She started singing: "Show me the way to go home! I'm tired and I want to go to bed ..."

My blood chilled a little and I started counting down again.

"Hush now, Lita. That's a good girl."

She stopped. "Oh," she said. "Okay." Then, a minute later: "How do you know my name? You're not my boyfriend are you?"

"It's a short story. Maybe I'll tell you sometime. Maybe I won't."

She shrugged and leaned her head back and resumed staring out the window at the sky. "You're breaking up with me, aren't you?" The night had become cloudy and overcast, but that didn't seem so spoil her fun. Lucky kid. Some really are born to sweet delight. "I have candy at home," she said. "Hidden in my secret place."

"You said that." I counted backwards some more.

## Chapter 8

As we pulled into the driveway outside the Wordstone mansion, I damn near thanked Lita for keeping her mouth shut for the rest of the ride. I would have done so in my usual fashion, dripping with pithy mordacity, if only to match the dried chocolate no longer quite dripping from her chin. But she continued to stare vacantly into space and would no doubt have been anesthetized to the slashing sting of my rapier wit. Her eyes were barely open. I wondered if she was even conscious.

I shut off the Camry's purring engine, silently cursing my piece of shit Jetta (in absentia) for no longer being able to do something as basic as purr. I climbed out.

Lights burned in the front of the big house but I detected no signs of activity. Prospect Avenue was very quiet. I crunched across the gravel. I had barely rung the bell when the door swung quickly open and Rosa the Puerto Rican housekeeper commenced yammering at me in a form of Spanglish I hadn't heard since my junior high school days on the west side of Manhattan.

"Oh! *Dios mio! Senior Phone!* Hang I glad to see choo!"

She peered around me out to the dark driveway where Lita sat in her Camry. She seemed to be simultaneously hiding behind me and helping herself to a gratuitous eyeful, as if gawking at a highway wreck for entertainment, without regard for the inherent tragedy.

"How cung choo dribing *la puta's* car?" she said, inquisitively and not a little suspiciously. "Chee hokay?" Her voice dropped several octaves, "Chee no dead?"

I don't know if Rosa hoped the answer would be "Yes" or "No." I smiled. "She's alive."

"Oh, chore. Lemme guess. *La puta* is dronk agang?"

I hooked a thumb over my shoulder the way I'd seen Clark Gable do while attempting to teach Claudette Colbert to hitchhike. "She's *something* but I'm pretty sure it isn't drunk. She'll need some looking after. You might want to call a doctor, if you know one who can keep quiet. I don't know if she's on drugs, or has a monster case of food poisoning. For all I know she's suffered a freakin' aneurysm. All I know is she's in a *wide* lunar orbit. If you get my meaning?"

Rosa put a hand to her mouth and shook her head, eyes pressed shut. For a moment I wondered if she had understood a word I'd said. If she hadn't it certainly wouldn't be the first time *that* had happened. "Oh, no! Chee do it agang!" Rosa said. "*Puta desgraciada!*"

"She do what again?"

"Chee allergic, but chee no pay no attenching what de doctor say."

Okay, we still weren't really making any progress.

"Allergic to what?"

"What choo thin' I talkin' about? *Chocolata!*"

"Chocolate?"

"*Si.* Jess. *Chocolata.*"

"That's ridiculous. How can anyone be allergic to chocolate?"

"*Pardona mi?*"

"It's a basic food group!"

"Oh, no, Senior Phone. Chee *muy alergico! Ella no puede comer el chocolata!* I tellin' choo, Senior Phone. One bite *la chocolata* the same one hundred bee stings."

"Except without the bee stings."

"*Si!*"

"In other words, not quite the same."

Rosa looked at me with that same expression she'd worn earlier in the day -- that is, as if I were some kind of mental midget (or is it dwarf, I can never remember which is which), but she couldn't make up her mind if I was being difficult by design or by default.

"Chee sleeping in the Toy-Jota?"

"Something like that. C'mon, I'll help you bring her in."

Rosa was all bustle now. Muttering to herself. Switching back and forth between English and Spanish. At one point I caught the phrase, "*Que noche!*" which I took to mean, "What a night!" Then, "*Y ahora esta,*" which I translated roughly as, "And now this!" But it was mixed in with a bunch of other nervous chatter and I didn't give it a whole lot of my attention. We worked fairly well as a team, once we put our minds to it. Jerry Lewis and Dean Martin without all the intense mutual animosity. Lita came along without too much struggle. We soon had her in the house and halfway down one of those long hallways that led God knows where.

We stopped suddenly in front of a large door and Rosa put up a hand like a traffic cop stopping cars at a busy intersection. Clearly my journey was over. I was to advance no farther. This was about to become women's work, or at the very least family business. Or maybe it was just that guys like me didn't get to hang around and watch Puerto Rican housekeepers strip the clothes off of stoned, chocolate-smeared young women. I don't know what her precise meaning was, but I got the general idea.

"By the way, could I have a word with Mrs. Buenavista?" I said.

"No!"

"No? Why not?"

"Chee no hone. Tha's why."

"Yeah, huh?"

"Chee out."

"Yeah, I made that connection when you said she wasn't home. What about Mrs. Wordstone?"

"What about her?"

"Can I see her?"

"No."

"Why not? Is she out, too?"

"Chee sleeping," Rosa said. "With the Fitches."

"The what?"

"The Fitches."

"The fishes?"

My mind reeled with images of Luca Brasi dying horribly at the hands of the Barzini-Sollozzo crime coalition. I pressed for details and eventually learned that an elderly couple named Doris and Karl Fitch, of the Litchfield Fitches (whom I'd never heard of, much to Rosa's shock and poorly concealed dismay), had come for Auntie Peg just before dinner. Together, they had driven to the Choate School in Wallingford where Doris and Karl's great grandson, Karl VI, was to play in a game of prep school ice hockey against Westminster, or was it Avon Old Farms? Rosa couldn't keep it straight and I couldn't make her understand that I couldn't care less.

"The Kennedy children, they go there," Rosa said, proudly. "Many, many jeers ago. Before they get shot."

The only thing I knew about Choate (and it was one monumentally useless piece of information) was its reputation for having the single coldest hockey rink this side of the former Soviet Union. *"Si,"* Rosa said, and explained that as such it was one of Auntie Peg's very favorite places in the world. According to Rosa, the *madrone* was going to stay overnight at the Fitch estate in Litchfield and return to Prospect Avenue sometime in the morning. "If chee live through the night," Rosa said, crossing herself. Then she excused herself to attend to Lita.

It didn't take long to finish putting Lita down for the night. But when she rejoined me, Rosa looked like she'd spent the last ten minutes wrestling alligators. Hair tousled, uniform askew. I thought I saw tooth marks on her left forearm. She straightened herself out as best she could and walked toward me with her head held high, oozing victorious dignity -- and a bit of blood.

"Choo should see the other guy," she said, pressing her hair into place.

"I'll just be going now," I said. "Here are the keys to Lita's car."

Rosa peered at me suspiciously. "Choo gonna *walk* hone?"

I turned and looked at her. The warmth had quickly bled out of our relationship. We were becoming more like Lewis and Martin by the minute. I wanted to go bucktoothed and squawk, "Lady!" at her, but I resisted the urge. "My pogo stick is double parked."

"I offer choo a ride, but Miguelito ..."

She turned away for a moment.

I wondered if she were talking about the kid in the tool shed.

"Miguel. He drive sontines for Mrs. Wordstone. In the Linking."

"The Linking?"

"Cong-tinental."

"Oh, he's the chauffeur," I said. I could not have made a more inappropriate comment if I'd called him a mincing fairy with a predilection for sticking his cock in underaged squirrels.

Rosa bristled and her dark eyes flared at me. I'm not sure exactly why. I meant no offense, and she herself had just described the duties rather adroitly. Still, I had rankled her. It seemed I had the gift.

"My boy is no ..." She stopped again. This time she clenched her teeth and said no more. Was she fighting back tears, or rage?

"Anyway, I don't need a ride. Thanks anyway."

"Fine. Be like that."

"Good. I will."

"*Muy.*"

I'd have tipped my hat to her at that point, if I'd been wearing one. But, alas, no hat.

I left the big house. Rosa didn't let the door hit me in the ass, but I could tell she was thinking about it. I hit the bricks and made my way sou th along Prospect Avenue. I passed a couple of locals walking their expensive pure breed dogs. I bade them a "Good evening." They bade me to "Go fuck yourself." I love this part of town.

On Elizabeth Street I turned toward the University of Connecticut Law School campus. A little out of way, but I needed a pay phone and I knew of only one in the area. With the explosion of cell phones, pay phones were quickly becoming an endangered species. I don't own a cell phone. I can hardly afford the crackling land line in my flat.

At the UConn campus I found the phone, dropped a couple of quarters in the slot and dialed Jolie's number. I hoped she'd be home, and was unsure how I'd feel if she were out at this hour of the night, or worse still, was home "entertaining." She picked up on the third ring, before I had a chance to massage my lingering doubts into a full-blown anxiety attack.

"Hey," I said, "it's me."

"Hey," she said. "You need dog food."

"I do?"

"Among other things," she added. Whatever *that* meant.

"Okay."

"So, what's going on?"

I hesitated. I was beginning to regret bringing Jolie into my mess. Oh, what the hell. What are friends for? "I hate to impose, but can you come out to play? I need a small favor."

"How small?"

I told her. She didn't ask why I wanted to go to Bloomfield at this hour, or why I couldn't drive there myself.

"Start walking up Whitney," she said. "Then cut over to Terry Road. There's less traffic. I'll pick you up along the way. I just need a minute to throw something on."

Before I could thank her, she hung up, leaving me with the nagging image of her having to throw something on. I headed for Whitney Street and hung a right, tacking north. I made it all the way to Asylum when headlights bathed the street in front of me. I looked over my shoulder. The headlights blinked off and then back on. I stopped and waited while Jolie pulled her rusty black Dodge pickup to the curb. The passenger door creaked and moaned as I pulled it against the better judgment of its rusty hinges. I climbed in beside Jolie and pulled the door shut. It clanged. I opened it again and slammed it shut again. Same thing. Clang. No click.

Jolie laughed. "You do that every time."

I looked at her. "Huh?"

"It's closed, Robby."

"You sure about that?"

"Don't worry, I promise not to drive over seventy."

"I feel better already."

"Don't forget your seat belt."

I did as I was told.

She hit the gas. After a small hesitation, the truck lurched forward and we were on our way. Without any directions from me, Jolie wheeled the truck to Albany Avenue, then hooked the same quick left and right Twannie Jefferson had and put us onto Bloomfield Avenue, heading north toward the general vicinity of Duncaster Road.

It only took a few minutes and Jolie didn't bother to fill the time by asking a bunch of questions. In fact, she had just one. "You want me to hang around and wait?"

"Nah, my car's there already. I can get home okay. But, thanks."

She nodded and said nothing. We rode along that way for a bit. A tape was running in her dashboard cassette player. She had it turned down low, as background music that wouldn't interfere in case of a sudden outbreak of conversation. *Bakersfield Bound.*

"You wanna turn that up, go ahead."

She took 189 to Adams before heading west, rather than using Terry Plains. It worked for me. I let her determine the route -- driver's prerogative. I cranked the volume just as the penultimate song began. Jolie sang along quietly, taking the high harmony on the chorus.

*If I take all the love that's in me and bet it on you*
*Would you promise me that I won't wind up broke and feeling blue*
*I would risk my life on love again, just tell me darling, am I still in?*

When we pulled in behind my Jetta around eleven o'clock, the street was dead quiet. No cops, no ambulance, no coroner's meat wagon, nothing. I was a little surprised. But also relieved. As I climbed out, Jolie cleared her throat.

"This your girlfriend's place?"

She was already grinning at me or I would have had to say, "Smile when you say that."

I closed the door behind me and leaned my forearms through the open window. For a moment I just looked at her. Jolie's a smallish woman, not much over five feet, with unruly auburn hair that she highlights when the mood hits her. A little younger than me. Not much, though. Slim and works at it. Shows some history in her eyes, but you can also see there's still a lot of life she wants to live. Cute nose. Killer smile. She's not from Hartford, either. I think that's what first drew us together as friends, being outsiders in a land of insiders.

"Have I ever told you you're too short to drive a pickup?" I said.

"About a hundred times," she said. "Why?"

"Well, you still are."

"Yeah, well you're too tall to stoop this low."

And with that, she jerked the truck into gear and hauled ass into the night, leaving me standing there with my absentee hat in my empty hands. It's one of the things she does very well.

I unlocked the trunk of my piece of shit Jetta to make sure the *iMac* was still there. It was. From the glove box, I retrieved a leather pouch, re-locked the car, and went back to Twannie Jefferson's place. A sinister hush seemed to fill in the air, but I'm pretty sure most of it originated in my imagination.

I kept looking over my shoulder, waiting for the cavalry to come out of the proverbial woodwork, or at least out of the woods. But it didn't. Apparently, no emergency call had gone out. No 911 report of shots fired. All part of the Great American Non-Involvement Act of 2001, which had apparently not yet expired.

I circled around to the back of the house and let myself in through the sliding doors. The lights inside were still on, just as I had left them. A few things jumped out at me immediately. None of them were cops or bad guys with guns. Somebody had been very busy. Or had called in one hell of an efficient all-night maid service. Every sign of a party ever having taken place had been erased. Gone were the trays of hors d'oeuvres. Gone the canapés. Ditto the caviar. The wet bar was nowhere to be seen, nor the ice bucket and array of liquor bottles. The plasma screen on which I'd viewed those few choice moments from that rather unique volleyball contest was now gray. No video boxes littered the coffee table in front of the couch.

And then my head snapped around. Holy shit! What the hell?

LaTwanda Jefferson was also gone. The woman of the house had taken a powder.

I could hear my third grade teacher, Agnes Grossman: "Well, Robert, she didn't just get up and *walk* away, did she?" Is it any wonder I hated third grade?

"How the hell should I know?" I said, then realized that a person may be stashed away indefinitely in the not-so-warm embrace of an institutional straight jacket and placed on a steady, Atkins-friendly diet of Thorazine for conducting these kinds of conversations with ghosts from the past.

I went to the spot where I'd last seen Twannie Jefferson sprawled out like a giant purple star. Someone had done some fast and effective work to eliminate the blood stain from the cream colored carpet. If you didn't know where to look, you might never see the thing. Must have used some of those magic enzymes. A CIA cleanup crew? I had my doubts about the gubmint's direct (or indirect) involvement in LaTwanda Jefferson's murder, or the crime's subsequent cover-up, even if she had been in violation of several federal statutes pertaining to the illegal importation and possession of Egyptian chocolate for purposes of trafficking. (Hey, it could happen. Inexplicably, laws remain on the books in Hartford prohibiting far lesser crimes -- such as educating a dog or kissing one's wife on Sundays.)

On a hunch, I went to LaTwanda's bedroom to check the closets, and immediately celebrated a rare moment of bullseye intuition. Like their owner, the furs were gone. I had a feeling they would be.

The party and the subsequent domestic violence was staged in the living room, and that's where most of the cleanup work had been done. Somebody -- or bodies -- had busted their singular or collective ass to to eradicate any evidence of wrong doing. For the life of me I couldn't imagine why.

It was time to have a crack at the locked room upstairs. If the police showed up now, the worst I'd face would be a charge of misdemeanor burglary, although I hadn't exactly broken into the house but had simply entered through an unlocked door. And I had no stolen merchandise on me, not counting the computer in the trunk of my car. I could claim it was a loaner if push came to shove.

Ernie Newman, my ex-cop friend, had long ago passed along to me the fine art of picking locks, which, if you have a little patience and a fairly steady hand, isn't nearly as difficult as it may seem. Ernie once said, "If you can play that fucking contraption," referring to my beloved pedal steel guitar, "you should have no problem picking a lock or two." Now I knelt before the locked door and selected the appropriate picks from the leather pouch I'd taken from the car. I worked them into the lock, pushed back the layers of the mechanism one at a time and listened for the satisfying click of a job well done. It took about forty seconds. I turned the door knob and let myself in.

The room smelled fresh and clean but looked like a private gymnasium. Exercise gear everywhere. A stair climber, rowing machine, stationary bike, full set of free weights neatly arranged by size order against one wall. Even a rack and boots used for hanging upside down, like a bat in a cave A small bed and a dresser with a built-in mirror completed the furnishings. I concluded this wasn't so much a workout room as it was the bedroom of a workout fanatic. There's a difference.

For one thing, it meant the free weights and exercise crap most likely weren't for Twannie, just in case I was tempted to entertain such an utterly preposterous notion. For another, it meant someone else lived here. Someone who might walk in any minute now.

Unfortunately, none of this told me anything useful about Twannie Jefferson's passing or her mysterious post-mortem disappearance, where she'd gone and, more importantly, how. All I knew for sure was that the police hadn't taken her body away or they'd still be here poking around, being inquisitive, suspicious, and bored all at once.

No, somebody wanted the fact of LaTwanda Jefferson's violent demise concealed. I wondered about the guy in the Monte Carlo Sport, but ruled him out for the time being. Judging by the way he tore ass out of Dodge, I couldn't see him circling back anytime soon. You don't run like a rabbit after killing someone, then come back an hour later and snatch the corpse and clean house -- unless you're a homicidal clean-freak with a conscience. Charlie Manson meets Felix Ungar.

This was crazy. I was beat. I couldn't be thinking straight if I honestly thought someone had grabbed Twannie Jefferson's carcass and hauled it out of there. The idea of stealing a dead body was too farfetched to be given any further consideration (Gram Parsons notwithstanding). Of course, if Twannie Jefferson ended up under a big rock in Joshua Tree, I'd wrestle the damn Stetson away from my dog, Rufus, one last time and eat it. With fava beans and a nice chianti.

I let myself out of Twannie's place and snuck stealthily back to my piece of shit Jetta safe under the cover of darkness and neighborhood apathy. The night had grown cold. The Indians had taken back their summer. Bloody Indian givers. I hooked a U-turn and headed home.

Cruising quietly back to Hartford, I pondered the day's events and periodically checked the rear view mirror for the swirling police lights I expected to see at any moment. If nothing else, it was nice to be united with distant family. No, not really. It had been interesting, odd, confusing, entertaining, even humorous at times, but I wouldn't go so far as to say the experience had thus far been nice.

I let myself into the apartment and the cats, J.D. and Buddy, immediately tag teamed me, each one wrapping himself around one of my ankles. Somehow I managed not to fall and smash the *iMac* to pieces. In the kitchen, laying on his padded mat and gnawing at the stuffing, I found Rufus. He looked up at me and wagged his tail furiously, banging it against the wall. When our eyes met, he jumped to his feet and trotted over to have his face pulled and his neck scratched. I spotted my Stetson crumpled in a ball in the spot on the mat where he had been sleeping. Rufus watched me pick it up and attempt somewhat unsuccessfully to beat it back into shape. The expression on his face was one of abject self-pity mixed with overwhelming remorse. I might have bought into his little canine melodrama if it weren't roughly the eighty-seventh time he'd pulled this particular stunt.

From the fridge I grabbed a beer and a white cardboard box containing the leftovers from last night's dinner of cold sesame noodles. I set the *iMac* on the kitchen table and attached all the cords. It booted up quickly and I started rummaging through Twannie Jefferson's Current Files folder as I ate. I went back to the list of names, where I'd found the Wordstone file, and scanned them. A few names popped. Big money locals, political types who perhaps had secrets they'd pay to keep quiet, a couple of well known philanthropists whose fabled generosity had apparently earned them a place on Jefferson's hit parade. This was what the *noir* guys called a sucker list. It gave me a bad feeling in my gut. But that could have been the cold noodles.

Even for a confirmed cynic, this represented a fairly lowbrow operation, vipering into people who already made a point of giving away their millions. (Not all of their millions, of course. They are, after all, millionaire philanthropists, not millionaire idiots.)

I was too tired to make any sense of it. In the morning, things might be clearer. I finished the noodles and cracked another beer but don't remember drinking it. I shut it down for night around 1:30 and crawled off to bed. Rufus and the cats joined me and we made a snooze fest out of it.

*The Farce News*

## Chapter 9

I awoke on Tuesday morning to the soothing strains of soon to be replaced Bob Edwards reading the news on NPR's Morning Edition. Naturally, most of the news was bad but the sonorous tone of Edwards' voice gave it the quality of a bedtime story. Having neglected to disable the alarm the night before, my punishment was to wake up to a litany of chaos and destruction, albeit delivered in the velvety baritone of a professional orator.

The dog and the cats had taken up positions at the foot of the bed, as they do every morning, one cat at each corner staring silently, the dog sitting between my feet panting happily, pinning the sheets and blankets so I can't move. This makes no sense, of course, because the three of them are anxiously awaiting delivery of their breakfast, which they're only forestalling with this tactic. But what should I expect? Their collective brains are about the size of a small tomato.

I wriggled free, staggered into the kitchen, flipped on the radio on the fridge, and poured kibbles and dog chow into the animals' respective bowls.

While they ate breakfast (their own and, inexplicably, each others), I spooned coffee grinds into a filter and set up the coffee pot. Once it began to drip, Chinese water torture style, I hit the shower. Five minutes later, shivering and wrapped in a towel, I grabbed the Hartford *Courant* from my doormat and settled down in the kitchen. The cats were giving themselves baths. The dog was chewing a rawhide bone.

The radio chattered. The regional affiliate had come on to deliver the local news report. I listened with one ear while I filled a large coffee mug. There wasn't much that grabbed my attention. A house fire in Newington -- smoking in bed, nobody injured. A case of ATM vandalism at a bank in Glastonbury -- kids in Richard Nixon masks, according to surveillance video. Another fatal car accident involving young adults. These catastrophes were becoming frighteningly commonplace. One of the victims was a seventeen-year-old kid from Simsbury, a high school senior who died from his injuries at one of the Hartford hospitals around dawn. The other young man, as yet unidentified, had been pronounced dead at the scene. His car plunged into a ditch under the Simsbury sycamore tree where Nod Road intersects Route 185.

In the sports section I checked the NHL scores for news of the Carolina Hurricanes (formerly the Hartford Whalers, before their carpet bagging owner moved them south). The 'Canes had played Florida to a 2-2 tie, leaving them winless in their first three games of the new season. Who could ask for anything more? I didn't gloat long, however, for my sad sack New York Rangers weren't faring much better.

I folded the sports page and turned to the Connecticut News section to check on the crooked governor. He wasn't having a very good season, either. One of these days, the woman currently playing understudy as Lieutenant Governor might have to give up her public access TV show and step up to the plate as boss of the state.

I was working on my second cup of coffee when the doorbell buzzed (or the door buzzer rang. I'm not sure which). Rufus became apoplectic, barking wildly and running in progressively smaller circles. The cats scrambled as if World War III had just been declared.

I put down the newspaper and the mug. I hoped it would be Jolie so I could fill her in on my adventures and thank her properly for jumping into the fray without hesitation.

I yelled, "Hang on," and hurried to pull on jeans and a tee shirt. When I opened the door I was a little disappointed to see my part-time drinking buddy Ernie Newman standing there in a crumpled brown suit and scuffed brown shoes. His shirt was unbuttoned at the collar, his brown tie was loosened. He looked like he'd slept in his car and his car had slept in a junk yard crusher.

"Woah," I said. "Don't you look like a pile of shit."

"Yeah, thanks loads," he said.

"No, I just mean the color scheme."

"Oh, in that case ..." He flipped me the bird.

"You'd better come in before one of my neighbors sees you and calls the cops."

He shouldered past me and made for the kitchen and the coffee pot.

I checked my watch as I closed the door behind him. I held it to my ear to make sure it was still ticking. "Mickey wants to know what brings you here at this hour of the morning. Did Jake's just close? Or did they finally cut you off? And how come you didn't bring donuts?"

"Mickey said all that? What a clever little rat bastard."

Ernie Newman is about fifty. Some days he looks closer to seventy. This was one of them. The stubble on his sunken cheeks was white. The bags around his bloodshot eyes were purple going toward black. His cheeks were rosy, but that was due to booze, not the brisk morning air. I had no reason to doubt he had come here directly from some gin mill barstool where he'd spent the last few hours drinking himself sober. Ernie had served and protected long enough as a soldier on the Hartford PD to come by his jaded world view honestly, which accounted for the hard outer shell. Underneath, he was totally different. Caring and considerate. He was also lazy as a summer afternoon and thoroughly lacking anything resembling ambition. Just like me. No wonder we were friends.

Despite his disheveled appearance, he was the nominal president and CEO of a private security company. It was strictly a hands-off enterprise. He'd set it up with retirement money when he left the force, hired a handful of carefully chosen experts to run it day to day. The company got most of its work on the strength of Ernie's reputation and word of mouth. Which was how Ernie came to know the Wordstone family. He'd updated their home security system. The fact that they turned out to be relatives (distant relatives, I reminded him as often as possible) was pure dumb luck. (Idiotic luck, in fact. The consequences of which were still to be determined.) He said this gig was a cake walk, a golden opportunity, a gift horse, a slam dunk chance to diversify my skill set. To say nothing of a tailor-made opportunity to get my fork in the family cash pie. (Was this Ernie's way of looking out for a friend? Also to be determined.)

At the moment, he was checking up on me, not looking out for me.

"So, whadja make of the old lady?" he said, helping himself to coffee. "She something else?"

"Enough to make you swear off ice cream for life."

He spooned way too much sugar into his cup. "Or hanging out in libraries."

"Not that you do much of that."

He smirked at me. "Oh, like you *do*?"

"Oh, I check out a book now and then."

"*Hustler* is a magazine, not a book." He blew steam off his cup.

"At least I have a library card."

"I've heard you prefer bus depots and soup kitchens."

I shrugged. "Fewer homeless. The smell of urine isn't as strong."

He looked at me sideways. "You mind if we change the subject?"

"You're the uninvited guest."

"The name Miguel Batista mean anything to you?"

I put down my cup. "Funny you should ask."

"Yeah? Funny *ha ha*, or funny *weird*?"

"Weird. I don't know many Miguels, but I heard of one last night. I didn't get a last name, so I couldn't say if this is your Miguel or not."

Ernie sipped his coffee and grimaced. "My Miguel, as you call him, isn't anybody's Miguel anymore. 'Cept maybe the good Lord's."

I was getting an ugly vibe. "No, huh? And why is that?"

"Because he's dead."

We stared at each other as his provocative report hung in the air.

"Well, *I* didn't do it," I said.

Ernie likes to adopt a *dumb-and-dumber* Columbo-on-Thorazine deceit, grinning like a village idiot, going around with the disheveled suit and the day-old beard, like some down-on-his-luck schlubb. But he's as sharp as anyone I know. Now he grinned at me and sipped his coffee. "Relax, kid. Nobody's accused you of anything."

I put together another cup of coffee. "So how'd Miguel Batista come to shed his mortal coil?"

"Car wreck."

"Ouch."

"Over in Simsbury. Well, technically Weatogue."

"Hey, wait a second," I said, pointing at the radio. "I just heard ..."

"Yeah, that's the one."

"Two cars? Head-on?"

"They took the one kid to St. Francis. He didn't make it. Miguel Batista was pronounced on the scene."

"The report on the radio said he hadn't been identified."

"Well, don't believe everything you hear on the radio."

"Not even NPR?"

He shrugged. "Maybe *Car Talk*."

"So how'd you catch wind of it?"

"I got a call from a friend who knows I've done work for the Wordstone family."

"The Wordstones? How are they connected to this?"

"Through the kid. Miguel."

"Yeah?" The tornado in my stomach was gathering strength.

"I'm on my way over there right now. Why don't you ride along."

"What's your interest in this?"

"My interest is your interest."

"Okay," I said. "I don't get it, but I'll play along."

I pulled on my cowboy boots and looked around for my Chicago Blackhawks sweatshirt and bomber jacket. Ernie watched me with silent chagrin. His silence didn't last long.

"What are you, thirty-five? When are you gonna start dressing like an adult?"

I looked him up and down, gave him the vaudeville once-over. "This from you?"

*The Farce News*

He finished his coffee in a single gulp. "Let's roll."

"Besides, I'm thirty-eight."

I pulled the plug on the coffee pot, killed the lights and locked the apartment. Rufus looked thoroughly forlorn. I wrote a note to Jolie -- *Emergency. Can you walk The Doofus. Back in an hour. Thx.* -- and slipped it under her door as we left.

Ernie's brown Pontiac was double parked outside my place, half-blocking traffic. He'd owned the car for at least twelve years and it had about 150,000 miles on it. Not as many as my piece of Jetta, but right up there. Once, outside a bar at closing time, a drunkard fiddling with the keys to his Acura asked Ernie and me if we knew what "Pontiac" stood for. Hell, we didn't even know it stood for *anything*. "Poor Old Nigger Thinks It's A Cadillac," the drunkard said, and laughed. The guy stopped laughing when Ernie balled up his fist and knocked him into a trash can with one punch. We forgot to mention that Ernie has no patience for bigots or drunken yuppie car snobs.

We cruised up Bloomfield Avenue, my third such trip in the last twelve hours, then headed west-northwest on Simsbury Road. After a few minutes of silence, Ernie cleared his throat. "How'd you like your cousin Lillian?" He asked it straight, but it came out all bent to hell, not unlike the grin on his grizzled face.

"Pretty theatrical," I said. "A virtual one-woman show."

"She's some great looking woman, though, wouldn't you say?"

"Didn't do much for me as a nun," I said. It was a lie, of course.

"A nun?"

"Just one of her many characters."

"Interesting."

"Yeah, she's a little hinky."

"But quite a knockout."

"You keep saying that."

"Makes you wonder why the husband would run off like he did."

"*The husband?* She's had two at last count."

"Blackie," he said, clarifying. "Didn't she mention him?"

"Actually, I was there to see my my aunt. As you well know."

"She was crazy about Blackie, too. Didn't the old broad bring him up?"

I looked over . "The old broad?"

He shrugged and kept his eyes on the road. "Don't get your panties in a knot. Twenty-four hours ago, you didn't even know her."

Just after East Weatogue Street, we came to the steel bridge which spans the Farmington River at Nod Road. It was newly refurbished. On the right was the fabled Simsbury sycamore.

A couple of uniformed cops waved motorists through at either end of the accident scene. Rubber-neckers slowed the process. Two cars bore Simsbury police markings. An ambulance from a local private company sat with its lights off, its back doors open. A couple of unmarked cars cruisers idled. I guessed these belonged to detectives. I had no idea which jurisdiction they represented.

The medical examiner's vehicle sat by itself, the back doors shut, and two flatbeds were parked nose to nose. One of the flatbeds already had a car on it, a silver BMW with a demolished front end and a shattered windshield. Like a soda can after some jock has smashed it into his own forehead. The empty flatbed was anchored at the side of the road with a winch played out to the wreckage in the ditch below.

We parked on the shoulder and joined the pack of cops standing near the edge of the embankment. Ernie shook hands with a man and women in plain clothes, and nodded casually to the officers who had Simsbury P.D. patches on their sleeves. He vouched for me but didn't bother with formal introductions. I didn't get anyone's name, or give mine. I still wasn't sure why I was here, but I had a nagging feeling it wasn't going to be fun. I nodded at those who nodded at me. We all stood around and did the bobblehead doll thing for a moment or two. Then the professionals settled back into their conversation -- yeah, the Celtics probably were gonna suck again this year -- and I drifted away from the group. I wanted to get a look at the wreck down below.

I strolled over to the flatbed truck with the winch and stood near the cab as the driver worked the levers while his partner down below worked the hook. When I peered over the edge into the ravine, I could see the car they were dragging back up to the roadway. It was a black two-door sedan. A Monte Carlo Sport with silver trim. In its present condition I couldn't tell if the rear end was jacked up on hydraulic shocks. But it sure as hell looked like the car I'd seen on Duncaster Road last night.

"They get the driver out yet?" I said.

The winch operator glanced over at me, not quite suspicious, but not exactly friendly either. He wore greasy coveralls and a NASCAR baseball cap with a sharply bent bill, the number three on the crown.

"You don't look like no cop."

"I'm with Ernie."

He stared at me. "What's that make you? *Bert?*" He grinned. One of his front teeth was gone. I wanted to congratulate him on completing the grease monkey stereotype with such style and panache.

I stared back at him, like I was thinking it over. Actually, I kind of liked his sense of humor. "What's that make you? Bert?" I said. "That's a good

*The Farce News*

one. Bert and Ernie. You watch a lot of *Sesame Street?*"

He grinned at me some more.

I grinned back so he could see a mouth that had all the dental work intact, just in case, in his world, he didn't get to see one too often. "Ernie Newman. Guy standing over there in the brown suit, bullshitting the detectives."

The grease monkey sighed. Lights seemed to go out behind his eyes. "They pulled some spic out," he said. "He was dead already."

I didn't argue with him. What was the point? "Where's the body?"

"Far's I know, they got 'im in the meat wagon." He pointed his unshaven chin at the coroner's car.

I strolled over toward the M.E.'s station wagon. Ernie Newman fell in step with me.

"Miguel Batista."

"Yeah?" I said.

"Guy in the Chevy."

"What about him?"

"Ever met him?"

"Not formally."

"I think you know his mother."

"You think so?" I had been thinking the same thing.

"Rosa Batista," he said. "Works for your aunt."

"So this Miguel was her kid, huh?"

"Afraid so."

"Bummer."

"Yeah, bummer."

His tone rang sour. "What?" I said. "What aren't you telling me?"

"I liked the kid. He was always a problem child. But not a bad kid. Hate to say it, but I'm not all that surprised, him ending badly."

I though it over. "He tried to shoot me last night."

Ernie looked at me sharply. "Want to tell me about it?"

"When that didn't work, he tried to run me over in his car."

"Spill it. Let's hear the story."

"Soon," I said. "I'm still trying to find out what this is all about."

Ernie didn't like my answer much. "Okay, have it your way."

"Gimme a couple of days."

"Fine. Just remember, I can't help you if you hold out on me."

"I get it." I didn't remember asking for his help, but I didn't say so.

We stood a few feet from the coroner's vehicle. Its chrome details sparkled in the morning sun, oblivious to its gloomy purpose.

*The Farce News*

"Miguel's been traveling rough roads for a long time," Ernie said, breaking the silence. Then he lapsed into a brief historical monologue. I didn't interrupt him. It was interesting enough, as unauthorized biographies go. Sex, drugs and rock 'n' roll, and, of course, violence. A true Hollywood tale of woe, but I wasn't sure what it had to do with Twannie Jefferson or a peculiar eighty thousand dollar extortion play, which was how I'd gotten into this mess in the first place.

According to Ernie, Miguel and his mother, Rosa, had come to the U.S. from Cuba in the mid-1990s. Cuba, not Puerto Rico. Which made me the schmuck of the moment for assuming, just because Rosa spoke with a heavy Hispanic accent, and just because there's a sizable Puerto Rican community in Hartford, that she was Puerto Rican.

In addition to a handful of juvenile raps currently under seal in Family Court in Waterbury, where they had lived before moving to Hartford, Miguel had been popped a few times for stupid stuff in Hartford County. Disorderly conduct. Petty theft. Possession of marijuana, although not enough to merit a charge of dealing.

Auntie Peg, for whatever reasons, had maintained a steadfast loyalty toward the Batistas, and had even picked up the tab for Miguel's legal representation whenever a criminal lawyer was required, which was comparatively frequently. She further vouched for him, as only a ceaselessly dedicated benefactor can, by hiring tutors to help him earn his G.E.D. The hope was one day he'd make something of himself.

"Question," I said.

"Shoot."

"How did my aunt conjure up all this faith in Miguel?"

"Many have wondered the same thing."

"Was he fooling around with Lita?" They were roughly the same age and she struck me as the kind of girl who might easily gravitate toward anything or anybody that looked like trouble.

"Not fooling around in the traditional sense. I think it went deeper than that. I think the kid was genuinely in love, which was way out of character. Might have been a two-way street for all I know. You just never know."

I thought about Lita and the behavior she'd exhibited in our two short encounters. Was she capable of being in love? One thing I knew for sure, it would be a big mistake to start assuming anyone, even Lita Wordstone, was incapable. Love is an equal opportunity terrorist.

The way Ernie told it, Miguel had been quite a lady-killer. A *young lady* killer. Two of the juvie busts in Waterbury were for statutory rape, although both girls -- one a sixteen-year-old, the other her fourteen-year-old sister --

swore he had not taken advantage of them, that they'd gone willingly. Miguel was seventeen at the time.

"Seems Lita struck some chord with Miguel," Ernie said. "She brought out the knight in shining armor in him. He treated her like a goddess. He'd have done anything for her."

"Think he'd kill for her?" I said. "If Lita was in trouble. Would Miguel take it upon himself to do something if violence were part of the picture? Seems like his crimes against society pretty much fell into the category of self-gratification."

"The three P's," Ernie said. "Pussy, pot, and pilfering."

"It's some jump from misdemeanor shoplifting and *shtupping* horny teenyboppers to cold-blooded murder. Was the kid capable of killing? You knew him. What's your take?"

Ernie didn't answer. Guess he thought it was a rhetorical question.

We strolled over to the front of the coroner's wagon. A guy sat in the passenger seat with a clipboard on his lap, filling out a form. He looked about thirty and wore a neatly trimmed calico beard and a tweed blazer. I'd have mistaken him for a college professor if Ernie didn't identify him as the medical examiner.

"Hello, Ernie," the man said, smiling easily. "You back on the job?"

"Nah. Friend of the family. What do you have?"

"Looks pretty straight forward. I'll know more after the post-mortem. Based on a preliminary examination, I'd say the vick died of massive head and chest trauma. No air bag in his car. Not even sure it has seat belts. If it did, he wasn't wearin' 'em. Still have to do tox tests. Check for the presence of alcohol or other controlled substances."

"If you find anything unusual, will you gimme a shout?"

The M.E. scratched his beard and looked a little uncomfortable. "Have to be off the record," he said.

Ernie nodded. "Goes without saying."

The M.E. looked over at me. "Who's your playmate?"

"This is Robby. He's related to the family Batista worked for."

The M.E. nodded. "Sorry for your loss." he said, but it sounded awfully rote.

Ernie hooked a thumb toward the back of the wagon. "Mind if we take a look in the bag?"

The M.E. shrugged. "Knock yourself out."

We went to the back of the wagon and opened the doors. Ernie slid the stretcher out halfway, then reached in and unzipped the top of the black rubber bag. Miguel Batista lay peacefully, exposed from the mid-chest up.

Miguel was the guy I'd seen ducking into the tool shed at the Wordstone mansion, the one who'd been watching me and pretending not to. So, this was the son of Rosa, the Cuban housekeeper. The guy who'd taken a shot at me in back of LaTwanda Jefferson's house and tried to run me down in his Monte Carlo. And now he was dead. His black hair was matted with dry blood. His features weren't badly marred. His injuries hadn't been so much facial as cranial. Even in death, he looked boyish. He couldn't have been more than twenty-four or -five. There was something sad about the whole thing. It wasn't as if Miguel was going to shake this off and put his life back together. This was it.

"This the kid who took a shot at you last night?"

"Yup."

Ernie zipped the bag shut and slid the stretcher back in place. We closed the doors of the wagon and Ernie went to have a word with the M.E. Moments later, he rejoined me and we walked back toward the wrecker where the greasy mechanic and his equally oil-stained partner were wrapping up their work. The winch was almost fully recoiled and the Monte Carlo had all four wheels on the flatbed. Ready to be tied down and hauled away. We walked around it, taking in the details. The right front fender and headlight assembly were totally gone, smashed beyond recognition. The left side of the car was badly dented and scraped. There was black paint on the guard rail of the westbound side of the road that matched the paint on the Monte Carlo. The roof of the car was also caved in, which I took as an indication that the car had flipped at least once before coming to rest at the bottom of the ravine.

After we finished our circuit of the flatbed truck, we waved to the cops on the scene and went back to Ernie's shit-brown Pontiac. We rode back to Hartford in easy silence. I don't know if Ernie was reflecting on this tragedy, or if he considered it a tragedy at all. Perhaps he saw it merely as a pitiable inevitability. We were halfway through Bloomfield before he spoke.

"Anything bother you about the Monte Carlo?"

I looked over. He wasn't grinning. This wasn't one of his usual jousting games. "Plenty," I said.

"Beyond the fact a kid died in it."

I thought about it for a moment, visualizing the damage. "The light panel on the right rear was smashed. The glass was completely gone."

Ernie glanced over at me. "What else?"

"Nothing else. No other damage to the back of the car."

"That's what I saw, too. What does it tell you?"

I thought about it for a minute. I wished I'd gone to the Police Academy,

*The Farce News*

or at least taken a class in critical thinking. "You think Miguel was tagged from behind?"

"What if he was?"

"It would explain why he crossed over and hit the Beemer."

Ernie nodded. The revelation provided no satisfaction, had no restorative power. It didn't bring Miguel Batista back to life or make it any easier for his mother to accept the news that her boy was gone.

"I'll make a couple of calls. See what comes off the back of the car. Maybe we can get a line on the third car. Sort this thing out."

I looked over at Ernie again. "We?"

He glanced at me for a moment. "You have a problem with that?"

"Not really," I said. I wondered when we had become partners, but it didn't seem like a very good time to say so. He seemed to sense my hesitation. As previously stated, Ernie's one sharp bastard.

"You want to find out who killed the kid, don't you?"

I wasn't going to dignify the question with an answer. Instead I let it hang in the air between us, along with some of the earlier ones still suspended in conversational animation. It occurred to me that if I rolled down my window, I might succeed in clearing the air a little -- and get rid of some these lingering issues. But maybe not. These were the kind of questions that possessed genuine staying power.

"This is way beyond the scope of what my aunt hired me for," I said. It sounded damned weak, even to me.

"Your great, great aunt," Ernie said. "Several times removed."

"Whatever."

"Look, I know all about Big Jeff. That's strictly small time. You can handle that with your eyes closed."

I let that comment join all the other ones hanging in the air. At the moment, Ernie did not seem to be aware of the fact that LaTwanda Jefferson, small time though she might be, was also dead and that I would not be handling her one way or the other, eyes open or shut. For the moment, I couldn't decide whether to come clean and tell Ernie about Twannie Jefferson's murder, or Miguel Batista's likely hand in it, or the fact that the bodily remains of "Big Jeff," as he called her (as Lita had also called her) were currently missing and unaccounted for. His reference to Jefferson in the present tense told me he was unaware that she was no longer drawing breath. Unless he was testing me. The moment passed. I decided not to say anything.

We navigated the midmorning traffic. Ernie dropped me at my apartment near Trinity College. He said he'd be in touch if he heard anything useful. I promised to do the same. I had my fingers crossed behind my back.

*The Farce News*

*

Rufus all but knocked me on my ass when I entered the apartment. I took this as a sign that he had, among other things, a full bladder (that Jolie was not home), that his patience was all but gone, and that if I didn't immediately take him out, he'd figure out a dastardly way to make me pay. I hooked up his leash and we headed for the Trinity College campus.

We smiled at all the pretty coeds who came over to pet him. Rufus has a very winning smile. My own smile isn't what you'd call winning. I usually play for a tie. For reasons I've yet to fathom, young women love Rufus. This morning I let go of my petty jealousies and let my mind work at the archeologist's job of sifting through the fragments of information I'd collected in the last 24 hours. It didn't feel like a hell of a lot. The heavier weight seemed to be on the side of the scale containing that which I had yet to discover.

Around noon, I locked up the apartment, slipped another note under Jolie's door -- *Ignore previous note. Dog's done his business. See you later.* -- and headed out to find my piece of shit Jetta, half hoping (as I always do) that somebody had stolen it overnight.

It was time to pay another visit to the phony card shop on Park Street, to renew my budding romance with the pretty if uninformed brunette, and to see if any of those impossible-to-find Wayne Gretzky rookie cards had come in.

## Chapter 10

If the bizarre and violent developments of the night before -- the murder of Big Jeff and subsequent suspicious death of her suspected killer, Miguel Batista -- had produced any measurable change in the general environment at Twannie Jefferson's Park Street card shop, it was not immediately obvious, at least from the outside. There were no police cars on the scene. No TV news trucks. No crowds of inquisitive onlookers eager for a dose of high drama to punctuate their otherwise dull lives. It was just another afternoon in Hartford's vaguely seedy north end.

I pulled my piece of shit Jetta to the curb a hundred feet from the store front and locked it (why, I'm not sure). As I crossed the street against traffic, a guy driving a minivan loaded up with flowers tried to run me down. I could tell there was malice in his heart by the evil smirk on his face. Maybe he was on his way to a funeral and thought he'd make it a package deal by delivering a fresh corpse.

The shop's cool interior had not changed. The harsh overhead light was as sterile and unwelcoming as ever. My sense was of entering a surgical theater where the operators were going sneak up behind me and carve out a kidney while some fast-talking frontman distracted me with a lecture on the virtues of organ donation.

The pretty brunette, Jennifer, was in her usual perch, idly flipping through a magazine. I doubt it was *National Geographic*. She looked up when I approached, but showed no sign of recognition.

"Can I do something for you?" she asked, exactly as she had the day before. Either she was extremely cool, or extremely out of the loop in terms of current events.

"Any luck on that Gordie Howe card?" I asked, smiling innocently. "Or the Gretzky?" I kept the nasal barking to a minimum, if only to avoid scaring her off, emotionally speaking.

A look of realization came over her pretty face. Her right eye brightened while her left eye narrowed. One eyebrow arched while the other flatlined. It was a neat trick, and it looked especially good on her. "Oh," she said. "I remember you."

"I was hoping you would."

"Um, I'm afraid I don't have any encouraging news for you."

"Doesn't matter. Is Big Jeff around?"

*The Farce News*

"I'm sorry," she said, without losing a beat. "Who?"

"LaTwanda Jefferson," I said. "LaTwanda Jefferson is Big Jeff. They are one and the same. Like Superman and Clark Kent. Like Batman and Bruce Wayne."

"Bruce Wayne?" she said, and frowned.

I guess she didn't watch much TV as a kid, or read many comic books. "Maybe I should speak with her directly."

The pretty brunette put up a hand and shook her head. "I'm sorry, but that's impossible. She's not even here. As a matter of fact, I don't know where she is. I haven't seen her all morning."

This declaration sounded oddly preemptive, as if to forestall further inquiry. "But you are expecting her, at some point?"

"Well," she said. "I don't see why she wouldn't ..."

"She doesn't spend much time here, considering she owns the joint."

"Well, I couldn't speak to that ..."

"She does own the place, doesn't she?"

The pretty young woman peered at me. Her right eye stopped brightening and narrowed to the dimension of her left eye so now she looked at me through matching gun barrels. Lovely gun barrels, if slightly disconcerting. Was she trying to decide how to answer me without giving anything away?

While she thought it over, I removed a chocolate bar from of my jacket pocket. It was a garden variety Hershey bar I'd picked up at a CVS drug store on my way here. Nothing fancy, but it got her attention. She watched me unwrap one end of it and take a small bite out of one corner. I chewed it thoughtfully while we locked eyes in our little game of No-No-You-Blink-First. I swallowed and said: "Not bad, really. If you don't mind domestic. It's got a slightly mass-produced quality. Care for a bite?"

She said nothing.

"Given my druthers, I prefer Egyptian. A nice Cairo dark ..."

She inhaled sharply, then caught herself and stifled it. "What do you want?"

I fixed the wrapper on the Hershey bar and stashed it. "Five minutes with Twannie Jefferson." I said, mildly, as if nothing had changed. "I have some business to discuss with her."

"And I suppose it has nothing at all to do with trading cards."

So she was in the loop after all, and not just loopy. I smiled. "You're as coy as a mountain lion," I said. I was just about ready to drop to one knee and propose marriage.

It would have given me great joy to continue our little sparring session. She was getting into the spirit of it now, giving as good as she got, and I actually thought we might be making some progress. But at this moment the door in the back of the shop, the door behind pretty Jennifer's desk, suddenly opened. And there stood Billie, or the woman I assumed was Billie, in her sleeveless biker jacket and painted-on black leather pants. She looked agitated, a thin film of perspiration dampened her brow. She looked briefly at me. The expression on her face darkened as she turned to Jennifer.

"Like to tell me what the hell is going on back here?"

Jennifer shrugged. "I don't know what you mean," she said.

"Yeah, right. 'Course you don't. Who are those two gorillas back there? And who told 'em to start emptying out the place?"

"Honestly," said Jennifer, sounding anything but honest. "I don't know."

"That's some bullshit," Billie said. Then she looked back at me, just as briefly as the first time. I didn't seem to be making much of an impression on her. She didn't ask my name. Didn't ask if there was anything she could do for me. Didn't invite me out for coffee or lunch or a drink or anything. Didn't even ask me what the hell I was looking at. Just shook her head at Jennifer, said, "Don't talk to this guy," and left, slamming the door behind her.

Before the door closed I got a quick glimpse into the inner sanctum. Billie was not alone back there. A couple of very large brothers sporting jailhouse muscles with jailhouse tattoos were busily stacking boxes. Lots of boxes. Big ones and small ones. In many colors, with labels printed in various languages. None of them in any way resembled the plain white boxes that were stacked neatly out here in the store front, the white boxes presumably containing the late Twannie Jefferson's legitimate inventory of trading cards -- assuming for a moment that the boxes in the storefront weren't in fact empty stage props. I made a mental note to check. Back there, behind the door guarded by pretty Jennifer, was the real, if illegal, gold mine. And now it looked as if someone had ordered a change of location for the goods. And Billie, apparently excluded from the decision making process, was none too thrilled.

I tried a new angle with Jennifer. "Is Big Jeff at home? Maybe we could call over and you could tell her someone's here who'd like to make a business proposition."

"That would be you?" Not just pretty. Sharp as a tack as well.

"That would be me."

"I don't think that's going to work. She didn't say she'd be available to take any calls. Besides, I'm not supposed to talk to you."

I smiled patiently. "Oh, come on. She must carry a cellphone. Who in their right mind doesn't, right?"

"I wouldn't dream of calling her cell. Not unless it was an absolute emergency. She's very strict about that. It costs money to receive calls, you know. Not just to make them. She showed me the bill one time, and, my God, the roaming charges alone ..."

"Jennifer," I said, interrupting her somewhat amusing attempt at a filibuster. "Listen to me."

"How do you know my name?" She seemed suddenly horrified.

"A great big orange bird told me."

"Oh," she said. I might as well have told her I got it from a fortune cookie.

"Listen, this is a whole lot closer to an emergency than you might think."

"I'm sure you're wrong," she said.

"I'm pretty sure I'm right."

"But, how ..."

"It doesn't matter. The time for games is over."

If I stuck with it a while longer, I might get her to admit that something was rotten in Denmark, but there was no guarantee she'd ever cop to any knowledge of her boss's demise. I could get physical, metaphorically speaking (perhaps metaphysically would better describe it), but chances were I wasn't going to shake any useful fruit from this attractive tree. I considered the likelihood that Twannie Jefferson had screened the help pretty carefully. Certainly it would have behooved her to do so. As a practical businesswoman in a frequently rabid dog eat dog world of cutthroats and back-stabbers, she'd have made damn certain the front-line soldiers were reliable, and not just pretty. Not that it had done her much good in the long run. From all outward indications, Twannie had been locked and loaded and headed for a major fall. The only question was, what kind of fall. Fortune cookies, tea leaves, Tarot cards, even the *New York Post* all say the same thing. You simply cannot drive around indefinitely in a tricked-out $60,000 purple Lexus SUV and expect to escape karma's exacting retribution. Bottom line: God hates a showoff. The lamentable fall from grace of the world's candelabra-wielding Liberaces is proof enough of that inescapable truism. If Miguel Batista's bullets hadn't done the job on her, some other combination of forces surely would have. They always do. You could just hear the argument. Heart Attack in a black tuxedo, Diabetes dressed in a sports jacket and slacks, and Stroke in sneakers and jeans, bickering like siblings on the last day of a long vacation when the airplane home has been delayed by bad weather, arguing among themselves about who was going to take the big girl out -- out for good, that is, not out for cheeseburgers and a movie. All the while the Grim Reaper lurking in the shadowy corner, scythe in skeletal hand, smirking evilly, proud of his agents of death.

But the question was: did Twannie Jefferson die because of business or was it strictly personal? I had no proof yet to support the notion that she'd been bumped off by a rival in the illegal import-export trade. In fact, at the moment, Big Jeff's shooting had all the earmarks of a crime of passion, a personal vendetta. But why? The connection between Miguel Batista, Lita Wordstone and Twannie Jefferson was somewhat bewildering. Batista's role would probably prove to be a thoroughly incongruous red herring or a spectacularly clarifying factor which would shine the blinding light of comprehension on all things. At the moment I had no idea which it would be. I was busy trying ito wrestle Jennifer to an intellectual draw, and in the words of Mick Dundee, making a bit of progress.

"Really," the pretty brunette said, edging toward the moment when she could either excuse herself and ride her high horse out of this Tombstone conversation, or simply dismiss me out of hand, having politely done all she could to be less than fully helpful. Meanwhile she seemed determined to maintain the facade right to the end. "I don't see how I can possibly be of any more assistance. Really, I don't."

If she'd said, "Really, I don't, *kind sir,*" then I'd have known for sure she was a graduate of the Dickens summer stock circuit.

At least we agreed on one thing. Her usefulness had indeed been exhausted.

Having had a but brief glimpse of the goings-on behind the secret door, and having witnessed the effect these goings-on had had on Billie, who either knew or didn't know that her boss, Twannie Jefferson, was dead, I thought it might be a good idea to take a peek around the back of the building and see how Billie and the Brotherhood of Bad Body Art planned to get all of this swag out of the building. And if, in fact, they were in cahoots. I assumed there would be some kind of loading dock back there because they certainly weren't going to haul that mess out the front door. Not with half of Hartford's north end rolling by in cars, walking by on foot, and otherwise idling by with an eye peeled for shady goings on.

"Well, if you do see Miss Jefferson," I said, then stopped. "Never mind."

Jennifer appeared to be genuinely relieved. I think it was the promise of my impending departure that did the trick.

"And if we get in any of those cards," she said, smiling, "what was the name? Jordie Howell?"

I laughed. "Don't push your luck." I was glad she had a sense of humor, even if it bordered on the the kind of absurdism even Samuel Beckett and Eugene Ionesco wouldn't have dared to attempt.

She wasn't laughing as I left the store.

I found a parking ticket stuck inside the windshield wiper of the Jetta --

which was totally bullshit and completely undeserved, just one more example of the voracious State of Connecticut reaching into my wallet and the wallets of my fellow Nutmegers to extract revenues where none were owed. Another example of taxation without representation. Hadn't we fought a war over this? I had fed and annoyed the goddamn parking meter and, what the hell, I'd only been in the card shop for ten minutes. Fifteen tops. I looked over and there were still twenty-five minutes left on the clock. Some frustrated meter maid was fucking with me. I was about to crush the undeserved ticket into a ball and drop it in the gutter when I realized it wasn't a parking ticket at all. It was a giant fortune cookie fortune, without the giant fortune cookie attached. Somebody had scrawled a message in thick black ink:

"Adam was but human -- this explains it all. He did not want the apple for the apple's sake, he wanted it only because it was forbidden."

I smiled and folded the message into quarters and slipped it into an inside jacket pocket. I guessed it was from Sully. He was reaching out in his own peculiar fashion. How he knew I was here on Park Street at this particular moment in the history of mankind, I couldn't begin to guess. He claims to know everything that goes on in this town. I don't believe him, but I'm smart enough not to write it down, just in case he proves me wrong someday. In addition to his claim of omniscience, he insists nobody loves Samuel Langhorne Clemens as much as he does, nor can anyone quote the great Hartford satirist with anything even approaching Sully's depth of intellectual appreciation. And he's got the doctorate to back it up. This message about Adam and the forbidden fruit was no doubt Sully's way of sending encouragement, and of reminding me to keep it simple. Sully once said, "People only seem complex until you break their codes. Then you discover they're really very basic. Find the key to the code and you're home free. That's how we brought the Third Reich to its knees. Hey, if it worked for Hitler ..."

Sully is quite a nut job.

I climbed back into the Jetta, cranked the engine to life and merged into traffic. I had to circle the block twice before I noticed the narrow entrance to the dead-end alleyway leading to the predictable loading area at the back of LaTwanda Jefferson's emporium. I parked up the street where I could keep an eye on the entrance without being too obvious. A beat-up panel truck had been backed in. An old step-up Grumman box truck. Beneath a remarkably cheap paint job it was still possible to make out the blue and orange insignia of Fed Ex. Presumably this truck had once been part of a delivery fleet until the odometer ticked over its trillionth mile and some middle management wag reluctantly scrapped it for something just a shade newer, with only a billion miles on it. I'll bet the muscle boys had picked it up for a song. I'll even lay odds the song was "How Much Is That Shitty Piece of Scrap Metal In the Window?"

I'm not sure what was currently motivating the pair of bearded Blutos, but judging by the quick work they made of emptying the storeroom at Twannie's place and filling the back of the battered Grumman, it might have been alternating current.

Within the hour, the front end of the loaded truck poked its nose out of the alley and crawled north toward Park Street. It rode very low on worn shocks. I fell in at a comfortable distance. Even my piece of shit Jetta could handle this rundown junker without putting more than a slight strain on second gear. Hell, I could have followed on foot, but I'm not a complete idiot.

I didn't see Billie anywhere, only the two barrel-chested mules. One was behind the wheel driving, the other was riding shotgun. I hoped he wasn't riding *with* a shotgun. The way the truck bounced and rocked, they must have been having the ride of their lives. Last thing they needed was a weapon discharging accidentally in their small cockpit. I figured there was no way they'd make Billie ride in back with the cargo, or that Billie, if she had an ounce of self-respect, would submit to such an indignity. That would be like hanging the Mona Lisa in a Hooters restroom. So, the question remained, where was Billie? I decided to stay with truck instead of doubling back to Park Street to look for the angel in the black leather painted-on pants.

The motley movers took a wide, swaying left turn on Sisson Avenue, and for a moment I thought the truck was going to tip over like a cow in the hands of a bunch of drunken Texas teenagers. Then they used the West Boulevard entrance to gain access to Interstate 84. They drifted into the eastbound lane. I followed, with a poorly crafted Chrysler minivan and two politically incorrect Japanese sedans as a buffer between them and me. Once we all made it safely onto the highway, I dropped back even farther. They were struggling to keep up with the pace of traffic, which despite the posted fifty-five mile-per-hour speed limit was cranking along at about eighty. Every once in a while a puff of black smoke exploded from the tailpipe of the Grumman. I hoped it wouldn't break down before the Bruise Brothers reached their ultimate destination. If the truck suddenly died, I'd have only two choices: to fly on by and head back to Hartford, or pull over and offer assistance. Neither option thrilled me. Thankfully, the Grumman kept chugging along and I managed to tuck myself into a steady stream of cars that periodically merged from the right lane.

Without signaling, the Grumman began to drift toward the off ramp at Exit 34, where Hartford more or less ends and Windsor more or less begins.

We proceeded north on Windsor Avenue past the Keney Park Golf Course and the Northwood Cemetery. At East Barber Street, the truck turned east and headed toward the Connecticut River. A municipal street sign identified the presence of a public boat launch at the far end of the street, in the shadows of the Bissell Bridge, still several blocks away. I had to give the Grumman more room now, but there was much less traffic in this sleepy residential neighborhood and it was even easier to tail them despite maintaining a greater following distance. Hopefully they didn't have a boat waiting. If they did, I was truly screwed.

We crossed some railroad tracks, and the truck suddenly veered to the left, into the oncoming traffic lane and abruptly stopped. I realized what was happening when the truck's back-up lights came on -- at least *one* of them did, the right one, the left one was burned out -- and the truck nervously backed into the driveway in front of an older home that hadn't had a new roof or a paint job in way too long. The Grumman was too tall to fit through the garage door. They edged up to the opening and stopped. I rolled slowly by, looking the other way so that even if they eyeballed the car and had any reason to wonder about it, they wouldn't get a good look at me. I drove down to the end of the block, made a series of left turns until I was back on East Barber Street, a couple of blocks west of the house where the truck was parked. I got out and locked it up. I walked slowly, hands dug into the pockets of my jeans, like a guy who has nowhere to go and is in no hurry to get there. The homes on this street ran the gamut from boarded-up to recently remodeled. I spotted a couple of late model cars among the rust buckets whose numbers dominated. Mine would fit right in, albeit at the less desirable end of the spectrum. There were a couple of FOR SALE signs hanging on posts in front yards. It was a quiet street. Not many people out and about. A couple of little kids racing back and forth on Big Wheels. I didn't see their mother anywhere. The children ignored me as I walked by and I didn't say hello or otherwise pretend I was someone they should notice or remember.

I stopped at a house two doors down from the one where the movers had parked the truck and rang the doorbell. After a couple of minutes I heard footsteps inside. A black woman in her fifties with salt-and-pepper hair pulled tightly back over her head and a broad if tentative smile opened the door and looked curiously at me.

"Yes?"

"Good afternoon, ma'am," I said. "My name is Lars-Erik Sjorbourg-Oddleifsson. It's hyphenated. Listen, I'm awfully sorry to bother you, but you see, it's like this: My wife, Bjorna, and I are contemplating the purchase of that house across the street." I pointed over my shoulder at one of the FOR

SALE signs. "I was hoping you could tell me a little about the area. You know how realtors can be, they only tell you what they think you want to hear. You know, to make the sale."

I smiled warmly, and she returned it a little cooler. "I suppose they do, don't they?"

"We've got a couple of youngsters, of course. Lars-Henrik and Brit. Five and two, respectively. Just adorable. Hang on, I have photos." I reached for my wallet, then put it back. "Oh, I'm sorry. How rude of me to bore you. Trust me, they absolutely delightful youngsters."

"Oh, no," she said. "That's quite all right."

"So, the neighborhood ..."

She looked up and down the street for a moment. I don't know if she was taking one last assessment before delivering the verdict, or checking to see if any of her neighbors were watching us. "I'm afraid it's been in a state of some transition for quite a while now. You can see for yourself. It's a little difficult to tell if the neighborhood is on its way up or on its way down. I like to think things are looking up, but that's because I've been here so long already and I'm not going anywhere any time soon. Our community hasn't received the kind of attention we deserve from the state, you ask me."

"I understand."

"We do have some young children on the block," she said, as if that was, indeed, a selling point. "But we have our share of problems, too. With the older ones. The teenagers, I mean. Not the seniors. Up to no good most times, you ask me. We have our share of break-ins, a mugging now and then. Some of the young men sell some drugs over on the avenue. They get high some nights and fight, just out of boredom. We know the police pretty well. A little too well, you ask me."

"I see." I kept a neutral expression so she wouldn't think she was talking me out of anything, or that I was passing judgment. I hoped to demonstrate in an understated way -- silently, in fact -- that I knew what she and her neighbors faced and that I commiserated. "How do you like the other families on the street? Generally speaking."

"Oh, just fine for the most part. The Johnsons next door? They're both teachers in the Hartford public school system, bless their hearts. And Barbara Hendricks, across the street there, she's a nurse at St. Francis Hospital. In the cancer ward. We do have a few rentals, so there's a bit of coming and going. That never helps build up community spirit, you ask me."

"What about the folks just down the street there?" I said, feeling like a complete phony as I nodded toward the house with the Grumman parked in front.

She put a hand to her chin for a moment, thinking hard. "That's one of the rentals. I'm trying to remember the name of the couple who live there now. He's a high-yellow Negro who dresses nicely but seems a little on the shady side, you ask me."

"Shady?"

"He's a player. I think that's what they call it nowadays. Works the street. No real job. At least nothing nine-to-five. They're mixed, you know. That attracts the wrong kind of attention."

"Excuse me."

"His wife, or girlfriend, or whatever she is, she's a white girl. Oh, my. I hope I haven't offended you by saying that. I don't mean any offense. I have nothing against the whites."

"No, not at all. None taken."

"I'm just an old woman, maybe a little set in my ways."

"Don't apologize," I said. *In fact, please say no more on the subject.*

"She's pretty, mind you, for a white girl. Has lovely long dark hair. 'Course she's a little on the skinny side. Ought to eat more, you ask me."

I thought that over. Hmm. A pretty brunette.

"Oh! I remember now. It's Brashear. That's the last name, like the man in that movie about the navy divers. His name was Carl Brashear, wasn't it?"

I furrowed my brow. "Divers?" I had no idea what she was talking about.

"Oh, what *was* it? With that terrible man from the *Taxi Driver* show and Havana Something."

"Danny De Vito?" I asked. She really had me flummoxed.

"You talkin' to me?" she said, and I thought one of us had suddenly gone stark raving mad.

And then ...

*Ding, ding, ding!*

I don't get to the movies much, but I had a flash and suddenly knew exactly what she was talking about. The navy divers. *Taxi Driver*. It all made sense (well, not quite *sense*). She was talking about a man-overcomes-the-obstacles melodrama with DeNiro and Cuba Gooding Jr. I found it pretty fascinating that this woman couldn't remember the name of the Hollywood celebrities who'd starred in the picture, but she could recall the name of the man who'd been portrayed in the movie. That was an unusual turn on the traditional stargazing cliché. But I had something a bit more pressing to consider. If I had my facts right, Brashear was the name of the dog who'd come sniffing for a bone after one of Lita Wordstone's previous indiscretions, long before Twannie Jefferson got her hooks into the girl.

"That's it," she said. "Johnny Brashear. Not a bad young man, really. Handsome in the face. Drives a fancy old car. Says hello most of the time. He's polite enough, just a little too *street*."

We talked for another couple of minutes, about some of her other neighbors, then I thanked her and said goodbye. She seemed disappointed that I was done with her so quickly.

"Don't you want to know about the churches?" she said.

"Another time," I said.

I was afraid that any minute now she was going to insist on seeing the photographs of my fictitious kids, and all I'd have to show her was a couple of snaps of Buddy, J.D., and Rufus. What would she tell the Windsor police about the strange white man who asked about the neighborhood and carried pictures of his pets in his wallet?

I strolled casually over to the Brashear residence. The movers were busy hauling boxes from the back of the truck into the garage, which already looked fairly well stocked with materiel. On a rolling garment rack toward the back, I saw some furs that looked strikingly like the ones I'd seen in Twannie Jefferson's closet. I didn't think a garage was the best place to keep that sort of thing, but maybe it was okay if it was only short term. It was entirely possible they had only just gotten here within the last twelve to eighteen hours. The two jail birds stopped what they were doing and stared at me as I stood in the driveway, hands buried in my pockets, staring right back at them.

"Hey, fellas," I said, smiling. "Johnny around?"

They looked at each other, then back at me and said nothing.

I pulled out my wallet and flipped it open. From a distance, two half-wits with a penchant for feeling guilty about the activities in which they were engaged could easily take it as a signal of official heat. Maybe I wasn't a straight city cop, but I could be some other agent of authority. And although they might spend ninety-nine percent of their waking hours bucking authority in words and deeds, I hoped it still worried them just a little bit to go up against it.

One of them decided to put his big toe in the icy waters. "Don't know nobody named Brashear," he said. He seemed pretty sure of himself, proud of his righteous indignation. I started to laugh and the other dude punched him hard in the arm.

"Dumb ass!" his partner said, a bit of the old junkyard dog straining at the chain.

"What?" the first one said, looking both perplexed and offended.

"He axed where Johnny at, you ain't know nobody call Brashear."

*The Farce News*

"Oh. Yo, I meant ..."

"Dumb ass."

The first man abandoned perplexed and offended and switched to ninety-nine and forty-four one-hundredths percent pure humiliation. He wasn't nearly so sure-footed once he began to furiously backpedal. "I *meant* Johnny. I meant I don't know nobody call ..."

"Forget it," I said. "Relax. I don't mean to bust your balls. I just want a word with Johnny."

The second man in muscles fielded this one. "Ain't seen 'im."

The first one nodded like he'd never heard anything he agreed with more. "And he ain't even 'sposed to be by 'til seven, seven-thirty."

I looked at No. 2 and shrugged. He stared back without changing his somber, no-bullshit expression. Then he turned to his partner. "Don't say no more. Just keep yuh mouth shut. You feel me?"

"How much he paying you to play moving man?" I asked.

No. 2 thought it over, no doubt trying to decide (a) if there was any point in trying to prolong the charade as to their relationship with Johnny Brashear, and (b) since there wasn't much to gain by extending the bullshit, would it hurt to answer the question about their daily salary?

"Hunnid."

"Each!" said the man who had only seconds ago been ordered not to speak anymore.

"Thought I tol' you shut the fuck up."

"And a box of cee-gars! From Savannah an' shit! That motherfucker in Cuba, yo. Them shits be for'n."

No. 2 looked at me. "I may have to kill this cocksucker yet."

"I understand."

"With my fuckin' bare hands an' shit."

I nodded. It's hard enough just to survive when the playing field is roughly level and the sides are even, but when your own teammates start diving at your knees, it can become a lonely and hopeless battle.

"Yo, whatchoo talking about?" the first man in muscles asked the second man in muscles.

"Don't talk no more," the second man answered. "Ever."

"What if I get hungry?"

I left them to their work. I knew where to reach Johnny Brashear, and roughly when. Whether a conversation with him would prove useful remained to be seen. These two might try to warn him, but that would reflect poorly on them. I figured they wouldn't bother to mention my visit.

I strolled back to my car and got in. I turned the key but it wouldn't start.

I let it sit for a minute. Maybe my piece of shit Jetta liked the neighborhood, felt right at home amid the squalor. Maybe I should take down the number of the realtor on that FOR SALE sign. Maybe it was time to move out of my Summit Street flat and buy a house, get a mortgage, start acting like a responsible adult. Find a woman who could tolerate me, start a family. Buy a lawn mower to cut the summer grass and a shovel for when the winter came and the snow piled up on the front walk. Maybe. On the other hand, maybe not.

I cranked the key again and the engine fired. I mashed the clutch, popped it and peeled out. Found my way back to the highway. Left-laned it all the way to Hartford, then hit Farmington Avenue and headed for the studio. Maybe there'd be some good junk mail on the floor or some good junk food in the fridge to help me take my mind off this bullshit case from Nowheresville. Served me right for getting involved with people who had more money than common sense, people who thought the rules of normal decency only applied to *everyone else*, people who came out of the chute with such a hard core sense of entitlement almost nothing or nobody could change the course of their thinking short of a guy with a sniper's rifle and the balls to squeeze the trigger. Sure, this was family I was talking about, but so what? I was ready to reach out to the Mormons. All that genealogical work they do, maybe they could give me some good news, tell me I was adopted.

*The Farce News*

## Chapter 11

I left my car in the Kinko parking lot on Kenyon Street and went inside. I slid a dollar into the soda machine just inside the front door and bought a bottle of Dr. Pepper. That officially made me a customer and entitled me to free parking. I left the copy shop and scurried across Farmington Avenue to a brick building on the south side of the street and used the freight elevator to get upstairs. There's a small alcove that separates the public hallway from the door to our practice studio. Because I live the closest, I keep the keys. The studio's basically just one big room with an old couch, a couple of beat-up lounge chairs, a desk that doubles as a liquor cabinet when we have any, a few antique guitar amplifiers, three mike stands, a modified practice drum kit, some guitar racks and my D-10 Emmons pedal steel guitar.

The alcove outside the studio, where the guys wait for me when I'm late arriving with the keys, is big enough for a couple of chairs and a low table where we keep some magazines so the guys have something to do other than curse my name when I keep them waiting. I swiped the magazines from my dentist's office. The magazines were originally addressed to some psychiatrist across the river over in Manchester. I view it as no more than a worthy recycling effort.

Now, sitting in one of the chairs in the alcove, was a woman. The way she sat gave it away. One leg crossed over the other at the knee, swinging easily. One elbow rested on the high knee. A cigarette burned in that hand, the other picked a piece of loose tobacco from her bottom lip. I found myself thinking, *Who in their right mind smokes unfiltered cigarettes anymore? Or filtered ones either, for that matter?* I also wondered why the woman, who I quickly identified as Mrs. Buenavista, and whom I would always think of as Lillian the Vaudevillian, was dressed from head to toe in the ornate and elaborate raiment of a 19th century Spanish toreador, complete with a small black hat sitting cockeyed atop her head and a large red cape draped elegantly over one shoulder. Needless to say, I was afraid to ask. What answer could she possibly supply that would put my troubled mind at ease?

I thought it best to play the whole thing super casual, even to the point of completely ignoring her ridiculous costume. I vowed not to be dragged into her troubling world of mental illness and codependency. Not without putting up a damn good fight. Nevertheless, I did extend common courtesy far enough to invite her into the studio. I'm just that big a fool, I guess.

It was hard to say if I liked Lillian Buenavista or not. She *was* family, but that doesn't guarantee anything. She wasn't a friend. She was barely an acquaintance. The problem was, I wasn't entirely sure I'd actually *met* the woman yet. I'd been subjected to a parade of caricatures, each one more goofball than the one before and it was entertaining as hell, in a frightening sort of way, like visiting the workshop of a mad bomber where you're never quite sure if something's gonna blow, and if you'll have time to take cover when it does. The Lillian Buenavista I knew was little more than a schizophrenic quick-change artist who, by all accounts, was a reincarnated throwback from a burlesque revue out of another era, a nickelodeon flip-card show flashing dizzily before my eyes. The only thing missing from her act was a drummer with a snare and a high hat to punctuate the punch lines with cliché rim shots. And this was what she called her therapy.

"Great to see you," I said, smiling broadly. "It's Lillian, right?"

She shot up out of her chair and stood before me, tall and erect, proud and dignified, despite (or was it because of) the ridiculous toreador outfit. She had excellent posture. "But, of courth," she said, bowing slightly. "Who elth?" I thought I detected a subtle Spanish accent. It was about as subtle as a chain saw. She dropped the cigarette on the linoleum floor and crushed it underfoot. Nice. (Note to self: carry cigarettes for this very purpose.)

I looked around the small alcove, under the chairs, beneath the low magazine table. I even peeked around behind Lillian Buenavista herself. She cocked an eyebrow at me, very imperious, as if to ask what in the world I thought I was doing. I suppose I could have been mistaken for a guy trying to get a quick glimpse of her rather attractive backside, but I wasn't. At least not this time. "I was just looking for your trunk."

"My *what?*" she said. The Spanish accent wasn't as thick as Rosa's, but Lillian Buenavista wasn't going for Havana so much as Barcelona. Make that *Barthelona.*

"You know, your suitcase. Your garment bag. With all your other getups."

She whipped the red cape off her shoulder and flared it once in the small space. She performed the flourish with great elegance. Then she gathered the cape and neatly draped it over one arm. "If you are referring to my attire ..." She was hellbent on sticking with the bogus Spanish affectation.

I turned to unlock the door to the studio. "Why don't you come inside?" Frankly, I didn't want her standing around in the hallway. If somebody walked by and saw me standing here, talking to a friggin' *toreador* for Pedro's sake, it could spell trouble. Most of the tenants in the building already consider the boys and me to be left of center, what with the strange hours we tend to keep, the loud music we play -- even with all the sound proof baffling we'd installed -- and the strange company we've been known to entertain. Lillian Buenavista was an excellent example of what they were probably talking about when they gathered around the community water cooler to gossip about the oddballs congregating in the rehearsal studio up on two. Good thing we're not a co-op. As it is they can't get rid of us because they pay rent just like we do, although they probably pay it on time with much greater regularity. Love means never having to say you're sorry, and life as a musician means never having to explain why the rent is late. It comes with the territory.

Lillian Buenavista followed me into the studio and I turned on the lights. The windows are infused with wire and covered with dirt. Sunlight has a hell of a time penetrating the grime, and usually doesn't try too hard.

I dropped into one of the lounge chairs. "Sit anywhere," I said, then watched with something approaching fascination as she meticulously folded the red cape, then sat on the edge of the couch and placed the cape on her lap. After a few snailish seconds crawled by she looked up. I couldn't help but wonder if she was taking a moment to get into character.

"I've been waiting an hour," she said. The phony Spanish accent was gone. I guess she'd been taking that moment to get *out* of character. What a whack-job.

I looked into her fabulous green eyes. They seemed to sparkle. "Sorry," I said mildly. "I didn't realize we had an appointment." I don't like to be pushed around by pushy people who think they're the only ones with places to go and people to see. And I particularly don't like it when these pushy types are dressed up like bull fighters. Even if they have fabulous green eyes that seem to sparkle.

"I left you three messages. You didn't answer any of them."

"Where?"

"Here, of course."

"I just got in," I said. "You witnessed my arrival. Have I had time to check for messages?"

"Well, you needn't bother."

"No? Why not?"

"I'm here now."

"Sure," I said. "You're here. But what if somebody else called?"

She looked at me like it was the last thing on her mind. "Well, if you actually think anyone else called, then by all means check."

"Thanks," I said. "I'll think it over and get back to you."

She placed the red cape carefully on the couch. It was arranged as

*The Farce News*

crisply as an American flag at a military funeral, but folded in a square instead of a triangle. She sat back and crossed her legs again. She looked tired and wired, as if she'd been up all night and was keeping the jag alive with bennies. It occurred to me that some people would say that youth is wasted on the young. I'd say bennies are wasted on the young. It's those of us starting to get a little long in the tooth who are most in need of the amphetamine performance enhancers.

"By the way," I said, "sorry to hear about Miguel."

Her head snapped up and her eyes got very hot for just a second.

"You know about the accident?" she said. "How?"

"It made the news. Friend of mine, ex-cop, he took me down to the scene."

"What friend?"

"Ernie Newman."

"Never heard of him."

"You don't have to know him. Your grandmother knows him. That's good enough."

"Well, if Nana knows him ..."

"So, how's Rosa holding up?"

She paused. "What do you mean?"

I sat back a little. "Come on, Lillian ..."

"Please," she said, "call me Lillian."

"I think I just did."

"Or Lilly."

"Whatever."

"Or Lil."

"Sure."

"Or Mrs. B."

"Should I be writing these down?"

"Some people even call me L.B. But I don't like L.B."

"I'll try to remember."

She reached into a small bag she had tucked under her ornate jacket. "Would you mind terribly if I smoked?"

"Mind? Hell, I'll light you on fire myself."

"Cigarettes," she said, holding up a red pack of Pall Malls.

"No, I don't mind," I said. "But I have to warn you, this building is full of cancerphobic fascists and they're likely to come down on you like trainload of screaming Rhesus monkeys if you light up one of those things inside."

She packed away her cigarettes and lighter. "Nobody stopped me when I smoked in the hall ..."

*The Farce News*

"Maybe they were afraid your *picador* would stab them through the brain if they made a fuss."

"Oh, honestly," she said. "What's the world coming to?"

I didn't have a ready answer to that one. "I didn't realize Rosa and Miguel originally came here from Cuba," I said, changing the subject as abruptly as possible.

"Waterbury, actually."

"Right, before Waterbury," I said. Lillian could be pretty tiresome when she put her mind to it.

"Before Waterbury they lived in New York City, and before that they spent some time in Miami."

"I stand corrected," I said and waited for her to point out that I was in fact sitting down.

"Miguel was extremely loyal. It's something he learned from his mother. As well as from Nana. She's very upset, as you can imagine. Rosa, that is. Nana knows nothing of this tragedy."

"That was a pretty hot car he was driving."

"I certainly hope you're not suggesting it was stolen ..."

"No, no. Hot. Souped up. Tricked out. Rigged for speed. Bit on the fancy side. A little out of his price bracket, wouldn't you say? Unless he was the best paid chauffeur in the State of Connecticut."

"Oh, Miguel was much more than just a chauffeur."

"That's what his mother said, too." That was last night, before I knew she was Miguel's mother.

"We'll miss him terribly. All of us."

That sounded like a line for a press release. "So, where'd he get the spiffy wheels?"

"What do you mean *spiffy*? You're completely overstating the case."

"Am I?"

"Yes. For goodness sakes, it was a 1985 Monte Carlo Sport with more than a hundred thousand miles on it. Nana purchased it for less than five thousand dollars, through a classified advertisement in the newspaper, if I recall correctly."

"Don't tell me it was your grandmother's car?" I couldn't see her behind the wheel of the hot rod. I couldn't even see her fitting through the door.

"No, of course not. Nana bought it to give to Miguel. As a gift."

I suppose there was a perfectly good reason for Lillian Buenavista to add the explanatory phrase, "As a gift." Even after she'd adequately established that Mrs. Wordstone had given Miguel the car by saying, "Nana bought it to give to Miguel." I wondered if she was making a subtle distinction in her own mind between a freely given present and some form of compensation. Had there been strings attached? Had Miguel done something special to earn the generous gift? Performed some valuable service? Or was I just another geographically challenged Siberian husky barking up a cocoanut tree?

"Nana paid extra to have a new engine put in," she said. "And a rebuilt transmission. And a new exhaust system. Oh, and an eight-speaker stereo system with a six-way CD changer."

"Very generous."

"Yes. Nana's wonderful."

"She should have bought him some driving lessons," I said. It was a harsh crack to make under the circumstances. I hoped it would piss her off. "To say nothing of seat belts."

Lillian sat up a little straighter and arched her back. "Miguel was an excellent driver!"

"If you say so," I said.

"And don't tell me to settle down," she said.

"I didn't." Christ, was she hearing voices?

She leaned forward and glared at me, breathing hotly through her lovely narrow nose. The nostrils flared ever so slightly. "Didn't you?"

I smiled soothingly. "Come now, Lillian. Don't make me use the red cape on you."

"Please, call me Lillian."

"I just did."

"Yes, of course." She calmed herself a little. Her breathing steadied. More stage craft. Couldn't anybody display a genuine emotion anymore?

"So, Robby ..."

"Please, call me Robby," I said. Hell, two could play this game, whatever game this was.

She ignored my remark. "How are you coming along on your business?"

"What business are we talking about?"

"The business Nana hired you for, of course. Don't be a simpleton."

I shrugged and made the old "who knows?" face. "Couldn't tell you if I wanted to. And, just for the record, I don't want to."

She stiffened. "Well, now that's just plain rude."

I shrugged. "Try to see it my way. You wouldn't want your psychiatrist telling me all about your various maladies, would you? Auntie Peg asked me for help in confidence. If she didn't tell you about it herself, I don't see how I could ..."

"Excuse me, what did you say?"

"Your grandmother asked for my help in confidence ..."

"Not that! The bit about my psychiatrist!"

"Oh, that was just to illustrate my point."

She relaxed a little and for a moment I was afraid she'd mistaken my explanation for some kind of apology. "Well, let me tell you a thing or two. While I was sitting out there in that sorry excuse for a waiting room, wasting half the day waiting to see if you'd ever show up, I did some serious thinking. That is, when I wasn't browsing through your magazines. By the way, who is this Doctor Frederick Mendelssohn?"

"I have no idea."

"Well, his name is on all the magazines."

"I'm aware of that."

"But ..."

"You still haven't told me a thing or two. Or even one."

She switched her leg position. "Basically, I've been trying to decide if I can trust you."

"Really?" I said.

"You certainly haven't given me any reason to so far."

I didn't reply to her non-charge, nor try to defend my honor. It was like standing accused of a crime I hadn't yet committed but which everyone -- in this case everyone being Lillian the Vaudevillian -- felt was inevitable, based on the dubious nature of my character.

"Is it important that you trust me?"

She laughed. She had a nice laugh and I liked the way it brightened up her face. For a moment, I thought I glimpsed the authentic Lillian Buenavista beneath the veneer. "Listen, just because you have a bunch of magazines you stole from a shrink doesn't mean you can start psychoanalyzing me. I get enough of that. Believe me."

I did believe her. "I didn't steal them from a shrink."

"Oh, I suppose they accidentally mailed themselves to you."

"No, I stole them from my dentist. I think he's being treated for a bipolar disorder. Or maybe it's the shrink who's being treated for a bicuspid disorder."

"That's not funny."

"Sorry."

"You can be very tedious."

"Is that going to have a measurable impact on your final decision regarding my trustworthiness?"

"I'm not sure yet. It might."

"Fair enough. In the meantime, maybe you can start by telling me a thing or two about why I need to be trustworthy?"

"Well, for one thing, you're working for Nana."

I sat back. I was having a hard time keeping a straight face during this syncopated conversation with this dazzling redheaded, green-eyed woman, who for reasons of her own was dressed up like a Spanish toreador. There were moments when I wondered who the joke was on, me or her?

"It's true that I'm supposed to be working for your grandmother," I said, glancing at my watch in the hopes that Lillian the Vaudevillian would get the hint. That is, that time was slipping away. "I think it's really more important that *she* trust me? Don't you agree?"

"Since you brought it up, that's actually part of the reason I came here to see you. I want you to work for me, too. I want to hire you. I can pay, of course. I have my own money. And, of course, we're family. So you can hardly refuse."

She was going to be very disappointed, perhaps even shocked, when I refused.

"What is it you want to hire me to do?" I asked, not that I really wanted to know.

"I want you to pay off a blackmailer."

I looked into her crazy green eyes again. For the first time, she seemed entirely serious. It was as if she was capable of lucidity on command, but preferred freestyle mania. I couldn't say I blamed her. Lucidity isn't all its cracked up to be. On the other hand, neither is cracking up.

Lillian Buenavista reached into her bag again. I hoped she wasn't going to repeat the cigarette smoker's lament. I still didn't know what the world was coming to any better than she did. I only knew the rules about lighting up in this particular smoke free environment. She'd been lucky once, but I didn't think she'd be so lucky with the nicotine nazis a second time. She wasn't smoking Lucky's, she was smoking Pall Malls.

But she didn't bring out the red pack of unfiltered cigarettes. Instead she produced a small flat package wrapped in brown paper. She handed it across the couch to me. It was about the size of a videotape box. I picked it up and peeled back the paper. It was a videotape all right. No wonder. I pulled it all the way out and looked at the cover. It was a colorful photograph of half a dozen young woman, all of them peroxide blondes, playing beach volleyball in their birthday suits. The video was entitled, "Volley-Ball!" I was pretty sure I'd seen a few minutes of it the night before at LaTwanda Jefferson's house.

"Where'd you get this?" I asked.

"It came to the house by messenger this morning, addressed to me."

I looked at the brown paper. There was no return address. I'd have been very surprised to find one. There was nothing else. "No note?" I asked.

"About twenty minutes after it arrived, I got a phone call."
"Ah."
"A man with a very smooth voice. I'd never heard it before. He said this could easily have fallen into Nana's hands if he wasn't such a decent and honorable guy. Then he said I should think seriously about ways to persuade him to make sure none of the other copies find their way to Nana, or the general movie going public."
"Did this smooth-talker suggest any particular ways you could do that?"
"Yes, as a matter of fact. He said a cash contribution would do nicely."
"And he called her Nana?"
"No, of course not. I'm parasailing."
"I think you mean *paraphrasing*."
"That's what I said."
"No, it isn't."
"Well, I won't argue about it if you won't."

I walked over to a beat-up oak desk we keep in the corner, where we keep gig contracts, show calendars, out-of-date band posters and other useless crap. I dropped the video on the desktop and opened a drawer. I spent a minute rummaging around for aspirin. I didn't find any. She watched without asking what I was doing. The effect was wasted. I shut the drawer. "So, how much of a cash contribution did he suggest?"

"Twenty-five thousand dollars."

A whole lot less than the eighty large Twannie Jefferson had demanded. More chump change from people who conducted their organized crime efforts like so many chimps, not chumps.

"Okay, and why would you bother to pay it? I mean, what am I missing here?"

"Take a closer look at the box."

I did. Nothing jumped except a couple of the models, but they had a reason. One was trying to spike the ball over the net while a second one was trying to thwart her attempt. I somehow could sense that one or both of them was about to end up sprawled in the sand with injuries requiring immediate, and, no doubt intimate, care.

"This is fairly tame stuff, a little silly," I said. "Everyone looks legal. What's the catch?"

"Silly? My God! How can you say such a thing?"

"Come on, Lillian. Aren't you overreacting a little?"

Lillian Buenavista stood up and came over to the desk. She put a slim fingertip on one of the blondes in the background. The girl's face was a bit obscured, a little out of the forefront. I looked more carefully.

"Is it you?"
"Don't be a pig."
"Oink."
"Look again."
I did. "I'll be damned."
"I don't doubt if for a minute," she said.
"Thanks."
"But that's irrelevant at the moment."
"You saying this is Lita?"
"Who else?"

I had to admit it did look like Lita. But then, I'd never seen Lita play volleyball. Nor had I ever seen her naked. I recalled she had a hell of an arm, though, hurling that taffy wad into the trees out in back of the Prospect Avenue place. And I remembered her telling me in the car how much she liked volleyball, but that she wasn't very good at it yet. "Have you watched the video?" I asked.

Lillian Buenavista looked down at her hands for a moment. When she looked up at me again, her cheeks were red. "I looked at the first few minutes. To be honest, I couldn't take very much."

"Sure."

"It's not that I'm a prude or anything, but ..."

"I understand."

"Do you?"

"It's your kid sister."

"Yes. Unmistakably."

I took a deep breath, slowly. I wanted to ask what Lita was doing in the tape, how involved was her participation. It might answer some questions about LaTwanda Jefferson and her hold on the Wordstones. But it didn't really matter anymore because LaTwanda Jefferson was dead. Now somebody else was making a play for a piece of the Wordstone money -- a laughably small piece, but a piece nonetheless. And it might have no connection at all to Twannie Jefferson, although I didn't believe that for a second. I also wanted to ask if I could hold onto the tape, but there would be no way to make such a request without appearing to be anything but a sadist or a voyeur. And if there's one thing I'm not, it's a sadist.

"How long ago do you suppose she did this?" I said.

"What? I don't understand."

"How? Old? Would? You? Judge? The? Tape? To? Be?"

"You don't have to be so rude!"

"So, answer the question. A year? Two years? A month?"

"Oh, I see. I think it must be very recent. There's a tattoo. On her right hip. She only got that done in January. That was ten months ago."

I thought it over for a couple of minutes. Then I went over and dropped into one of the lounge chairs and looked Lillian Buenavista in the eye.

"Anything else you want to tell me?"

"Such as?" she said.

"I don't know. This is your drama, not mine."

"You're really quite mean, aren't you?"

"Look, Lillian, there's something fundamentally wrong with this entire setup."

"What do you mean?" she said. At least this time she didn't ask me to call her Lillian.

"Let's start with the money."

"Yes, okay. The money. What about it?"

"Twenty-five grand isn't much for you people, but it's a lot to keep such a small secret."

"What do mean 'a small secret'?"

"It's a ridiculously small sum, considering the vast resources a clever extortionist might exploit if he were brazen enough to make the Wordstone fortune his personal gold mine."

"How can you say such a thing? That's my baby sister! Your own cousin."

"Yeah, yeah. I'm looking into that."

"And I don't think twenty-five thousand dollars ..."

"This is the twenty-first century, Lillian."

"What does that have to do with anything?"

"Look, we might prefer our loved ones not to appear in skin flicks, but it's barely against the law anymore. Freedom of expression, right? Lita's old enough to make her own decisions. Even bad ones. What's more, she hasn't done anything very shocking. You can buy videos of college girls getting drunk and naked off the television at five o'clock in the morning. If that's your cup of tea. At five in the morning, I prefer coffee. But that's neither here nor there. The point is, it's no big deal. Not in today's climate of excess. Look around. Pretty much anything goes, right? You can traipse around in a bull fighter's costume and nobody even says boo."

"Yes, but I can't smoke a cigarette without risking persecution by a horde of neo-fascists!"

"True, but let's consider the bigger picture. For a kid with her resources, showing up in a soft core dike porno might make her a target for petty extortionists, but it isn't exactly going to hold her back or ruin her life, or irrevocably damage her future. Christ, Lillian, it isn't as if she's planning to make a career out of this. No more than you're planning to make a career of bull fighting."

She glared at me. "It really bothers you, doesn't it?"

"What's that?"

"That I'm free enough to express myself in costume."

"Doesn't bother me one bit. I find it extremely entertaining."

"Entertaining!"

"I'm sorry, isn't that what you were going for?"

"Rude, rude, rude!"

"My bad."

I shrugged and let her stew awhile. Finally she broke the silence: "Anyway, if Nana ever found out, it would kill her."

"I seriously doubt that. Auntie Peg hasn't spent her life in vacuum, you know. Half the books in her sub-arctic library are trashy sex novels. I doubt she keeps them around just for decoration. Look," I said, holding up the video box. "There must be quite a few copies of this thing if this extortionist readily gave you one."

"That's very logical of you, Robby."

"Paying twenty-five thousand dollars isn't going to reduce the threat of disclosure."

Lillian Buenavista would not be swayed. "Yes, I see. But we must pay. I can't risk it."

"What about your sister? Have you discussed this with her?"

"No, not yet. She's home in bed. She spent the night vomiting. Food poisoning, I think."

"I suppose you know she's allergic to chocolate?"

"Yes, of course. But she takes meds to counteract the effects. Why?"

"Ask Rosa when she's up to it. Last night, Lita got into some Egyptian fudge ..."

"Oh, my God ..."

"I think that's the source of your food poisoning."

"That's awful. Who would give it to her?"

"No idea," I said, lying through my teeth.

"And why would she eat it without first taking her medication?"

"Why don't you ask her when she's back on her feet."

"You bet I will."

"And while we're on the subject, where were *you* last night?"

"Me?" She stopped short. I watched her train of thought switch tracks and jump the rails. All vestiges of sisterly concern evaporated like so much mist on an ocean breeze. Her voice became throaty and emotional. At last, it was time for her close-up. Had we been sitting in that huge room in her private wing of the Prospect Avenue mansion, she would no doubt have excused herself to change into her version of the bewildered Norma Desmond in *Sunset Boulevard*.

"I was at the Simsbury Dinner Theater with a gentleman friend, if you could call him that."

"You mean a *friend?*"

"No."

"You mean a *gentleman?*"

"No."

"Okay, I give up."

"It's not important. The point is, that's where I was. We saw a production of *Les Miserables* and ate fillet mignon with mushrooms. We drank champagne and laughed the night away."

"I didn't know *Les Miserables* was a comedy," I said.

"Absolutely. The way *they* did it."

"I see."

"Of course, the food was simply dreadful. The food there is always dreadful."

"Maybe it's something in the water."

"I think it's something in the kitchen, actually."

"And the play?"

"Worse still. I'm afraid theater is not the strong suit at the SDT. It's always atrocious."

"Interesting," I said. "Just out of curiosity, what would be their strong suit?"

"Well, the valet parking is excellent."

"I see."

She continued her monologue as if William Morris were sitting in the room scouting talent.

"The actors, if one could call them that, lack any of the basic artistic integrity and honesty required to deliver a truly memorable, or even competent, performance. They lack soul, individually and collectively. I don't know why I keep going back. Do you know, I've seen *Les Mis* four times this month alone? And my God, it isn't even the fifteenth. It's absolutely shocking, Robby. May I call you Robby? Really, I'm appalled. Last month they attempted to stage *Miss Saigon* as a musical.*"

"I thought it *was* a musical."

She paused. "Oh. Are you sure?"

*The Farce News*

I had to admit I wasn't.

"Anyway, it doesn't matter," she said.

On that we could agree.

"It was even more ungodly awful than *Les Mis*. I've learned one thing, Robby ..."

"Please, call me Robby."

"... The only thing worse than Andrew Lloyd Webber done well is Andrew Lloyd Webber done by a troupe of dinner theater hacks who can't sing or dance or deliver their lines on cue."

"I can only accept your word for it."

"And yet I keep going back. It's astonishing, really."

"It is a bit peculiar," I said, just to be agreeable.

"It's almost as if I can't get enough of a bad thing."

"Almost."

As I watched her, I realized she was no longer talking to me. Rather she had turned her attention to a spot on the wall, a spot that must have served as a portal into another dimension where all the stage lights shined on her face, where all eyes were cast upon her riveting countenance. Of course, I'm only paraphrasing for her troubled psyche, which at the moment may well have been off parasailing somewhere in the South Pacific. I may have stolen some magazines from the guy, but I never actually went to shrink school myself.

I was about to add something clever about the inescapable hammerlock of addiction, how like a Full Nelson dependency could forestall all forward motion, both physically and psychologically. And how, eventually, it played havoc with your respiratory system if you didn't somehow break the hold before the referee counted you out. I decided not to say anything. I was pretty sure she wouldn't have heard me anyway.

And then a bell rang somewhere in my head and I found myself thinking about all her costume changes and this bizarre and insatiable appetite she had for lousy theater. There was a connection. If only I could find the right psychological chain saw with which to sever it, I might even be doing the woman a favor. Probably not.

"So, Lillian -- may I call you Lillian? -- what time did you get home?"

"Yes, of course, I insist. It was well after midnight."

I nodded. "That's a bit too specific. Could you be more vague?"

She looked at me funny and seemed to snap out of whatever daze she'd lapse into. "You really are tiresome, aren't you?"

I shrugged and yawned. "I didn't sleep too well last night."

She was getting pissed, but at least the spell was broken. Norma Desmond was gone. In her place Antonio Ordonez had returned, thankfully *sans* the phony Barcelona lisp.

"There was a time when I thought I could like you," she said with a wistful sigh.

"So you're a dinner theater junkie, huh?"

"My close, personal friend Venus Edwards keeps a table for me up front. Of course, dinner is complimentary."

"I thought you said the food was no good."

"All the more reason not to pay." She winked and smiled.

My skin tried to crawl away and hide under the desk. *"Ole,"* I said.

She arched an eyebrow at me and her smile dripped away.

Venus Edwards. Now there was a name you heard around town without even trying. Rich beyond even the highest Prospect Avenue standards. Millions stacked on each other like cords of wood at the lake house. The Wordstones and their Old Money cronies might entertain themselves by peering haughtily down their noses at Venus Edwards and her *nouveau riche* compatriots. But it was a sham. The old school farts accrued what modicum of self-righteousness they could by convincing themselves, and each other, that their own wealth was genuine. That is, legitimate, deserved. And that the fortunes amassed by the Venus-Come-Lately crowd were no more than the fortuity of sweaty gold miners who gained wealth not from ingenuity or creativity but merely as a byproduct of their mulish endurance. Any monkey could get lucky, given enough opportunity. But that wasn't the case with Venus Edwards. She was an entrepreneurial genius. She not only owned half of all she could see, but also commanded respect, fear, admiration, loathing, disgust, adoration ... It depended only on the angle from which you viewed her. Some people in my home town said the same sort of things about a guy the mainstream media had designated The Donald. Not the duck, the other one. The tower tycoon. I'd never seen anything there but bad hair and a peculiar disdain for good taste.

Anyway, Venus was The Donald of her domain.

Different strokes for different folks, right? One leaves you paralyzed on the left side and drooling. The other leaves you speaking fluent Portuguese even though you spent your entire adult life in a Medicine Hat, Alberta.

"How'd you get so chummy with Venus Edwards?"

"Oh, it's very complicated," she said. "Or very simple. I'm not sure which."

"Try the simple version first. I'm not too smart. You might lose me with anything elaborate."

She sneered. "My sister said you're a prick. Maybe she was right."

*The Farce News*

"She said that? After all I did for her? I'm shocked."

"She said you're a dickhead and you don't know your place."

"A dickhead? That's nice. So refined. Guess she straddles both sides of the fence, huh?"

Lillian recoiled a little. "That was uncalled for and extremely uncouth."

"You started it."

We stared at each for a minute. The toreador get-up was really working my funny bone to a frazzle. I just couldn't get over how she was able to take herself this seriously while decked out so preposterously. It was a remarkable demonstration of egocentrism. I thought about saying so, but she was regaining her composure and I decided not to ruin it.

"Venus Edwards and I share a common mortification."

"Really? Not many people can claim a *common mortification*."

"Do want to hear it or don't you?"

"Sorry. Please continue."

"It's our husbands." She stopped and stared at me.

I counted to twenty. "Yes? I'm afraid I'll need a little more."

"They abandoned us," she said. "Technically."

"Technically? How does that work?"

She bowed her head for dramatic effect. "They ran off."

I thought about that. "Together?"

Her head snapped up. She fixed me with a cold stare. "Of course not!"

"Well, the way you said it ..."

"Listen here, Robby ..."

"Call me Robby."

"My husband was a lot of things. Hold on, I have a list." She began to fumble in her little bag.

"Forget the list." I wondered if Blackie Buenavista had ever been a toreador, or a nun, or a French maid, or a construction worker, or, for that matter, a belligerent Finnish midget on ice skates.

She looked up. "Anyway, one thing he was not, was a faggot."

I cringed. "Ouch, that's such an ugly word."

"Okay," she said. "How about homo?"

"Not much better."

"Fudge packer?"

"Yikes, the imagery."

"Rump ranger?"

"Rustic, but still rude."

She threw her hands up. "Oh, you're just too hard to please. I don't like playing with you."

"Hey, this is your party. I just stopped by to check for messages and pick up the mail. You're the one who killed half a day waiting to see if I'd ever show up, remember? Whenever you get tired, the door is right behind you."

She composed herself again, or pretended to. "Honestly, I don't know what Nana sees in you."

Well, now she had me because I didn't really know what dear old Auntie Peg saw in me either, other than someone she thought was streetwise enough to solve her icky problems with the great unwashed masses. And I'd forgotten why Lillian had come to see me. In any case, I thought it was time to tie a ribbon around this gag gift of a colloquy.

"Look, Lillian. Let's talk about your problem."

"My problem?"

I pointed at the videotape. "Remember?"

"Oh, that. Yes, of course."

"How about we just tell these blackmailers to go take a flying leap off the Bulkley Bridge?"

"Do you think it would work?"

"If I were you, I'd tell 'em, 'Yeah, nice movie. Thanks for sharing. Not exactly Mary Poppins, but I've seen worse.'"

Lillian Buenavista didn't like my idea. I could tell right away when she said, "No way."

"Why not?"

"For one thing, it would imply that I've actually seen worse."

"Actually, it would be an open admission."

"Exactly. No can do. I have a reputation to protect."

This from a woman in a toreador suit.

"Okay, then I suggest you go scrape together twenty-five thousand dollars. Maybe you have it in your piggy bank. Maybe you cash a check at the *Super Stop N Shop*. While you're at, give some thought to where you're going to get the next twenty-five grand and the twenty-five grand after that, because once you start this chum line, the sharks are going to gather. Eventually, they'll want to climb into the boat and get cozy."

"Yes," she said, suddenly very thoughtful. "I *saw* that movie."

I rolled my eyes. I don't think she noticed. I didn't really care.

"Just get the money together and call me. We'll work out how to make the drop. Or better still, figure out how not to make the drop."

Lillian Buenavista was still thinking about the movie she had seen. "Don't you think Roy Scheider is dreamy? I didn't take a bath for a year after I saw that film. Just showers."

I decided to stay out of this parallel universe conversation.

She stood and smoothed her wrinkle-free outfit with a brush of her palm. Then she picked a corner of the red cape which was folded on the edge of the couch. With another great flourish, she unfurled it and waved it over her shoulder.

"*Ole!*" she said, and turned for the door.

She was way too fast for me. I didn't even have a chance to stand up and say good-bye -- or *Adios!* -- before she was out the door, mumbling something in Spanish in what sounded to me like a totally phony Barcelona lisp. I decided at that moment, that I quite liked Lillian Buenavista after all. Call me a pig, but I liked her best when she was walking away, leaving me alone, getting the hell out of the rehearsal studio, making her grand exit stage left. "I'll be in touch!" she said, and vanished, slamming the door behind her.

The trembling quiet that followed was perfect for the kind of reflection my life seemed to require. I'd only known the Wordstone clan for about twenty-four hours and already the dead bodies were starting to pile up. And one of the corpses was now missing. Too weird. And not one but two witless extortion plots had been hatched, one of which was now a moot point. And two seriously twisted sisters were conspiring to drive me crazy -- no mean feat considering both of them were (at least figuratively) out to lunch at the buffet of the truly bewildered.

Which reminded me, I hadn't eaten all day.

Half an hour later I was finished sorting the junk mail and ready to head home. I was about to lock up when the phone rang. I reluctantly picked it up, wishing to hell I could afford Caller I.D. Lillian Buenavista couldn't possibly have put together twenty-five grand that fast, not unless she had large sums of money stashed around the mansion -- although that wasn't entirely out of the realm of possibility.

I let the phone ring five times before picking it up. "Hello," I said, in a mock-mechanical voice. "You have reached the offices of Elvis Jihad. We can't take your call right now, but if you ..."

"Knock it off, Robby."

It was Ernie Newman.

"Hey," I said. "I thought it was someone else. What's new?"

"The Monte Carlo. Somebody definitely put it into a spin."

"No kiddin'. Just like those NASCAR rednecks?"

He ignored my crack. "Found paint on the right rear panel that wasn't from the Chevy."

He paused. "Keep talking," I said. "You had me at hello."

"Take a guess what color the paint is?"

"Help me out here, Ernie. My last girlfriend broke up with me because I'm color blind."

"Yeah, bummer. I hate when that happens."

"You get used to it."

"Maybe *you* do."

"But you digress. What about the paint?"

"Would you believe purple?"

"No way, Max."

"Way."

"Beautiful."

"You like purple, huh?"

"Not that way, no."

"They're running the chips through spectrographic and chemical analysis. Should be able to tell us where it came from, who did the paint job, if it's a factory job or a special custom order. The whole shebang. It's a big break, Robby. And there's more."

"Don't keep me in suspense."

"There was a heater in the car."

"Really? How about air conditioning?"

"A gun, asshole. A .38 snubby. All six shots fired."

"Recently, I'll bet."

"Time will tell."

"You're a pal, Ernie. I owe you."

"Indeed you do."

I locked up the studio and headed down to my car. Invigorated by all this new information, I decided to go home and take a nap. I hadn't slept well the night before, thinking about Twannie and Billie and Lita and Lillian and Jolie. All these women keeping me up nights and some of them I'd never even met.

Twenty minutes later, I let myself into the apartment. J.D. and Buddy attacked my ankles like a veteran tag team on the Saturday night wrestling hour. Rufus bounded over from his mat. He stood up, put his paws on my chest, and barked a big, stinky dog-breath hello in my face. It was good to be home. Good to feel the love of adoring companions. Or maybe the cats were just hungry and the dog had to pee. Who really knows?

On the kitchen table was Twannie Jefferson's *iMac* to remind me that I was nowhere with her coded list of potential blackmail targets, or customers, or whatever the hell they were. Inside that computer were all the secrets that could set this case on a course toward its final resolution. And here I was, a virtual computer illiterate.

On the *iMac's* black screen, someone had taped a note. It was Jolie's handwriting. Broken script with a slight forward slant. I tore it off.

*"The Doofus has been out. Did no business. Kitties need more tuna. See ya later."*

I held the sheet of paper to my nose. It smelled like Jolie. Her shampoo, that funky Indian incense she burned. And that lovely smell she had all by herself without even trying. Made me want to run down the hall and bang on her door. Not sure exactly what was holding me back. Fear of rejection? Fear of acceptance? Fear of flying? No, I love flying. Just don't like the idea of crashing very much.

## Chapter 12

There are some things that can make you feel pretty stupid pretty quickly. Math riddles about trains that leave the station an hour apart, et cetera, et cetera; anagram-laden crossword puzzles from the *London Times;* balancing a goddamn checkbook. That's always a treat. If I were married I'd leave that tedious task to my wife while I worked on the *London Times* crossword puzzle. I'm sure it would ultimately lead to our divorce, but *c'est la vie,* can't have everything.

At the moment, however, I didn't need this kind of demoralizing experience.

An hour of staring at LaTwanda Jefferson's computerized target list was about all I could take without going cross-eyed and drooling like a washed-up heavy metal drummer. She was better at this sort of thing than I'd originally given her credit for. Her alphanumeric code was the work of a pure evil genius. The kind of thing only a fifth grader could crack, the labor of someone a lot smarter than I'll ever be. It didn't take long to realize I was never going to break the cypher. The closest I'd come would be if I took a sledgehammer to the computer itself. (And I was thinking about it.)

Other problems occupied my mind like so many squatters in an SRO hotel room. The problem of this new blackmail pitch, for one. I didn't think it was a very good pitch. It was low and outside, way off the plate. Nowhere near the strike zone. And yet Lillian Buenavista wanted to take a swing at it, and not just to make contact. She wanted to dig in and take a home run cut, as if smacking this one out of the park would end the game and enable her to trot off the field like Mr. October -- or in her case, Mrs. October -- in the seventh game of the World Series. But this wasn't the bottom of the ninth inning. Not by a long shot. This was about the middle of the fourth. There was a long way to go before a winner emerged and somebody offered up another sad rendition of Harry Carey's legendary cry of "Cubs win, Cubs win!"

Right now Lillian Buenavista was playing a loser's game. My only hope was that she didn't have a Red Sox uniform hanging in that magic closet of hers. Or, if she did, that she had the good sense to leave it on the hanger where it belonged. The last thing I needed right now was to get stuck babysitting some Carl Yastrzemski wannabe, trying to convince her to take a pitch. Nobody ever had to tell Yaz to take a pitch. But he knew a screwball when he saw one. And so did I. Lillian the Vaudevillian definitely qualified.

Lita Wordstone, on the other hand, was more of a knuckler. Or maybe a spitter. Something about that young woman was fundamentally against the rules.

I decided to forget about Twannie Jefferson's purple desktop computer for the time begin. There were still unanswered questions waiting for me back at Big Jeff's house and, if the cops still weren't there nosing around, I'd like to finish the search I'd begun the night before. I wanted to get a look at the rest of the house, the basement, the attic, the whole deal. I didn't know what I'd find, or what would be left for me to find.

Had the same crew that did such a crack job on Twannie's place also taken the opportunity to clean out the big girl's merchandise? That was the burning question and so far the only thing I had on hand to put it out was a fresh can of Curiosity Brand Turpentine.

The fact that someone had removed Twannie Jefferson from the murder scene made me cringe a little, not just because she was so big and so fat and so dead when she was carted off. Whoever had absconded with Big Jeff's super-sized carcass must have used some kind of heavy duty cart to do it, or the kind of steroid-boosted musculature not found on normal people. The movers I met at Johnny Brashear's house could probably pull it off, if they were smart enough. I doubted they were. And neither of them looked like they could be trusted with a forklift.

But that wasn't all that creeped me out. It went far beyond my fundamental aversion to direct contact with the recently deceased.

It was the cold-blooded nature of the act. It's one thing to kill in a moment of overheated passion. At least I think it's one thing. I've never done it myself -- killed in a moment of overheated passion, that is. But I'm fairly certain it doesn't qualify as two or more things. On the other hand, pilfering goods and stashing a corpse -- now that's definitely two or more things. Well, two things, actually. Three if you count moving the body and hiding it as individual acts.

On the subject of two or more things, I was currently of two or more minds on the entire matter of LaTwanda Jefferson having gone missing in the first place. One mind had already filed her disappearance under Acts of Bizarre Depravity Bordering On -- no, Entering Freely Into -- the Macabre. The other mind was actually casting about looking for someone to thank. If only I knew who. As far as I was concerned, *absent* wasn't the worst thing Twannie Jefferson could be at the moment, so long as she was dead anyway. As long as Big Jeff stayed missing and didn't suddenly reappear like some ghoul out of *Night of the Living Dead,* the long overdue 911 call would not have to be made.

If LaTwanda did turn up again -- and I couldn't think of a single set of circumstances in which her return could be viewed as a positive thing -- I'd have no choice but to drop a dime and start conjuring up a storm of bullshit and half-truths to assuage the various law enforcement agencies who would not be happy with me on any level. Worse yet, at such a juncture my case (if it could be called a case) would be history. My job would be done. Over before it ever got started. Certainly before I'd ever had a chance to talk LaTwanda Jefferson out of sticking up dear old Auntie Peg for eighty thousand dollars, which no longer mattered. Absolutely worst of all, my chance to earn a modest fee for services I never had a snowball's chance to render would be shot to hell. Just like Twannie.

There were other reasons to keep banging away at this human math puzzle, even in the aftermath of Twannie Jefferson's untimely departure from the station considerably more than an hour before the rest of us (with the possible exception of Miguel, who seemed to have left the same station within a couple hours, at most, of Twannie). I wondered if Miguel traveled quicker in death and had yet overtaken Twannie on the Journey to Wherever, passing her in the breakdown lane as only an inveterate juvenile delinquent would.

There were issues to be addressed. It remained to be discovered, for example, how many copies of "Volley-Ball!" were in circulation at the moment. And on that subject, it sure would be interesting to find out who was holding the tapes, who controlled their distribution.

There was no question in my mind but that Lillian Buenavista was jumping the gun on this particular ransom demand. When one stopped to consider (as I had done at some length) the object being held over her head as leverage, it was hard to avoid feeling it was no big deal, much ado about very damn little. There are certainly those people among us who have decided that any kind of sex but the kind they practice is somehow dirty and immoral. By the same token, however (and not the sort of token you might use to operate a peep show Viewmaster), this is often the same crowd of moralistic finger waggers so often found sneaking in and out of sticky-floored movie theaters cloaked in sticky trench coats. You'd never get them to admit they read D.H. Lawrence or any other periodically banned *smut*, but they could tell you the page numbers with all the really lewd parts.

If Lita Wordstone had participated in a bit of girls-only fun in the sun, it was nothing to me. The only question of note concerned the extent of her willingness to play along. If she had jumped on board like some happy-go-lucky sailor bound to see the world, then more power to her. If, however, she'd been dragged into the hold like a slave en route to the land of the free and the home of the brave, then there was a problem. I'd have to ask her about it when our paths next crossed, provided she was at least partially coherent at the time.

As for keeping this big secret from Auntie Peg, I judged Lillian Buenavista to be guilty of practicing a form of benign age discrimination. We're all damned good at overlooking the fact that before all the old folks around us got to be old folks and began to forget stuff, like which flower pot they put their shoes and socks in, and whether they left the frogs boiling on the stove again, they'd had a fair amount of fun of their own. Most of them raised some hell, most of them raised some kids, most of them made a few mistakes along the way just to prove they were human, and most of them, at one time or another, dabbled in their own generation's version of antisocial behavior. They didn't get to be old living in vacuum-packed baby food jars, even if, here in the homestretch, that was where they ended up getting much of their nourishment. Lillian's beloved Nana was surely a tad over her ideal fighting weight and arguably a few miles down Slap Happy Highway, but she still had the constitution to withstand major shots of expensive whiskey.

My bet was Auntie Peg could probably handle a little mortification from Lita's corner of the world (if it ever came to that). I also thought it was a prohibitive long shot she'd ever be tested. After all, who among the D.A.R. sisterhood populating the Wordstone social circle was liable to call and say, "Oh, Maggie, dear, you'll never guess where I saw Lita? Why, in a soft-core lesbian porno flick!" How much more secure could any secret be than the one about which no one dares to speak?

Meanwhile, it was my hope that Twannie Jefferson's house had a few secrets it was willing to share. A little inside dope to help an amateur snoop make sense of this extraordinarily dopey situation in which the wacky witches of Wordstone manor had become ensnared.

Duncaster Road was just as quiet and empty in the middle of the afternoon as it had been on my previous two visits, though the hour had been much later. Maybe this was just one of those streets that didn't get much action, save the odd homicide the seemed to go completely unnoticed. I parked my dented black Jetta around the corner on Duncaster Hollow and locked it. Call it habit. In my hometown, you had to lock up your trash or someone would steal it and sell it for a profit. I pulled a Hartford *Courant* baseball cap a little too low on my head carried a battered wooden clipboard with me as I headed for Twannie's front door.

Anyone watching from their home would see a subscription salesman hocking home delivery service, making me the ultimate in sad sack working stiffs, the kind of poor bastard from whom anyone in his right mind would immediately run and hide. I walked up the driveway with a pathetic limp. Hell, it worked for Kevin Spacey in *The Usual Suspects.* What's good enough for Kyser Soze is good enough for me.

For no particular reason, I took a look through the windows of Twannie's spacious two-car garage. I was hoping for a look at the purple Lexus -- particularly its front end. See if there any signs of damage. Maybe a smear of black paint from a Monte Carlo Supersport.

But the Lexus wasn't there.

In its place was another vehicle, one I hadn't been expecting to see any time soon. And yet it was a vehicle whose presence, I must admit, didn't surprise me all that much, considering how things had gone in the course of the last 24 hours. The car was a late model silver Toyota Camry with spinning gangsta rims. Lita Wordstone's rig.

Which made me think: Uh, oh. If Lita's Camry sits here cooling off, can Lita be far away?

Instinctively I spun around, just to make sure the girl wasn't sneaking up on me from behind again, *Psycho* style, with a kitchen knife in one hand, a half-eaten chocolate bar in the other.

I didn't make any pretense of ringing the front door bell. Instead I slipped around back, to let myself in through the patio doors. I turned the corner and there, sitting on a built-in wooden bench with her back to me, was the girl herself. The white blonde hair gave her away. But fair's fair. In turn, my footsteps gave me away as well. She turned suddenly, an expression of fear and guilt on her chalky face.

"Oh!" she said. "You scared me."

It wasn't much of an Alfred Hitchcock moment after all. Her eyes were red-rimmed. She had a couple of expensive Louis Vuiton handbags hanging from the lower lids. Her skin had the pallor of someone getting over food poisoning or, in her case, a cocoa overdose.

"Well," I said. "Fancy meeting you here."

"I know you," she said. Her eyes did a valiant job of trying to focus on me. She said she knew me, but she didn't sound all that sure. Maybe she was trying to convince herself I wasn't a homicidal maniac.

"Dr. C. Everett Koop," I said, holding out my hand. "Pleasure to see you again. What's it been? Hours? How are you feeling?"

She didn't stand up to shake hands. Oh, well.

"I was just ..."

She stopped abruptly. I gave her some time to finish the thought. But she didn't. Apparently she was having second thoughts about finishing the first thought. Instead she stood up and backed away from me, the way the B-grade actress backs away from the swamp killer in all the cheesy teen creature features. I was definitely scary. Clearly she'd never heard of C. Everett Coop. Or perhaps it was the Hartford *Courant* hat I wore too low on my head. Maybe she thought I was going to try to sell her a subscription to something. That would explain the full-blown look of horror.

"What do you want?" she said.

"Take it easy," I said. "Is that your car in the garage?" It seemed like a good enough place to start. Ask her a simple question, one to which I already knew the answer. See how she responded.

"What garage?" she said.

I sighed. Maybe this wasn't going to be so easy after all. "Um, you know, the one attached to the house. And please don't ask ..."

"Which house?" she said.

"... which house."

"Sorry."

"No problem. Let's start over. That's your Camry in the garage, the garage attached to this house. Right, Lita? I mean, those spinners ... They kind of give it away, you know?"

"Spinners?"

"The rims."

"Oh. They were Miggy's idea."

I filed that away for future reference. "First things first. How'd you get it in there? You have a clicker?"

"You mean a garage door opener?"

"Yes, Lita, a garage door opener."

She had slowly backed up to the house. Now she had her palms flat against the horizontal wooden siding. I don't know if she thought the house was holding her up or she was holding the house up, but they were like siamese twins, and she wasn't going to be easily separated from her newfound appendage. I wondered where she'd picked up the instinct for protecting her back side. It hadn't been doing her much good thirty seconds ago when I came around the side of the house. Clearly she was flying by the seat of her pants and her wing flaps weren't providing any lift whatsoever.

"I didn't need a clicker," she said after a pause. "It was open."

I made a rude noise, like a game show buzzer when a contestant rings in with an incorrect answer. "Sorry, that'll cost you a thousand dollars."

"I mean it was unlocked," she said. "You know. You touch the button, the door goes up."

I thought it over. It seemed implausible. But the same could be said about damned near everything that came out of Lita Wordstone's mouth, and yet some of it had to be true. If nothing else, the mathematical law of averages suggested that at some point she had to stumble across the truth if only long enough to give it lip service "You hit the button again and it goes back down," she said.

"I get how a garage door opener works, but thanks for the scientific analysis."

She stared at me like I was the chief idiot in this battle of nitwits. "That's okay," she said with a miniature smile. "You're welcome." I wondered if she was kidding. If so, she had the deadpan delivery of the century.

"If you could get into the garage, why didn't you let yourself into the house? Why are you sitting out here?"

She bit a nail. A fingernail, that is. The day she started gnawing on hardware was the day I walked away from this deal once and for all, family or no family, my fee be damned.

"The breezeway is locked," she said.

That made a little more sense. Twannie Jefferson wasn't a fool. And this was still America, even if we were out in the sticks a fair piece.

"Did you try the sliding doors?"

Lita looked over at the deck doors as if seeing them for the first time. I walked over and dragged one of them smoothly along its rail. A strong odor of disinfectant and violence wafted out.

"Oh," she said.

"After you," I said, holding out a hand like some obsequious monkey-suited *maitre d'* in some overpriced *trattoria,* hoping against hope for the kind of gratuity that would make life worth living.

She edged along the side of the house, then backed into the empty darkness, watching me like a mouse who's trying to sneak past a hungary snake, ready to run in case I decided to strike, but knowing she wouldn't get far. I followed her inside and closed the door. The wall switch activated some inset ceiling cans and illuminated the room in diagonal sprays of soft yellow light. It was a little seventies for my taste, but at least it wasn't purple light, which I imagine would be pretty tough to read by.

"Wait just a minute," she said. "You aren't C. Everett Koop."

"I'm not?"

"No."

Maybe it was my lack of Captain Ahab chin whiskers that tipped her.

"You aren't Sammy Sosa, either."

"I'm not?" Maybe she was a baseball fan after all.

"My sister told me about you."

"Oh, she did, huh?"

"And why Grannie hired you."

I was about to ask her why she called Auntie Peg "Grannie" while her sister used "Nana," but all of a sudden I realized I didn't care.

"What did she say? I hope she was charitable."

"Nothing."

"Nothing? That must have been illuminating."

"It wasn't."

"Did she tell you how I took you home last night in a semiconscious stupor?"

"That's a lie."

"If you say so."

"You're my cousin, aren't you? Like twenty times removed."

"Innocent until proven guilty."

"Meaning what?"

"I'm trying to find out if maybe I was adopted."

"What's the matter? We're not good enough for you?"

It was time to change the subject. "Your sister still doesn't know, does she?"

"Know what?"

"That you were here last night, getting ripped on Egyptian fudge. That you were here when Twannie Jefferson was shot dead."

"That's a lie," she said. "That's two lies. Three altogether, counting the one about the coma."

"I guess Rosa didn't rat you out."

"That bitch."

"You don't even remember seeing me last night, do you?"

"No! Of course not. Because I didn't."

"Well, you might not have at that," I said. "You were in a bit of an altered state. And I don't mean Alabama."

She seemed to be having a bit of trouble keeping up. Her eyes darted around the room. I glanced around to see what it was she found so interesting. I saw nothing.

"Looking for something special?"

"No!" she said, with a little too much emotion. "Yes!" This penchant for sinking into daytime TV melodrama was definitely a family curse, as was the accompanying lack of stage craft. Lita didn't have anywhere near the acting bug that afflicted her big sister. Thank God. I didn't think I could handle two like that, always breaking into one character or another, playing out scenes in their own minds. It made you want to sprint for the concession stand in search of a box of Jujubees. Or to knock your knuckles on the sides of their respective skulls like a door-to-door vacuum salesman. "Hello, hello? Anyone home?"

I waited for her to stop looking around the room and come back to focus on me. I had to wait a while. "So," I said. "Who killed Twannie?"

"What!"

"I said ..."

"I heard what you said. I don't know what you're talking about."

"You were here."

"That's a lie."

"You saying you didn't see anything?" I almost laughed at her.

"I'm saying I wasn't here."

Now I did laugh. "Stop it, Lita."

"And anyone who says I was here is a damn liar."

"Oh, sorry," I said. "My mistake. I thought that was you smeared in chocolate. I'm not surprised you don't remember, but please don't tell me you weren't here."

"What do mean smeared in chocolate? That's ridiculous."

"All over your face. You had the classic shit-eating grin."

"That's disgusting" she said.

"I hear you have a problem with fudge."

"It's not a problem. It's an allergy. I take medication for it."

"Yeah, well, it's a problem if you're allergic and you snarf it like there's no tomorrow."

"It's an allergy," she said. "Not a problem."

"You're the expert."

"And it's not my fault."

"Me, I'm allergic to *Liquid Plumber.* Never go near the stuff."

"Excuse me?"

"Man's got to know his limitations."

"Huh?"

"Woman, too."

"What are you talking about?"

"A death in the family," I said.

"What do you mean? Who's dead?"

"Your pal, Big Jeff."

"Who?"

"Come on, don't play dumb. You called her that yourself."

"Who?"

"LaTwanda Jefferson. The woman who lived here until about ten o'clock last night."

"Ten o'clock ..."

"She's dead, you know."

"Who?"

"Twannie. Big Jeff. C'mon, Lita, follow the bouncing ball."

"What?"

"Shot to death."

"When?"

She'd already used up *who* and *what* and *when*. Before she could get to *where*, I intercepted her: "Right here in her own home. You ever heard of anything so unfair? Some cheap hood with a Saturday Night Special did the job on her. And it was only Monday. Life is so ironic, don't you think? And death, too. I counted three wounds. He wasn't very efficient, but that's amateurs for you. No clue. I'll give him this much, he sure was determined."

"He was?"

"Is it coming back now? Twannie was lying right here. And you were sitting at the dining room table with your face smeared and your brain on an extended dessert break."

"You're a liar," she said. She drawled it, southern belle style, but she didn't quite earn the Scarlet O'Hara Prize for self-centered delusion.

"Excuse me," I said, my hands balling involuntarily into fists. "Did you just call me a lawyer?"

"I called you a liar."

"Oh," I said, relaxing. "That's okay, then."

"Wait," she said. "You're confusing me."

"Sorry." I took no pride in this dubious accomplishment.

Lita Wordstone shook her head, much like a person who couldn't make heads or tails of a conversation in which they've become inexorably trapped. That made two of us. I decided to try a different tack. I wanted to throw a little gasoline on the fire before it died down.

"So, Lita, you know a guy by the name of Johnny Brashear?"

"What?" she asked. Either she was hard of hearing, dumber than a burlap rug, or the persistent use of such simplistic expressions as *Who?* and *What?* had become a tried and true stall tactic she was neither able nor willing to abandon.

"Johnny Brashear," I said. I jumbled the name to a state of near gibberish (not Alabama). It came out "Jommibuhjeer."

"Huh?"

"So you do know him?"

*The Farce News*

She shook her head and blinked hard. "What's his name?"

"Who?" I said.

"Johnny Brashear," she said, exasperated.

"Never heard of him," I said with a shrug.

Her eyes got very round, her face turned a deep shade of crimson and for just a moment I thought Lita's head might explode. I wished I had a Polaroid camera to capture the moment for posterity. Maybe Sully could run it in *The Farce News* with a story about a young socialite who lost her head, blew her mind, and otherwise suffered the ultimate brain cramp.

"Wait," she said. "You, I mean, I ..."

"Catch your breath, kid. It'll do you a world of good."

"He's ... he's ... he's the one," she said, finally.

But then she didn't say anymore.

"He's the one *what?*"

"He's the one who ..." Again, she stopped short of delivering the goods.

If she said "He's the one *where* ..." I would slap her, so help me.

"He's the one who killed Big Jeff!" she said.

"Bullshit," I said. She recoiled as if I had slapped her. "Nice try, but if this is your idea of coming clean, we're gonna need a bigger bar of soap."

"It's true."

"I don't think so."

"How do you know? You weren't even here." She said it with the kind of egocentric petulance only the truly spoiled can pull off.

"Oh," I shook my head at her, hands on hips, "and I suppose you were." This was getting fun.

She put a hand to her mouth and started looking around the room again. I put a hand to my own mouth and made a big, faggy show of joining in her fruitless search. I even thought about lisping when I said: "What are we're looking for, Lita, honey? Tell me and I'll help you find it?"

"I'm not looking for anything."

"Lawyer," I said, dropping the faux queer act. She hadn't gotten it anyway.

And now she didn't get my crack about the lawyer either. I'm not much of a standup comic. I'm better sitting, particularly if I have my feet up on a desk. But if she wasn't going to sit down, neither was I. And she was too hopped-up on nervous energy to sit still. Maybe that was a side effect of the cocoa overdose. Lot of caffeine in that stuff, or so I'm told. On the other hand it might have been genuine fear coursing through her veins.

"Look," I said. "I don't know where Big Jeff kept the videotapes. If that's what's worrying you."

She snapped her head around. "What!"

Here we go again.

"Please, Lita. You have to stop it. Really. Say anything, just don't keep saying *What!* In fact, no more pronouns. Okay? You're killing me."

She ignored my appeal. "You ... know ... about ... the ... film?"

I nodded and shrugged, just to show her I considered it to be no big deal, and left it at that. I thought it was pretentious to call it a film.

"Have you seen it?" She looked coquettish, almost batting her eyes at me. I wanted to vomit.

What did she want me to say? That I had seen the movie, or that I hadn't. I had the feeling she was going to be disappointed either way.

"Not all of it, no."

She made a dismissive face and waved a hand as if batting at a fly. "Doesn't matter," she said. "That's not really me, anyway, you know."

"Sure, Lita. Whatever you say."

"It's just someone who looks like me."

"Fine."

"It isn't me!" she shouted. Then, even louder: "It isn't me!"

I put my hands up in mock surrender. "Lita," I said. "Catch your breath before you faint. I really don't want to carry you home again. "

"Then say you believe me."

"Why should I?"

"Say it!"

"What difference does it make if I believe you?"

"Say it!"

"Look, everyone's entitled to a little hinky fun now and again. You didn't hurt anyone, although those injury time-outs were interesting."

She looked at me for a long moment. "You don't think I'm a terrible person?"

"A terrible person?"

"You know," she said. "For ..."

"A terrible actress, maybe."

She looked hurt. "You're cruel."

"And a really terrible volleyball player."

"Meanie."

"I don't know you well enough to know if you're a terrible person."

"Or a whore?"

"That's a bit excessive."

"Or a slut?"

I shook my head. "What do you want from me, Lita? Maybe you are, maybe you aren't. I'm not ready to pass judgment. Not on the basis of a few minutes from some half-assed skin flick."

"You don't think the movie is wicked?"

"Wicked? No. A little silly, maybe. But not wicked. Why? Does it turn into a snuff film or something?"

"A what?"

"A snuff film. Does anyone actually die?"

She didn't answer right away. She frowned and made the mistake a lot of people make, dignifying my questions with actual answers. "Die? No, of course not. Don't be silly. No one even has a real orgasm!"

What a revelation.

"And nobody held a gun to your head?"

"How do you mean?"

"To take part in the movie?"

"Oh, that," she said, waving me off. "No."

"Fine, then I don't see a problem. What do you say we just forget about it for the time being."

"Forget about the film?" She stuck out her bottom lip, clearly unhappy with the idea of changing the subject away from what a naughty little girl she could be, but I got the feeling she wasn't going to push her luck too far.

"Why don't you tell me who shot Liberty Valance?"

"What?"

"Twannie Jefferson? Who put the slugs in her?"

"I told you already."

"Yeah, yeah. Johnny Brashear."

"Right. Johnny Brashear."

"And who is this Johnny Brashear?"

"He's a man," she said. "An awful man."

"How do you know him?"

"He used to be my friend."

I was on the verge of believing her, even though I knew this could be foolish. At least the part about Johnny being a former friend. If he used to be a comrade and had become an enemy (for whatever reason) it would certainly provide Lita with the motivation she needed to stick a bogus murder rap on him.

"Why?" I asked.

"Why *what?*"

"No pronouns," I said. "Tell me why Johnny Brashear did it?"

"Did what?"

I closed my eyes and shook my head. This was why I didn't become a special ed teacher. One of the ten thousand reasons including several hundred that had to do with the hours. "Why did Johnny Brashear shoot LaTwanda Jefferson?"

"Oh. Well, how should I know?"

"I don't know, Lita. Make something up. You've done okay so far stringing the bullshit together."

"Hey!" she said, and crossed her arms like child who feels she's been unjustly scolded for spilling the milk when this is the first glass in thirty she didn't actually knock on the floor.

On the bright side, *"Hey!"* was better than *"Who, What* and *Where."*

On the dark side, she showed no inclination to budge from the Johnny Brashear angle. What if I'd offered a different name. Like Newt Gingrich. What were the chances she'd heard of him? Maybe she'd like Newt for killing Twannie if only I'd planted the seed. I also wondered why she thought it necessary to cover for Miguel when Miguel was already just as dead as LaTwanda Jefferson. Surely, she knew Miguel was dead. Was it possible she didn't? Better find out.

"By the say, sorry about Miguel," I said.

She looked at me like I'd slapped her. "I have to go."

"To the bathroom? It's down the hall."

"Home," she said. "I have to go home."

"But, Lita, we're just getting to be friends."

"I have to go. Right now."

"Maybe you'd feel better if you had something to eat. Not chocolate, of course. Maybe I could make us some popcorn and we could watch a movie. Excuse me, a film."

Lita didn't answer or tell me where I could stick my popcorn.

And then we stopped and turned toward the front of the house.

A car was pulling into the driveway outside. Through the sheer curtains, I could make out a large luxury sedan, a Lincoln maybe, or a Caddie. Black and well polished. Definitely an American gas guzzler. I looked at Lita Wordstone. She had transformed herself into a statue. I was beginning to wonder if this trance routine was a legitimate condition or simply a conditioned response. Maybe she'd been a chameleon in another life. Maybe she was a chameleon in this one. Maybe she was just full of crap. I walked over to her and snapped my fingers an inch from her nose. To my surprise she snapped out of it on the first try. If my Jetta was as responsive to the turn of the ignition key, I'd consider keeping it. Of course, if I had two dimes to put toward a new car ... wait a second, then I could afford a twenty-cent car, which I already had. The Jetta.

*The Farce News*

"I have to go," Lita said, or rather hissed.

"We're alone," I said. "You don't have to whisper."

Then the door bell rang. It was a chime, three notes. A major triad. It reminded me of the Three Stooges: "Hello, hello, hello," with the fourth greeting on the minor seventh, "Hello!" Twannie Jefferson's chime had no minor seventh. But whoever was out there pushing the button apparently didn't mind. Whoever it was, they were satisfied with the three simple notes. And content to play them over and over again.

After about seven times through the basic arpeggio, there came the jangling of keys, followed by the unmistakable metallic sound of a key sliding into a lock. We were still standing there in the middle of the living room. I suppose we had time to bolt out the back door, but I was curious. And Lita was paralyzed -- or putting on a show. In any event, we were still standing there like a couple on a blind date, not quite sure how close to dance, when the front door opened.

In a rectangular box of sunny backlighting there stood a woman, her feet slightly more than shoulder width apart. She was very well dressed, with a fur wrapped around her shoulders and coiled around her arms. The skirt she wore had the shimmer of raw silk. The jacket was dark and perhaps cashmere. I'm not only color blind, I also don't know my way too well around most fabrics and wools, natural, synthetic or otherwise. In many ways I've lived a sheltered life. I hope it continues that way.

"Come on in," I said to the stranger. "We were just about to make popcorn and watch a *film*."

Lita backed away from me and collapsed onto one of the couches.

"And who are you?" the woman said, staring at me with placid curiosity.

"Oh, nobody," I said, just as placid. "Just the guy who pops the corn."

## Chapter 13

She stood in the middle of LaTwanda Jefferson's living room, looking me over as if I were underdressed, under-qualified, and quite possibly under the influence, a pathetic applicant for a gig on one of her elite squads of chauffeurs, gardeners or house butlers. I assumed, by her expression, that she wanted nothing more out of life at this moment than to look down her nose at me. But I was too tall. To really give me the full length of her nose and its full deriding effect, she would have to crane way, way back, probably spraining her neck in the process. Of course, it wouldn't have taken much to look down her nose at me as she had a rather small, well-shaped nose, a pleasing nose, in fact, as noses go. Probably not the original equipment. In any case it wasn't nearly long enough -- or gnarled enough -- for the job she had in mind.

But it didn't stop her from giving me a professional once over.

She began at the spot on the floor where I stood and meticulously worked her way up, taking in the splendor that isn't me. It was instantly -- and abundantly -- clear that, like so many before her, she highly disapproved of the splendor that isn't me. My *Adidas* running shoes, for starters. They're a little old, but I view them not as antiquated but as classics. She scowled at them. Maybe she didn't care for green stripes. Who knows? The sour expression she wore on her roundish face suggested she didn't think much of my faded blue jeans, either. But maybe she was a rodeo style Wrangler woman, and here I was wearing beat-up Levi Strauss. One thing I've learned: you can't always win, but you can *always* lose. I had on one of my favorite black t-shirts, with a silk-screened image of Gram Parsons on the front and a bunch of outdated concert information about the annual Gram Fest in Joshua Tree, California, on the back. You couldn't see much of Gram's face as I still had on my leather bomber jacket. She eyed Gram and he gazed back. In this particular staring match, my money was on her to blink first. Finally, she appraised my beloved leather jacket. Judging by her arched eyebrows and upturned lip, she behated it. God only knows what she thought of the *Courant* ball cap on my head. I didn't even like the thing.

I knew if we spent enough time together she'd eventually get around to telling me how her shoes alone cost more than my entire wardrobe, including the stuff I had at home folded haphazardly in dresser drawers and hanging on hooks in various closets. It was my fervent hope that our relationship wouldn't last nearly that long.

Meanwhile, if I was a wardrobe disaster on wheels, she was a model of fashion grandeur, which just goes to show you: money may not buy happiness but it sure comes in handy if you have a big league jones for snappy designer duds. She was dressed as if by a loving (and perhaps fearful) tailor, one whose personal health and welfare depends on the satisfaction of the malevolent monarch at whose pleasure he (or she) serves. Despite the mature curves that had accompanied this woman's inexorable voyage into what looked like pretty well-fed middle age, her sartorial sails were so neatly trimmed you couldn't tell if she was twenty pounds overweight or twenty pounds underweight. Her fingers and wrists sparkled with the shimmer of gold and jewels. Her throat was bedecked in a string of milky white pearls the value of which I could only estimate, since I haven't the vaguest idea how much a pearl necklace sells for on today's open market, or today's black market either. My guess was they were real. She didn't strike me as the kind who settled for costume jewelry. There was enough make believe in her life without playing the games herself. Besides, why would one drink Schlitz when one can sip chilled *Dom Perignon?* (Unless, like me, you can't stomach champagne.)

She didn't know me, but I knew her. At least I knew who she was.

Venus Edwards.

Rich and powerful, the self-proclaimed real estate matriarch of north central Connecticut. Owner and proprietor of, among other properties, the Simsbury Dinner Theater where Lillian Buenavista spent an admittedly inordinate chunk of her free time.

"Is the *resident* about?" Venus Edwards said, breaking the silence.

"About what?" I said, smiling at her, friendly, not at all wise ass. There was time for that.

"I would like a word with Miss Jefferson," she said. "Immediately."

"Let me guess: *Immediately -- if not sooner.* Right?"

She stared at me as if were speaking Farsi. "Look here, I'm a very busy woman." The only thing that kept her from a frightful resemblance to one of those stuffy English marms was the lack of a broad accent and the fact that she didn't begin her question with the phrase, "Dare say." Or proclaimed that she "... *should* like to see Miss Jefferson." I never got that particular form of speech. I *should* like to do this, I *should* like to do that. Yeah, sure, you should, but what if you don't. Whose fault is that? All things considered, Venus Edwards didn't sound very *New* England, let alone merry *old* England. She was more like Litchfield County via Passaic, New Jersey, with a pit stop in Larchmont for a jaw-replacement.

"We haven't seen her," I said, speaking for myself as well as for the dazed and confused Lita Wordstone, who seemed incapable of verbal communication at the moment.

Venus Edwards took some more time to look me over, perhaps in greater detail this time. Or she might have been thinking about her grocery list. You couldn't tell from her expression if she was trying to figure out who the hell I was or contemplating that pound of olive loaf she planned to pick up at the *Super Stop N Shop.* At least I couldn't tell. She shifted her gaze away from me for a moment and focused on Lita Wordstone, who sat perfectly still on one of the couches.

"Dear, you may go," Venus Edwards said, the benevolent nanny, the forbearing school teacher releasing a favorite student from yet another unfortunate detention.

Lita Wordstone's head snapped up and she practically jumped to her feet. I'd have torn something loose in my lumbar had I tried to launch myself in such an explosive manner, but Lita was young and, if nothing else, quite lithe.

If I thought it would do any good, I would have objected. If only for the fun of it. After all, who did Venus Edwards think she was, barging in here and acting as if she owned the place? But, I didn't see any percentage in filing an official complaint. Best I could do was countermand the order and ask Lita to stick around. But why would I do a stupid thing like that? And why would she listen to me? In any case, before I had a chance to put in my three cents, she was up off the couch and out of the house. The curtains wafted in her wake. If I ever decided to assemble an amateur track team, Lita would be my girl for the fifty yard dash -- and maybe pole vaulting; the first because she was so quick out of the blocks, the second because it might be fun to watch her break her pretty little neck.

Quiet fell on the room like a velvet comforter. I twitched and twisted. I'm allergic to velvet, did I mention that? Venus Edwards and I stared placidly at each other, in measurably wary silence. The only sound was the secondhand rumble of the garage door going up, a car engine starting with a nervous rev, and the diminishing whine as the Camry left the immediate area.

"You know something," I said. "I think I'll just be running along."

My declaration brought the expected response. Venus Edwards stepped just slightly into my path and put up one hand.

"Please," she said. "Cease and desist. I wish to speak to you."

"Ah, if only the feeling were mutual," I said.

"Pardon me?"

"What am I, Gerald Ford?"

"Say again?"

"Look, I'm willing to do a fair bit of ceasing, if only momentarily, just to show I'm an all right guy," I said. "But I'll be damned if I'm gonna desist just 'cause some woman I've only just met thinks she can boss me around. That would be you, by the way. In case you were wondering."

She stared at me, immune to my cheeky rudeness. "You and I need to engage in some intercourse."

I blanched and took big step backward. "I'm not even forty." I said. She had to be pushing sixty.

"How nice for you," she said. "Now then ..."

"Oh, you mean *conversation*," I said.

She looked perplexed. "Of course."

"Well, that's different."

"For starters," she said, but got no further.

"You're absolutely sure it's a *need?*" I said, interrupting. "And not just a *want?* You know, a selfish desire? A lot of people confuse the two. Particularly folks with a twisted sense of entitlement. Spoiled children, for instance."

Now she stopped looking perplexed and shifted to an expression of impatience. "Despite the fact that I have only just met you," she said, "you are already giving me a considerable headache."

"Sorry."

"Do you have this effect on everyone?"

"Everyone? I'm not sure. Why don't you ask them. I'll work up a list of their phone numbers if that's any help. Of course, it could take a little while. Couple of years, at least. I'll need a grant."

"I think I feel a migraine coming on."

"Oh, gosh. That's just awful. If it makes you feel any better, I've got a bit of a sore throat myself."

She peered at me some more. "You are exceptionally irritating," she said. "And I sincerely wish you would stop it." To her credit, she scolded me without wagging a finger. I hate finger waggers.

I shrugged and twisted my face into an expression that asked the eternal question: "Who cares what *you* think?" It was the same face I used to make when elementary (and middle and high) school principals and guidance counselors rebuked me for not giving it the old college try. Of course, I rebuked them right back for jumping the gun, since I wasn't even in college yet. It was the same face I made for girl friends who broke up with me for being too immature. "No I'm not," I said.

"Yes, you are," said this matronly woman, just as the girls had always said.

"No I'm not," I responded, to show how really mature I had become. I was going to add a gratuitous "So there!" but didn't. I have my limits.

She took a breath. "Sadly, I have come to expect this sort of insolence from your generation."

I laughed at her. Out loud. "You gotta be kiddin'."

"You find something amusing?"

"Lady, if you think I'm going to shoulder the weight of some sweeping cultural guilt for the behavior of faceless millions who happen to populate my general age group, then I'm afraid we're going to have a serious problem getting along."

She thought it over for minute, then changed the subject rather abruptly. At least she tried to. "I could have you arrested," she said.

"Why, because you think my generation is rude? Wow, you really *are* delusional, Mrs. Bonaparte."

"You are an intruder," she said. "There are laws against burglary."

"Wanna frisk me, see if I have a TV under my shirt?" I held my hands out wide and smiled.

"Why are you here, then, if not to rob and steal?"

Since I had been waiting on the edge of my proverbial seat for permission to address the *grande dame,* I cleared my throat rather ceremoniously and began.

"You see," I said, "it all began with what I thought was a completely innocent invitation to a candy tasting."

"Candy tasting!"

"Don't laugh. We -- the young lady and I -- were led to believe there would be some rather rare dark chocolates from Nigeria and Croatia on hand. And that we would have an opportunity to sample it as a precursor to a potential subsequent purchase opportunity. As instructed, we arrived at the appointed hour. We rang the doorbell. We knocked. We even shouted 'Yoo hoo!' Well, *she* did. I don't go around shouting 'Yoo hoo' unless someone's holding a gun to my head. But I digress. The fact is, alas, nobody answered."

I hoped Venus Edwards would go for all the "appointed hour" crap. She seemed like the type. I also hoped she'd like the bit about us coming "as instructed," the implication being that we were good at following orders from superiors. "After several minutes, we came around back. The door was open so we let ourselves in. It's simple, really."

"And why on earth would you do such a thing?"

"Let's see, because it was cold outside?" I said, offering up a lame excuse I was sure would meet with instant disapproval.

"That's utterly preposterous."

"Well, I hate to do anything in half-measures."

"Answer the question. Why did you let yourselves in?"

*The Farce News*

"Um, let me think. How about if I said we had to use the facilities?" I smiled her. "Better?"

She didn't smile back at me. "Ridiculous," she said.

"Hmm," I said. "You're tough to please. Remind me never to cook for you. Or sing."

"Why don't you try telling the truth, if you're capable."

"That's not very nice of you," I said, and looked down at my shoes.

"Regardless." She didn't care one bit if she hurt my feelings. She'd have made a damn fine elementary school principal, or guidance counselor for that matter.

"Okay, I'll come clean. We just love Nigerian chocolate.?"

"Nonsense. I don't believe a word of it."

"Really? Not a word? How do you feel about the punctuation?"

"Your story is patently absurd."

I nodded sadly. "Story of my life. If only a had the patent, you know?"

"Your only saving grace is that you're not a very skilled liar."

"I'm not a liar at all! Worst you can say is I'm *imaginative*. Admit it, I'm a very compelling storyteller. You *want* to believe me. You *want* to buy in. I'll bet you can't wait to see how this one comes out."

"Are you on medication," she asked, apropos of (I hope) nothing.

"I beg your pardon!"

"You must have had another reason for committing a felony ..."

"Felony! Why I never!" I said, in my best Alec Guinness voice.

"Breaking and entering."

"Now just hold it a second," I said, holding up my hands and dropping the heavy English accent. "We entered, as I've already explained, but we damn sure didn't break anything. And I resent the implication, if not the accusation itself, which I'm inclined to simply ignore. Now, if you doubt my veracity, as you seem intent on doing, I strongly suggest you take a look around."

"I plan to."

"Good. And if you find anything broken, I'll buy it. Just like at the Pottery Barn."

She squinted her eyes. I wondered how her migraine was coming along. If she was seeing colors yet. Prisms flashing in her brain. "It occurs to me that you still haven't adequately explained why you are here in the first place? Let's get back to that, shall we?"

"Sure, of course," I said. "The truth is we wanted to get in out of the rain."

"Oh, please, Mr. Vaughn. It hasn't rained in a week."

"We were running late."

She had let it slip that she knew my name. So I let it slide that I noticed her slip. Between us we were like an amusement park water ride from Hell. I wished I had a towel.

"What utter nonsense."

"You see, that's just the thing," I said. "No matter what I say, you're determined not to like it, or to believe it. So what difference does it make if I say we wanted to get in out of the rain, or we had to use the bathroom, or we wanted to surprise Twannie when she got home. I bet you'll just tell me it isn't even her birthday."

"It isn't."

"See! See what I mean?"

"You're rather loathsome, aren't you?"

I shrugged. "The better you get to know me, the worse it gets. Exponentially, according to my last three girlfriends."

"I don't doubt that for a second."

"But let's keep in mind the fact that the back doors weren't locked."

"Apropos of what?"

"Apropos of you ceasing and desisting from any further talk of my alleged breaking and entering. Because, frankly, that flag won't hunt."

"Excuse me? Won't hunt?"

"Go ahead. Run it up the dog path if you want, but believe me, but nobody's gonna salute."

She stared me, almost open mouthed. Not quite. "Are you by some chance mentally ill?"

"What do mean, by some chance?"

"Well, I don't mean one out of a hundred," she said. "More like one out of two."

I thought it over for a moment. Should I cop an attitude or address her concern in a serious manner? "That's an excellent question," I said. "I suggest you ask my psychiatrist -- just as soon as she's released from prison. My mental health is an issue under some debate, for reasons I don't quite grasp. Of course, it depends largely on who you ask and how much alcohol they've consumed at the time you pop the question. I've found that some people will agree to anything if they're drunk enough. Others you have to pay. Some you have to threaten with physical violence to get them to play along."

She looked as if she wished she were my mother just so she could slap me across the face and get away with it. I wasn't too worried. She looked strong enough to give me a fair stinger, but with me in my *Adidas* sneakers and her in those stupid Calvin Klein stiletto heels, if that's what they were, I was pretty sure I could outrun her if it came down to a foot race.

*The Farce News*

"Please have a seat, Mr. Vaughn. There on the couch. I intend to have a look around and I would rather you didn't interfere."

"Hey, that's the second time you've called me that and to tell the truth I'm getting a little sick of it."

"What?"

"Mr. Vaughn," I said.

"It's your name, isn't it?"

"Sure it is, but who gave you permission to use it?"

"You can't be serious."

"Well, it is my name."

"You are serious, aren't you?"

"I'll bet you're one of those people who constantly helps herself to stuff without asking. Like it's all just one big smorgasbord to sate your personal appetites, the rest of us be damned. I mean, here, we haven't even been formally introduced, and already you assume we're on a last-name basis. What unbridled arrogance."

"You really are quite ill, aren't you?"

"Which reminds me, is there any such thing as *mitigated* gall?"

"You need help."

"Nonsense. I've never felt better in my life. Except for last Tuesday when I did seventy-five sit-ups without stopping once to vomit. Otherwise I'm fit as a cello."

"You mean a fiddle, don't you?"

"No, a cello. I hate the fiddle. In fact, I hate just about anything to do with Arkansas or country music."

Now she tilted her head way, way back and successfully looked down her nose at me. "That isn't what I hear."

I shrugged. "Okay, so I voted for Clinton. So, sue me."

"I meant about the music," she said.

"Then I suggest you change radio stations. Or see your dentist about getting new fillings."

She looked at me with a new expression, this one more curious than anything. "Honestly, why are you behaving this way?"

"Me! If you don't mind me saying so, you're one to talk. Christ, you come barging in here, pretending you don't know who I am when clearly you do, and immediately start accusing me of all sorts of high crimes and misdemeanors."

"All right," she said. "Stop it. Really. Enough!"

I nodded and shrugged -- and nearly pulled a muscle in my neck in the process. God playing a little joke on the marionettes. "You saying 'when'?"

"I have business with Miss Jefferson."

"Yeah, me too. Take a number."

"Where is she?"

"That's the question of the hour. Although I'm not sure it's worth the sixty-four bucks."

"She has suddenly become extraordinarily difficult to locate."

"So I've noticed."

"Several attempts to contact her at her Park Street establishment have been fruitless, and the sales clerk reports Ms. Jefferson never came in today."

I liked that. "The sales clerk? You mean Jennifer?"

"Yes, that girl of hers. In any case, I find it extremely unusual, not to mention irritating. Now I come here and find you."

"You mentioned irritating."

"Yes?"

"You said you weren't going to, then you mentioned it."

She stopped herself. "Excuse me."

"Make up your mind."

"Sit down," she said, pointing at one of the couches.

I didn't move. I wasn't anywhere near ready to start taking orders from Venus Edwards, not without the benefit of a real and palpable threat to my health and well-being. Gunpoint would probably do the trick, but so far as I could tell she wasn't packing any heat.

"I have every intention of getting to the bottom of all this."

"Good luck," I said, hoping to sound like I actually meant it.

She kept an eye on me as she moved about the place, poking her head into the kitchen, checking the rooms down the hall. I suppose I could have run out the front door at any time. But I hung around. She had tweaked some little part of my curiosity. Moreover, I was actually having fun playing the schmuck role in this ad hoc vaudeville act. And she probably didn't get enough roughage in her social diet. If I could be of any assistance, why, I owed it to her as a fellow human being in this challenging civilization of ours to help out wherever and however I could.

While she was busy poking around the place, I took a look out the breezeway windows and noticed that Venus Edwards had not traveled to Duncaster Road by her lonesome. Behind the wheel of the large black sedan (which turned out to be a Cadillac Brougham) sat a uniformed chauffeur. So, I guess that position wasn't available after all. Maybe something in gardening, about which I know nothing. It also looked like there was another dark suit riding shotgun. Not literally, I hoped.

Venus Edwards strode past the enormous plasma screen TV and muttered something that sounded like "decadent," but I couldn't be sure. She opened a cabinet under the TV and pulled out a few videotape boxes. Held them up for me to see. "What is the meaning of this?"

I shrugged. "How should I know? I don't live here."

"Pornography. Disgusting."

"Hey, I don't live here," I said again, just so she didn't get any ideas about adding insult to injury as far as the continued denigration of my character was concerned. "I didn't put it there."

She stopped looking around the house and stared at me. "Let's start over. Why are you here?"

"No special reason," I said, "I'm just the guy ..."

"Who pops the corn. Yes, yes. How tedious of you to repeat what wasn't even remotely amusing the first time. Again I ask, what is your business here?"

"I'm hooked on illegal fudge. I've tried detox, but without health insurance, who can afford treatment?"

"Vaughn," she said, ignoring my tale of woe. "What kind of name is that? Irish? Welsh?"

"What difference does it make? You going to report me to the INS? I'm an American citizen. Just like you. You are an American citizen, aren't you?"

"And what are you doing here?"

"Here? You mean in Bloomfield?"

"In this house."

"This is roughly equivalent to badgering the witness, your honor. We've already been over this. Several times, in fact. You just don't like my answers. But that's your problem, not mine. Tell you what, why don't you take a turn on the stand and answer a question for me?"

"Don't be ridiculous. Why on earth should I?"

"Hey, what's fair is fair. Even in your world."

She peered at me with a whole new level of suspicion. "What do you mean my world? What do you know about my world?"

"Oh, y'know. Your world of cutthroats, thieves, and institutionalized deceit. I'm referring, of course, to real estate."

"And what makes you think I'm in real estate?" Funny, she didn't seem to mind that I had characterized her world of real estate in disparaging terms, only that I had associated her with it.

"Well, Mrs. Edwards, to begin with ..."

"Ah, so you know me?"

"Sure, I subscribe to all the gossip rags. You're quite the rising star. Or is it shooting star? Maybe it was a five-pointed star. I can't remember which one they said."

She didn't like that very much. I don't think she liked me much, either. "What is your question?"

"How is it that you happen to have keys to this house?"

She made a guttural noise in her throat. Not quite a laugh, not quite a snort. Somewhere in between, like a bemused Miss Piggy after too many tequila shooters. "Sonny, I own this house."

"Oh." Learn something new every minute. "Good reason," I said, mildly. No wonder she'd barged in and started acting like she owned the place. I hate when that happens. "So, you're ..."

"I am Miss Jefferson's landlord."

"Yeah, I was just gonna say that."

"My turn. What was Lita Wordstone doing here with you?"

"You know her, do you?"

"Of course, I do. Don't be absurd. I've known her all her life."

"Huh! Small world, wouldn't you say?"

"No, it's a very, very large world. But it is filled with many smaller, interconnected circles."

I stared at her. "Wow, that's deep." I was about to ask if I could take some notes, but then I remembered I don't carry a notebook. Have to remember to get one. And a pen, too. Never know when they'll come in handy.

"Now, tell me again, how did you gain entry? And this time tell the truth."

"Through the back doors. I told you, they weren't locked."

"And because the doors were not locked, you let yourself in to the home of a perfect stranger?"

"Oh, please," I said. "Who among us is perfect?"

"What are you doing here?"

"We were invited. Remember? For the chocolate."

She peered at me. "Why do I doubt the veracity of everything you say?"

"How should I know? Maybe you're incredulous by nature."

She smiled but I didn't see much humor in the expression.

From her jacket pocket she extracted a very small silver cellphone. She unfolded it and pushed a couple of buttons, speed dialing someone. She said one word, "Come," then refolded the phone, and slipped it back into the same pocket. Within thirty seconds the two suits from the Caddie came silently through the front door and positioned themselves like stone gargoyles at Venus Edwards' side.

They were a regular Mutt and Jeff team, except I'm pretty sure this was a man and a woman. They had a distinctive Asiatic look, but not Chinese or Japanese. Maybe they were from some other Asian locale. Mongolia perhaps. The woman was tall and and thin and mean as hell looking with sharp features and dark, sunken, vaguely Oriental eyes. If Morticia Addams had been ugly instead of beautiful, this broad could have played the title role and made millions. She had long black hair pulled tight against her bony skull and tied in a stringy ponytail. She wore a black suit jacket and pants that had been tailored for a man, but she was making the worst of an already bad situation. Her shoes were large black boxes of polished leather. If she laid one of those bad boys on you, you wouldn't get up for a week.

The guy seemed to be the Gomez Addams end of the partnership -- although I refused to let my brain tinker about with any images of coital intimacy between them. He was shaped like a large cardboard box, the kind in which a dishwasher might have been delivered. A box that's been kicked in on one side by a kid with no other outlet for his aimless aggression. He stood wrenched to the left at the waist. It didn't look like he'd ever straighten up again.

"These are my associates," Venus Edwards said, then turned to them. "Fran and Sam, meet Mr. Vaughn." She turned to me. "Mr. Vaughn, meet Fran and Sam. By the way, in case you're wondering, those are not their real names."

"I wasn't wondering."

"Naturally. You don't take me for the curious type."

*"Touché."* Bitch.

The gargoyles glared at me coldly, as if I were the one who'd called them on the cell and interrupted their lunch break. Or whatever it was they were doing out there in the Caddie. Maybe they were playing Rock-Paper-Scissors. I seriously doubted they were discussing the novels of Tolstoy, or the fall of the Ming Dynasty, or the global implications of trickle-down economics. They already didn't like me and I hadn't even done anything to them yet. I nodded, just to be sociable and, for a moment, wondered which one was supposed to be Fran and which one was supposed to be Sam. Sam and Fran. Fran and Sam. It occurred to me that everyone probably wondered which one was which, and that Venus Edwards no doubt enjoyed this little enigma as much as any contrivance she could concoct. I could just see the Classified Ad: *Wanted: Freakish couple possessing no measurable sense of humor for security detail. Must be willing to adopt androgynous names and wear ill-fitting clothes.*

"Keep on eye on him," she said to Fran and Sam, using very deliberate speech, pointing to her own eyes and then pointing at me. Sure that they understood, she walked out toward the breezeway and the garage beyond it.

"I don't think you'll find anything there," I called out, just to be helpful.

Fran and Sam took a small step in my direction and said, in perfect unison: "Mutter baloney don't."

"Sorry?"

Fran and Sam simultaneously reached into interior jacket pockets and produced small red leather booklets. They flipped through the pages, consulted with each other in a series of feral grunts, then put their books away and looked up at me. "Shaddup!" they said, in perfect unison, her voice just a little deeper than his. "Nyet bullshlitz."

"Nice harmonies," I said. "Like half a barbershop quartet."

They took another small step toward me and in perfect unison, barked: "Making words stop."

"You mean Shaddup. Right. Nyet bullshlitz, whatever that means."

Venus Edwards wasn't gone very long. "Are you behaving?"

"You found nothing, right?" I said.

"Yes, how did you know?"

I rolled my eyes at her. "I peeked."

She snickered, "Barbarian."

"Hey! I'll have you know I speak excellent Greek. One *falafel, Spiro.* There, you see!"

"I find the garage extremely suspect."

"To say nothing of extremely empty," I said. "It is completely empty, isn't it? Not a single rake or gardening implement."

"Not a snow shovel to be found." she said.

"Nor a leaf blower."

"No bikes hanging from the ceiling," she said.

"No lawnmower. No recycling bins."

"No weed whacker. No piles of cardboard."

"No firewood," I added.

"No sports equipment at all."

"Not even a sack of *bocce* balls."

Venus Edwards mulled it over. "I have never seen anything quite like it."

"It's a pity, really," I said.

"In what way?"

"All that room going to waste."

"Meaning"

"That garage has about twice the floor space of my apartment."

"Oh," she said. "Of course I am not surprised in the least."

"And it gets a lot more direct sunlight."

*The Farce News*

"The fact that you live in comparative squalor is not surprising."

"Social climber," I said in my most obnoxious, childish tone. "I'll just call you Ivy from now on."

She ignored me and began to pace the living room again. During all of this, Fran and Sam stood in their spots, glaring at me. I smiled at them, just to be a pain in the ass. Once, I considered winking at Fran, or was it Sam? (The woman.) But I refrained. She might be the kind to suddenly snap and become seriously violent. Enough blood had already been shed in this house to last a lifetime. LaTwanda Jefferson's lifetime, to mention just one. I didn't feel like adding to the patchwork of stains lurking deep within the thick carpeting beneath our feet.

Now Venus Edwards became suddenly flustered.

"All right, where is it?" she said, peering at me sternly.

"Where is what? You'll have to be more specific."

"You know what I'm talking about, don't pretend you don't."

"I haven't the foggiest idea what you're talking about."

"Liar."

"Slumlord."

"Where is it?"

"Describe *it*."

"My bust."

I cleared my throat and averted my eyes. It was my gentile way of letting her know I was biting my tongue damn near in half to avoid saying something entirely crude and inappropriate. "I, er, um, uh ..." God, I hoped she would catch on soon. I looked at Fran and Sam. "Help me out, fellas? Huh?"

"My Alice Walker!" said Venus Edwards.

I looked back at her. "Oh, of course. Why didn't you say so?"

"You know where it is?"

I shook my head. "Sorry, no clue."

"Listen to me, you impertinent reprobate. Here is the pedestal right before your eyes. You see it don't you? Good. Now follow along if you're able. I'll try not to speak too quickly. Where there should be an extremely expensive and valuable piece of art, there is nothing. Empty space. See for yourself. No sculpture. No bust. Now, then ..."

"Did you just call me an impertinent reprobate?"

"Mr. Vaughn, if you know what is good for you, you will not toy with me any further."

"Well, I know orange juice is supposed to be pretty good for you."

"Orange juice?"

"Not to be mistaken with O.J."

"What?"

"O.J. can be very bad for your health."

"Stop it! Stop it this instant! This is not a trifling matter. Tell me what has become of my Alice Walker bust or I will not hesitate to have you arrested for grand larceny."

"You can try," I said. "But I doubt you can make it stick."

"Don't test me."

"I think I will."

"You think I won't call the police?"

"There's the phone," I said, pointing at a purple cordless sitting on a small table beside one of the couches. "If you can't get a dial tone, use your cell. I think the number's still nine-one-one for the quickest service."

She was studying me again as if I were a cryptogram. She turned to the gargoyles, Fran and Sam. "Go wait in the car," she said, again speaking very slowly, gesturing outside, and using the international sign language for steering a car. They abruptly turned and left, without even looking my way, let alone grunting goodbye or offering any kind words about how nice it was to have met me. Couple of creature feature ghouls playing dress-up. That's all they were. Exactly why I despise suits. They're so deceiving. You never know what kind of genuine Grade A shit heel is going to be hiding inside a respectable suit of clothes. Just check our nation's capital for proof of that.

When we were alone, Venus Edwards spoke. "What game are you playing at, Mr. Vaughn?"

"If I said Russian Bank, would you believe me?"

"Am I to understand correctly that you are not necessarily in favor of the authorities joining us, but neither would you object very strenuously if they were summoned."

I shrugged again. "I wouldn't object strenuously, or at all for that matter. You call the cops and I'm out of a job. That's all. I'm on the clock, here. This isn't exactly my Indian Summer vacation."

"On the clock? Who exactly are you working for?"

"Oh, you can forget that line of questioning right now."

"Maybe you would prefer to tell the police."

"Yeah, maybe. But I don't think so."

"They have ways of extracting information."

"You can't scare me. This isn't Nazi Germany, Mrs. Edwards."

"They can force you ..."

"Tell you what, let's call 'em and find out what they can and cannot force me to do. While we're at it, maybe we can get a lot of other questions answered. Like a package deal."

*The Farce News*

"You have no preference?"

"Let's just say I'm both here and there."

She began to lose her temper again. "The expression is *neither here nor there*. Can't you get anything right?"

"Call me greedy. I want it all. Just like you, Mrs. Edwards."

"Let's change the subject, Mr. Vaughn. What do *you* think has become of Miss Jefferson?"

"I thought you were worried about Alice Walker's bust."

"Unlike some people, I'm capable of working on more than one problem at a time."

"Oh, you're a thief *and* a multi-tasker. Impressive."

"Why do you insist on hectoring me?"

"Hector? Who the hell is Hector?"

"What do you hope to achieve?"

I thought about that. I didn't want to be having this conversation with Venus Edwards. I had hoped to be dismissed, just as Lita Wordstone had been dismissed. That's what I hoped to achieve. To be sent home. Even to be sent to my room without dinner. Anything rather than this. But she wasn't going to be put off quite so easily. I decided to give her some morsels to chew on. Hell, I'd already annoyed the piss out of her, I might as well break all the rules of the zoo and feed her, too. "Listen," I said. "It's a two-headed monster, but it's still pretty simple. First of all, someone's making a move on Big Jeff's action, or at least trying to. Meanwhile, and I could be wrong on this -- it happens once in awhile, okay, twice in awhile. But I think someone got very pissed at Twannie, for something personal, nothing to do with business. It's mostly guess work. I haven't been on the gig very long. Some kind of melodrama is unfolding but I'm still getting to the know the actors."

"Oh?" She stood back and appraised me again. "Do you enjoy the *theater*?" She pronounced *theater* in a smarmy English accent, the way some low class schmuck might say it if he were trying to sound high class.

"I don't get to Broadway much, if that's what you mean."

"I'm a bit of a theater aficionado, myself," she said. It was remarkable how quickly she'd been distracted, like a lab monkey with a shiny trinket.

I played it dumb. "That right? Are you, like, an *official* aficionado?"

"Theater happens to be one of my passions."

"How many do you have? Passions, that is. Not theaters."

"I simply adore the smell of grease paint."

"I see. And is that a separate passion or does it fall under the omnibus category of your general passion for the theater?"

It was no use. I'd temporarily lost her. She was adrift in a fantasy world.

"The hot lights, the spontaneity. You know, in live theater there are no second takes."

"Really?" I said. "What about injury time-outs?"

"One must possess the gift of improvisation!"

"Yeah, but the only thing around here, outside of Hartford at least, is that crappy little dinner theater over in Simsbury. You know the place I mean? The way I hear it, the grub they're passing off as food makes Burger King look like friggin' *haute cuisine*."

That snapped her out of it fast enough.

A dark cloud passed over Venus Edwards and her face took on a decidedly funereal caste. I wondered who had just died. The light went out of her eyes and it was very clear she no longer found me interesting or charming or someone with whom she wished to spend even one more minute.

"Well!" she said with great haughtiness. I half-expected her to finish it off with a heaping helping of *"I never!"* but it didn't come. Maybe she *sometimes* ... I almost felt bad for her. I guess she didn't have the gift of improvisation. But I couldn't quite dredge up any real sympathy for her. Not after the way she'd dissed me and judged me on the relative demerits of my clothing. The superficial twit.

"Listen, Mrs. Edwards, you have your business with Twannie Jefferson. Fine. That's nothing to me. I have my own interests which, I'm sure, don't concern you in any material way. Why don't we just skip the hand shake and go our separate ways. By the way, which way are you going? Y'know, just in case."

"I am afraid that's not possible."

"Why the hell not?"

"Because I don't trust you."

"That's because you don't know me well enough."

"I don't believe you possess the necessary discretion to conduct your own business without negatively effecting me and mine."

"Well, thanks very much for the vote of confidence. If I ever need a letter of recommendation, I'll be sure not to ask you."

"I will be watching you, Mr. Vaughn. Of that, you may be certain."

"Knock yourself out. But eventually you'll be reduced to little more than a Peeping Tom. Let that be on your conscience. If you have one."

"I'm talking about keeping tabs on you."

"I prefer *Post-It* notes," I said. "Feel free to take notes if it helps you remember. I drive a beat-up piece of shit Jetta. It's black. I live in Hartford. It's mostly black. I share a small studio on Farmington Avenue with some fellow musicians. They're mostly alcoholics and drug addicts. My residence is listed in the white pages and our band is listed in the yellow pages under 'E' for Elvis Jihad -- in case you need to get in touch, or you want to hire us for a private party. I don't conduct the majority of my business under a big cloak of secrecy. Like any natural born fool, I go for honesty first whenever I can. That's probably why I'm broke. In the end, I'm just a working stiff trying to earn a living and stay one step ahead of the steamroller. You get all that? "

"Quite a speech."

"Thanks. I cribbed it from the Internet. Amazing what you can find on the web ..."

"I will be keeping an eye on you," she said again, just in case I didn't hear it the first time, or just so she could have the last word.

"Super! I look forward to it. More than I can say. Maybe I'll even drive out to Simsbury some night and take in one of your shows. Have a little dinner -- if I can find a date with a strong constitution."

Her eyes flared again. What the hell nerve did I have to treat her this way? That's what she wanted to know. But she didn't ask, for to do so would mean lowering herself to my level. And prolonging our visit, which she clearly did not want to do.

"You like danger, Mr. Vaughn?"

"Not so much," I said. "I had my fill of it growing up in New York City. Ever ride a subway, Mrs. Edwards? Bone-chilling."

"I think perhaps you should be on your way," she said.

"Yes!" I said. "Now we're thinking alike."

"And I don't think you should come back here anymore. This is private property. I intend to have all the locks changed if Miss Jefferson does not contact me within twenty-four hours. If I hear of you coming back, I will not hesitate to alert the authorities and have you arrested and jailed and prosecuted to the full extent of the law."

"Just like a shoplifter at Target, huh?"

"Tread very carefully, young man."

"Yeah, yeah. Believe it or not, Mrs. Edwards, I get it."

"Good. I'm very glad to hear it."

"Oh, and Mrs. Edwards?"

"Yes, what is it?"

"Give my regards to Mr. Edwards," I said. "That is, if you see him."

"What's that supposed to mean?"

I shrugged. "I understand he's been away."

"It is most certainly no business of yours."

"So, is he back yet, from ... wherever?"

"You have been duly warned, Mr. Vaughn."

"Right," I said, and saluted as a lowly private might salute an especially despised colonel. "Nice talking to you, too."

She walked to the front door and opened it. I strode past her. Now I felt like the mouse trying to get past the snake. If she was going to take a swing at me while my back was turned, so be it. That was pretty much the microcosm of life as I knew it. But I'd be damned if I was going to give her the satisfaction of seeing me flinch.

I walked down the driveway past the Cadillac and its two saturnine occupants. I decided it was best to think of them as Morticia and Gomez from now on. At least then I'd know which was which, and perhaps even which was witch and which was warlock. On the other hand, if I never saw either of them again, it would be an early Christmas on Summit Street. I waved cheerfully at them. They glared at me, but didn't wave back. I wondered if they stood in front of a mirror practicing this ridiculous glaring routine. I tried to suppress my disappointment at their failure to wave good-bye. It wasn't easy, though. So far, eight out of every ten people I'd met on this job seemed to detest me on sight without even getting to know me first. After a while that sort of thing begins to wear on you. After a while, your feelings get hurt.

Not really.

I strolled casually down to my piece of shit Jetta. The Caddie didn't try to run me down from behind. I got into the car, threw my *Courant* hat in the back seat and cranked the ignition key. The engine started on the third try. It didn't explode or anything dramatic. I popped the clutch and wheeled on down to the intersection and hooked a left to start my journey back to the city.

Venus Edwards was standing in the doorway of Twannie Jefferson's house -- Venus Edwards' house, as it turns out -- watching me take off down the road, hoping no doubt that I'd crash headlong into the first available oak tree. I waved cheerfully at her as well. Just like her two goons, she neglected to return the gesture. So much for breeding. Maybe dear old Auntie Peg was right about the *nouveau riche.* They were all about the money and the intoxicating effects of wielding influence, but they had no clue about basic civility.

I flipped Venus Edwards the bird and gunned the Jetta's motor. I doubt she even saw it, but I felt better anyway.

All the way home, I thought about one thing. The farther I got from Big Jeff's house, the more frustrated I became. By the time I hit the outskirts of Hartford, I was genuinely pissed. Three trips to the house on Duncaster Road and I still hadn't so much as set foot in the basement, let alone found any secret cache of illegal goods. I was starting to doubt I ever would.

In twenty-four hours, I'd have a whole new set of locks to pick, if Venus Edwards was a woman of her word. She didn't strike me as one to make idle threats. She didn't strike me at all, in fact. And given my behavior toward her, it showed excellent self-control on her part. She also didn't seem like the type to enter casually into a world of pointless violence. Of the many strategies I might employ with her, the safest seemed to be to keep her off balance, and I thought I could probably handle that task pretty easily. And who knows, along the way I might even find out why Twannie Jefferson and Miguel Batista were dead. I wished I had some clue about what the hell I'd gotten myself into. In many ways I felt like Hellen Keller in a world of perpetually rearranged living room furniture.

*The Farce News*

## Chapter 14

The afternoon sun dropped steadily toward its final resting place out of sight below the western horizon. As it sank, so did my mood. A chilly, meat-locker frost insinuated itself throughout Hartford, casting a dull gloom over my entire unproductive day. The breeze no longer had the sweet aroma of Indian summer. Instead the afternoon wind blew no one good, least of all me. It bore the dank stench of another harsh winter lurking just around the next corner. Winter, cold and spiritless, killing everything it can, sending the rest into lifesaving dormancy. A cold day in hell? Welcome to Hartford in the dead of winter.

I headed home to change my clothes, scan my phone machine for messages, sift my personal mail for junk, and check my pets for signs of life. If they were happy to see me, they did a masterful job of concealing the fact -- except for the dog, of course, who's a worse actor than Keanu Reeves. He jumped me like a dark alley hoodlum and ran circles around the kitchen until even I was dizzy. They say every fifteen minutes is a new day for dogs. I guess I'd been gone about three years, by Rufus's inner clock. I'm surprised he remembered me at all. Maybe he didn't. Maybe I was just somebody who was going to give him food, and that was enough reason for him to form an immediate lifelong bond. Fair enough.

I spooned something called *Formule poisson de mer* for the cats. Bilingual cat food. Stinks in two languages: shit and *merde*. And what the hell was Ocean Fish Formula anyway? Its odor made me want to throw up, as did the sight of Buddy and J.D. hungrily lapping it up. Meanwhile, no sooner had I poured out the dog's crunchy kibble dinner than it was gone and he was at my heels, harumphing and groaning for water. One day, he'd learn to chew his food, but apparently not in this lifetime.

I left the animals to their business and went to the bedroom where the air was heavy with the weight of lonesome bachelorhood. The unmade bed yelled out to me what had been in the back of my mind for several days now. Bonnie ain't comin' back. Get used to the idea.

I cursed the unmade bed and moved to the closet. I pulled a black wool turtleneck over my Gram Fest t-shirt and swapped out my sneakers for a pair of tan suede cowboy boots that were currently on their fifth set of heels and soles.

I killed half an hour taking Rufus for a walk. He was so grateful I actually felt bad for making him wait so long. After a few minutes of recklessly jerking me around in explosions of pent-up energy, he finally settled into his usual ritual of snatching the leash in his jaws and, I think (in his mind, at least), walking me. If he could speak, I'm guessing he'd say something like, "C'mon, Billy Bob, it's this a-way to the crick." Don't ask why he'd speak in a Mississippi drawl. Or why he'd want to take me for a walk. Or head for the crick. I never completed my undergraduate work in Fundamental Canine Psychology. That's what I think *he* thinks he's doing. I go along with him because it's just too hard to talk him out of it.

After our walk, I left him in the kitchen, slurping water from his stainless steel bowl, spilling half of it on the linoleum floor, looking up at me periodically with an expression of abiding devotion and love. I'd have spent the next few minutes tugging his ears and scratching his neck, but I knew it would only make good-bye that much harder to say. For him, that is. Okay, for me, too. Meanwhile, the cats had long since finished eating their revolting chum and had gone back to work (their jobs, apparently, to watch us with expressions of something approaching unparalleled pity). There are times when I feel it is a significant shortcoming of mine that I allow a cat or two to reduce my self-esteem to virtually nil. If I could somehow learn how to adopt that round-eyed scowl of contempt, I could probably get a lot more accomplished in this great big world of intimidation and disrespect. On the other hand, maybe God is punishing cats for their intrinsic disdain for everything and everyone non-cat by making them go through life nine times. Once around this psychotic merry-go-round was already proving to be more than enough for me.

On my way out, I knocked on Jolie's door. No answer. I noted the onset of minor nausea and a momentary increase in my heart rate. Both conditions receded somewhat as I headed for the street and my piece of shit Jetta, but I was still thinking about it as I wheeled out of Hartford with the setting sun in my rear view mirror. It was nothing. Minor hunger pains. That's all. She was out. No big deal. Jolie had gone off before, sometimes for days on end. I guess the difference was that this time I had taken notice earlier in the process, instead of going, "Oh, yeah," like some high school dope, when she reappeared. It also occurred to me that, prior to the unmade bed in my apartment speaking to me in perfect English on the subject of my most recent (if as yet unofficial) breakup, Bonnie hadn't occurred to me in several days. Not in any meaningful way, at least. In fact, I half expected the phone call saying she'd be by for her things. But if I remembered correctly, she hadn't actually left any of her things at my place (shifty female that she was), so that was one phone call I wouldn't have to be a grown-up about. Another call I was probably in no danger of receiving was the one saying she'd made a mistake, all was forgiven, and she wanted me back. Well, it wasn't like I'd been holding my breath. Bonnie was okay but she wasn't worth turning blue over.

Jolie, on the other hand ... Inexplicably, the thought of her driving away in her beat-up truck made my pulse quicken.

Traffic in town was the usual cacophonous crawl but I eventually made my way to the waiting line for I-84 East, then inched my way over to the right lane and the entrance ramp for I-91 North. Traffic progressed with an almost palpable reluctance. At one point a very old man hobbling along with the aid of an aluminum walker passed me in the breakdown lane. I gaped at him and he gave me the finger. It was a gnarled, bony thing that sent home the message in astonishing and bitter clarity. But I managed not to take it personally. I figured we'd be hearing about this old coot on the eleven o'clock news. Another not-so-happy wanderer, escaping the death sentence of his nursing home incarceration to explore parallel dimensions visible only from his unique vantage point (that of irreversible dementia). More power to him. I'd have offered him a ride if I didn't have places to go and people to see. Or if I had room in the trunk for his aluminum walker.

It was nearly six o'clock before I got to Windsor Locks and found East Barber Street. I pulled the Jetta to the curb three houses east of Johnny Brashear's rental and parked. The dilapidated Grumman box truck was gone. In its place was a red Mercedes-Benz that looked even older than my VW. Maybe by a decade or two. It had once been candy apple red. Now it was faded to a strange shade of burnt pink. A few rust spots pitted the bottom of the doors and side panels, a victim of too many New England winters -- or one spring in St. Paul, Minnesota. I'd have traded my Jetta straight up for it without even asking for a test drive. It had that kind of dignity, even in its state of advanced automotive infirmity. Like the old guy on the highway with the walker. They were old and headed, with grim determination, for their respective scrap yards, but they still had their pride. I turned and gave my Jetta the finger. It clicked and popped as the metal cooled. Either that or "click-and-pop" are Jettaspeak for, "Up yours, *Scheisskopf*."

In addition to the car sitting in the driveway, there were lights burning at Brashear's place. The little kids I'd seen earlier racing their Big Wheels were nowhere in sight. Perhaps home wolfing macaroni and cheese and watching Bart and Homer Simpson on the tube. Living *la vida loca*.

I walked up the driveway, crossed the dewey lawn to the front door and rang the bell. There was a harsh firehouse ringing from within, followed by the sound of footsteps approaching. Then the door opened a few inches. A face that reminded me immediately of Bruce Lee, the karate guy from the seventies, filled the space. But the guy was black, not Chinese. He had a short, tight Afro, not straight black Asian hair. He wasn't particularly dark-skinned and I took him for a mixed breed, just like the rest of us. A mulatto with a some obvious Asian thrown into the mix. This had to be the *high yellow Negro* I'd heard about from the long-suffering neighbor three doors up. Johnny Brashear. I hoped he didn't know karate. Or, if he did know karate, I hoped he had the discipline and self-awareness those people are suppose to be famous for. Last thing I needed was for him to start showing off what a hot shot he was by practicing that kung fu nonsense on me. *Arrigato* very much, dude. And pass the *sake*.

He was a pretty good looking guy, in a peculiar way. He had china blue eyes -- not to be mistaken with Chinese blue eyes, which would constitute a very rare genetic occurrence indeed. His blue eyes threw me much the way a 500-pound sumo wrestler might toss aside a 98-pound DMV clerk. He reminded me of one of those funky sled dogs. Malamutes or Alaskan huskies. I thought about what they say about the life of a sled dog, and I paused to consider Johnny's lot in life. I wondered if he was a front runner, or if he took the view, like that of the pack; that life was more or less a bunch of assholes and the only way he'd ever get anywhere was to chase vigilantly after the assholes directly ahead of him.

"Good evening," I said, giving it my best non-threatening smile.

"Yeah, fabulous," the guy said. "What's up? You're not from the Clean Water Act, are you?"

"No," I said. "Actually ..."

"Police Benevolent Association?"

"Er ..."

"Community Chest?"

"As a matter of fact I'm looking for Big Jeff," I said.

That stopped him. Credit where it's due, he was pretty cool when I named-dropped on him. I half expected him to slam the door in my face -- or at least to try. But he made no such gesture. Instead, he presented me with an expression of startling indifference. I started counting silently in my head, waiting for him to say, "Who?" I got all the way to six alligators before he spoke.

"Sorry, who's Big Jeff?"

I smiled and chuckled a little. "That was pretty good," I said. "Not great, though." He continued to peer at me like I was some kind of nut and he didn't know what I was talking about. Of course, that's because he didn't.

"Sorry, pal you lost me. What's pretty good?"

"Your version of aplomb. You do know what aplomb is, don't you? Credit where it's due, you have a fairly good sense of dramatic timing. You don't get flustered and you don't jump your lines or give away anything. For pure dramatic effect, I'd give you about a six on a scale of one to ten. So tell me, where'd you learn your craft? On the yard?"

Needless to say, I'd been waiting years to use that phrase, "on the yard," on someone. Finally!

"The what?" he said, taking two thirds of the wind out of my sails.

Maybe I should have given him an eight. I jibed the jib and reversed tacks. Clearly, he needed the direct approach, slang-free and entirely non-euphemistic.

"Prison, my man. The yard. Tough-guy proving ground."

He frowned a little. Maybe he didn't appreciated the direct approach after all, or my bold insinuation that he was some kind of cheap jailbird. "I think you should beat it," he said. But he still didn't slam the door in my face. Yet.

"How about acting class? Where'd you study? Not Stanislavski."

He peered at me. A lot of people had done a lot of peering at me lately, and most of them weren't what I'd have called peers. Barely acquaintances, really. Damn near total strangers. I was getting a little sick of it. "You serious?" he said. Great, now he was questioning me.

"Sure I'm serious. Why wouldn't I be?"

"I mean about the acting school thing."

"Yeah, sure. Why not? Everyone I meet lately, seems they're one kind of drama school dropout or another. So, why not you? You're about as bad an actor as the rest of them, although I'm not sure you know what your motivation is supposed to be."

"You looking to get your ass kicked, man?"

"No," I said, very casually. "Not really."

"Then I suggest you take off," he said, and started to close the door.

I made a face like he was hurting my feelings with that kind of talk. I guess I'm not that good an actor either, because he didn't seem taken in. So I put my hand on the door to keep him from closing it. Turns out I was the stronger of us. Or he wasn't as committed to his role. He lacked that certain thing, whatever the opposite of *joie de vivre* is, that ingrained angst which enables one to engage enthusiastically in physical violence. I don't have it, either, but I bluff better. At least better than this guy. Comes from hanging out in too many bars, probably. Have to talk to Artie about booking us into some better rooms.

"Don't be rude," I said. "I just want a little conversation."

"Fuck off."

"I don't think so."

"I don't know you and I got nothing to say to you."

"How about Big Jeff? You going to tell me you don't know Big Jeff? Because if you do, I'll have to call you a liar. I'm not calling you a liar yet, mind you. Or otherwise doubting the depth and breadth of your character, so don't get all bent out of shape. But, if you do start down that road, you know, lying and making a mockery of everything that's true and good, well, I won't have any other choice but to call you a flat-out bold-faced prevaricating fabricator. I'm pretty sure you'd like to keep that from happening."

He stopped peering at me (which was a welcome change) and gawked at me as if I were some kind of sideshow freak (which wasn't). "Am I supposed to know who you are?" he said. "Or give a flying fuck?"

"Only if you're part of a circus act that does that sort of thing."

"Then why don't you take a hike?"

I shook my head. "I just got here. And we have so much to discuss."

"Yeah?"

"Look, my name's Robby. I think you know my great, great aunt, several times removed."

"Yeah?"

"Yeah."

"And who would that be?"

"Margaret Waddley-Wordstone."

"Yeah?"

"Yeah, Johnny. Yeah, yeah, yeah. Just like the song. And now that you know who I am, maybe you could start to work on giving a flying fuck. Or we could just stand here all night. But that would just get your neighbors curious. One of them might call the cops, and the cops might eventually like to see what's in your garage. I'm pretty sure you don't want that kind of heat. Do you?"

My casual use of his first name grabbed his attention. His eyes narrowed a bit. That's one thing about guys who suddenly realize they don't have the best cards at the poker table. Their eyes always narrow. It's the *tell*. Least that's what they say in all the movies. I wanted to reassure Johnny, tell him to relax and go with the flow. But I also thought it would be a waste of breath. These guys usually don't get it. Takes 'em forever to learn that *life goes on*. We all make mistakes, some of them are even honest mistakes. Regardless, we clean up the mess with life's version of two-ply paper towels, then we move on with the hope that tomorrow will be an improvement on today, with fewer spills and, failing that, better paper towels.

If Johnny Brashear still wanted to slam the door in my face, he was just curious enough to delay until he established what my face was doing there.

*The Farce News*

"Is this going to take long? We're baking."

His smirking insolence was a pathetic pretense. I saw dread in the curl of his sneering lips and decided to cut him some slack. Besides, now that he mentioned them, I could smell the cookies. I love the smell of cookies in the early evening. Smells like ... well, if not victory, at least a hell of a lot like chocolate chip oatmeal, which is the next best thing to victory.

"Look, I'm just an ordinary schmuck," I said. "Like you. The only difference is I have an *iMac* on my kitchen table. You don't by any chance have an *iMac* on your kitchen table, do you? I only just came into possession of mine last night. It's one of those colorful desktop models. Purple, of all things. Amazing, huh? Has all sorts of interesting files on the hard drive. I don't know shit about computers, but even I could figure some of this stuff out. It's mostly names and addresses and phone numbers. Stuff like that. But it isn't your typical little black book. These are players, Johnny."

"Players, huh?"

"Heavyweights."

"Yeah?"

"Sound familiar?"

He sure as hell wasn't going to admit it if it did. He shrugged a little. "Purple, you say?"

"Purple," I said. "I got it from LaTwanda Jefferson."

He nodded. "I don't suppose she just gave it to you?"

"Er, no." I smiled a little, just to let him know I got the joke and almost found it hilarious.

"You rip her off?"

"Not so's she'd notice."

He paused. "You better come in," he said. "I don't need to heat the neighborhood."

I graciously accepted his magnanimous invitation and followed him into the house. The living room was surprisingly cozy, with a warm lived-in quality. Floor lamps lit the space, nothing fancy. A bunch of brown furniture that looked comfortable and inviting if a little tattered around the edges, as if a cat or two had done their nails on the fabric. I know a little about that. The couches looked broken-in without having reached critical mass on the worn-out scale. You could still sink into one without bottoming-out and ending up with springs up your ass or feeling the floorboards beneath you. At the moment, I was just bone weary enough to find the appeal in any stuffed furniture I encountered. The walls had some mediocre artwork hanging on them. No dogs playing poker, however. No Elvis sweating to the oldies in Vegas. Not *that* brand of kitsch. This was mostly still life crap. Bowls of apples and oranges -- somebody apparently thought you could, in fact, mix the two. A couple of landscapes that might have been an attempt to capture the Pacific Coast. Stock stuff. Waterfalls with distant rainbows. Amateur efforts, half-a-rung up the culture ladder from Painting By Numbers. It was the kind of yard-sale artwork that gave the room a peculiar aura of impermanence, the way a hotel room can never feel like anything but a stopover no matter how it is appointed.

"Sit over there," he said, pointing at a large brown couch with a wooden frame.

I didn't move from my spot. "Why is it people think they can boss me around all the time? Do I have that kind of face? Do I give the impression of being overly passive?"

He stopped and studied me for a moment. "I don't know what you're talking about, man."

"You're the second person in the last couple of hours who thought it was just fine to order me around like some kind of lackey. Offer me a chair, but do me a favor, don't tell me where to sit."

Johnny Brashear continued staring. "Hey, relax, huh?"

"Sure, I'll relax."

He shrugged and took a seat on the couch opposite the one he'd offered me. "Sit anywhere."

I sat down and looked across a small coffee table at my reluctant host. His neighbor three doors away had called him "a little too street." I found Johnny Brashear to be more urbane than inner-urban. He carried himself like a man who might be right at home throwing bones and playing the dozens with the brothers on a Friday night, but he could also circulate casually at a black tie cocktail party on Saturday night, schmoozing whomever crossed his path.

"So, let's talk about Big Jeff?"

"What about her?"

"You know her?"

"What if I do?"

"Tell me about her?"

"What if I don't want to?"

"Then we sit around and waste a lot of time."

"I'm not going anywhere. I live here."

"How about Venus Edwards?"

"Nobody by that names lives here."

"But you know her?"

"No. As a matter of fact I don't believe I do."

I didn't believe it either. "Are you by any chance a congenital liar?"

"Piss off."

Maybe he couldn't help himself. Maybe he was one of those chronic bullshit artists you're always reading about in the *Washington Congressional Weekly*. I decided to give him a little piece of unsolicited advice.

"On the off chance you're telling the truth, and you're really don't know her, let me suggest you keep it that way."

"Ooh, I'm shaking. She doesn't scare me."

"Well, if you're as smart as you think, you know that Venus Edwards is hip deep in big stakes games that earn a lot of money. I doubt she's going to allow some small fry like you to spoil her fun, to say nothing of threatening her profit margin."

Apparently Johnny Brashear didn't like me referring to him as a small fry. I got that feeling when he leaned forward, pointed a finger at me and said, "Who the hell are you calling a small fry?" If his finger had been a gun I'd have been forced to dive for cover, or at least duck behind some furniture. As it was I simply stared down the barrel of his manicured index finger.

"Oh, please, mister. Don't shoot!"

He put the finger down. "I'm not afraid of some old broad."

I nodded at him like I shared his tough guy attitude. "You're never to old to start."

He grunted and dismissed the whole idea. If he was going to be afraid of Venus Edwards, it would be in private. "Let's change the subject," he said. "Let's talk about your new computer."

"What about it?"

'What's in it? And I don't mean the *iTunes*."

"Okay," I said. "But before we do, why don't you ask your girlfriend to join us?"

"My girlfriend?" he said. He did *innocent* about as well as he did *nonchalant*. Not well enough to impress life's casting agents or win a SAG card. Or me. "What girlfriend?"

"What girlfriend? I suppose that's your perfume in the air?"

"Watch it, pal."

"There's a pretty good-smelling woman somewhere in this house. No point making her strain at the keyhole. The cookies will bake themselves."

Johnny Brashear smiled and called out over his shoulder. "Come on in, Jenny. This guy's harmless."

The kitchen door swung open and Jenny walked in. I stood up, because that's the polite thing to do when a woman enters the room. She looked at me rather coldly. I'd have been disappointed if this was our first meeting and we were getting off to such a bad start. But this was by no means our initial encounter. I'd seen Jenny before, even spoken with her, a couple of times, in fact. Jenny was the pretty brunette who worked the Customer Relations & Disinformation Desk down at LaTwanda Jefferson's House of Whacks down on Park Street. Jenny was the whack job who told me all about the fictitious trading cards they didn't currently have in stock. She had, of course, neglected to tell me it was because they don't exist, never had and never would, but I let it go. After all, what's a little treachery among friends?

"I told you he'd find us," she said, scolding Johnny, while referring to me as if I weren't in the room. I hate when people do that. Makes me feel small and insignificant, as if I'm not especially important in their lives, just another ancillary carry-on bag they could just as easily have left at home. Actually I couldn't care less.

Jennifer plunked herself down on the couch next to Johnny. Tonight she was wearing designer jeans that hugged her nicely, along with a beige pullover sweater whose snug fit it would be inappropriate of me to describe in any great detail. The perfume I'd detected in the air was hers all right, and it was even nicer with her in the room as chaperone. Oddly enough, the fragrance mixed well with the aroma of baking cookies. How many perfume manufacturers can make that claim? Jenny would have been a real knockout if fear and loathing weren't busy playing havoc with her features. Her mouth was drawn tight, her eyes were wary and shifty. Her jaw was clenched. I wanted to tell her to relax, but it was fun to speculate on what it was she might be worrying her pretty little head off about.

I sat back and smiled. "Well, I certainly hope you two schemers have a good exit strategy."

Johnny Brashear fielded this one like a Caribbean shortstop, smooth and elegant. Then he muffed the throw to first.

"You'll have to be more explicit," he said. "We don't know what you're talking about."

"Nobody ever does," I said. "Swear to God, I just don't get it."

"It must be you, huh? And not the rest of the world."

"You might be on to something," I said. "But I doubt it. Listen, let me try a different approach. See if talking straight works any better."

"Go ahead. We're all ears."

"I'm not all ears," said Jennifer, smoothing the front of her sweater.

"Okay, it's like this. Now, don't take offense, but it's been my experience, and I read a lot of cheap detective novels, that, historically speaking, when people like you two double-cross people like LaTwanda Jefferson and Venus Edwards, the repercussions tend to be, in a word, harsh."

"Is that right? Repercussions? That's a pretty big word."

"It's the same as effects. Impacts. Influences."

Johnny Brashear smiled at me, and said to Jennifer: "He's a regular thesaurus, isn't he?"

Jennifer didn't answer. It was a rhetorical question, and like so many people I admired in this overly verbose world, she didn't waste a bunch of time answering rhetorical questions.

I went on. "You do understand the basic principles of cause and effect, don't you?"

"Let's just say I do. For the sake of argument."

Great. Another guy who liked to argue.

"Super, then this conversation has a chance to really go places. Here goes nothing. Far as I can tell, you lovebirds are guilty of nothing worse than acting out of turn, taking what isn't yours. Seems you dreamed up some harebrained scheme to rip-off LaTwanda Jefferson. And maybe Venus Edwards, too, for all I know. Anyway, let's just say that was the cause. As for the effect, I'm guessing that these people, Jefferson and Edwards, or more likely their people will soon be dispatched to exact a pound or so of flesh. Your flesh."

"Really?" Johnny was interested, just not very articulate.

"And," I said, ignoring him and turning to Jennifer, who was much better to look at, "I'm afraid they'll want a pound or two of yours as well, honey, particularly if it turns out you conspired against your boss with Johnny, here."

"Conspired," he said, laughing nervously. "That's another awful big word, chief."

I turned back to him. "Not really. Only nine letters. *Antidisestablishmentarianism*. Now, *that's* a big word."

He threw his hands up. "You're friggin' nuts. I can't talk to you."

"Try. For argument's sake."

"Okay, so what makes you think anyone's been double-crossed?"

"Come on, Johnny. You're too smart for the Dumb Guy routine. Even the little old lady down the street has you pegged as a player. You're not fooling anyone. Besides, you have a track record. I know about your tap job on Margaret Waddlely-Wordstone. The way I see it, your problem is you can't make up your mind what sport best fits your skill set. Extortion is quick and easy, but it tends to piss people off because you get to keep the goods you have on them even after they pay you to go away. Ultimately that's a loser's game that could eventually get you killed. You don't want to get killed over a little money, do you, Johnny?"

"Keep talking," he said, pretending to stifle a yawn.

"Porno's probably got the potential to be a regular cash cow, but it tends to be greasy and rife with lowlife hoodlums. I believe the expression is 'all mobbed up.' Know what I mean? Busting at the seams with wise guys? So you have to ask yourself, who wants to spend all day trying to remember which one's Vinny, and which one's Vito, and which one's Salvatore and which one's Guido. God help you the day you mix it up and some cheap thug in a thousand dollar suit takes a Louisville Slugger to the back of your skull. That would suck, don't you think?"

"You watch too many Joe Pesci movies," Johnny Brashear said.

"You might be right, but we were talking about you, and the dangers of dabbling in pornography."

"At least *you* were."

"Do you think producing skin flicks will ever get you the kind of legitimate business reputation you really want? Be honest. Isn't it true that most pornographers are degenerate dirt bags or repressed fags?"

"I don't give it that much thought."

"Okay, so let's explore other possibilities."

"Such as."

I smiled at him. "C'mon, Johnny. Don't be coy. What have you got sitting out there in the garage? I know it isn't lawn furniture."

"What do you know about that?"

"I know where you got it. I'm pretty sure it wasn't a gift from Twannie Jefferson. The thing is, you have to be damn careful about the people you do business with, and who you double-cross."

"Double-cross?"

"What? You think all that merchandise actually belonged to Big Jeff?"

"I don't follow."

"Clearly you don't. I'm suggesting to you that Twannie was a middleman, so to speak. She had people above her to answer to. And those are the people who are gonna be just a little peeved at whoever it was that ripped them off. In broad daylight, no less. I do have to give you points for brass balls."

"We had a deal, me and her."

"No you didn't."

Actually, I didn't know if Johnny had a deal with Twannie Jefferson or not. But I had my doubts.

"She said if anything ever happened to her, that ..."

"Stop right there."

Johnny glanced over at Jennifer. It was an involuntary reflex and he immediately tried to call it back. But not fast enough. He looked back at me. "You got something to say, say it. Otherwise, there's the door."

*The Farce News*

I shook my head and stared at him like he already had the rope around his neck and didn't know they were about to yank the trap door out from beneath his feet. "Let's try to keep it real, shall we?"

Jenny grabbed Johnny's arm. "What does he mean?"

I turned to her. "You lovebirds are heading for some serious hard times if you don't figure out a way to cut and run. And I mean *soon*. You're sitting on a stockpile of goods but I'm guessing you have nowhere to lay 'em off. You were quick this morning, but sometimes quick can be mistaken for impetuous."

"More big words."

"Your haste could get you wasted, Johnny."

He glared at me for a moment. "You come here to warn me?"

"No, Johnny. I came to make a deal, just like Monty Hall. You see, I've got this list of names. They mean nothing to me. I'm just an underemployed musician trying to get along it life. But I think you could probably turn it into a pretty healthy stable of regular customers if you handle it right. I'd be willing to guess there's a considerable degree of repeat business built-in."

"This about the *iMac*?"

I smiled. "You're a quick study. That's good."

"What's the pitch?"

"LaTwanda Jefferson was no dummy. Her files are encrypted. I can't tell by looking at the names who's into what, whether it's dike porno, or tax-free fudge from halfway around the world, or illegal furs from Scandinavia. Point is, you've got the product and I've got what I believe to be Big Jeff's customer accounts."

Johnny Brashear looked me over, trying to make up his mind whether to trust me or invite me to use the door again. "How'd you find me anyway?"

"It wasn't hard. In the last couple of days, your name's been batted around like a crippled rat at an alley cat convention."

"*What?*"

"Never mind. Point is, if you're serious about moving up in the world, you'd better get smart, and soon. You don't want to end up like LaTwanda Jefferson."

"Meaning what?"

I smiled. "Meaning horizontal. And not quite room temperature."

Jennifer became very agitated. "What's he mean, Johnny?"

She was quite lovely to look at and I took a moment to look at her, admiring her features the way one might admire scenery from a speeding train. Pretty in passing, but one doesn't necessarily want to interrupt one's journey to stroll around in it. Not if one cares very much about one's ultimate destination. (Whoever the hell *one* is.) Me? I didn't particularly want to get off and stroll around in Jenny right at the moment, although she was pretty as a field of clover (and about as sharp). It had dawned on me by now that, in all likelihood, she and I were never going to hook up. In the biblical sense or any other. Fetching as she was, she wasn't imbued with what you might call a staggering intellect and I could see getting tired of answering the *"What's he mean?"* question after about three minutes. Besides, if I was interested in fetching, I always had Rufus waiting at home to play that game. I stopped gazing at Jennifer and wondered for a moment about how they'd connected in the first place, she and Johnny. Maybe he'd used her to get to LaTwanda Jefferson. Or maybe he'd known her first and had planted her in the card store to gain access. Or maybe Jennifer was one of LaTwanda Jefferson's protégés who had fallen under the influence of the charming Johnny Brashear. Perhaps I should give Johnny a little more credit for his gifts as a manipulator. Perhaps I should watch my back a little more carefully. I turned my full attention back to him now, though my eyes filed an immediate protest with my brain because he wasn't nearly as good looking as Jennifer.

"I met your moving men this morning, Johnny. They weren't particularly subtle."

"You get what you pay for," he said with a shrug.

"I'd say you have a refund coming," I said.

"Don't I know it."

"I was at the shop this morning when your muscled-up Laurel & Hardy tandem were downloading Jefferson's inventory out the back door. I couldn't help but notice how much of it looked absolutely nothing like boxes of trading cards."

"So?"

"Lucky for me, I had already seen some of LaTwanda Jefferson's stash."

"Yeah, when was that?"

"Last night."

"And where would that have been?"

"At her place, Johnny. I was there just after you. We must have just missed each other."

"Me!"

"C'mon now, don't start the Dumb Guy thing again."

"You're nuts. I was nowhere near her house last night."

"I have a witness who swears up and down you killed Twannie."

"What! That's nuts. I don't even own a gun."

I looked over at Jennifer, then back at Johnny. "Who said anything about a gun?"

He hesitated, then retreated to safe ground: "I don't own a gun."

I suppressed the urge to laugh in his face. "Not now, you don't. Even a dumb guy would have ditched the murder weapon by now, and you're not a dumb guy, are you, Johnny?"

"I've never owned a gun."

"Never?"

"Not ever. I don't believe in guns."

"That's not the story my witness tells."

"Witness, what witness? Who is this witness?" He was incredulous, or fairly convincing in the title role of "The Incredulous Man," a low-budget picture destined to go straight to video. "Who's spreading these lies about me?"

I admired his restraint. He stopped short of calling them vicious lies.

"An old friend of yours," I said. "As a matter of fact, she did a little acting for you recently, when you were still in the movie business."

Johnny Brashear shook his head as lights went on in his brain. "That bitch."

"No need for name calling."

"Lita Wordstone has never been anything but a pain in my ass."

"Well, if it's any consolation, she's not too happy with you at the moment, either. And I strongly suggest you take a moment to consider the situation. It's he said, she said. And you're dealing with the wrath of a woman truly and thoroughly scorned. She's ready to swear on a stack of motel bibles that you're the man who put LaTwanda Jefferson on her back."

He snorted. "No man's ever put LaTwanda Jefferson on her back, if you catch my drift."

I shook my head. "Are you always this clever?"

"Anyway, she's just pissed off about the film."

"Yeah, sure, the *film.*"

"And what's more, it turns out she's a lousy actress."

"We can critique her performance another time. Maybe over a large bowl of popcorn."

"She was never committed to the project. It was just a flight of fancy for her. A game for a rich, spoiled brat. And that was reflected in her performance, which, I might add, totally lacked luster."

"Or to paraphrase the song, *She lacked lust, she was so lackluster.* Does that about get it?"

"What the hell are you talking about? What song?"

"Nothing, never mind."

"Jesus, you're some piece of work" he said, not unkindly.

I sat back and put my feet up on the coffee table. "But enough about me, let's talk about you. What was your part in this ridiculous movie malarkey anyway? You were the producer, right? You were the guy who rounded up the talent. And I'm assuming you were the director, too, right? Not exactly a Cecil B. DeMille epic, though, was it?"

"Gotta start somewhere."

"You didn't finance it yourself, did you?"

"I was the worker-monkey. I didn't have the operating cash, but I did everything else." He seemed almost wistful, as if reminiscing on an experience for which he'd had genuinely high hopes but was now just a pile of dying embers in the overflowing ashtray of his life.

"What else was there?"

"Editor."

"Oh. Sure, of course."

"And sound tech."

"Yeah?"

"And lighting coordinator."

"Right, right."

"And key grip."

"Wow, I had no idea. I certainly didn't mean to diminish the scope of your participation."

"And gaffer."

He was slipping away down memory lane. "You're quite the jack of all trades."

"And best boy."

"I'm sure you were in charge of wardrobe, too."

He looked at me warily. "Have you seen the film?"

"A couple of minutes of it."

"And ...?" He seemed on the verge of asking me what I thought of it, then apparently thought better of soliciting my opinion. Maybe his ego was especially vulnerable this week.

I decided to switch topics. "Did you handle distribution, too?"

"Well, I was supposed to."

"How many have you made?"

"Adult films? Just a couple."

"No, Johnny. How many copies of 'Volley-Ball!' have you made?"

"Oh, not very many. Maybe a hundred?"

"Maybe a hundred? You're not sure?"

"Okay, it was a hundred."

"And how many do you still have?"

"A few. Why? What do you care?"

"Answer the question. How many?"

"Ninety-eight."

I gave him the old "you kiddin' me?" look. He shrugged. "Why so many?"

"I haven't had time to follow-up on promo."

A pitiful excuse, but classic from the kind of guy who dreams large and produces small, who can't finish the job he starts. A great idea man, maybe (probably not), but he couldn't cash the ticket at the end. So, here he was holding ninety-eight copies of "Volley-Ball!" It was good news for the Wordstone family if it was true. It meant he had them all, except the one he'd sent to Lillian the Vaudevillian, and the one I'd seen playing on the large screen TV at LaTwanda Jefferson's place.

"This is good, Johnny. Very good."

"Yeah? How so?"

"Because now that we know what's behind door number one, we can work a deal."

"What kind of deal?"

"For starters, I want you to give me all the remaining copies."

"What! You gotta be joking!" He seemed genuinely shocked, then quickly crestfallen, as if reality was smacking him in the back of the head, knocking a little sense into him.

"I want all the copies, Johnny. And I want you to leave Lita and her big sister and their grandmother alone. Permanently."

"You know about that?"

"I read all about it in *The Farce News.*"

"The what?"

"Forget it."

He took a minute to forget it, then asked: "What's in it for me if I give you the tapes?"

This was another favorite of mine. The "what's in it for me?" gambit. As if every human act was contingent on the expectation of reciprocation. I wanted to throw up, metaphorically speaking (which is a hell of a lot easier to clean up).

"You give me the tapes, and I give you Twannie Jefferson's computer. If you're clever enough to crack her codes, you'll be in business with a nice list of customers with all kinds of interesting and unique tastes and desires. But there's a catch."

"Yeah, right. There's always a catch."

"You take the computer and the list, and all that crap you've got out there in the garage, and get out of town. Move to the country. Lay low. Be inconspicuous. Take time to set yourselves up."

"But we live here."

"Not anymore. You can't stay here. You're too hot. You'll have to work your business from a remote location. You can use FedEx to ship your product. Or the post office. They're a little cheaper. Hell, see what brown can do for you if you want. I don't care. The point is, stay the hell out of the limelight. Don't draw attention to yourselves or you're likely to end up dead. And, for the love of Pete, leave the Wordstone family out of your plans?"

"Who is Pete?" Jennifer said.

"One of the disciples," I said. "But that's a story for another day."

"Why do the Wordstones get a pass? What's your interest in them?"

"Much as it saddens me to admit it, they're family," I said.

"Oh," was all he could managed.

"Look, you want to step up in the world. This is your chance. Trafficking in illegal merchandise might suit you. But you gotta be smart or you'll have to answer for the LaTwanda Jefferson."

I glanced quickly at Jennifer to see if she was going to ask, "What's he mean?" She kept her pretty little mouth shut this time and I silently thanked whatever God is in charge of such things.

"I'm telling you, me and her, we had a deal," Johnny said.

I don't know if he was bluffing. God knows *I* was.

Besides, he didn't like me telling him how to conduct his business any more than I had liked him telling me which couch to sit on. But I think he recognized the up side of the picture I was painting for him. I guess he saw the potential in taking his stash and starting over. If he played it smart, his pot of gold would be bigger and better than ever. No more blackmail. No more petty crap. No more living in rentals and driving cars old enough to be in college. If he got stupid -- or greedy -- he could very easily end up stepping on the rainbow and find himself sucking potato salad through a straw at the same picnic where LaTwanda Jefferson was no doubt currently belly-up to the eternal feeding trough.

"So, where's the *iMac*?" he asked.

"Where are the tapes?" I asked.

"I've got 'em here," he said, without saying specifically where.

"Good," I said. "Go get them. I'll wait here with Jennifer. We'll make small talk while you're gone. She and I have a lot to talk about. Gordie Howe, for one thing."

"Why should I?" he said, practically whining.

It's pitiful when grown men devolve into classic elementary school obstinacy. If I had a nickel for every time I'd seen some wannabe tough guy collapse into infantile bitching, I'd have almost $3.25 by now.

"You should because if you don't, you'll probably end up spending the next several weeks negotiating a plea bargain with the local prosecutor instead of negotiating the price of contraband with your new clientele. The Hartford police will certainly want a crack at you. Ditto the Bloomfield police. And let's not forget the Windsor Locks constabulary. Want me to go on?"

"Get the tapes, Johnny," Jennifer said, tugging at his sleeve.

It was the first intelligent thing she'd said all night. (At least since I got there. For all I know she'd been lecturing Johnny on the sociological effects of quantum physics as they related to space exploration and the challenges of successful suspended animation of laboratory rats in the twenty-first century scientific community. But I doubt it.)

"Do as the pretty lady says, Johnny. Get the tapes."

Now we had him outnumbered. It was only a matter of time before he saw the light of day -- okay, about twelve hours if you're going to be persnickety about it. I could see that he wanted to do the right thing. But I could also see that he had to sneak up on the right thing from behind and throw a rope around its ankles before he could be sure the right thing wouldn't take off on him, leaving him standing there like some loser boy scout with no old lady to escort across the street. You could look in his eyes and see the wheels turning. I'll bet you could listen to his ears and hear the gears grinding.

"They're out in the garage," Jennifer said. "In a box marked 'Sports Videos'."

Johnny gave her a dirty look.

"I'll bring the car around, Johnny. You get the box."

We were just getting up from our respective couches when the doorbell rang.

It was like we were playing musical chairs, only in reverse. The music started up and we froze. We looked at each other.

"You expecting anyone?" I asked.

"What the hell, I wasn't even expecting *you*," Johnny said, clearly not thrilled with his new role as *ad hoc* Suzy Homemaker.

The doorbell buzzed again. We froze some more. It was starting to get awfully cold in there.

"I hope you didn't bring the heat with you," Johnny said to me.

"Funny you should mention it," I said. Nobody laughed.

As if on cue, Jennifer scurried back out to the kitchen. I'd seen this act performed in hotel rooms, usually when only one person is officially registered. There's a knock on the door and all the unregistered squatters scatter like cockroaches, just in case its the hotel dick or some other middle management trouble maker.

We waited to see if the doorbell would ring anymore. We didn't have to wait long. It rang yet again, although without any particular sense of urgency. As for the person causing it to ring, we could only guess at their relative urgency without first meeting him, or her.

## Chapter 15

Maybe it was something about my visit that had put Johnny Brashear off the notion of entertaining any more guests. I hate to think I could have such a negative impact on someone's natural instincts toward hospitality. But it was a possibility I had to at least consider as now he clearly didn't want to answer the doorbell. Despite his reluctance to respond in any palpable sense, it kept on ringing with a dogged perseverance I found almost admirable.

"You have a lot of friends who drop in unannounced?"

"No," he said, the glum petulance in his tone suggesting perhaps he didn't have a lot of friends of any particular description.

"You do *have* friends."

"Would it matter? You dropped by unannounced."

"And ...?"

"I wouldn't call you a friend."

While I'm nowhere near the antisocial sonofabitch Johnny Brashear was quickly turning out to be, I could think of a few people I hoped it *wasn't* on the other side of the door. The list began with Venus Edwards and her two gloomy tag-alongs, Gomez and Morticia. They hadn't been too happy with me when we parted company earlier in the afternoon. If she'd pinned a tail on me like some kind of birthday party donkey and followed me here to Johnny's place, things could get ugly in a New York minute -- or its Connecticut equivalent, a Hartford half-hour.

Then there was the Windsor Locks police. If they'd been tipped off, we'd have a whole lot of explaining to do. I wasn't making much money in this amateur private eye racket (I wasn't making any, as a matter of fact), and the last thing I needed was to have to post bond to get out of jail.

There was also a chance the two jailbirds from this morning, Bluto I and Bluto II, might have come looking for their pay. But we'd have heard the Grumman approach the house if it were them.

The doorbell jangled yet again.

"I don't suppose you ordered a pizza?" I asked.

"No." The subtle subtext of his monosyllabic monologue was obvious in his dour expression. I won't go into what I think Johnny Brashear thought of me at that moment. Suffice to say it wasn't very flattering. And I don't think my mother would have appreciated the canine reference. But I didn't hold it against him. He was having a pretty lousy evening.

"Take it easy," I said.

"I sure picked a lousy time to quit smoking," he said, growling at himself.

"When did you quit?" I asked, just to demonstrate my inexhaustible wealth of compassion.

"Four years ago."

That killed the mood. "Answer the door, Johnny."

The buzzing stopped, but was now replaced by knocking.

"Maybe it's Jehovah's Witnesses," he said. "Nobody else is this pushy."

"Except girl scouts."

"And those clean water freaks."

"There's no getting rid of those people."

"I thought you were one of them.*"*

"That hurts, Johnny."

He reached for the doorknob but didn't get very far. He had only turned the knob far enough to release the locking mechanism when the door shot open, knocking him off balance.

The good news was it wasn't any crew of religious zealots come to sell a little piece of their eternal paradise. Nor was it girl scouts bearing high-priced low-flavor cookies. It wasn't one of those environmental kooks. It wasn't any high-rolling matron of the arts and real estate power hitter -- with or without her creepy henchman and henchwoman in tow. It wasn't the two muscle-bound moving men come to even the score in a game whose very rules and regulations remained an indecipherable mystery to them. It wasn't even the local law come to serve arrest warrants to all of us on suspicion of committing various and sundry deeds of a particularly evil and miscreant nature, the details of which would have to be filled in as they became apparent.

It was none of these nightmares.

Unfortunately, it wasn't the pizza guy, either.

It was worse. It was Lita Wordstone, lit up on something with way too much caffeine in it. Her eyes had the flash of a crack-smoking headbanger in search of an all night blow.

She barged in, half falling into the room. She stumbled, regained her balance, then stopped to look back and forth between Johnny and me, as if she were trying to figure something out -- like, what I was doing there. Or who I was. But I didn't think so. Lita Wordstone didn't seem to make much of a habit of stopping to consider very many things. She just forged ahead on the strength of whatever might currently be the foremost inclination lingering in the Gratify-Me-Instantly segment of her psyche. And damn the consequences (which in her life seemed to reap effects eerily similar to those of warship torpedoes of yore). She scared me in all the worst ways, like a fantastic wave you're bodysurfing and all the while you can't stop thinking about the corral reef into which you're about to be slammed.

Life with Lita Wordstone.

She was wrapped in an enormous sand-colored trench coat. Probably something very expensive from England. Lined in plaid cloth, wind proof, water resistant. The way she held it closed in front made you wonder (okay, made me wonder) what she had on, or didn't have on, underneath. I made a mental note to myself: Grow up.

"What the hell do you want?" Johnny said by way of greeting.

At that moment, Jennifer came bursting in from the kitchen. On her hands she wore thickly padded oven mitts patterned in red and white checks, and she carried a large tray of cookies that had apparently just come out of the oven. Their aroma had replaced the lovely perfume I'd smelled earlier. We all stared at Jennifer for a moment.

"Cookies?" I said. "How nice."

"I told you we were baking," Johnny said.

"Where's my movie?" Lita said, interrupting our digression.

We all turned to her. "Your movie?" I asked.

She spun and looked at me. Again I wondered if she thought she recognized me from somewhere, but couldn't quite place me. She had that glazed half-there, half-not-all-there expression of a bewildered, hyperactive child who wants to blame everyone for shaving the dog when she herself was still holding the Remington electric in her trembling hand. Figuratively speaking. Her hands were currently buried deep in the pockets of the trench coat. No doubt sore from all the bell ringing and door banging they'd been doing.

"Who are you?" she asked, confirming my suspicions that she had the shortest attention span in the history of A.D.H.D., and whatever other letters went with it. L.M.N.O.P.?

"Oh, nobody," I said, with a slight smirk.

"What's he mean?" Jennifer asked, apparently confused about the substance of my answer. I was disappointed in her, but I didn't say so.

Lita Wordstone turned to Jennifer. "You!"

Jennifer blanched and took a step backwards. "What?"

Johnny stepped between them, just in case violence broke out, which seemed like a very real likelihood just then.

"Why doesn't everyone just calm down?" I suggested.

"I don't want to calm down," Lita Wordstone said. "I want my movie and I want it now."

I could hear her uttering the exact same phrase throughout her life, at different ages, substituting the phrase "my movie" with "ice cream," or "to go shopping," or "a trip to Europe," or "a new car," or "some candy." Maybe her parents should have named her Lola instead of Lita. Maybe they should have experimented in drug therapy.

"Take it easy, kid," Johnny said, and she turned on him.

In retrospect, I think that of the countless expressions in our rich lexicon of linguistic clichés and hackneyed bromides, Johnny's choice at that moment to go with "Take it easy, kid" was probably among the least advisable. It was gasoline to Lita's fiery temperament and it sparked her fury as no other phrase could have. I suppose something along the lines of, "Go piss up a tree you toady shit-eating troglodyte," might have done the job as well, but now we'll never know.

In a flash, the cozy living room erupted into a swarming hailstorm of viciousness and destruction. From the depths of her trench coat, Lita produced an ivory colored bowling pin with three red stripes painted around its base. She wielded it over head, holding it by its neck, and charged at Johnny, intent no doubt on braining him with it. "You dirty, rotten mother- ..."

"Stop it," cried Jennifer, lurching forward in an attempt to block the bowling pin attack with the aluminum cookie sheet. "You'll hurt him."

I thought about sharing with Jennifer the essential detail that inflicting hurt upon Johnny seemed to be the whole purpose of the exercise, and that pointing it out would only confirm that Lita was, in fact, on the right track and that she would therefore be encouraged to proceed apace with her frontal assault. Needless to say the opportunity to call such a time out and convene a meeting of the rational minded among us -- if I could find any -- did not present itself.

Instead, cookies went flying everywhere. I snatched one out of the air and took a bite. Waste not, want not. It was still warm. Chocolate chip oatmeal. One of my favorites. "Mmm, delicious," I said to no one in particular. No one in particular heard me. No one in particular answered me.

Lita was still swinging the bowling pin like a homicidal juggler who's lost two thirds of the original set. No wonder kids are afraid of clowns. Lita was trying to connect just once with Johnny's skull, as if one good shot was all she needed. I had no doubt it was. But, bless her pretty little heart, Jennifer had Lita successfully blocked. The two of them juked and jived, bobbed and weaved in a kind of frenetic modern dance whose choreography would have sent Georges Balanchine pirouetting in his crypt. There was quite a racket from the bowling pin hitting the cookie sheet over and over and over. Like the cheapest gong you've ever heard. Lately, nobody had been responding much to shots fired. I wondered if this clamor would bring out the cavalry. I had my doubts.

*The Farce News*

I looked around for Johnny. He was cowering behind a couch.

I put two fingers in my mouth and whistled, as if I were still back in my hometown trying to hail a cab on Lexington Avenue at five o'clock on a Wednesday afternoon in the rain.

All activity suddenly ceased and there was an eerie stillness in the room.

"Jesus Christ, knock it off!" I shouted.

To my surprise, someone responded, "Praise the Lord." It had come from not too far away. We all heard it and turned to one of the front windows. And there we spied Johnny Brashear's neighbor, the woman who'd called him a "high yellow Negro." She was peering in at us. She smiled and waved at me. I noticed a bundle of brochures in her hand. They looked an awful lot like the kind of pamphlets Jehovah's Witnesses carry around when they go door to door.

"Okay, people?" I said, turning to Johnny, then to Lita, then to Jennifer. "Are you satisfied now? Do you see how close we came? Another minute and she would have rung the doorbell."

Johnny ran to the window and pulled the shades down.

"Everybody just relax." I took the bowling pin from Lita. "Where'd you get this?"

"Miggie gave it to me."

"Mickey? Mickey who?"

"Not Mickey. Miggie. Miguelito. Miguel. He loved bowling."

"Yeah, well spare me the details."

Jennifer giggled. I spun around and looked at her.

"Don't tell me you actually got that one?"

She nodded and I wondered if she'd been pulling the wool over my eyes the whole time.

"Y'know," she said. "The details thing. Everyone knows there's no details in bowling."

"Jennifer," said Johnny. "Shut up. I'm begging you."

"And you!" Lita said, pointing at Johnny. "Where's my movie?"

"Lita," I said. She looked at me. I took her by the elbow and led her towards the front door. "I've got everything under control, okay? Please leave it to me. Or failing that, please just leave."

"I have a right to be here."

"Right now I need you to take your toys and go home."

"It's not a toy, it's a bowling pin."

"Have a nice glass of milk."

"I hate milk."

"Or a cookie."

"Chocolate chip?"
"Chocolate chip oatmeal."
"I hate oatmeal."
"Okay, how about you go pull some taffy."
"Ooh, I love taffy."
"Great. Whatever it is you do to entertain yourself when you're not tormenting me and the rest of the world, go do that. I'll see you later."
"And you'll have my movie?"
"Yes."
"Oh, goody," she said and twisted her face into a sickening grin. "Maybe we can watch it together and eat some licorice. I love licorice. Red or black. I don't care. Do you like licorice?"

I didn't answer. But that wasn't a broad enough hint for her. She just kept staring at me. "No," I said. "Not particularly."

"Do you have any brothers or sisters?"
"No."
"If you did, do you think they'd like licorice?"

I was edging Lita toward the door. It was all I could do to keep from shoving her out the door like some party crasher, which in many ways is exactly what she was. I hoped the neighbor woman would take an interest in her, maybe give her a little talking to. That would kill a couple hours. Give me a chance to wrap up this business with Johnny and Jennifer. "Be a good girl," I said, "and don't hit anyone else."

She turned and looked at me. Her eyes may even have come into focus. I couldn't really tell. "You're the man who thinks he's Sammy Sosa, aren't you? I think you're sweet. I like sweets. Candy is sweet. I like candy. Do you like candy?"

It was painful to see how her mind worked. In fact, just listening to her, my teeth began to ache.

I closed the door on Lita and turned to find Jennifer crawling around the room on her hands and knees, picking up chocolate chip oatmeal cookies and putting them back on the badly dented cookie sheet. I watched her for a moment. She looked damn good crawling around on all fours, even if it made me feel like a pig for noticing. I didn't like feeling like a pig. It made me feel bad about all the bacon I've eaten in my lifetime. Jennifer looked up and saw me watching her. She blushed a little, then shrugged.

"Hate to see them go to waste," she said. I thought about that and wondered who she planned to pawn the cookies off on. Johnny and me, maybe? I didn't know about Brashear, but as for myself I hadn't stooped so low yet that I was going to start eating cookies off the floor. Even if they were homemade chocolate chip oatmeal cookies.

In a few minutes the mess was cleared away. I tried to return to the salient points of our earlier conversation. "Now do you get it? Do you understand why you need to get the hell out of town? Do you grasp the breadth and scope of the grief someone like Lita Wordstone can cause you. And the bad news is she may be the least of your troubles. If you stick around."

They nodded in unison. I glanced at Jennifer to see if she was going to ask her special question. But this time she seemed to know what I meant without me having to spell it out.

"You know I wasn't there last night," Johnny said. "Twannie's house. You know I had nothing to do with that business."

I thought it over. "I'm not ready to make up my mind yet. I don't know for sure where you might have been last night. But if it makes you feel better, I don't think you killed Jefferson. Lita's your problem. She's holding a grudge. And Venus Edwards could be your problem, too. I haven't quite figured that part out yet. Which reminds me, Jennifer. Why is Lita so torqued off at you? You steal her man here?"

"No, nothing like that."

"Well, what then? You eat some of her candy without asking?"

She continued to hesitate. Johnny shrugged and gave her a nudge. "You might as well tell him."

Jennifer didn't want to say the words, but she finally managed to spit them out. "I'm the one who got her into ... you know, acting."

Oh.

"So, you ...?" I asked

She nodded, then blushed some more.

I wondered if Jennifer could be found among the cast of "Volley-Ball!" With all that pretty brunette hair, she was the wrong type. But with a little makeup and a wig ...

"Well that answers that. We still don't know for sure who else might be tangled up in this business. But whoever it is could take an active interest in you when it becomes common knowledge that you grabbed Twannie's merchandise."

Johnny thought it over and smiled. "Yeah, but for the moment, nobody knows about that except you and me and Jennifer, here."

"You left quite a trail when you hired those two steroid junkies."

The smile slid off his face like melting snow from the hood of a sun-baked automobile. "They won't talk."

"I hope you're right."

"They're too dumb."

I let it go. If Johnny wanted to believe he was safe, I wasn't going to waste time trying to convince him otherwise. "Okay."

"Okay."

"Okay," Jennifer said, chiming in, I guess, just to prove she got what everybody meant.

"Good," I said. I turned to Jennifer. "While Johnny here helps me load that box of videotapes, why don't you get started packing a couple of suitcases." I turned back to Johnny. "And before you leave town, I'd put some new locks on this place. Sew it up tight so nobody cleans you out while you're figuring out how to make your next move without getting yourselves killed."

"How do I get the computer?" he said.

"I'll give you the address and phone number of my rehearsal studio on Farmington Avenue. You can give me a call and come by for it."

"And how do I know you won't drop a dime on us? Call the cops?"

"I know what 'drop a dime' means, Johnny."

"Anyway ..."

"Think about it, in your copious free time. Add up all the reasons I might call the cops and weigh them against all the reasons I wouldn't and you'll probably sleep a whole lot better."

"He has been restless," Jennifer said, as if Johnny had already left the room, which he hadn't. Always trying to be helpful. Always failing miserably. You had to love her. Some part of me hoped Johnny did. Otherwise it would be a pretty cold and lonely winter coming up.

"C'mon, Johnny," I said. "Let's get the tapes."

We stood and had taken a step toward the door when the bell rang again. We all stopped. Johnny got a flustered look on his face.

"Shit! Not again."

From Jennifer: "You don't think she's come back, do you?"

I knew I should have taken away the bowling pin.

"This is ridiculous," Johnny said, full of piss and fire. "Man, I've had it."

He went to the door and opened it. I heard a woman's voice. It didn't sound like Lita. It said, "Hello, Johnny." Then, "Good-bye, motherfucker."

Johnny didn't answer, just staggered backwards and fell to the floor, his arms splayed out like a horizontal Christ, his eyes open, staring lifelessly at the ceiling where the plaster was cracking. A song in my head: "Was he afraid, was he afraid, was he all worn out by the end of the day? Did he have brown skin, did he make a good friend, did he ever get together with Magdelain?" Unless I missed my guess, Johnny Brashear was dead before he hit the floor.

*The Farce News*

## Chapter 16

"Oh, my God!" Jennifer screamed and ran from the room.

Johnny Brashear lay on the living room floor. His last words, it seemed, had proven prophetic. I envied him for that. Sure, he was dead and that was hardly an enviable position, but he'd taken a moment to deliver one final edict, and he'd been right on the money. I thought a man's last words should carry some weight. His certainly did.

I knelt beside him. He'd had it, all right. I could find no pulse, nor any breath in or out of his lungs. No movement in his eyes. My eyes fell upon the instruments of his destruction. To say I was surprised would have been something of an overstatement, even though my eyes have known to be goddamn lying bastards at times. But not this time.

Two rather large lawn darts were stuck firmly in Johnny Brashear's chest. One must have punctured his heart, killing him. His shirt was dotted with two small stains at the points of penetration, but the bleeding had already stopped.

So much to live for and now he was dead, just like the woman whose lucre he'd recently appropriated. A moment of reflection seemed to be required, so I posed the rhetorical question: what did Johnny Brashear have to show for his brief time on the planet? A couple of schemes to get rich quick (although not nearly rich enough nor quickly enough) and a pretty gal pal who would now have to fend for herself? His remarkably prescient parting words notwithstanding, it wasn't much of a legacy.

And what's worse, now I'd have to load the videotapes myself. Me with my bad lumbar.

Footsteps on the sidewalk snapped me out of my reverie and I ran from the house to give chase, damn fool that I am.

Night had fallen in the quiet Windsor neighborhood where Johnny Brashear and Jennifer Last Name Unknown had lived. It was dark under a half-formed moon. The temperature had steadily dropped. Still, a trickle of sweat formed on my brow as I took off down the street in pursuit of the fading footsteps of Johnny's killer. Sweat from exertion, sweat from fear, sweat from excitement, sweat from (d) all of the above. My brain tried to do a little miscellaneous filing as I ran along, but the drawers were all full, their contents had been shuffled and haphazardly replaced. I couldn't tell the difference between a shopping list and a tax return. Not much made sense.

Twannie Jefferson was dead. Johnny Brashear was dead. When someone comes along and starts plugging away at us with various weapons of destruction, it flies in the face of all that we hold to be socially acceptable and morally right. In any event, Johnny had enough to live for that his own sudden death must have constituted a major change in plans. I didn't know Johnny well enough to guess at his inherent capacity for spontaneity, but I'd guess this turn would push the limits no matter how skilled he was at going with the flow.

Twannie Jefferson was shot dead on her living room floor. Now Johnny Brashear lay dead on his living room floor, the reason for his murder as yet to be determined. Cause of his death: lawn darts.

What was the world coming to?

Who was it who'd asked me that very question so recently? Was it the daffy Lillian Buenavista while decked out in one of her ridiculous "therapeutic" costumes? And what had been the context of the conversation when she popped the rhetorical question?

I had other matters to consider at the moment. Johnny Brashear's killer was one quick-footed bugger. I soon regretted my decision to swap out sneakers for cowboy boots. They might be better for shit-kicking and cockaroach-in-the-corner hunting, but when it came to giving chase down dark streets in pursuit of homicidal maniacs, they were a poor choice. In my *Adidas* runners, I'd have tracked my assailant without hesitation. Now it was all I could do to register the retreating footsteps over the steady drum beat of my own pointy-toed footfalls, to say nothing of the timpani banging away in my head as my heart and lungs worked overtime to keep up with the rest of my body's selfish demand for oxygenated blood. I expected a load of adrenaline to pull into the station on the night train, but it was already overdue.

Meanwhile, we ran west toward Windsor Avenue, the killer and I.

There weren't many people on the streets, mostly kids. Teenagers in baggy pants and baseball hats they inexplicably wore sideways. They watched me with mild interest as I ran by. Obviously they didn't think I was the heat, or they weren't afraid of cops one way or the other, or they were too bored to be moved. In any case, they stood idly by as I raced past them. I heard one say, "Nigger can run," and I wondered if, like me, the guy was color blind.

After about three blocks I stopped to listen but I heard no footsteps. Only the rasping of my own breath. Sure, I can run. Just not indefinitely. I leaned against a wooden telephone pole to catch my breath. My heart was pounding but otherwise I felt good. I could probably take a little more of this action without bonking, but I was no hound dog. Like anyone else, I could track the sound of footsteps running on the sidewalk. If I lost my quarry for any reason, however, I'd be screwed. Down some dark alley? Screwed. Into a waiting getaway car? Screwed. Lost in the heavier traffic of human beings on Windsor Avenue? Screwed. So many ways to get screwed, and none of them any fun. What *was* the world coming to?

I bent over and put my hands on my knees. My breath was returning to normal, my heart rate was dropping out of the red zone. But it wouldn't last, for at that moment, I heard a whistle. Not a human whistle. Not some neighborhood guy signaling his dog to stop mauling the mailman. This was the unmistakable whistle of incoming. As in artillery. It was instantly followed by the dull thwap of one object embedding itself into another. I looked up. And there, stuck in the pole where my head had been a moment earlier, was a bright red lawn dart, with a couple of inches of its brass spike stuck in the wood, still vibrating.

I heard the footsteps again. Well, goddamn!

Before taking off once more in pursuit, I pulled the dart out of the telephone pole. Carefully, I took it by the plastic plumage and eased it into my jacket pocket. It was about eight inches long, from the tip of the dart to the back of the flights. It had a nice weight. This was no child's toy.

I ran.

At the next intersection I spotted my quarry. I could hardly believe my eyes. But what other choice did I have? The street light showered the killer in a hazy halo, and in my moment of recognition my heart sank. The beaded hair extensions provided an immediate source of identification. I never would have spotted her in her black leather if she'd simply stayed in the shadows.

And now, as I watched and caught my breath, she slowed her pace. She was a good deal younger than I. And very athletic. But the mad dash must not have been her strongest event. Oh, well. Nobody's perfect. I took off after her once more, now staying on the opposite side of the street, keeping her in my view, running along the grassy edges of front lawns to silence my footfalls, and ducking behind available parked cars as I tracked her. Even if she turned and glanced over her shoulder, I was confident she wouldn't immediately spot me. In a minute I pulled even with her, then ran ahead a few yards. She had slowed to little more than a casual jog. And then she stopped running altogether and began to walk, those lovely arms swinging at her sides, carefree, as if nothing in the world was amiss. I got about a hundred feet ahead of her, then (excuse the expression) darted across the street to her side. (I thought it appropriate to dart across the street, all things considered. If she'd gunned down Johnny Brashear in more traditional gangland fashion, perhaps I would have shot across the street. Don't know *how* I'd have gotten across the street if she strangled him, but thankfully I didn't have to waste too much time thinking about it. Anyway, if she was going to be different -- c'mon, lawn darts? -- then, damn it so was I.)

I concealed myself in the shadow of a mailbox and listened as her footsteps on the sidewalk grew louder. Then, as she drew even, I stepped into her path. She looked up, a little surprised. But she played it cool. She was radiant, no doubt from the thrill of the hunt, the rapture of her perceived escape, and finally the triumphant sense that she had made it. All was well. Mission accomplished. Cue the music. Role the credits. Turn up the house lights and start scraping juji fruits off the soles of your shoes.

She was just as beautiful as she'd been when I saw her on Monday attending to her boss at the card shop on Park Street. But now I'd seen her in a different light, engaged in another kind of service, dispensing violent retribution for untold sins committed against her boss. She was the ultimate loyal employee, unless there was more to it than that.

I probably should have been a bit more nervous. After all, here I was confronting a more or less cold-blooded murderer. Maybe I wasn't smart enough to be scared. Maybe I wasn't scared enough to be smart. Maybe some part of my brain figured she'd done all the killing her system could tolerate for one night and she'd be more interested in beating a hasty retreat than in racking up carcasses. *Yeah, but she just threw a friggin' dart at you, Einstein! And damn near nailed you.* Okay, so I guess it was back to me not being smart enough to be scared. Still, it could be argued that the third dart had only been meant as a warning.

"Yo, excuse me," she said, and began to walk around me. Not too good at bluffing, either.

I blocked her path again. "Hang on just a second," I said and withdrew the lawn dart from my pocket. "Didn't you drop this?"

I saw something resembling extreme distaste in her expression. And it was a huge letdown. To think, just twenty-four hours ago I'd been deeply in lust with this astonishing beauty -- without the benefit of a formal introduction or the advantage of even the briefest conversation. I'd been prepared to commit to a long and fulfilling relationship. But for her part, after meeting me only once, she was prepared to hate me enough to fire a lawn dart at my head. This was a record, even for me. But that's the kind of week I was having. Ever since I'd picked up those goddamn prescription Ray Bans first thing Monday morning, women seemed to find me loathsome with a growing frequency and increasingly deeper conviction (if I was wearing the damn things or not). I was thinking seriously about dumping the shades all together

*The Farce News*

and going back to my John Lennon rose-colored specs. Not that they'd brought him much luck.

"Yo, whatchoo want, be-yotch?" she said. Or rather snarled. She was catlike in many ways. I hoped I wouldn't be introduced to her claws.

I turned to see who might have snuck up behind me. There was no one there. We were still alone.

"Are you talking to me?" I asked.

"You de only be-yotch I see at the moment," she said, truculence in the extreme. "Be-yotch."

This was a new one for me. I'd been called a lot of names over the years, none of which could be found anywhere on my birth certificate, not even in anagrammatic form. Some of the names, while hurtful and insulting, had even been reasonably accurate, if only at the precise moment of their emotionally charged delivery. But this was in no small way bewildering. To say nothing of belittling.

For the second time in the last hour or so, I felt the pressing need to call a time out and review the official play book. For this, I knew, was the ultimate fourth-and-long dilemma. If I punted, the game would be lost. Then I'd be the guy nobody remembered in the morning. At least, I think that's what the current lexicon of sports clichés says about losers in general. The point was: if I didn't play this right and regain field position, tomorrow might not find me playing armchair quarterback, it might find me playing wheelchair quarterback, sucking Jell-O through a straw and wondering when my diapers were next going to be changed, and by which grim-faced, dispassionate stranger in white nursing home garb. I slammed the play book shut, snapped the imaginary chin strap on my symbolic helmet and trotted back out onto the existential grid iron where this metaphorical battle was fated to be waged, prepared to conduct warfare at its most savage, come what may.

My nemesis looked, in a word, bored.

"Yeah, yeah, okay. Now I get it," I said. "I think I saw this on Jerry Springer. Real tough. The whole macho-chick transformation thing. Complete with role reversal and gender re-identifcation. Impressive, but also extremely tedious after about thirty seconds."

"Man, whatchoo talkin' 'bout, be-yotch?"

"I'd say you're at about the fifteen second mark right now, Billie, so why don't you go ahead and rant and rave for a bit longer, try on all your favorite postures. Get it out of your system. Then we'll talk."

"How 'bout I kick your narrow white ass?" she said.

I shook my head. "I don't hit girls. And frankly, I don't think you can take me."

I certainly hoped she couldn't. That would be both painful and humiliating.

"Keep messing me with, be-yotch, and you gonna find out."

"Look," I said, holding up one hand in a "stop right there" gesture. In the other hand I showed her the lawn dart she'd recently hurled at my head. "You're not thinking straight. You don't want to go to jail without passing 'Go' and collecting two hundred bucks, do you?"

"Whatchoo talking about jail, be-yotch? I ain't did nothing."

I wished she would stop calling me that, but at the moment I couldn't think of a good way to tell her without sounding weak or whiny -- or giving her the idea it was getting to me. It was more irritating than hurtful, and of course, patently stupid.

"Well, okay," I said. "You just run along then. I'll just take this back to Johnny Brashear's place with me." I dangled the lawn dart in front of her. She eyed it greedily but didn't make a move to grab for it. "I'll hand it over to the police when they come. Then they'll have three. This one and the two you stuck in Johnny's chest. That will constitute a matching set. Maybe the cops will find a matching set of finger prints on them, too. What do you think are the chances? You think the police have such technology at their disposal? And what if those prints belong to somebody with a record? Think they can figure all that out and make a positive identification? Maybe even get some judge to sign an arrest warrant with your name on it?"

"Whatchoo want with me, be-yotch?"

"First of all, stop calling me that. You sound like a moron."

"Yeah, well fuck you."

"That's not much of an improvement," I said. "But it's better than be-yotch. More interactive, at least. My name's Robby."

"Yeah?"

"And you're Billie, right?"

She paused and thought it over before telling me.

"Billie Billie," she said.

I had to give her credit for saying it with a straight face and looking me dead in the eye to make sure I didn't laugh.

"What shall I call you? Miss Billie? Or just Billie?"

"Billie." She didn't get the joke and I didn't bother explaining it.

"Okay, Billie," I said. "What do you say we take a little walk."

"Where we walking to, be- ...?" She stopped herself. I smiled.

"My car's up the street. Let's get lost before somebody calls the cops to report an assault with a deadly lawn dart."

She fell reluctantly into step with me. I had no hold on her other than the threat to turn her in to the police, but it was enough at the moment. We

## The Farce News

didn't speak. It was nice to have a break from being called a be-yotch. A block or so from my piece of shit Jetta, we came across the same group of teenagers I'd raced past only a few minutes earlier. They watched us with vigorously renewed boredom. We must have made an attractive couple. Couple of *what*, I couldn't say.

"Yo, what's up, Holmes?" one of the teenagers said. He was going to play me, see if I was one of those white, middle class dweebs who's afraid of the brothers on sight.

I was about to respond with something clever and neutralizing about how he had me mixed up with some other white, middle class dweeb. "Inflation," I said. "Unemployment. Price of gas."

The brothers shared a look among themselves, perhaps trying to decide if I was fucking with them, or if they cared enough to do something about it if I was. One of them took a step toward us, apparently ready to punctuate his boredom with a little senseless violence.

Billie Billie stepped to the plate and faced the kid down with bunch of hand gestures and a tilted head. "Step away, be-yotch. This here ain't none of your *got*-damn bidness."

The kid had, if nothing else, great instincts. He backed off as if Billie Billie were conducting electrical current and he didn't want to fry.

"Have a nice night, fellas," I said, cheerfully.

As we passed, I heard the voice again, saying, "Nigger got some balls."

I don't know if the kid was talking about me or about Billie Billie. Either way, he had at least some of the relevant facts wrong.

We got to my car without further incident. I unlocked the driver's side door and held it open. "You handle a stick?" I asked Billie.

"I ain't into no dick, be-yotch," she hissed at me.

"Stick," I said. "Can you drive a stick shift? It's a manual transmission. Jesus."

"Oh," she said, sheepishly. "No problem."

"Good," I said. "Get in."

She got in. I climbed in on the other side and gave her the keys. I held the lawn dart between us, the sharp end pointed at her rib cage. I felt like an idiot. Wait til the guys in the band heard about this. They wouldn't believe a word of it. And I wouldn't blame them.

Billie Billie cranked the engine and listened for a second. Then she smirked. "Beater," she said.

"Yeah, it's no Lexus," I said, "but at least it isn't purple."

She gave me a dirty look and for just a second I thought maybe I'd gone too far. We didn't really know each other that well yet. Well enough perhaps for her to be comfortable hurling all kinds of epithets -- to say nothing of lawn darts -- at me. But not well enough, apparently, for me to offer a little good-natured dig here or there. Talk about your double standard. I just can't figure out women. And even if I could, what good would it do me?

"Where we going?" Billie Billie asked. I waited a second for her to punctuate the sentence with the customary "be-yotch," but this time it didn't come.

"Duncaster Road," I said. "I think you know the address."

She offered no response other than to twist the steering wheel and mash the clutch. And then we were off, into the night, a pair of strangers drawn together by crime, tragedy, violence and, well, lawn darts. A fugitive from justice and a half-wit amateur sleuth waltzing into a charge of aiding and abetting. I can't speak for Billie Billie, but I'd sure as hell had better weeks.

She handled the car with a combination of fluid grace and controlled fury. I understood the fury part well enough from driving the piece of shit Jetta around Hartford myself. I don't know how she pulled off the fluid grace. I guess that's how I suddenly knew I was in the presence of real talent. If I could get her to stop talking for a while -- or, specifically, to stop calling me "be-yotch" -- there was a chance, a small chance, I could fall in lust with her all over again, and maybe even win a little piece of her heart. Yeah, sure, said the little voice that taunts me from time to time. Keep dreaming.

"Ain't nothing for you there," Billie Billie said.

I turned and studied her profile, illuminated only be the dashboard lights. I wondered if she was referring to Twannie Jefferson's house or if she had somehow managed to read my mind regarding the acquisition of her affections. If it was the former, I had my doubts about the accuracy of her statement, for I still felt that the house on Duncaster Road held the answers to a handful of lingering questions. On the other hand, if it was the latter subject to which she referred -- that is, my silent musing on the subject of her elusive adoration -- then I completely bought the notion that there was nothing to be harvested (at least not tonight) from her dark and broken heart. I sat quietly and pondered this as she drove. She knew all the back roads and dark streets. I let her pick the route. We were headed in the right general direction. I didn't care how we got there.

After a while, I broke the silence.

"Would you mind telling me why you killed Johnny?"

Billie Billie made no immediate sign that she even heard my question. We drove another minute or two without speaking. I tried to understand her, to better figure out if she was just being rude, hadn't heard me, or was simply lost in a shattered world of her own. In the low light, I continued to study her profile. Her jaw was set. I expect she was in the midst of a tooth-grinding marathon, but the lines of her face remained soft. She hadn't lost her femininity despite the tough-guy front she put on. I felt like telling her she was beautiful and should consider dropping the hard-core biker-chick routine. But, really, it was none of my business.

So I kept my mouth shut. If it was an act, she was entitled to play it out. And if it was a legitimate lifestyle choice she'd made, maybe an option born of a direct response to some unknown stimulus, then I had no right to try to talk her out of it. If it was some self-protective mode she'd gone into and could no longer turn if off, who was I to play Dr. Freud with her (although I could have used the $150 per hour fee). In any case, it slowly dawned on me that this astonishingly beautiful and ornery woman, Billie Billie, was yet another carefully contrived character hiding behind an impenetrable facade. There seemed to be a lot of that going around lately.

"You already took care of Miguel Batista. Why bother with Johnny?"

If she had an answer, I wasn't about to get it wrapped in ribbons and bows. Barbed wire? Maybe.

We were almost to Twannie Jefferson's house when I tried one last time to shake her loose.

"You must have loved her very much."

Billie Billie slammed on the brakes. I shot out my hands to brace myself against the dashboard as the Jetta skidded to a stop. She turned to face me. With only the light of the instrument panel on her face, I could just make out the glint of tears in her eyes. Not the kind of tears that well up and flow down your cheeks and drip off your chin. These were shallow pools of sorrow which had collected like mourners outside a church after a funeral, in no hurry to disperse. Her jaw tightened again.

"We're not going to talk about that," she said. "Not now. Not ever."

There are times when hitting the nail on the head is just about as satisfying as hitting your thumb. This was one of those times.

## Chapter 17

Not ever. That's when Billie Billie said she'd talk about it. That was one hell of a declarative statement coming from a woman whose future now hung in a rather precarious balance.

I thought about it as she gracefully guided my piece of shit Jetta over the last mile or so of dark road up to LaTwanda Jefferson's dark house. There was another way of thinking about not ever. And that was, of course, never. Not only was that another *way* of thinking about it, it might well prove to be a good time to think about it. That is, never. What would be the point, after all? Billie Billie clearly didn't know how long not ever would last. Who among us has that particular gift of prognostication? Or wants it?

Furthermore, while we may attach egocentric expectations to the concept of not ever, we're usually hard-pressed to apply true values to such intangible notions of immeasurability. Not ever was when LaTwanda Jefferson was scheduled to come back to life and resume management of her successful if dubious import-export business on Park Street. Not ever was roughly the time Johnny Brashear was going to get over being pierced through the heart (not metaphorically by some *noir* blonde in stiletto heels, but quite literally, by a pair of lawn darts in the hands of a vengeful *noir* mulatto in black leather and hair extensions). Not ever was when I was scheduled finally to figure out women, how they work and why, and probably when I'd find one who could tolerate me over the long haul.

Sadly, not ever was also when Billie Billie was scheduled to prowl the earth again as a free woman. If I did nothing else tonight, I was determined to put Ernie Newman's ex-colleagues in law enforcement on the trail of this dangerously beautiful -- and tragically misguided -- murderess. Hopefully before she killed anyone else. Like me.

It chipped off a little piece of my heart to recognize that her life was pretty much finished, like the lives of Miguel Batista and Johnny Brashear. The only benefit to Miguel and Johnny was that they wouldn't have to do any more laundry, or have their teeth cleaned by some under-zealous government-provided dental hygienist with a water pick, or look over their shoulders every time they took a shower for the next twenty-five to life.

"If you change your mind," I said to Billie Billie in the darkness of the car, "I'm all ears."

She turned to me. "That ain't the body part you all of."

*The Farce News*

Oh, well. So much for reaching out to touch someone.

We got to Twannie Jefferson's house with no further conversation. Fifty feet down the road sat another vehicle with its motor running, its tail lights glowing red in the dark night. I recognized it immediately. A rusty black Dodge pickup truck. There's a million rusty black Dodge pickup trucks in the world, hundreds of them in the Greater Hartford area, no doubt. But only a few have a missing tailgate and only one I know of sports an *I Love Emmylou Harris* bumper sticker, with a red heart in place of the word *love*. Unless I missed my guess or there were, miraculously, two vehicles fitting this description, the pickup belonged to my neighbor, Jolie. I never expected to see it there. Not ever.

Billie Billie pulled my Jetta into the driveway and stopped with the nose of the car a couple of inches from the garage doors. If she had taken any notice of the rusty black Dodge pickup truck, she didn't let on. Instead, she cranked back the emergency brake lever, which I never do, and pulled the Jetta's keys from the ignition. I put my hand out and she sullenly dropped them into my palm. We climbed out. As we did, the driver's side door of the rusty black Dodge pickup truck opened. The interior light came on for a moment, and Jolie hopped out. She didn't wave hello, or call "Yoo hoo," or offer any kind of formal or informal greeting. She simply strode up the road toward us, purposefully, a girl on a mission. I tried to guess what her mission could possibly be, but it was impossible without the benefit of some clues. Or coming attractions.

Billie Billie had turned at the sound of the truck door slamming. Even in the darkness, I saw her face harden, her posture stiffen.

"The fuck ...?" she mumbled. I ignored her for the moment.

We stopped and waited for Jolie to join us in the driveway.

She was dressed for camping in faded blue jeans, a red and green plaid lumberjack shirt, beat-up denim jacket with the cuffs turned up. She wore cowboy boots similar to my own, tan suede with low heels and pointy toes. She had a black and navy Mets baseball hat on her head, with the bill turned to the back. It gave her a tomboy carriage I rather liked, without hiding any of the attractive woman underneath. It fit her well, made her damn sexy as a matter of fact. In the time it took my brain to process all of this and become utterly sidetracked, a trap door opened in my frontal lobe and I completely forgot to ask the obvious question; that is, what the hell was she doing here?

"Before you ask me what the hell I'm doing here," she said, "I got a phone message."

"Who from?" I asked.

"Guy named Sully."

"Sully!"

"Left a message. Said he was a friend of yours."

"That's a bit of a stretch."

"Said you needed me. You weren't home when I knocked."

"Yeah, it's this business ..."

"He said it was important. I wasn't sure where to look. Figured this place was as good a place as any to start."

"I'm impressed," I said. And bewildered. (I didn't say that part.)

"Anyway, here I am."

"Wow," I said. "How long you been sitting there?"

"'Bout five minutes."

"Your timing's uncanny."

"Wait'll you see me dance the *bossa nova*."

Sully claims to have the inside track on everything going on in Hartford. I don't buy his line of shit. It could be argued he's just a lonely guy in an unnecessary wheelchair, afraid to go outside, with too much free time. But he's proven me wrong a couple of times, so I withhold final judgment. I don't know what he meant, telling Jolie I needed her. Was he trying to be funny? Or helpful? And what was she supposed to make of such a pronouncement, considering the source? How would anybody take it? And yet, here she was. No questions asked. So far.

Billie Billie cleared her throat. "You ladies wants to catch up on old times and shit, that's cool. But, me? Fuck it, I gotta bounce." She was back in character. I hadn't even heard the director call for quiet on the set, let alone "Action!"

I turned to her. "Hold on, Billie. You can't leave us now. We have unfinished business. Oh, by the way, Billie Billie, this is Jolie. Jolie, meet Billie Billie."

"Yeah, fuck all that," Billie Billie said. "We ain't got no bidness."

"Hey! In case you didn't notice, you've pretty much hit the jackpot for antisocial behavior. By my count, you're on the hook for at least two murders. Three if you count the teenager in Simsbury. Maybe there's stuff I know nothing about. Maybe you're habitually homicidal. Maybe you're a regular serial killer."

"Shee-it, I ain't no Ted Bundy."

"Good. Right now I'm more concerned with Twannie Jefferson."

"She dead. But I ain't did it."

"Yeah, I know," I said. "I'd sure like to know who moved her body."

"Why you care one way or the other?"

"Call it morbid curiosity. You know where she's being stashed?"
"What difference does it make?"
"That's the question, isn't it? Why? Why would anyone do it?"
"Why? Shit, why ain't nuthin' but a letter in the alphabet."
I stopped and stared at her for a minute. Steam was pluming from her nostrils. "Look, I'm not a complete idiot. I can put two and two together on the Miguel Batista business."
"Oh, you smart all of a sudden?"
"I know you ran him off the road, along with that other kid."
"Who says I did?"
"I do."
"Well that just shows you ain't know nuthin."
"You were driving the Lexus. I figure it was retaliation for Miguel gunning down your girlfriend."
"You best watch your mouth, be-yotch."
I put my hands up in mock surrender. "Hey, you want to go the diminished capacity route, it's up to you and your attorney. It's certainly worth a try."
Billie Billie scowled and blew some more steam out of her nose. She was beautiful when she scowled. I had a feeling she'd be beautiful with a mess of half-chewed linguine and clam sauce hanging out of her mouth. "I ain't got no attorney, be-yotch."
Again with the "be-yotch." Clearly we were regressing. I should have known that not ever was also when Billie Billie permanently would drop the belligerent act.
"If you want to make things a little better for yourself," I said, "you'll think about joining our little gabfest. As an active participant, that is, not as a mere observer. You have a lot to offer."
"Instead of that, why don't I just slap the shit outa you?"
I shook my head at her, then glanced at Jolie. She was giving me a look that said: "You gonna take that?" I shrugged at her and smirked.
"What do I do now?"
It was Jolie's turn to shrug and smirk.
"Don't take this the wrong way, Billie," I said, returning to my reluctant guest, "but you're starting to sound like a ninth grader who just doesn't grasp the concepts of trigonometry. I can certainly relate. Trig was never my best subject. But nobody's going to let you off the hook just because you're a sympathetic figure. I get it that you're pissed. Maybe you have good reason. But while you're out here kickin' ass and taking names, it's becoming increasingly clear that violence isn't the answer."

*The Farce News*

She glared at me and held up the middle fingers of both hands, the old double-barrel bird.

"Here's your fuckin' answer, white meat."

"Wow," Jolie said, talking to me as if we were alone. "Beautiful *and* classy. She must get all the dates to the prom."

Billie Billie remained in her pose, giving me the side-by-side finger. She had lovely hands. Not like those of the bony old man who'd been staggering along the shoulder of I-84 earlier this evening. The nails on her middle digits were neatly clipped and coated in a clear polish. "I'm sorry," I said. "Could you repeat the question?"

"By the way," Jolie said, "does anybody have keys to the house? Or are we just going to stand out here in the cold all night?"

Billie Billie shifted her sneer to Jolie. "Who axed you, be-yotch?"

"All I'm saying ..."

"Shoot, don't make me no never mind one way or the other," Billie Billie said, interrupting with a wave of her right hand. "Just stay the fuck out my face and we be cool. You feel me?"

Jolie turned to me. "Quite a mouth on her. I'll bet she was the valedictorian at juvy hall."

I shrugged. Jolie had a way of putting into perspective that which I was completely willing to overlook, based on a foolish testosterone-driven crush.

Billie Billie tilted her head to one side and pointed at Jolie. "Oh, no. Uh uh. I know you didn't just say that."

Jolie laughed out loud and I bit my tongue to keep from giggling.

"Ladies, please," I said, stepping slightly between them. It was turning into a full evening of fisticuffs. First, Lita Wordstone and Jennifer in a lightweight preliminary warm-up bout that ended in a frustrating double TKO that had the crowd screaming "Refund!" But, really, what choice did the judges have? Bowling pins and cookie sheets? Beyond ridiculous. The Marquis of Queensbury had to be doing the Ali Shuffle in his grave. Now it was about to turn into Friday Night At the Fights with a cruiserweight scrap between Billie Billie fighting out of the black leather corner and Jolie fighting out of the blue denim corner. The fact that it was only Tuesday seemed to have no impact on the speed with which hostilities were developing. And here I was playing Zebra In the Middle. Where the hell was my striped referee shirt when I needed it? Oh, yeah. I don't have one.

"Fuck all this," Billie Billie said, and came at me brandishing a pair of beautifully knuckled fists. Was there nothing ugly about this woman, other than what came out of her mouth? I looked over at Jolie and could hardly believe me eyes.

Jolie was a woman I'd known for a couple of years. Someone I considered to be a good friend, patient and considerate. And above all, patient. She adored my pets, which is more than a lot of my ex-girlfriends could say. She had talked me through some tedious breakups. I'd done the same for her, but I think the score was about 17-4 in her favor at this point. She didn't seem to have very many relationships, while I didn't have very many that lasted longer than a couple of weeks, or if I was lucky, a month or two. I always saw Jolie as a comfortable place to land after a rough flight (and history had shown I was a comparatively bad pilot). Anyway, I thought I knew her pretty well.

But I'd never seen her move as she did now.

Before Billie Billie could land the intended haymaker on my chin, assuming that's where she would have aimed her assault, Jolie stepped between us. As Billie Billie came with a right roundhouse, Jolie shifted to what looked like some kind of Praying Mantis martial arts stance, but without the funky hand gestures or the one-footed crane stance or the weird high-pitched Asian sound effects. Her weight was distributed more or less equally between the one forward foot and the other which stayed slightly back. Her arms came up in quick circular motions and before any of us knew what had happened, she had blocked Billie's punch with the outside of her left forearm and grabbed hold of Billie's arm, completely immobilizing her.

"Maybe you should rethink this strategy," she calmly advised Billie Billie. Her tone was remarkably neutral, a college counselor telling a high schooler with a C average not to pin his hopes on a Yale scholarship. "Maybe Robby won't hit a girl, but I have no such hang-ups."

"Yeah, be-yotch?" Billie Billie said, struggling to tear herself loose. It seemed to take forever to dawn on her that it wasn't going to happen.

Jolie brought her right boot forward and planted it in Billie Billie's midsection. Then, falling backward, she took a handful of her sleeveless leather vest in her right hand and flipped her into the hedge row that lined the side of the driveway. Before Billie Billie had even landed, Jolie was back on her feet, ready for whatever might come at her by way of a retaliatory counterattack.

With no clear role to play, I merely stood back and scratched my head in amazement. Just when you think you know someone.

Billie Billie wasn't finished. Not by a long shot. At least she didn't think she was. If she knew then what she was about to find out, she might have scrounged up a white towel and waved it in well-advised surrender. *"Mais oui!* But of course I geeeve up!" Unfortunately, Billie Billie didn't have the benefit of well-focused foresight or an academic understanding of French history. She had only the rage of the moment, so she charged like a little bull in black leather. Which was a bad choice.

With none of the pomp and ceremony of Lillian Buenavista's absurd toreador charade, Jolie lithely sidestepped her attacker, then kicked out the back of Billie Billie's right knee as she flew by. Consumed with hatred and frustration, Billie Billie climbed to her feet. Despite a pronounced limp -- one pronounced "Ouch, this shit hurts!" -- she began a shadow boxing routine that would have made Joe Louis proud, or blush, depending on how the Brown Bomber responded to girl fights.

Jolie was very serious now as Billie Billie circled.

I backed away to give them room. I had a sudden yearning for popcorn. But it's a fairly well established fact that I'm a pig.

In any case, there was no chance in the world I was going to get in the middle of this scrap. I don't break up girl fights. Not this one or any other one for that matter. I'd learned that lesson way back in sixth grade. (In fact, it was among the only lessons from that painful year that I've never forgotten it.) Along with about a hundred other shocked 11-year-olds I had watched Gerta Mae Olafsson, the 275-pound principal of our elementary school lose most of her yellow satin blouse and a fairly nice pair of horn-rimmed glasses when she attempted to break up a particularly nasty donnybrook between Danny Ortiz' sister, Yolanda, and LaMarr Watson's sister, Brooke, over who was the prettiest girl in school. In the ensuing wreckage, Yolanda lost three teeth and Brook took twenty-five stitches over her right eye, pretty much rendering the debate moot. On the other hand, our intrepid principal, Gerta Mae Olafsson (also known as Mrs. Loaf) required several weeks of treatment at the Payne Whitney psychiatric unit of New York Hospital. According to many who knew her well, she was never the same again. Certainly her outward appearance undertook a great shift. She took to wearing heavy jackets made of something resembling burlap and which she held in place with lengths of heavily knotted rope. These jackets gave her the look of an inflated shipment of hemp and made her the laughing stock of the school. Children can be so cruel. (To say nothing of vicious in a street fight.)

Now, Billie Billie jabbed with her left fist and tried to land a few rights. Jolie easily dodged them, all the while trying to talk Billie Billie down off her emotionally charged ledge, to no avail. They circled and sparred. I fought off the urge to go find snacks. Billie Billie trashed talked, called Jolie all sorts of unfriendly names. Jolie just watched and stayed out of reach of Billie Billie's slashing punches.

"This is a bad idea," Jolie said, calmly. "It won't end well."

"Yeah, be-yotch," Billie Billie said. "For your narrow white ass."

Jolie looked over at me and smirked. "Do I have a narrow ass."

I shrugged and smirked right back at her.

Frankly, I was growing a little weary of Billie Billie's recalcitrant ethnocentricity. It was beginning to tarnish the luster of her otherwise impeccable nature. Okay, maybe that's a bit of a stretch. But I might have been a little blinded by her inexpressible beauty. At the moment I was also quite distracted by Jolie's categorically expressible derring-do as well as her astonishing equanimity in the blistering heat of battle.

And just like that, Billie Billie suddenly seemed to lose her patience. Without warning she lunged wildly at Jolie. Another big mistake. Jolie calmly stepped back, took Billie Billie by the right wrist and deftly turned the hand backward at an angle that didn't seem humanly possible. Billie Billie was looking at her own palm as if for the first time ever. If it hurt, which I figured it must, the level of pain was such that it effectively sucked all the wind out of her lungs, rendering her incapable of screaming out, which was probably just as well. Instead she collapsed to her knees, grimacing and gasping for breath. Jolie maintained the pressure on Billie Billie's wrist with her left hand, then moved her right hand to a spot just below and behind Billie Billie's ear, and pressed. Hard. I'd never seen a more benevolent act of kindness in my life.

Billie Billie didn't make another sound. Like a baby who's stayed up past her bedtime, she stopped struggling and suddenly dropped off to sleep. Right there in the driveway. As consciousness vanished, so did the aggression in her face.

Jolie laid her down gently. "She's pretty."

"When she isn't awake."

"Or talking."

I shrugged. "If you go for that type."

Jolie looked up at me and laughed. "You're so full of crap."

"C'mon," I said, feeling transparent and superficial and shallow, but mostly transparent. "Let's get her inside."

We carried Billie Billie to the front door. She seemed very light. Under a hundred pounds. I scurried around back, let myself in through the sliding doors on the rear deck, and unlocked the front door for Jolie. For all her talk, Venus Edwards not only had neglected to change all the locks on the Duncaster Road house, she hadn't even bothered to lock the back doors. Unmitigated arrogance on her part, figuring she'd scared me off sufficiently with her veiled threats. We carried Billie Billie to one of the living room couches and put her on it. Jolie went to the kitchen and came back with two lengths of rope. I didn't talk her out of it when she hog-tied Billie Billie's hands and feet. I'd seen enough fighting for one night. When she came out of her current stupor, Billie Billie would be one pissed-off assassin. For her, the game was now officially over. Five for fighting, 10 for killing Miguel Batista (and the Simsbury kid), another 10 for doing Johnny Brashear, and a game misconduct for calling me a be-yotch. Gone. Suspension to follow. She had played with her heart instead of her head, and now, right or wrong, she'd have to pay the price for her impetuous-slash-homicidal predilection for wreaking havoc. You just can't go around running people off the road and sticking lawn darts in people's chests. There are rules of conduct and Billie Billie had broken them at a world record pace. I shared Jolie's unspoken reasoning that it would be a good idea for this beautiful hothead to be physically restrained when she came around, just in case she got a little crazy.

When she was finished knotting the ropes, Jolie took a small leather wallet from the front pocket of Billie Billie's sleeveless jacket. She opened it and took out a driver's license. She grunted. "Says her name's Willemina Williams. She's twenty-two years old."

"A kid."

"Willemina Williams? Some name."

"Billie Billie."

"Go figure."

I left Jolie to watch over Sleeping Beauty and headed straight for the basement. I'd been waiting for this opportunity all day. I expected the phone to ring, or the doorbell to chime, or the roof to fall in. But none of that happened. Maybe my luck was changing. The door to the cellar was in the kitchen where I expected it to be. No one had moved it. If only Twannie Jefferson were so lucky. The door wasn't locked. I opened it and a cool draft washed over me. I flipped on the light switch just inside the door. The stairs were polished wood. The walls on either side of the steps were covered with framed photographs. Twannie Jefferson alone. Twannie Jefferson with others who looked just like her. Family, no doubt. They all kind of looked like James Brown, the king of soul. Even the men. There were photos of Twannie and others who weren't family. I recognized some of them. There were pictures with Jennifer and photos with Lita Wordstone. There was one with the late Johnny Brashear. Just a nice little community of petty thugs, all playing nicely together until one of them decided they wanted to be the new king of the hill and suddenly all manner of ugliness had broken out. That's what comes of leaving the kids home without a baby-sitter. Another photo showed Twannie with Venus Edwards at some fancy function, some kind of theater opening. Everyone dressed to the nines, except some guy in the background who wore a big yellow cowboy hat that looked like it was made out of straw.

*The Farce News*

I went quickly down the stairs. The basement was a good deal cooler than the rest of the house and I soon discovered why. A lovely bentwood rocking chair sat in the middle of the room with small Shaker tables on either side, and a gooseneck floor lamp shining its mellow light from over the left shoulder. A large free standing television against one wall was turned on. The sound had been turned down low. I looked quickly at the screen.

It was bowling, of all things. Professional bowling.

The quiet whirring sound which emanated from the console suggested the show was a video tape.

Jesus, how perverted can you get?

There are two spectacles I had vowed never -- that is, not ever -- to watch on television, no matter how desperate for entertainment I might become. One was bowling, be it professional, amateur, or performed by blindfolded chimpanzees on Thorazine. What was bowling, after all, but a pointless repetition of an inherently stultifying activity, aiming one object at a series of other objects all lined up ready to be knocked down by the first object? Now, if they could get the pins to *move* while the bowlers rolled the ball at them, that might be fun to watch, or at least interesting. In its present form, however, no way. The other spectacle I had sworn to avoid at all cost was the exclusive in-depth interviews, which seemed to number in the thousands, of disgraced and defrocked newspaper reporters who'd been shit-canned for fabricating stories and who then made millions of dollars, ironically enough, writing books about their painful ordeals. *Oh, the poor fucking dears.*

I turned away from the bowling.

At the moment I wasn't particularly interested in what was playing on the TV screen. I was just happy it wasn't more volleyball. I was much more curious about the occupant of the bentwood rocking chair, whose eyes were wide open and who, though I knew this could not be, appeared to be watching the prerecorded bowling competition. My mind reeled with the grave coincidence of the situation, for this was precisely how I thought *I* would turn out if I were ever forced to watch bowling on television. Which is to say, stone cold dead.

It was, of course, LaTwanda Jefferson in the flesh -- the stone cold dead flesh. She was wrapped in a flowing purple robe that didn't seem to be keeping her very warm. On the other hand, I didn't hear her complain. I wondered (if only in passing) whether she'd really been shot to death after all. What if she had expired as a result of the transcendent soul-killing boredom wrought by watching the Professional Bowlers' Association championship, and Miguel, as an agent of the PBA -- after all, he loved bowling, did he not? -

- had only shot her to cover up the true cause of death, to prevent the bowling industry from shouldering the blame for yet another senseless death-by-boredom. God knows what that would do to their reputation, to say nothing of their TV ratings.

I shivered.

At least now I knew why the heat had been turned off.

I walked the perimeter of the basement, examining the workmanship. The room had been skillfully remodeled and tastefully decorated, if you absolutely had a thing for purple and no other color would do. There were a couple of doorways. One led to a furnace room with a standard water heater and an electrical fuse box. I tapped the sheet rock walls and found the studs at sixteen inch intervals. According to code. No short cuts here. No cheap labor. This was good and bad. It meant if there was a secret storage room, I might have a hell of a time finding it.

Ten minutes later I was beginning to think I wasn't up to the job.

On the television screen, some tall, painfully thin lefty with a nine-inch neck, an Adam's apple the size of a cocoanut, and a handlebar mustache that reached down past his jaw line, was staring over the top of his blue and silver speckled bowling ball. He wore a black leather wrist brace on his throwing hand. It had naughty S&M fun written all over it. He seemed to be sharing some intimate moment of mental telepathy with the ten pins arranged neatly at the far end of the alley. I could just hear him talking to them in that special way only a trailer park bowling champ could. "I'm a gonna git ya, ya garl dang motherfuckers. All nine a y'all."

I couldn't take the suspense. I picked up the remote control on the table next to Twannie Jefferson's rocker and started hitting buttons. The STOP button didn't work. It refused to kill the bowling tape. I tried the PAUSE button. Nothing. I jammed my thumb into the EJECT button, hoping against hope. No luck. I mashed EJECT and PAUSE together, desperate to get the damn show to stop. While it did nothing for the television or the VCR unit, it wasn't totally without effect. A panel in the wall behind the television suddenly started to slide open. It barely hissed. I walked over and let my amazement build up a head of steam. Fluorescent tubes flickered and came on although I'd triggered no obvious light switch.

The room beyond the false wall was large and spacious. The walls were lined with floor-to-ceiling metal shelves and storage racks. On them I found hundreds of boxes of chocolates from all over the world. Turkey, Egypt, Singapore, Nigeria, Croatia, Libya, Iran, and even Iraq, although it was my understanding that we currently had some kind of trade embargo with Iraq. I found several cases of Iranian caviar. Yeccch. And twenty large boxes of

Canadian maple taffy. I thought about Lita Wordstone and her insatiable sweet tooth. In another section, I came across a lifetime supply of tea from Uganda. Uganda? The land of Idi Amin, brutal dictatorships and recreational cannibalism. I wondered how their tourist board was faring. Probably not too well. More to the point, I was pretty sure the U.S. State Department didn't even have diplomatic relations with that particular country. I'd have to check it, though. Elsewhere, I discovered a giant humidor the size of a small bank safe. It was filled with Cuban cigars of all variety and flavor, and all of them illegal. The climate-controlled room also contained a number of clothing racks, on most of which there hung all manner of furs and skins. More of the same Norwegian seal furs I'd seen in her bedroom closet. Another no-no.

Twannie Jefferson had been very busy. Into all kinds of action.

But now she was dead and her punishment seemed to be to spend eternity watching old bowling shows on videotape.

I'd take Hell over this brand of torture any day of the week.

I went back out, took up the remote control again and hit the EJECT and PAUSE buttons. The lights in the secret room went out and the wall slid silently back into its original position. The seams were invisible to the naked eye. Bob Villa and Norm Abrahams would have been impressed.

There wasn't anything I could do for Twannie Jefferson at this point. Hell, I couldn't even figure out how to turn off her damn television. There was no electrical cord connecting it to the wall -- which I added to the list of things that made no sense. I left it alone and went back upstairs, turning off lights and shutting doors behind me as I went.

Jolie was in a chair near the no-longer-sleeping beauty, Billie Billie.

"Find anything interesting?

"You wouldn't believe me if I told you," I said. Then I told her. She said she didn't believe me. I said I didn't blame her.

"I'm sorry, Billie," I said. "There isn't much I can do for you now other than to put you in the hands of people who, at least, won't try to kill you."

"Don't do me no favors," she said. Still hard core, and now an ingrate as well. I was almost ready to abandon my adolescent crush.

I went to the purple telephone on the table beside the couch where Billie Billie was sprawled. I punched in a series of numbers and waited. When the connection went through, I said: "Ernie, it's me. Write down this address and get out here as fast as you can. I found Twannie Jefferson. I've got a girl here who goes by the name of Billie Billie but it's really Willemina Williams. You might want to get your friends on the Hartford P.D. to check her out. She's the one who killed Miguel Batista, and earlier tonight she put a pair of lawn darts in Johnny Brashear. Needless to say, he didn't take it very well.

Do me a favor, Ernie. Hurry. I'd just as soon you got here before the Bloomfield cops storm the bastille. Something tells me they're gonna want a piece of this action."

I recited the address and hung up the phone. Then I collapsed on the couch opposite Billie Billie.

"Sorry, kid," I said.

She snarled beautifully at me. "Fuck you, be-yotch."

I looked over at Jolie. She shrugged at me and smiled. Jolie has a killer smile.

"Ever think you'd end up spending the evening this way?"

"Never," she said.

I nodded. "Me either." Not ever.

And it wasn't over yet.

*The Farce News*

## Chapter 18

It was late Tuesday night, nearly midnight, when we pulled our two-car convoy to the curb in front of the state courthouse. The streets of Hartford where nearly deserted, just the way I like them. Ernie had agreed to act as liaison between me and my prisoner, if you could call her that, and one of the Assistant State's Attorneys. It was time for Willemina Williams, who was in a fractured state of disbelief and denial, to be turned over to the State of Connecticut. I wondered if I'd miss her in the aftermath of our whirlwind relationship. I had my doubts. If nothing else, it would be nice not to have someone call me "be-yotch" every 23 seconds.

Ernie made a call, got the prosecutor he wanted and arranged the meet. I went along for the ride.

The Assistant State's Attorney was a good-looking former street cop in her mid-forties. Ernie said she'd cut her law enforcement teeth with the Los Angeles Police Department. Now she wore expensive suits and cut her hair in the style of a page boy. Ernie told me she went by the name of Dee Dee McCool. She hated her first name, which was Daisy (who could blame her?), and despised her middle name, which was Delores (poor kid), even more. Her last name made up for it though. She'd started her criminal justice career as a radio car patrol officer in the Hollywood division. In fifteen years on the job, she steadily climbed the ladder through Vice, Arson, and Fraud on her way to a gold shield and a slot in Robbery Homicide. While others around her reached positions of middle and upper management, she achieved the rank of sergeant but could advance no further (through no fault of her own -- short of lack of male plumbing). Instead of signing up for anymore LAPD tests she went back to school. On the day she graduated from the law school at UCLA at the age of thirty-five, she filed her retirement papers and moved three thousand miles east. She took the Connecticut bar exam, passed on her first try and soon thereafter joined the Connecticut Division of Criminal Justice in the Office of the Chief State's Attorney. She'd been there ten years now. According to Ernie, she was having a hell of a time. Ernie said she was trustworthy and his word was good enough for me. He also said she was a killer prosecutor, so to speak, with a conviction rate of about ninety-seven percent. Ernie said she didn't give a second thought to the scumbags she sent to prison, but agonized long and hard over the ones who walked thanks to their scheming scumbag lawyers. She once told Ernie the worst day of her

*The Farce News*

adult life was the day Orenthal James Simpson walked.

Ernie Newman had more actual experience transporting prisoners (certainly more than I, who until tonight, had none at all), so he drove the lead car, with Billie Billie shackled in the back seat. I followed in my piece of shit Jetta, just to make sure he got where he was going in one piece. Jolie went home before Ernie got to Duncaster Road. I thought it better to keep her out of the mix once the law got involved on an official basis. She didn't argue the point, but neither did she behave like someone who was all that worried about answering to any beleaguered ex-cops or hot shot prosecutors. What had she done, after all, other than subdue a fugitive double-homicide suspect with a couple of moves anyone could plainly see were executed in self-defense? They should be thanking her, no? Good questions. Still, I'm glad she didn't hang around to ask them.

Ernie made record time getting to Twannie Jefferson's place, pushing his hideous brown Pontiac to its mechanical limits, and no doubt running every light along the way. Still, it was a long wait and I half-expected the Bloomfield cops to kick down the doors at any time and haul us off to the slammer, or for the Windsor cops to arrive en masse with billy clubs and pepper spray. They would have to get a tip on the Johnny Brashear killing pretty soon. Guys just don't get lawn darted to death without the cops hearing about it, even if lawn-darting a guy to death doesn't make much actual noise. Once they caught the squeal and started poking their noses around, how long would it be before Jennifer spilled what she knew -- provided she was able to articulate at least some of it coherently? On second thought, Jenny might slow them down quite a bit.

Ernie sized up the situation quickly. The cop in him came to the fore and he shifted modes to all business. I showed him the basement shrine where Twannie Jefferson sat gazing sightlessly at the World Championship of Bowling -- the only way, in my opinion, to watch bowling. I also revealed the hidden wall panel, the hidden room behind it, and the hidden cache of illegal treasure stored therein. He looked without touching anything, then said, "Close it up, Robby." And that was it.

Ernie and I went out to the kitchen and he listened as I gave an admittedly bare bones recap of the events of the last two days. Some of it he already knew. He identified these bits by saying, "Yeah, yeah, I know that part already." Some of it was news to him, and he indicated his surprise with such comments as, "Yeah? That's news to me," and "No shit, huh?" Some of it he never learned because I left it out of my monologue.

To lie or not to lie, that wasn't the question. To skip over some parts, that *was* the solution, at least for the time being.

*The Farce News*

I didn't bother to tell him about Lita Wordstone's surprise visit to Johnny Brashear's place or the fact that she arrived armed to the teeth (or, in true bowling-related trailer-trash terms, armed to the tooth), wildly brandishing a potentially lethal 10-pin, or that she clearly had violence and revenge in her cold, rich heart. It was too absurd a development to repeat without making this entire business seem conclusively untoward and embarrassing. I also left out any mention of the rich broad, Venus Edwards, who owned the house in which LaTwanda Jefferson had lived and died. While she appeared to play some role in this fractured drama, it remained as yet to be determined exactly what that role was. I hoped it was nothing more sinister than perhaps usher or ticket taker. Since I hadn't figured it out, I didn't see the benefit to anyone if I spilled this particular can of beans.

"You should get some rest, Robby," Ernie told me. "You look like ten miles of bad road."

"Thanks."

"I'll smooth things with Dee Dee. She'll be hacked off about you withholding evidence from last night's killings and running with a fugitive tonight, but don't sweat it. When I hand her the keys to this little killing machine" -- he nodded to Billie Billie, seated silently on the couch -- "and tell her the story and she sees how it wraps up all neat and nice, maybe she'll forget to be pissed."

"That would be nice."

"Just remember, what they like best around here is clearing cases. Putting criminals in jail and moving on to the next pile of human garbage."

It was simple to go along with Ernie. He knew the system and how best to manipulate it. He knew the rules and how to bend them. I didn't want any face time with any Assistant State's Attorney, even if Ernie vouched for her. I liked what little anonymity I had and wished to hold on to it for as long as possible. A meeting with Dee Dee McCool was bound to go badly, providing no chance for me to make a good first impression. She'd play hard ball with me, and I'd soft soap her. Maybe I'd get first base on a wild pitch but maybe we'd both slip in the shower and break our necks. In any case, it wasn't a promising match up.

Furthermore, I didn't feel like wasting a bunch of time defending myself against the idle threats of some knee-jerk law enforcement hack bent on breaking my balls just because I had played a little fast and loose with the rules. Like Ernie always did. They weren't going to make me squirm, not based solely on their ability to intimidate and brow beat. I do have some pride.

"If your friend wants to have a pissing contest with me, tell her to bring it," I said. "Tell her I'd love to talk to her, and maybe the newspapers, too, about Twannie Jefferson's home style supermarket for illegal merchandise, how she ran it right under the noses of Hartford's finest. No offense. Maybe your friend can explain how the city cops knew all about it and did nothing, or how they knew anything about it in the first place."

Ernie stared at me. His expression grew a little hard at the edges.

"Which newspaper? *The Farce News?* Nobody reads that rag."

Before we left, Ernie sat down next to Billie Billie on the coach where she remained hog-tied. She was still a bit groggy, but as harshly uncommunicative as ever. Ernie was exceedingly patient, almost fatherly, clearly playing the part of The Good Cop. I thought it an odd strategy considering there was nobody on hand to play The Bad Cop, unless he expected me to jump in with the hostile threats and imprecations, which I was neither prepared nor willing to do. He asked a few basic questions. Her name. Her connection to the resident of the house. How she came to be in Windsor with a set of lawn darts. Did she like spaghetti? Where she got her charming tattoos. Did she prefer light beer to taste great or be less filling?

Billie Billie said nothing. At one point she cleared her throat, but then only sighed.

After a few minutes of this, Ernie got up. "Guess you'll talk when you're ready," he said.

Billie Billie hadn't been Mirandized and Ernie wasn't officially on the job anymore, so it wasn't as if a confession at this stage was going to carry much weight. She was too fuzzy headed even to call him any of the foul names she'd hurled at me. I found her newfound silence to be truly golden.

We drove downtown without incident. Billie Billie never made a move. With her hands cuffed behind her back and her ankles shackled in chains, she'd have had to pull a major Harry Houdini escape act to get loose. And then Ernie would have had to beat her down. It occurred to me that, had she somehow gotten free, thus forcing Ernie to put the thumbscrews to her, I'd have ended up as the only one all night who didn't get a chance to take Billie Billie down the hard way. The irony left me embittered. Here I was, bent sideways with a schoolboy crush, and everyone but me gets to wrestle her to the ground. The world is so unfair.

A Hartford Department of Corrections car was parked in front of the courthouse when we got there. Ernie and I helped Billie Billie out of his hideous brown Pontiac and into the police car without banging her head. She didn't say thank you or anything. I shrugged. I was so over her.

"Go home and get some rest," Ernie said. "I'll call you later."

I climbed back into my piece of shit Jetta, but I didn't go home. Instead, I circled the block and headed back for Windsor. There was hardly any traffic and I made good time getting to East Barber Street. The teenagers I'd encountered earlier were nowhere to be seen and the street was quiet. No police were visible in front of Johnny Brashear's place or in it, no unmarked cars seemed to be staking it out, waiting for some unenlightened criminal to return to the scene of the crime. (Would I have seen them if they had been?) I pulled to the curb a few houses away and watched for a minute, just to be certain. No lights burned in the house. I drove down the street, turned the car around and parked directly across the street from Brashear's driveway.

A concrete path led around to the back of the garage where I found a side door. It was locked, but the mechanism was old and the wood around it was dry and brittle. I leaned heavily into it, twisted the knob, and it gave up without a fight. The garage was dark. It dawned on me that I was now a true burglar. For the first time, I was legitimately guilty of breaking and entering. Where was Venus Edwards to gloat and say, "I told you so"? A thousand miles away, I hoped.

Unlike Twannie Jefferson's immaculate carport, this one was a mess. The boxes brought from Park Street by Johnny's movers were here, but they were carelessly arranged, as if thrown down without any regard for their size, their shape, or their contents. By the dim light of a street lamp which shone through a row of small windows built into the main garage door, I searched for the box marked "Sports Videos." It wasn't hard to find. Of course, it was one of the biggest and heaviest.

As quietly as I could, I moved boxes around so I could drag the heavy box to the side door. I dead- lifted it off the ground and muscled it across the street to my car. I managed to open the trunk and lower the heavy box into it without dropping it, or wrenching my back, or suffering a double hernia.

I sat in the car for a moment, catching my breath and watching the house for any sign that Jennifer might still be in there hiding. I wondered if Johnny was still in there, too. Dead people had been disappearing from their death scenes with remarkable regularity lately -- LaTwanda Jefferson's one-time vanishing act made it regular enough for me. And I knew that as soon as Ernie got around to telling Dee Dee McCool about Billie Billie and the lawn darts, she'd have the local cops swarming. For all I knew, they were already on their way.

There may be a hell of a lot of boozing and carousing that goes on in the music business, as well as a fair amount of other behavior one might, at best, call adolescent. But on the whole, there's quite a bit less gun play. Indeed acts of random violence tend to be fairly few and far between, except perhaps among the 12-year-old girls at Kiss concerts. In any event, I was genuinely beginning to miss the relative timidity of the bar scene, with its dim lights, thick smoke and loud, loud music. And missing the bar scene is something I never do. Not ever.

I fired up the Jetta and idled slowly up the street. Turned south at the end of the East Barber and began to pick up speed. A block later, I heard sirens in the distance. I wondered if they were headed for Johnny's place. I didn't stick around to find out.

The streets remained deserted and I made it back to Hartford without being pulled over. I drove the last few blocks to my apartment on Summit Street with a sense of having successfully run some invisible (but no less deadly) gauntlet. A few late-night stragglers wandered aimlessly along dark sidewalks. A couple of teenagers trying to break into a black Honda Accord ran off when they saw my headlights. An HPD sector car idling at the corner contained a couple of snoozing patrol cops. I wondered if they were friends of Ernie Newman. Somehow I doubted it.

There was an open space a block from my apartment house. I parked the car and walked back, feeling a weight dragging at me. It was the millstone of anticlimax. The moment of letdown that accompanies completion-without-closure. Like playing the last note of the last song of the last set, when the house lights come up and the party's officially over. That moment when those lucky enough to have companionship find their way to private encounters and the rest of us slink off into the night, disheartened, discouraged, lonely. It's closing time, the fun and games are over, the adventure is complete, and hopefulness is unfulfilled. And what's worse, there's nobody to sit around with and recount what (and sometimes who) went down. I couldn't identify exactly what was bothering me about this whole affair, other than the people in it and their collective knee-jerk proclivity for choosing violent resolutions to every dispute, large or small. Maybe Ernie was right. Maybe I just needed some sleep. I staggered to the door, fumbled for my keys and let myself in.

Outside my apartment door, on my "No habla Englais" welcome mat was a folded copy of *The Farce News*. Still warm. I picked it up and tried to focus my weary eyes on the front page. The date on the masthead was for the following morning, which made no sense at all, as *The Farce News* had always come out on Friday, not Wednesday.

The headline chilled my blood.

## HARTFORD HOODS TRY FOR TYCOON'S FAMILY FORTUNE

The story carried no byline, but that was Sully hiding behind the old "By the Editors" scam, his way of entertaining himself at everyone's expense. He was the editor. Everyone knew that. The only editor. I tossed it on the kitchen table next to Twannie Jefferson's purple *iMac*, which would have to be brought to Assistant State's Attorney Dee Dee McCool sometime Wednesday. Johnny Brashear sure as hell wasn't going to need it, and I doubted Jennifer, the pretty brunette, had the brain power to make much use of the computer, other than perhaps as an oversized paperweight. It was time to divest, to put this sordid debacle behind me.

Buddy and J.D. swarmed around my ankles. I spooned out some tuna for them and they retreated. Rufus came over and wagged his tail so hard he knocked over a kitchen chair. I fed him, too. Then I took him out for a short walk. And all the while my mind wandered, drifting, wondering what the hell Sully was up to.

I don't make a habit of reading *The Farce News*. It's my basic opinion that city news (regardless of the particular city in question) usually doesn't amount to much more than a postmodern rendition of *Much Ado About Nothing*. Sully may have been trying to do good work, but I wasn't very interested in his subject matter.

A year or so back, the self-proclaiming nonpartisan state legislature had gone to war over a budget which, after months of contentious debate, contained a considerable "area of disagreement." That was how the politicians themselves had characterized it. The dispute arose in the form of a two hundred million dollar gap. Sully published an article in which he identified the legislators as hypocrites and suggested they put their special interest back room deals aside and consider the needs of Connecticut citizens for once in their miserable lives. They more or less told him to shut up and go away. That was their first mistake. Sully responded by launching a privately funded investigation of the key players involved in holding up the budget resolution, determined to find out who was protecting what, and why. If there was a logjam, he planned to be the dynamite that broke it apart. He compiled the curiously inconsistent voting records of all concerned, chronicled their surprisingly voluminous police records (a staggering portion of it DUI related, no pun intended), obtained by hook and crook their abundantly incriminating telephone records (much of it phone sex-related), and even sent away for their quite revealing academic records (quite a bit of it cheating-on-exams-related). Where and how he obtained all of his information remains something of a mystery. He claims the Freedom of Information Act is a wonderful tool, but it clearly wasn't the only screwdriver at his disposal. In the end, he published a series of scathing reports in *The Farce News*, with charts and graphs and cross-referenced lists of offenses. The offended party hacks banded together and tried in earnest to shut him down, threatening him with lawsuits and worse. He responded by publishing a detailed account of their campaign of harassment, including transcripts of taped conversations. He pointed out that, ironically enough, it represented the most unified, nonpartisan cooperation he'd seen between the Democrats and Republicans in his entire adult life. Now, if they could just come together on education funding and tax relief for the middle class ...

After that, Sully was left alone. The politicos realized that they couldn't beat him, so they turned to a campaign of self-denial, hoping that if they simply ignored him, like a lump in their collective armpit, he would eventually go away. But he didn't. He grew an audience and and a de facto layer of protection from his critics. Sully was, and is, a fearless gadfly, an intrepid shit disturber. His critics dismiss him as a kook, calling his articles works of pure fiction. But time has proven that he usually gets it right.

Most people now feel it will take a mugger's bludgeon or another hit-and-run traffic "accident" or some other trumped-up, phony act of premeditated vengeance to bring Sully down. But he almost never leaves his apartment, which makes him a particularly frustrating target for any would-be assassin, professional or otherwise.

Half an hour later, I unleashed the dog and, despite my abject fatigue, scanned Sully's article. My eyes kept dropping shut, but I fought it off as best I could. From the very beginning, there was something about it that made me feel as if I'd been spied on, manipulated like a puppet, and otherwise abused in ways I couldn't quiet describe -- or didn't want to contemplate. It was like being molested by a horny octopus. Where does it feel worst?

Sully's piece read as follows:

*Violence erupts in our happy little town and the bodies are falling like tenpins in the path of a twenty-pound bowling ball. But there's good news, folks. Looks like the hoods don't have all the moxie. Our own version of Puddin'head Wilson has been on the job in pursuit of truth, justice and a piece of black cherry pie. As a result of some derring do by said sleuth, the dashing Assistant State's Attorney Dee Dee McCool is set to tie a bow around a nifty little triple homicide and deliver it to the Grand Jury for indictments all around.*

*Local musician Robby Vaughn, distantly related to one of Hartford's foremost millionaire families, was asked to handle a would-be blackmail scheme. Along the way, he uncovered and subsequently reported to all the relevant authorities -- and a few less relevant ex-authority figures -- an illegal operation in which one of the three victims in our Triple Threat Death Dance, the late LaTwanda Jefferson of Bloomfield, is alleged to have trafficked in contraband in direct defiance of several specific U.S. federal trade restrictions currently in effect. Sources close to the investigation suggest at this point that the word alleged is little more than a courtesy. That is, Twannie done what they said she done. And for all the miscreant behavior she's undertaken, she's won a date with the undertaker.*

*According to reports, Ms. Jefferson was the first felon to fall in this macabre march of destruction. Early Tuesday night, her body was discovered in the basement of her Bloomfield home along with a sizable stash of contraband commodities. The woman, also known by the street name 'Big Jeff,' was thought to have been in situe for twenty-four hours, putting the time of her death at around eight o'clock Monday night, give or take a few minutes. Do you know where your children were?*

*Authorities believe her assailant was a locally employed chauffeur with a lengthy police record and a personal vendetta vandalizing his badly broken heart. Miguel Batista, a Cuban national in the employ of Mrs. Margaret Waddley-Wordstone, won't have to carry a torch any longer, however. His cooled-off corpse was fished out of a gully beneath the Simsbury sycamore tree on Route 185 early Tuesday morning, several hours after he apparently lost control of his Chevrolet Monte Carlo. After bashing a Beemer headed in the opposite direction, Mr. Batista's sedan flipped and tumbled off the road. Sources have told TFN that the suspect (or is it victim?) was forced into the fatal fracas. Indications are that a third car pushed Mr. Batista into the path of the oncoming 700 series BMW driven by a Simsbury high school senior (la dee freakin' da). Somebody's been watching too much NASCAR on TV.*

*But it does beg the question: Who was at the wheel of the third car? Authorities have detained a woman for questioning in this matter, as well as in connection with a killing Tuesday night in Windsor in which the resident of a rental home on East Barber Street was slain when a pair of (get this) lawn darts were planted in his chest. The assailant's identity is being withheld at present. The victim of the bizarre attack was identified as thirty-something street hustler Johnny Brashear, an ambitious if, by all indications, not a particularly successful small-time businessman known to dabble in adult film making and other scurrilous enterprises. He was rumored to be making a play for Ms. Jefferson's import-export concern in the aftermath of Big Jeff's sudden demise.*

*Ms. Jefferson was seemingly surprised by her aggrieved assailant Monday night while hosting a small soiree for one of the stars of Mr. Brashear's latest video production, "Volley-Ball!," all copies of which have mysteriously disappeared. Brashear leaves behind a bewildered brunette lady friend as well as a garage full of objects whose ownership will surely be the subject of some heated debate.*

*Mr. Vaughn turned over his findings to ASA McCool who, in turn, is formulating a prosecutorial strategy, the successful execution of which will no doubt be quite a bold bit of plumage for her sartorial head wear. Word is Dee Dee always gets her man, unless the bad guy is a woman.*

*Meanwhile, one is hard pressed to ignore the ignominious fact that trouble seems to trail Mrs. Margaret Waddley-Wordstone like a mongrel dog too long separated from steady nourishment. Her granddaughters, Lillian Wordstone Tuomaleinin Buenavista and Lita Wordstone, are known to be quite the pair of pretty little migraine headaches. It's said, and repeated as necessary, that if it weren't for bad news, those girls would provide no news at all.*

*In a related story, there continues to be no further word in the matter of the as-yet-unexplained disappearance of Lillian's adventurous ex-husband, Benizio. Readers will no doubt recall that "Blackie" Buenavista, a self-proclaimed Central American freedom fighter (proof of this claim has yet to be produced), apparently walked away from friends and family nearly a month ago, and has not been heard from since. Wherever he is, telephone and/or mail service does not appear to have been installed. Concurrent with Blackie's departure from the scene is the similarly strange disappearance of Hubert Frobisher Edwards, husband of wannabe socialite entrepreneur Venus Edwards. Rumors that Blackie and Hubert ran off together have been vehemently denied by all parties, with the obvious exception of Blackie and Hubert, who remain at large (whether singularly or in tandem).*

*In a final note, aficionados of alternative country rock (you know who you are, you just don't know why) can see and hear Robby Vaughn when Elvis Jihad, the quartet in which he picks the pedal steel guitar, plays the Bristol Road House Friday and Saturday night. Admission is $5.00. There's a two-drink minimum. You may need more.*

I threw down the newspaper and waited for my fury to ratchet down a few notches from Boiling Over back to merely Smmering. One of these days, Sully's idea of fun and games was going to get someone killed. When that happened, I didn't want my name to appear on the list of victims. In addition to making me feel violated, his article also plunged me into deep, dizzying bewilderment.

*The Farce News*

For one thing, I didn't know anything about any gig in Bristol. Artie hadn't called and there was no message on the ... Now, wait a minute. I went to the answering machine on the table beside my bed. The red light was indeed blinking. I hit REPLAY and waited as the tape whirred. In a moment, Artie Johansson's cheerful baritone sounded. "Clear the weekend, Robby. We've got the Bristol Road House for two nights. Pays twelve hundred. We'll do it as a four piece. I'll call Tony and Al."

I stopped the tape, picked up the phone and punched in seven digits. After four rings, the connection went through.

"Hello, Robby," said Kareem Abdul Sullivan, proprietor, editor-in-chief and publisher of *The Farce News*. His voice was beyond serene.

"Fuck you, Sully. And fuck your stupid caller I.D. And most of all, fuck your stupid fish wrap."

"Robby, what ...?"

"You trying to get me killed?"

"I don't know what you're talking about."

"Your little article. What else? Jesus, Sully. What kind of shit is that? And where did you get it?"

There was a brief pause. I had asked the unanswerable question.

"What article?"

"The one in your paper, of course. It's right here." I looked around, but didn't see it. I'd thrown it somewhere. Maybe under the couch.

"Robby, are you drunk?"

"Not drunk enough."

I stopped barking at him. There was a long period silence. I wondered if he'd had hung up on me.

"You still there?" I asked.

"Yes."

The guy actually sounded like his feelings were hurt. What a putz.

"Where'd you get the *missing Blackie Buenavista* angle?"

"Blackie Buenavista, now there's a name I haven't heard in a while. What ever happened to him, anyway?"

"How the hell should I know? I've never even met the guy."

"Men like Blackie Buenavista don't just fall off the face of the earth, you know. And they don't just walk away, either. Not from a friend like Margaret Waddley-Wordstone, a friend who can be very beneficial to a cause, if you know what I mean."

"Yeah, well I'm not my brother's keeper. And he's not my brother. And it's not my fault Margaret Waddley-Wordstone is my aunt, so don't throw that in my face."

"We are all our brothers' keepers, Robby."
"Bullshit. Not me."

I didn't wait to see if Sully was going to hang up on me. The putz. I slammed the phone down and went to the fridge for a beer. There wasn't any. A perfect ending to a perfect day. I called Jolie to see if she knew where Blackie Buenavista was, or cared. She wasn't home. Great. At this hour?

I went to bed. Wouldn't you know it, I dreamt about Blackie Buenavista, some guy I'd never even met. Then I dreamt about some guy named Earl Anthony, whoever the hell that is. (Only later did I learn that Earl Anthony was once a world champion bowler. Boy, was I gonna need some serious therapy by the time this ordeal was over.)

## Chapter 19

I didn't sleep very well what with images of would-be Central American freedom fighters and pro bowlers dancing in my head. But the fact that I was already tossing and turning wasn't much consolation when I was jolted awake around three o'clock in the morning by the sound of knocking on my apartment door. This unwelcome noise inspired the dog to commence growling angrily at whomever was standing on the other side doing all the knocking. His message seemed to be: At this hour? You'd better have treats!

It crossed my mind that it could be the Bloomfield cops. Maybe they'd finally caught on to me and were going to haul me in for obstruction of justice. Or maybe the Windsor police wanted to know what was in the cardboard box I'd taken from Johnny Brashear's garage.

I dragged myself out of bed and pulled on a tattered, blue terry cloth robe I've had for about twenty years. I stumbled through the living room and kitchen, turning on lights as I went, not so much to boost a low sense of my own safety and security as to keep from barking my shins on the furniture. I was trying to imagine all the laws I might have broken in the last forty-eight hours and for how many of them the irrepressibly charming Ernie Newman would be unable to talk Dee Dee McCool out of pressing charges. As I prepared to face the music (Richard Wagner style, long and mournful) I vowed to go down to the *Super Stop-N-Shop* in the morning and apply for a deli job -- if morning came and I was still a free man. The work would be duller than a one-trick pony with a one-track mind but it would be steady and safe if you didn't count the stainless steel circular saws they used to slice the Swiss cheese and Genoa salami. Anything had to be better than this foolish business of risking life and limb for practically no money, no benefits whatsoever, and hardly any sense of personal achievement. It was especially depressing that my so-called clients were in fact family, and that they seemed hellbent on systematically sucking all the fun out of my life.

Rufus, his back hair up to demonstrate just how tough and agitated he could be, growled and snarled and whined and made himself busy sniffing at the front door. I fumbled with the locks. Logic suggests it might have been prudent to take a quick look through the peep hole, considering the time of night and the circumstances of the last two days. But logic lives in a different tax bracket from me (as well as a different neighborhood) and doesn't get out of bed at three in the morning unless the house is on fire.

*The Farce News*

I opened the door a foot or so, expecting to see uniforms and badges and maybe even a couple of guns drawn. At least a stun gun. Instead I was treated to a couple of badly animated cartoon characters. Three o'clock in the morning and I get a visit from a pair of walking, talking pen-and-ink drawings. Would my luck never change?

"Lady quarterback thirsty for words on you quickly," said Gomez Addams, the squat, box-shaped limousine driver, bodyguard and errand boy to Venus Edwards. Standing beside him, a foot or so taller, was the sallow Morticia in her manly suit of shiny black cloth. She clearly was not impressed with me, my terry cloth robe, or my growling dog. If only I gave a shit.

And if only I knew what the hell Gomez was talking about. I was about to say, "Would you remind repeating that?" But I didn't honestly see the point.

"Well, if it isn't Fran and Sam. Or is it Sam and Fran? You two should think about adding a third member to your little minstrel show. Call 'em Cisco, then you can introduce yourselves as Sam, Fran and Cisco. Has a certain ring to it, don't you think?"

"Lady quarterback ..." Gomez began. I cut him off.

"Yeah, yeah. I didn't get it the first time." I turned to Morticia. "What the hell is he talking about? Do you know? I sure don't."

"The coverings on your frame," she said. "Presently make them."

I gazed at her. She was even creepier than the last time I'd seen her, but that may have been a function of the late hour. She was the closest thing to a zombie I'd laid eyes on since running from the theater when *Dawn of the Dead* premiered in 1978. No, that's not quite right. I'd also seen quite a few walking dead on the boob tube much more recently. On the Fox News Network and on a few reality TV shows. Dead from the neck up, that is.

"You, too?" I said.

They looked at each other, then extracted their little red leather books from inside jacket pockets. "Hark ..." she said.

"No, you hark," I said. "I want you to go away. The sun will be up in a few hours. You don't want to be exposed."

"The transportation apparatus," Gomez said. "Inside for anticipation of estimated arrival. Minutes of time four."

I looked back down at him. He was hooking a thumb over his shoulder just in case I cared where he'd parked the car in which they would wait.

"If you're waiting for me, you'll be waiting a long time," I said, no longer caring if they understood me or didn't. "To be honest, you guys don't look like you have long. Ever thought of mixing in a salad, maybe a nice London broil once in a while? Zombie cannot live on roadkill alone, y'know."

"Not to harden punishings on yourself," Morticia said.

I looked at her and translated what I gathered was her version of a threat. "Piss off."

She looked, in a word, mortified. It suited her features and complexion. But so would death by starvation. Or a dose of ante-mortem embalming fluid. I guess she understood short words best.

Gomez said: "Talk manners not at lady to receive extra punishing violence extremely."

I was getting a sore neck from looking down at him, up at her, down at him, up at her ...

"I'll be closing the door now," I said. "If you're still here in thirty seconds, I'll have to set Rufus on you. If that doesn't work, I might start shooting."

Gomez turned to look up at Morticia, plainly confused. "Rufus?"

"I'm kidding, obviously. No way the dog would go anywhere near you ogres. He likes fresh meat, not the lifeless, flaking sinew of the long dead."

Morticia looked back down at Gomez and shrugged. "Rufus?"

"Good night, now," I said. "Next time, call ahead so I can be sure to be out of town."

And with that I closed the door, carefully re-locking it, still not sure they wouldn't reach through the cracks in the wood and grab me by the throat and drag me screaming into some Fourth Dimension of Terror and Abomination. I'd seen it happen. In the movies. I didn't look through the peep hole to see if they were still there. I preferred to believe they were gone.

Rufus bravely retreated with me to the bedroom. While I was turning the lights off in the kitchen and the living room, the mutt beat me to the warm spot where I'd been trying to sleep and proceeded to make himself at home. It was quite a process to kick him out while J.D. and Buddy watched superciliously from the foot of the bed. Then I had to flip the pillow to the dry side because Rufus had already managed to drool all over it. I swear the cats were laughing.

I lay there staring up at the blackness where the ceiling would be if I had the night vision of an owl or a vampire bat. For all their grotesque appearance, Gomez and Morticia had thus far proven to be fairly harmless, except perhaps to the psyche. I hoped I'd seen the last of them, and to this list headed by Gomez and Morticia I added the names of just about everyone else I'd met in the last forty-eight hours, including Lillian Buenavista, Lita Wordstone, Rosa Batista, Venus Edwards and Billie Billie. I also added the names of those no longer drawing the sustaining breath of life: LaTwanda Jefferson, Miguel Batista and Johnny Brashear. Running into any of *that* crowd again would be extremely bad news.

Ten minutes had not elapsed before the dog began to growl again and the tapping on my front door renewed. It was a different kind of knock this time. Call me a sexist pig, but I'd have laid down money that this was a woman's hand at work. Which meant it was neither Fran nor Sam, nor vice versa. So, who? Jolie? At this hour? Ready to start something that had maybe been hanging in the air for several weeks now, like a trial balloon nobody is willing to acknowledge for fear it'll fall out of the sky like some obsolete NASA hardware from the 1960s. I didn't feel that lucky.

I hadn't bothered to shed the blue terry cloth robe before returning to bed. So I was at least spared the hassle of trying to remember where I'd thrown it, or the embarrassment of putting it back on inside out and backwards. Dressing in the dark was never a strong suit of mine.

With the dog grumbling at my heels (not quite hiding behind me, but close) I went back through the apartment, turning on lights and honing the edge on my rapier wit in preparation for Round Two of Mystery Unwanted Guest. I had a sneaking suspicion who it would be. It wasn't going to be my beguiling neighbor looking to start anything. More likely it would be a certain hatchet-faced matron looking to finish something. And not a moment too soon, if you ask me, so long as the business she wished to conclude was our brief acquaintanceship.

I went through the routine with the locks again and swung the door open. I hate always being right.

Venus Edwards was alone and dolled up as if she had either just come from a very fancy dinner party or was on her way to one. I suppose either could be true if you lived in those circles where they keep vampire's hours.

"If you're looking for your two illiterate ghouls, I sent them packing. When you see 'em, try to explain that Halloween isn't for three weeks."

Venus Edwards peered at me with bald disapproval. "Mr. Vaughn, your impudence never ceases to amaze me."

"No shit? You must be pretty ceaselessly amazable."

Rufus took the opportunity to bark. He might have been laughing at my pithy witticism, or simply letting Venus Edwards know what he thought of her for in fact arriving without treats. She ignored both the dog and my futile attempt to deliver a stinging insult. Instead of offering a caustic retort or launching into another haughty criticism of my manners, she stretched her neck to get a better look at the apartment behind me. I shifted a little to block her view but she wasn't about to be put off.

"Aren't you going to ask me in?"

"Hell no," I said. "And just so we're sure to cover all our bases, I'm not going to ask you out, either."

"Is this how you treat your guests?"

This time I laughed out loud. And Rufus barked again. "Seriously?"

I was about to tell her to get the hell off my welcome mat.

Before I could stop her, she squeezed herself through the opening between the door and the jamb. The look of triumph on her face confirmed what I expected: her gaining entry to my apartment was a lot more important to *her* than my keeping her out was important to *me*. To my disgust, Rufus backed off, whimpering. Some guard dog.

"Ah," she said, standing in my living room. "That's a little better."

I remained at the apartment door, the knob still in my hand, watching her with what I hoped would be construed as stoney indifference. "Maybe for you."

"I do so enjoy seeing how the other ninety-nine percent lives."

So she had a sense of humor after all. "Won't you barge in?" I said.

"I wish to speak with you," she said.

I shut the door and went to the only couch in the living room and flopped down on it, leaving her nowhere to sit but a hard-backed chair, a wicker rocking chair, or the low, padded reading chair that faced the other away. I hoped she would pick the reading chair. Not only did it face the other way, but it was also covered in cat fur and would leave her outfit completely despoiled. Rufus immediately trotted over to the couch and jumped on it with me, pinning me up to the backrest before stretching out and making himself comfortable. Venus Edwards gave us a look of consummate pity (which we probably deserved) and went for the hard-backed chair. She lowered herself into it as if she were trussed up in an orthopedic spinal corset. Clearly the woman didn't know diddly-squat about the merits of slouching. I could show her a thing or two, but to do so would require spending additional time with her, which at the moment was a concept to which I was unequivocally and intractably opposed. And I thought the feeling would probably last a while.

"Since there seems to be no way to get rid of you, why don't we just cut to the chase?"

Venus Edwards arranged her hands somewhat more primly on her lap than I would have thought possible for someone who so enjoyed wielding ham-fisted authority. She fixed me with a cool, appraising look even though I didn't need fixing at the moment. Without clearing her throat to presage the start of her rambling oratory, she said simply: "You worry me."

I didn't answer. For one thing, I didn't care if I worried her or not. For another, I thought if I shut up she might get around to explaining herself, and this visit would end that much sooner.

"I understand you had some interaction with members of the law enforcement community this evening," she said.

I smiled. "At least you didn't accuse me of having intercourse with them. Congratulations on updating your vocabulary to nearly the 20th century." Why she couldn't just say contact or conversation or dealing was a mystery to me.

"It's true then?"

"If you say so. Unofficially, it's none of your business."

"I understand you made certain disclosures in regard to events which transpired in and around Hartford in the last couple days."

"Where did you learn to speak English, the Institute for Smarmy Anal Retentives?"

"Just answer me, if you don't mind."

"I do mind. And what's more, I forgot the question."

"I said, you made certain disclosures ..."

"That's not a question, it's a declaration."

She waited for me to elaborate. The dog yawned and scratched himself behind one ear. I yawned as well, but resisted any manner of scratching which might unduly offend my guest.

"You and I had an unsatisfactory exchange yesterday," she said.

"That's because I didn't get anything out of it."

"Our discourse did not evolve as I would have liked."

"Yeah, and the intercourse wasn't that good, either."

She gave my comment all the attention it deserved. None. "I feel we got off on the wrong foot."

"The wrong foot? You could lose both legs in a wood chipper and still get off on the wrong foot. Your problem is you don't comprehend the concept of Option B. It's your way or the hard way. Case in point: coming on heavy with the freaky creature-feature bodyguards. I don't like your style. I don't like the company you keep. And I sure as hell don't like you turning up at three o'clock in the morning for your version of a little chat. Having said that, the floor is yours. Dance your dance and then get the hell out."

She stared blankly at me. I guess most of the astronauts in her orbit didn't speak to her this way. That or she was having a *petit mal* seizure and had lost the ability to blink her eyes.

"C'mon," I said. "Let's hear it. Gimme the speech, then scram." I tapped my wrist watch, to indicate the lateness of the hour. I was beginning to enjoy this. She didn't squirm well. Lack of practice.

"That's just the thing," she said. "You see, it isn't so much what *I* have to say as what I'd like to know regarding what you've said."

"To whom?" I could have said "to who?" but she only would have corrected my grammar.

"To the relevant authorities."

"That narrows the field. Which authorities are the relevant ones?"

"I'll put it simply," she said. "I would appreciate it if you to relate to me the details of what you divulged to any law enforcement personnel in regard to our impromptu *tête-à-tête* at the Duncaster Road property on Tuesday. That would be yesterday."

I smacked my forehead with the palm of my hand. "You mean it's Wednesday already!"

"Yes," she said, tentatively. "Why? What difference does *that* make?"

"All the difference in the world. Wednesday is garbage day!"

She sighed. "Please, Mr. Vaughn."

"And recycling. I'll bet you don't recycle, do you, Mrs. Edwards?"

With some difficulty, I shifted my position on the couch. Rufus, whose presence was at the very root of my difficulty, shifted his position as well. I think he got the better of it. I was getting a cramp in my left leg. Rufus looked perfectly content. I think he even smiled.

I addressed Venus Edwards, wishing I had a postage stamp to glue to her forehead so I could mail her somewhere. Like Ethiopia. Or Katmandon't. Or Timbuk-Three.

"Maybe for Christmas, Santa Claus will bring you everything you ever wanted. Me? I don't drive a sleigh or keep reindeer. Just a dog and a pair of cats, and they don't handle physical labor very well. Bottom line: I don't think I can help you. And even if I could, why should I?"

Now I was just being rude. I could easily have told her what I'd told Ernie and, by proxy, Dee Dee McCool, which was next to nothing. If I did, maybe Venus Edwards would fulfill my wildest dreams and go home, leaving me to wrestle with my nightmares in peace and solitude, not counting Rufus and the cats. But it scraped me the wrong way to have her sit there and quiz me like a school teacher, work me like some sleazy real estate agent, massage me like a chiropractor with an overdue payment on his Porsche. And all the while expect me to pony up information just because she had some inflated sense of her own importance. It was high time somebody brought her down a notch or three. Maybe I was the wrong guy to do it, but it might be fun to give it the old junior high school try.

"If I tell you what you want to know, will you go away?"

"Mr. Vaughn ..."

"I mean it. Will you go away?"

"Well, I don't see ..."

"Forever? Never come around here again? For any reason? Ever again. Will you do it?"

"Don't tell me what you think I want to hear, Mr. Vaughn. Just what was discussed. I'm a realist. I like to be prepared for any contingency. It's the key to survival."

"Yeah? I've survived pretty well by minding my own damn business. You should try it some time."

As I stared at Venus Edwards and she stared back, I wished Rufus was one of those highly trained attack dogs who responded to key catch words. So if I were suddenly to say, "Bouillabaisse!" he would leap off the couch and tear out her throat (after he stopped laughing at me for picking such a stupid attack command) or at least he'd grab her expensive Louis Vuitton purse and ferociously spill its contents onto the living room floor, then paw through them like a horse pretending he can count. Then we'd see how tough she was, and how well she dealt with contingencies. But, alas, Rufus had fallen asleep. His heavy breathing and drooling gave him away.

"Please," she said, "try to pay attention."

Jesus, if I had a dime for every time someone had said *that* to me.

"Look you want me to share, but I don't feel like it. You and I don't have the kind of relationship where sharing comes into play. And why is that? I'll tell you. Because you're the kind of person who takes and takes and takes, but never gives. This is a perfect example. You want me to share, but you offer me nothing in return. You come barging into my home in the middle of the night and you didn't even bring donuts or a treat for the dog. That's just plain thoughtless."

She deliberated over that. If she thought I had a valid point, I'd probably die of old age waiting for her to acknowledge it. "I may have some information that will be of use to you," she said.

"I seriously doubt it," I said. As far as I could tell, my work on this nutty case and all its nut cases was over. According to the answering machine, I had a gig in Bristol on Friday night and the next few days would be best spent woodshedding hot licks on my Emmons D-10 pedal steel guitar. That's if I ever got some decent rest. At the moment I felt like I was stuck in the clutches of some mushroom induced hallucination.

Venus Edwards smirked. "I understand you have a going interest in Benizio Buenavista."

Blackie again. "You're woefully misinformed."

"Nonsense." she said. "You must wonder what became of him."

"Not in the least. If he took a long walk off a short pier and disappeared in the muck of low tide, more power to him. What do I care?"

"Men like him don't just fall off the face of the earth, Mr. Vaughn. And they don't just walk away either. Not from a friend like Maggie Wordstone, who can be very beneficial to a cause, if you know what I mean?"

Jesus. Where had I heard this riff before?

"And there is the matter of his little sex toy."

"Lillian," I said. The vaudeville quick-change artist.

"Exactly."

Now the hair was standing up on my back, but I wasn't feeling very tough. Just agitated. And confused.

"What the hell do you people want from me?"

"I want to know what you told the authorities."

"In regard to the property on Duncaster Road, its contents, and events which may or may not have taken place there?"

"Exactly."

I looked her in the eye. She was dead serious now. No more tea time with the Queen of England. No more phony good manners and manicured cucumber sandwiches. Rufus raised his head and looked at me. He raised one eyebrow. "Well, ain'tcha gonna to tell 'er?"

"As far as I'm concerned, you were never there."

"What about your little friend, Ernie, the former policeman?"

"Your name hasn't come up."

Venus Edwards raised an eyebrow, just as Rufus had. No doubt she was trying to decide whether to believe me, if I were worthy of being believed, if I was trustworthy. She seemed to conclude, eventually, that I was leveling with her and that she had heard all she needed to hear. Or that I was completely untrustworthy, and so nothing else I said would hold water anyway, rendering any further conversation pointless, just in case it hadn't been pointless enough already. She unfolded her hands and stood, her spine perfectly straight.

"I have a rehearsal hall on Firetown Road in Simsbury, across the road from the main theater building. Come see me there tonight. We're auditioning parts for our next production."

"I'm not an actor."

"It's a musical version of *Who's Afraid of Virginia Woolf?* By Edward Albee. The playwright?"

"As opposed to Edward Albee the proctologist from Terre Haute?"

"Whatever."

I was about to say "Well, I'm not a musician," but that would have been a lie and I didn't want to spoil our relationship with a quilt work of fibs.

"You might find it interesting. And I might have some information to share with you."

"You might?"

"I can be a very caring and sharing woman, Mr. Vaughn. Once you get to know me."

We seemed to be circling back dangerously close to the subject of intercourse again. I was about to confess to being a seminarian on my way to Catholic priesthood -- but this was another prevarication which would undermine our budding relationship. Instead I sat still, waiting for the moment to pass. Or for her to leave. Which ever came first.

Without another word Venus Edwards strode purposefully to the door and let herself out, without bothering to close the door behind her.

Rufus barked at the door as it swung back on its hinges and clicked shut.

"Oh, sure," I said to him. "Now you're a tough guy."

I climbed wearily from the couch and went over to refasten the locks. Then I went to the phone and dialed. After several rings, a voice I didn't think I'd ever heard before came on the line.

"Wordstone residence," it said. Too deep for a woman, too high for a man. Too wide awake to be a normal human. Could it be Morticia moonlighting?

"Is Rosa Batista there?"

There was a pause. "No."

"Isn't she a live-in?"

"Yes."

"So, where is she?"

"There's been a death in the family."

"Did Rosa buy the farm?"

"No."

"Okay. What about Lillian?"

"I believe she is sleeping. It *is* after three, you know."

"I know damn well what time it is, sister."

I took a guess it was a woman on the other end of the line. If it was a guy, well, I'd just made another mistake, and perhaps another enemy. I do it all the time without even trying.

"Is there any message you wish to leave?"

"Yeah, when she wakes up, tell her the tapes have been secured."

"The tapes?"

"All of them."

"She will understand the meaning of this diagonal communication?"

"One can only hope," I said. "One can only hope." Then I hung up.

That felt good. Let someone else spend a few dead-of-night hours shaking their head and asking, "What the hell?" Why should I be the only one?

I went back to bed. Rufus was sprawled in my spot again, snoring. He

*The Farce News*

was already into deep REM sleep, twitching and occasionally whimpering. He was probably dreaming of squirrels and climbing trees, and not about missing freedom fighters from Central America. Lucky dog. I curled up beside him and eventually dropped off to sleep. I managed to get through the rest of the night in complete oblivion, without interruption or disruption.

I didn't stir again until around eight o'clock the next morning, when the light of day and the smell of coffee combined to ease me from my slumber. Wait a minute, coffee? Who the hell in my household knows how to operate the coffee maker, other than me? Certainly not the cats. They can barely turn the TV set on and off by themselves. What's more, they don't even know where I keep the grinds. Rufus? Please.

Groggy and bleary-eyed, I staggered into the kitchen and found Jolie drinking coffee out of my ceramic New York Rangers Stanley Cup mug (my favorite mug) and reading the Hartford *Courant* (not my favorite newspaper). A platter of bagels sat on the table, along with several side dishes in plastic containers. I surveyed the spread. Lox. A tub of cream cheese. Some herring in wine sauce. A jar of almond butter. Some raspberry jam. Also a pot of coffee. And another mug, one from the San Diego Zoo with a giraffe on it. Had I slept straight through to Sunday? If so, Artie would be pissed.

I glanced at the front page of the newspaper Jolie was reading. It was Wednesday all right, not Sunday. I didn't know whether to be happy or disappointed.

"Find everything okay?" I said.

Jolie didn't look up from the paper. "Yup."

I went back to the bedroom, got some clean clothes and headed for the shower. Ten minutes later, Jolie was still reading the paper. I pushed my wet hair back over my head and sat down opposite her. The giraffe mug was now full. I reached for it and took a big sip. Excellent. Just the right amount of sugar and Half & Half. Almost as good as the coffee I make.

"Anything interesting in the paper?" I asked, doubtfully.

She looked up and flashed the killer smile. "Gotta say it. We have some extremely creative people reporting the news in this town."

I immediately thought of Sully.

"Is that right?" I said.

"According to this story in the Metro section, the Hartford police, in cooperation with units from Windsor and Bloomfield, solved a double homicide last night. Pretty impressive, wouldn't you say?"

"A double homicide? Not a triple?"

She tapped the paper as if that action alone would confirm the accuracy of her accounting. "They've got Billie Billie in custody for killing Johnny Brashear."

I took another sip of coffee. "Yeah, we know about that one."

"Meanwhile, Johnny Brashear has been credited with the LaTwanda Jefferson shooting."

"What? No way."

"Says so right here, cowboy."

I took the paper and turned it around. I read through it with a growing sense of awe and disbelief. Sure enough, the cops had gift wrapped the thing like a fire truck from Toys-R-Us. They had Johnny Brashear doing Twannie in what was characterized as a "hostile takeover attempt." So much for honor among thieves. It also said Billie Billie was on the hook for killing Johnny as payback. There was an oblique implication that Billie and Twannie were "an item." There was nothing at all about Miguel Batista. Nothing about Lita Wordstone's career in the adult entertainment industry. Nothing about Johnny reaching out to Twannie for distribution. Nothing about Venus Edwards or her connection to Twannie Jefferson or the Wordstone family. And, thankfully, nothing about a moonlighting pedal steel guitar player obfuscating the law and obstructing justice in his bumbling attempt to foil a blackmail caper against his distant relation, Margaret Waddley-Wordstone.

Ernie Newman had cut a pretty lean deal with Dee Dee McCool. Kept me out of it. Kept the Wordstones out of it. Kept the kid, Miguel, out of it.

"This sure as hell ain't how Sully's running the story," I said.

Jolie adopted a puzzled expression. "What do you mean?"

"His version's a hell of a lot more accurate, for one thing."

"He told you he's doing that?" she said.

"I saw it."

"You saw what? Like, an advance copy?"

"He left a copy on my doorstep last night."

"But it's only Wednesday. I thought he published on Friday."

"If you don't believe me, take a look for yourself. It's right here."

I rummaged around on the kitchen table, checking under the plates, rooting among the various sections of the *Courant*, then ducking under the table itself for a look. Nothing. I looked on the kitchen counter, then checked the top of the fridge. No luck. No copy of *The Farce News,* either. I searched the living room, under couch cushions and chairs. I even tipped the couch back to see if it was under there. It wasn't. Rufus barked. His tennis ball, or what was left of it, was there. It looked a hundred years old, but that didn't stop Rufus from being delighted to have it back. But there was no copy of *The Farce News* anywhere to be found. I gave the bedroom a look but came

*The Farce News*

up empty. I even tried the bathroom, in honor of all the times I'd told Sully what his paper was good for. But no luck. I wondered if maybe Venus Edwards had taken it, but recalled her leaving empty handed -- besides which, she sure as hell would have said something about it had she known of the article's existence. In fact, she would have had a friggin' cow. And I would have paid to watch.

Jolie stood in the doorway, watching me.

"You okay, Robby?"

"Yeah, sure," I said. "If it's okay to lose your mind."

I went to the phone beside the bed and punched in Sully's number. He answered right away, sounding chipper and energetic.

"What's on the front page of your next edition?" I said. I didn't bother to identify myself.

"Who is this?" he asked.

"Don't screw around, Sully. You know who ..."

"Oh, Robby. Hi."

"Just answer the question, Sully. No games."

"The front page? Well, it's only Wednesday, so I'm not entirely sure. Right now I'm working on a story about the governor getting a free roof on his lake house in exchange for accepting rigged bids on state construction jobs. But things could change. Why do you ask?"

"Are you saying you're not running a story on the Twannie Jefferson murder? Or Billie Billie's arrest for killing Johnny Brashear? Are you saying you didn't have someone deliver a copy of *The Farce News* to my apartment late last night. Jesus, it was still warm when I got here. I still remember the headline. It said ..."

Of course, I couldn't remember the headline at all. If I *wasn't* trying to remember it, I would no doubt be able to recall it word for word. But now it was gone.

"I have to go," I said, and hung up.

Jolie was still standing in the doorway, munching a bagel and holding my Rangers mug under her chin, poised for another sip.

"That's my favorite mug," I said. "Please don't break it."

She winked at me, held it up in a mock salute, and took a big gulp.

I triggered the REWIND button on the answering machine bedside the bed. J.D. and Buddy picked up their heads to watch me. I couldn't tell if they were really interested, or just wanted to see who had interrupted their naps. They scowled at me. They're always scowling at me, unless they're hungry. I punched the PLAY button.

And there was Artie Johansson's cheerful baritone voice, just as I'd heard it the night before. "Clear the weekend, Robby. We've got the Bristol Road House for two nights. Pays twelve hundred. We'll do it as a four piece. I'll call Tony and Al."

I looked at Jolie. "At least I'm not completely out of my mind."

She shrugged and turned her back. "Let's not jump to conclusions until all the facts are in."

I pointed in the general direction of my front door. "Out," I said.

She wasn't looking at me so the effect was lost. I fell on the bed, face down, and scared the cats out of their skins. Rufus came over and began to lick my hand. A great start to another promising day.

## Chapter 20

The stretch of land known collectively as Central America, with the Pacific Ocean to the west and the Caribbean to the east, holds many centuries of complicated history and secrets. For all I knew it held the key to discovering Benizio "Blackie" Buenavista's current whereabouts, or could at least provide some clues about the general heading he'd taken since lambing it out of Hartford a month or so ago. Of course, I had no evidence to support such a theory. In fact, I hadn't the requisite evidence to support any supposition whatsoever -- even that he'd left Hartford. I was by no means sure I cared one way or the other. But it sure seemed that every time I turned around, somebody was working way too hard trying to persuade me that (a) I was already busy searching for him, (b) I should be busy searching for him, (c) if I wasn't that somebody should be busy searching for him, and/or (d) all of the above.

My only question at the moment went something like: Where the hell was (e) none of the above when you needed it?

Frankly, I was sick of the whole sordid affair. It was not turning out to be one to remember.

Moreover, I was growing damn weary of the notion that these nagging Nellies might be right; to wit, that somebody, perhaps me (but preferably someone else) should take a moment or two to inquire into Blackie's unexplained and (if you believed the polls) uncharacteristic vanishing act.

At least one person -- and perhaps one phantom as well -- had insisted that Blackie wasn't the sort of man who simply fell off the face of the earth. Not unless someone snuck up from behind and gave him a big ol' nasty shove right between the shoulder blades. None of the nagging Nellies was prepared to come right out and say for certain that Blackie had been the victim of foul play, but neither was anybody willing to accept his apparent desertion as a viable and tolerable choice, or one that should escape a focused examination by some objective third-party observer. Where they got the idea I was the man for the job, I'll never know.

Meanwhile it had not escaped my notice that nobody was exactly leaping to the front of the line to pay me to find Blackie. It was one thing to do a favor for one's family, even this troubled tribe, but it was quite another feat of arrogant entitlement to expect me to perform this new task *gratis*, out of the questionable goodness of my heart or some even more dubious sense of obligation. This presented a problem, a big one.

Thus far nobody had paid me for the two errands I'd officially been requested to complete: specifically, talking LaTwanda Jefferson out of her extortion threat against Margaret Waddley-Wordstone, and thwarting the Johnny Brashear porno blackmail strategy against Lillian Buenavista. What I needed was someone with a checkbook and a generous spirit. And a working pen. And a functioning conscience. Or, failing on those counts, an updated To Do list with my name on it.

So it was left for me to blunder forward with little or no help.

And what I didn't know about Blackie would fill a book, although probably not a cookbook or, say, an address book. Word on the street was he'd been some kind of freedom fighter in Central America before migrating north like a Canadian snow goose with a malfunctioning radar. It was a story Blackie Buenavista himself had propagated. All I knew for sure about him was he'd been married to Lillian for about twenty minutes and that nobody had seen him for about a month. The abridged marriage to Lillian was not a surprise. Modern matrimony was rife with stories of the short-and-sweet concluding in protracted bitterness. What was strange was that the abrupt cessation of the marriage in no way heralded the end of Blackie's friendship with his grandmother-in-law. What was that all about?

According to the family, he'd spent a good deal of time in Auntie Peg's freezing cold library, gobbling ice cream treats while she guzzled expensive malt whiskey. But nobody seemed to know what they talked about or what the mutual interest between them could have possibly been. Was he playing her for money to fund some nationalist (or anti-nationalist) military activity in his homeland? Or was it she who was using him, feeding her soul at the trough of his nourishing (if suspect) attentions? He was said to be a young adventurer with charm and manners. She was known to be a gargantuan antique with a major alcohol problem. What a combination.

And what did a would-be 21st century banana republic freedom fighter do when the bullets stopped flying? Run for political office? Perhaps. It had happened. Or emigrate to New England, consume large quantities of ice cream and squire rich young women -- only to disappear into the mist? That seemed unlikely.

And in which of the many chaotic theaters of geopolitical discord that made up Central America would Blackie be apt to have conducted his overt, covert or otherwise openly clandestine operations? I didn't even know which country he hailed from, or which nation, if any, currently held the claim check on his nationalistic loyalties. The two weren't necessarily mutually exclusive.

Could he have been a rebel warrior in El Salvador? Plenty of that sort of thing had gone on there. But the warring factions had signed some kind of treaty back in the early 1990s. And what, aside from cocaine, was El Salvador trying to sell to the world? There was shrimp, but I didn't see much evidence of shrimp among Twannie Jefferson's stash. And besides, who'd kill (or risk dying) over a load of shrimp?

Had he been a gun runner to the Nicaraguan communists? The Sandinistas were part of the national government now, Hadn't their rebel leader lost the last presidential election in Managua by a rather slim margin? And what was Nicaragua chief export? Aside from cocaine? Cotton. Gold. Coffee. Shrimp. More shrimp? A connection? Nah.

What if Blackie was in bed with the Costa Ricans? They had arguably the most stable government in the region, and by far the most successful tourist trade. But in the absence of political strife, what was their most pressing economic concern, aside from the uninterrupted exportation of cocaine and heroin? Was he smuggling coke out of Costa Rica, or maybe pineapples? And what about shrimp?

What if it turned out Blackie was part of some Guatemalan money laundering operation? That was supposed to be a big deal down there. They had conducted a lovely little civil war lasting nearly four decades. According to tourist brochures, roughly 100,000 Guatemalans died in the fighting. They had endurance, those Guatemalans, but no palpable sense of urgency. Americans had buried six times that number of men, women and children in only four years of 19th century domestic violence. (Then again, with the exception of the Canadians, North Americans had always loved a good fight if they could start one. History has shown that Canadians do much of their best fighting while strapped into ice skates, but from a national perspective they come off as hopelessly nonviolent. They can't even figure out what to do about those troublesome xenophobes in the Province of Quebec.)

And where did this leave me?

Why look for answers so far from home when the possibility surely existed that Blackie was still in town, laying low and running his games from behind the scenes. Had he played any part in the extortion drama against his so-called pal, dear old Auntie Peg? Was he trying to finance insurgency somewhere south of the border using the Ice Queen's lucre? Was he just a thief? Had he asked her for money up front and been rejected? Did that permanently queer the rather queer friendship between them? I didn't think so. The old broad had given no such indication. And she would have. If I read her right, she genuinely liked Blackie, if only for his incomparable capacity to consume vast quantities of ice cream, and missed him.

*The Farce News*

And why would he ask for a paltry $80,000 when millions were available? That number (eighty grand) raised all kinds of red flags. None of them had any stars or stripes or hammers and sickles on them, however, and certainly none seemed worthy of salutation.

So what did I have?

Nothing but dead ends with only the occasional philosophical cul-de-sac.

I turned my attention to other aspects of this puzzle and found myself wondering about Hubert Frobisher Edwards, the husband of Venus Edwards. How did his disappearance tie in with Blackie's, if at all?

I decided I owed Ernie Newman a thank you call and this seemed like as good a time as any to make it. He'd done a great job of keeping the State's Attorney's office off my back, to say nothing of assisting in the delivery of the homicidal maniac, Billie Billie. I also thought Ernie could shake a few peach trees and get me some information. I punched up his number and hoped it wasn't too early for him to be up.

Expectedly, he sounded pretty groggy when he finally answered the phone, but he insisted I hadn't awoken him so I stopped feeling bad almost immediately. Maybe he was just getting in, drinking himself sober again. I told him what I was after. He listened patiently and suggested I get some breakfast and call him back at noon. I wasn't sure if that was his way of saying he'd have the information for me by then, or that, at that time, I could restate my case; that, at present, he was busy. I didn't press the issue. His voice became muffled for a moment, as if he were covering the mouthpiece with his hand. As if something was going on in the background and he didn't want me to hear it. I guess I could have been imagining things, but I thought I heard him say, "Dee Dee, knock it off for a second." If Ernie was in the sack with the Assistant State's Attorney, I was probably a lot further in the clear than I'd originally dared to hope.

I rang off and went down the hall to Jolie's apartment and tapped lightly on the door. She didn't answer. I knocked a little louder. I thought I could hear activity inside, and yet she continued not to come to the door. "C'mon, I know you're in there," I said, guessing. But she refused to take the bait and say, "Oh, no I'm not." I knocked a few more times, growing weary of the game, if that's what it was. "You have my Rangers mug," I said. "You can't hold it hostage forever."

But she was clearly determined to ignore me. My fault for kicking her out. A voice somewhere in the back of my head announced that I was officially an idiot and that she was perfectly within her rights to give me the cold shoulder. I told the voice to shut the hell up and mind its own goddamn business. I won't repeat what it said back to me.

*The Farce News*

Back in my apartment I finished the coffee alone. Then I made another pot just to be spiteful. I wasn't especially hungry but I cut up a couple of bagels -- one garlic, the other cheddar cheese -- and applied cream cheese and lox and had a proper sit down breakfast. I ate slowly, brooding. I picked up the *Courant* to see what was going on in the National Hockey League. My Rangers hadn't lost again, which was a small consolation. Of course, they hadn't played, either. They were in the midst of a five-day layoff before the Atlanta Thrashers came to Madison Square Garden on Thursday night. Just what the doctor ordered, a chance for the Rangers to crank up their anemic scoring attack against a young team. Fill the net with goals, get the season going in the right direction. So why did I have the overwhelming sense that no such thing would happen? That, in fact, they would lose on home ice to the Thrashers? Too many years of watching them, I guess.

I finished breakfast, cleaned up the dishes, then took Rufus for a walk. He didn't have his usual spunk and I wondered if he was still getting over the creepy middle-of-the-night visit from Gomez and Morticia Addams. I know I was. We cut it short and headed for home. A block from the apartment building, a short, stocky kid on a skateboard nearly killed us as we stepped off the curb to cross the street. I swore out loud. Rufus snarled at him, then stopped to take a dump. I guess he was feeling better.

While I waited around for the rest of the morning to get on its horse and ride west, I stashed Twannie Jefferson's purple *iMac* in the trunk of my piece of shit Jetta next to the box of video tapes I'd taken from Johnny Brashear's garage.

At noon, I called Ernie again. He sounded even more exhausted.

But he had been busy, and not only with the draining task of being shagged by the Assistant State's Attorney, if that is, in fact, what he was doing when I first rang his number.

He told me there was no case file open on Blackie with the folks at Missing Persons. And why not? Because nobody had officially reported him as missing. It wasn't an official source of concern. There was talk on the streets, of course. There always is. Rumors. Not much of it useful. Some fingers pointed at Venus Edwards, but only because her husband, Hubert, had coincidentally vanished around the same time.

Ernie had narrowed down the last day anyone remembered seeing Blackie. He gave me the date and I wrote it down, just for the record. It meant nothing to me, rang no bells. I didn't expect it to. He'd been seen jumping into a taxi on Prospect Avenue outside Auntie Peg's mansion. Cab company records indicated that he'd been taken to an address in Simsbury, on Firetown Road. Some kind of theatrical enterprise.

*The Farce News*

"The Simsbury Dinner Theater?" I asked.

"As a matter of fact, yes. How'd you know that?"

That put Venus and Hubert Edwards right back in the middle of it. I asked Ernie what he knew about the husband. He grunted.

"Not much about Hubert catches your eye or makes you lose your breath. He's a Certified Public Accountant who got rich on investment counseling. He's suspected of insider trading but the Securities Exchange Commission can't catch him. He's too smart."

"What if they were about to lower the boom and he knew it," I said. "That would be a good reason to take off."

"Nah. I hear Hubert's a mastermind when it comes to laying down an audit proof paper trail. All of Venus Edwards' holdings are jointly held, and he does all the paperwork. If the Internal Revenue Service or the SEC wants a piece of him, they're going to have to study up and get a whole lot smarter. Right now, they're not even in his league."

"Think a Good Time Charlie like Blackie Buenavista would hit him up for revolution money?" I said. "Or use some revolution story as a scam?"

Ernie didn't waste time speculating on that subject. He didn't buy the freedom fighter angle. Said he had no reason to believe it was even remotely true. Besides, he'd found no passport activity on Benizio Buenavista in the last six months. He was an American citizen now, with a U.S. passport. But the trail ended before leading to the actual time when he'd held a foreign passport, if such a time had ever existed. So, unless he was currently traveling on forged papers -- and not the kind Hubert Edwards might provide -- Blackie was still in the country, if not right here in Hartford somewhere. Laying low.

I'd had the same thought earlier, but didn't say so.

"So who the hell is this guy?" I asked. "What do you know about Blackie Buenavista?"

There wasn't much to tell. Ernie ticked it off like items on a grocery list. Tall, dark, and handsome. *Milk, eggs, and cheese.* Movie star looks. Bedroom eyes. Charisma coming out of his ass. *Hair gel. Visine. Preparation H.* He could play the good guy in a spaghetti western, or knock off every bank from Boston to Bolivia and you'd root for him to get away with it. Clint Eastwood meets Paul Newman meets Antonio Banderas meets Cantinflas. With subtitles for those who can't understand the thick, phlegmy accent.

"So what do you make of the idea that Blackie and Hubert ran off together?" I said.

"What?" he said, snorting. "A pair of fags going bump in the night? That's pretty weak."

"Why? What if Hubie got bored pushing paper around his desk? What if he wanted to get his hands a little dirty, just once in his miserable little white collar life? You never know. Maybe he goes for the tall, dark and handsome *caballero* type."

Ernie laughed. "Blackie might have had an interest in Hubie's money, but I doubt he was the type who'd grab his own ankles to get it, if you know what I mean. I hear he was a hard core womanizer. You can ask the ex-wife about it. Story is she caught him at it more than a few times. And even if Hubert was half-a-queer, I don't see Buenavista starring in *Pillow Talk* as Doris Day."

I suggested the Venus Edwards connection, but Ernie didn't bite.

She was well known for her single-minded pursuit of her own interests, whether it was the acquisition of real estate holdings or the production of staggeringly bad dinner theater productions. She had all the financial expertise she needed from Hubert. She didn't need, or apparently desire, his personal attention. It worked this way: Venus wrote the checks and Hubert made sure the money got into the appropriate account on time. It seemed they lived parallel lives with very few occasions for, as Venus would probably put it, intercourse. Plenty of marriages worked that way. Still, it left lingering mysteries. Where the hell was Hubert? How come nobody had seen him?

"That's a fair question," Ernie said. "At the moment, however, you're the only one asking it."

"Venus Edwards isn't asking?"

"The company line is that Hubert is away attending to affairs."

"And she gets away with that?"

"There's nothing to get away with, Robby. Maybe he's in the Bahamas setting up offshore accounts. Maybe he likes snorkeling with *cabana* boys and sipping rum punch on the beach and doesn't want to come home right away, particularly to a wife who doesn't put a whole lot of value in his companionship. Anyway, no crime has been reported. Or, for all we know, committed. Aside from you, nobody's squawking."

"Yeah, I'm stunned by the resounding silence."

I was also frustrated at being no closer to understanding what the hell was going on. And at how easy it was to get sidetracked. I was supposed to be tracing the movements of Blackie Buenavista, even though nobody had officially hired me to do so, and instead I was talking about some squirrelly Poindexter pencil-pushing bean-counter and where he'd gone. Why? What the hell did I care if Hubert Frobisher Edwards had skipped off into the sunset with a boyfriend or a girlfriend or one of each? And why did I automatically think of him as the kind of guy who skipped? Had to be that middle name.

*Frobisher.* And the fact that he was married to a human battle ax.

"So, Blackie disappears," I said, "and nobody officially reports it. Fine. But the minute I agree to do a favor for the old lady, on a completely unrelated subject, everyone leaps to the conclusion that I'm looking for him. When I say I'm not, nobody believes me. And when I say I couldn't care less one way or the other, everyone keeps bringing it up like it's the most important event on the fall social calendar. But not important enough to call in the police. What's wrong with this picture?"

"Plenty," Ernie said.

"No shit."

"But that's the nature of the beast."

"Beautiful."

We hung up and I put the leash back on Rufus. He looked confused. Not because he was getting another walk so soon after the first one, but because he's a dog and dogs frequently look confused even when they aren't. Maybe he didn't recognize me. They say every fifteen minutes constitutes a new day for a dog. I'd been on the phone with Ernie Newman for at least twenty minutes.

Without a particular destination in mind, we started out for the Trinity College campus. At worst, I figured some cute coeds would come over to cuddle Rufus and pull his ears. With any luck, some cute coed would come over to cuddle me and pull my ears, too, although I didn't think I'd enjoy it as much as the dog would.

There was no hurry. After two days of running around the county half-cocked and two-thirds bewildered, there was an almost measurable tranquillity to the day. I'd be rid of the computer by mid-afternoon. This evening, perhaps, I'd drop by the Wordstone mansion and give the box of videotapes to whomever raised their hand first and said, "Please," and "Thank you." I might even hint my way to a paycheck or two. I'd hate to come right out and say, "Pay up, you bastards." But if it came to that, I'd do it.

As we stepped off the curb to cross the street, a short, stocky kid on a flashy skateboard raced by and nearly wiped us out. For a moment I thought I was having one of those weird deja vu moments. But that quickly passed and was replaced by an even stranger sensation that it was the same short, stocky kid on the same flashy skateboard who'd nearly taken us out earlier that morning. The kid had the speed of a cannonball rolling down a hill. He was almost beyond earshot before I could properly gather my senses and curse him out, or condemn his mother for her misguided decision not to go through with that back alley abortion after all. I turned to check for traffic coming the other way, and discovered Jolie standing there, smiling.

*The Farce News*

"Miss me?" she said.

I laughed. A nervous response. Rufus barked. No clue what *his* emotional state was.

"I'm being stalked by a lunatic on a skateboard at the moment," I said. "So let me save your question for another time."

"Fair enough. Where you headed?"

"Nowhere special."

"Mind if I come along?"

I made no objection. Rufus was clearly delighted. He proceeded to demonstrate his enthusiasm by jumping up to throw a cross-body block at Jolie. I thought about alerting him to the fact that Jolie apparently held some advanced belt in one of the many branches of martial arts. But I don't speak dog. And besides, he would learn his lesson soon enough. All's fair in love and war.

Jolie caught Rufus in midair, squeezed half the air out of him, then put him down gently on all fours. Rufus never knew what hit him. He looked up at me with the expression of an eight-year-old kid who's just had his first roller coaster ride and says, half-terrified, "Can we go again?"

We strolled around the campus for a while, not talking much. I don't think Jolie was waiting for me to explain everything that had gone on in the last forty-eight hours. Frankly, I think she had figured out most of it for herself, based on what she'd seen first hand, the contents of our breakfast conversation, and what she'd read in the mistake-filled newspaper.

"Know why I didn't answer the door when you knocked?" she said, after a period of comfortable silence.

I looked at her. "Because you weren't there?"

Which, of course, was patently ridiculous. How would she know I knocked on her door if she wasn't there in the first place? No wonder I made a lousy investigator.

She put out one hand. "Can I walk him?" she said.

Rufus looked up at me again. "Yeah!" he barked. "Let her! Let her!"

"Sure," I said, shrugging. Hell, she walked him almost every day anyway.

She took the dog's leash from my hand and wrapped the strap around her right fist.

We continued walking quietly. There were no cute coeds out on the campus square. I hardly missed them.

After a few minutes, Jolie broke the silence again. "I just wanted you to know how it feels."

I turned to her again. Seems like I was forever looking for excuses to feast my eyes on Jolie. I wished I'd realized it at the time. She wasn't smiling.

But she didn't look particularly sad, either. Or angry. More like tranquil.

"How what feels?" I asked.

"How it feels to knock on someone's door and get no answer."

Oh.

We walked along. I stared down at my *Adidas* sneakers and thought about what she'd said. Or what she meant by it. The fallacy was that she had been there when I knocked. Maybe I didn't hear her right.

When I looked up, I noticed the short, stocky kid on the flashy skateboard again. He was a couple of hundred yards ahead of us, cruising slowly in our direction. He was compact and greasy, with long hair, baggy jeans, huge sneakers, a loose black shirt, and a denim jacket with no sleeves. He might be twenty years old. Certainly too old for children's toys. Or foolish games.

"Come on," I said, and took Jolie by the hand. We cut across the grass heading back toward Summit Street. I didn't want to be obvious, but I wanted to know if the kid would try to follow us. He did. He couldn't ride his skateboard across the grass, ao he picked it up and sauntered in our direction. "Let's pick up the pace a little. It's the skateboarder from Hell."

Jolie was obviously a spy movie veteran, one who knew better than to look over her shoulder and tip off our stalker that we knew we were being pursued. We walked at a brisk pace, without panic. Why would she panic? She could probably break the skateboarder in half, to say nothing of turning the skateboard itself into a pathetic pile of laminated splinters. A block from the apartment, we came to my parked car. There was a folded leaflet pinned under the windshield wipers. I grabbed it, stuffed it into my back pocket, then fished out my keys and unlocked the front and back doors.

"Climb in," I said.

Jolie hopped in. Rufus jumped into her lap then clamored over her into the back seat. Meanwhile I stood holding the back door for him like some sad sack chauffeur with a spoiled child for a client.

I ran around the front and slid in behind the steering wheel and fired the engine. Miraculously, it started on the first try. The skateboard stalker was back aboard his machine and pumping hard with one leg, closing the gap between us. I pulled out into traffic and gunned it north toward Park Street. I figured my piece of shit Jetta, bad as it was, could outrun a fat kid on a friggin' skateboard. Still, I kept checking the rear view mirror until I was absolutely sure we'd lost him.

## Chapter 21

We drove around aimlessly, Jolie and I. Chuck Berry riffed in my head. *Ridin' along in my automobile/Baby beside me at the wheel/Cruisin' and playin' the radio,/With no particular place to go.* It would have been perfect if only the radio in my piece of shit Jetta actually worked. The only thing it picked up was some wacko station called the E.I.B. Network, and the only programming broadcast on it was a steady diet neofascist propaganda, pretty much around the clock. I figure the car's original owner must have been some kind of modern day Hitler Youth dweeb who'd maliciously rigged the antenna to achieve this psychotic result. As an antidote, I had torn the knob off so nobody would ever turn it on again.

Jolie said she had no plans. The worst of the morning was behind us -- now that we'd lost the short, stocky kid on the flashy skateboard. It had taken about ninety seconds and a series of left and right turns to drop the greasy stalker. I was almost proud of my piece of shit Jetta for a job well done and almost stopped hating the rusty bucket of bolts. But the feeling only lasted about three minutes, until I pulled to a stop at a red light and the engine coughed twice and stalled.

I continued to check the rear view mirror periodically, just to be on the safe side (and because that's what they tell you to do at driving school when you're sixteen, and what's good enough for a sixteen-year-old is good enough for me). But I didn't notice any particularly conspicuous cars back there that might be tailing us, assuming the Bam Margera wannabe had upgraded his means of transportation to some form of conveyance featuring a combustion engine. For the life of me, I couldn't think of who was left in this preposterous misadventure who might have any reason to sneak around in such a laughable and irritating manner. Or to terrorize Rufus and me while we're out enjoying a civilized walk, just a dog and his faithful master. Then again, it had been that kind of week. And it was still only Wednesday.

I'd found myself waiting for Jolie to say something along the lines of: "My knight in shining armor," and to thank me profusely for saving her from some untold catastrophe. Instead, after a few minutes, she broke the silence with a challenge: "So, what was that all about?"

No suitable answer popped into my mind, since I didn't know what it was all about. Jolie accepted my shrug at face value (or perhaps shoulder value) and let it go. We rode along for a few more minutes in easy quiet. The dog had gone to sleep in the back seat. His snoring and the half-stifled roar of my car's pitted muffler were the only sounds.

Soon, I changed our heading and steered us back toward Summit Street. We were about to go our separate ways when Jolie suddenly had a bright idea. I imagine she has several bright ideas each day, but this was the first one she'd shared with me. And I liked it immediately. Rufus was a little miffed when it dawned on him that he wasn't part of the great scheme, but he got over it when I took him upstairs gave him some water and a couple of marrow bones. I put on a clean shirt, and ran back down to the street and got back in the car where Jolie was waiting with the engine running.

If she noticed that I'd changed my shirt, she didn't embarrass me by mentioning it.

For the next half hour we cruised the neighborhood in search of decent lunch fare. Fast food was out of the question for all the obvious reasons, among them basic health concerns, some philosophical postures, and a fundamental revulsion for the available products in question. "I've never quite grasped the appeal of super-sizing," I told Jolie as we cancelled a number of choices.

"It's the culinary version of adding insult to injury," she said.

"Exactly," I said. "When the injury itself is self-inflicted."

We were clear to West Hartford before Jolie finally suggested this two-story joint opposite the West-Farms mall on New Britain Avenue in a shopping center known as Corbins Corner. It was casual enough, no tie was required, but every table featured a white tablecloth and carefully folded cloth napkins. The interior was dimly lit and arranged on different levels, which had to make waiting tables something like an olympic endurance event designed by M.C. Escher. A bar was situated in the central pit. A single bartender was down there mechanically drying glasses, no doubt battling valiantly to ward off the onset of midday ennui. We skipped the lonely bar scene and grabbed a corner table somewhat off the beaten track. The traditional lunch hour had come and gone, so there wasn't much traffic. A couple of salesmen drank their way through the early afternoon, some professional mall crawlers took their midday feed in preparation for an afternoon of no-nonsense power shopping.

We studied our menus and mumbled about the choices. Jolie ordered a rack of ribs. I eventually settled on a Cobb salad that came in a large bread bowl. Our waitress was (I thought) excessively jubilant over our choices and swore what amounted to a food-service-industry blood oath to return almost instantaneously with a bread basket and our drinks: a Guinness for me, a diet coke for Jolie. Neither of us touched the bread. But as we sipped our drinks and waited for the food to arrive we shared a few immature comments about our fellow diners, particularly a pair of young lovers who looked about seventeen. We decided they should be in school taking a World Civ test, not cuddling like kittens in a public restaurant. Neither of us wanted to be the one to tell them, however. We ultimately decided to live and let live.

There were some stretches of silence as well, but they felt right.

Our food arrived and we became absorbed in consuming it.

"This is so stupid," Jolie said, putting down a stripped rib, licking the barbecue sauce from her fingertips.

"What is?" I said. "The ribs?"

She looked me in the eye. "How long have we known each other?"

I put down my fork. I actually had to think about it. I honestly didn't know. A couple of years? Three? More? I'd been in the Summit Street apartment for a few years. Was it four? Five, maybe. My short term memory has been failing with increasing regularity. My long term memory is all but nonexistent. Had she always been there? I couldn't even remember when we met, or what the circumstances had been. Had fate thrown us together at the mailboxes in the lobby? Had I chivalrously held a door for her while she wrestled an armload of grocery bags? Or had she held the door for me?

"A while, I guess. Why?"

"How many times have we gone out for a meal together?"

"You mean in a restaurant?" I had to think about that, too.

"Don't get a cramp," she said. "The answer is never."

"You mean not ever?" I said. She smirked. She got the reference.

"Never," she said. "Not ever."

"That can't be right."

She dabbed perfunctorily at her mouth with a napkin. I'd never seen anyone eat a rack of ribs and so deftly keep the barbecue sauce from covering her face. The way she handled her food was nothing short of an art form. "It isn't right," she said. "But it's a fact."

"Okay," I said. "So, let this mark the official beginning of the non-stupid era. What are you doing for dinner?"

"After this?" she said, holding up another rib. "Fasting."

We went back to our respective meals. She attacked hers with a good deal more gusto than I applied to mine. It's pretty hard to get really worked up over a Cobb salad, no matter how good it is. Now, linguine and clam sauce is a different story. But this restaurant didn't serve it. "By the way," I said. "Where the hell did you ever pick up karate, or ju jitsu, or whatever that was you used on Billie Billie?"

She put down her napkin and gave me a long, inscrutable look. "Robby," she said. "You don't pick up karate, or ju jitsu, or whatever that was that I used on Billie Billie."

"My bad."

"It's a discipline. A lifestyle."

"Okay, I get it." I didn't, really. But I hate to be scolded.

"It's Kempo," she said. "I studied for fifteen years, back when I lived in California."

"So, you're from the west," I pointed out. The amateur detective in me bubbled to the top, like cream -- in my case, sour cream -- as I demonstrated my dexterity in the area of Pointing Out The Obvious. I could only hope she wouldn't hold it against me.

"Bakersfield," she said.

"Ah, Bakersfield," I said. "Home of Buck Owens and *the sound.*"

"You're a fan of Buck Owens?"

"I'm a fan of his steel guitar player," I said. "I prefer Wynn Stewart and Merle Haggard, but Buck's okay." I didn't want to say too much. I've often gotten in trouble for admitting that the only thing I really like about most country music is the pedal steel guitar riffs. People often respond by telling me that such an attitude could easily be construed as selfish, egocentric and snobbish. If only I gave a shit what people thought.

Jolie smiled and dabbed her mouth with a napkin. "Personally, I prefer Buddy Miller."

"How could you not? *Midnight and Lonesome* is a personal favorite."

"*Poison Love* tops my list. Why he isn't more popular I'll never understand."

I put down my fork and peered cautiously at her. She didn't look away. She was inching toward a dangerous mine field. For years, Artie Johansson and I had shared a dream, and drained our share of bourbon bottles, and killed someone else's share of endless nights writing songs and bemoaning the sorry state of the music industry. I guess that's what you do when you don't make it. You blame *them.* Our lament went way back, long before we grew too old to sustain any real hope of landing that elusive record deal that would launch us into the stratosphere of musical fame and fortune. We'd bitched long and hard about everything that was wrong with the music business, but had never come up with a productive solution to our ongoing quagmire of dilemmas and conundrums.

"If the people who run Nashville didn't have their heads up their asses, the Buddy Millers of the world would be headliners and all the big hat and hairdo acts would be off playing the smokey bars and VFW halls where they belong."

I winced. We play our share of VFWs. They're fun, but a far cry from the dream gig. "Actually," I said, then stopped and shrugged. "Never mind."

"Mind you, I have nothing against smokey bars and VFWs," she said, "except that all the wrong people play them. But that's the world."

I agreed. "Not much of it makes much sense."

"And few things are what they should be."

I smiled sadly at her.

She smiled. "Since you asked."

I thought about asking her something else, specifically: to be the mother of my children. But we hadn't even finished lunch yet. Our first meal together, apparently.

She shrugged and attacked another rib.

I picked at my Cobb salad without much enthusiasm. The turkey had gone dry. The croutons were soggy. The ice berg lettuce was just one more victim of global warming. Furthermore, I felt a little sick to my stomach, and wondered if I was coming down with some kind of flu bug. I hadn't slept well for a couple of nights. Maybe I was just worn out from all the lowbrow high drama. But I didn't really feel worn out, either. Just nauseated.

"So, what belt are you?" I asked, to change the subject.

She gnawed on a rib for a moment, then put down the bare bone. I was sorry when she finished it because it was kind of fun to watch. "Black," she said. "Fourth degree."

"I suppose you can pretty much break a brick if you wanted to."

She flashed the killer smile. "Thank God I haven't had to do that for a while. Believe me, it isn't all it's cracked up to be."

I don't know if that was some vague attempt at a pun. I let it go.

"So why'd you leave Bakersfield?"

She made a face. "Why does anyone leave home?"

"Family."

"Bingo."

"The Marine Corps didn't want you? With all your special skills?"

"No," she said. "And the feeling was mutual."

"Do you still study martial arts?"

"No, not really. I practice what I know, to keep it current, but I'm not motivated enough to do the work to earn any more degrees. I got turned off."

"Why?"

"My instructor, guy named Max Crayton, had a few loose screws. He used to pretend he was some ex-CIA spook or some such thing. On one hand he was all the time talking about the importance of discipline and self-control, then on the other hand starts showing us his private stash of kill moves. What he could do with just his thumbs. He thought it was really funny."

"Kill moves?"

"Yeah."

"Tell me that isn't what it sounds like."

"It's exactly what it sounds like."

"Nice."

"It gave me the creeps."

"No kidding. I'd take that as a sign of your sound mental health."

"A bunch of us quit together because of him. His antics really took the fun out of it."

"The old turd in the swimming pool, huh?"

She stopped and stared at me. "Hey," she said, after a moment. "I'm eating, here."

"My bad."

"Anyway, I'm satisfied. I can protect myself if I have to."

I snorted. "That's quite the understatement."

The waitress came by for about the fifth time to ask how everything was. I was a little weary of assuring her that my patently ordinary salad was *simply fabulous*. For a moment I considered launching into a clever, William F. Buckley-esque lecture on the state of the union, or perhaps I'd regale her with a detailed description of an imaginary rash on my inner elbow. But I seemed to be fresh out of snappy repartee at the moment. Or maybe it was just her lucky day.

The waitress eventually retreated, dragging her abject boredom behind her like an invisible rag doll, and Jolie stepped to the microphone to take over as *ad hoc* interviewer.

"So, how in the world did you ever become a pedal steel guitar player? I mean, it's not exactly your typical boiler plate instrument. What happened, was the music store all out of harmonicas when you decided on a career in show biz?"

Unlike all the rhetorical questions I'd been facing (and posing) in the last few days, this was a question to which I possessed an actual answer -- if only I could overcome Jolie's withering sarcasm. I put down my fork. (Putting down cutlery always serves as a fairly dramatic preamble to any significant reminiscence. Why? Who the hell knows.)

"Once upon a time," I said, and she rolled her eyes, "in a land far, far away ..."

"Please."

"I was just a kid. Fourteen or fifteen, maybe. Went to this concert at Roosevelt Stadium in New Jersey. Ever hear of it?"

"What? You mean New Jersey?"

"No, Roosevelt Stadium. It's gone now. Tore it down years ago to make room for a Wendy's or something equally useless."

"But you digress."

"Anyway, so I'm at this Grateful Dead concert ..."

"Oh, my God," she said. "I knew it. You're a Dead Head!"

She looked incredulous. I studied her expression for signs of deal-breaking disappointment but could not immediately identify any.

I shrugged. "What can I say?"

"It sure explains a few things," she said. "Like the ponytail. And the hippy attitude."

"Thanks."

She cracked the killer smile. "But where's all your tie-dye stuff?"

"I'm in recovery."

"Oh," she said. "Okay. Go on."

"Anyway, the opening act was this five-piece country rock group ..."

"Let me guess," she said. "New Riders of the Purple Sage."

"You know 'em?"

"Sure," she said, and began singing. "Panama Red, Panama Red, he'll steal your woman, then he'll rob your head ..."

"Panama Red, Panama Red," I sang back, tapping out the rhythm on the tablecloth with my fingers. "On his white horse, Mescalito, he comes breezin' through town, bet your woman's up in bed with old Panama Red."

The young lovers across the room looked up from their insufferable cuddling to register disapproval of our singing -- both in style as well as content. Expressions of intolerance twisted their adolescent faces. Jolie ignored them. I stuck out my tongue at them.

"So, the New Riders had this steel player, a Canadian guy, Buddy Cage. A real hippy looking dude. Long hair, handlebar mustache. If you didn't know better, or you hadn't heard him play, you'd think he was some skinny Hell's Angels biker. But, man could he pick. For no particular reason, fate maybe, I ended up standing down in front on the side of the stage where he had his rig set up. Before that day I had no idea what a pedal steel guitar was. I'd never even heard of the thing. But the stuff he played just blew my mind. Then, a few weeks later, I heard this other guy, Jay Dee Maness, backing the Byrds on *Sweethearts of the Rodeo.* He played riffs with melody lines moving in opposite directions simultaneously. I'm a sucker for counterpoint. The licks he played were ridiculous. Upside-down chords. Chromatic fills up the ass."

"Good, huh?"

"You never wanted the solos to end."

I paused, remembering what it was like to be young and mind-boggled by something that could grab you that way and not let go. How it made you slightly sick to your stomach. In a good way.

"Don't stop," she said.

"That it was it. I was hooked. One free taste and I became a pedal steel guitar junkie. Took me a few years to get around to buying a steel guitar and learning how to play it. Sometimes I'm a bit slow on the uptake."

"Really?"

"Seems like the higher the stakes, more I want something, the longer it takes me to screw up the courage to go after it."

"It's a charming trait," she said. "Up to a point."

"You think?"

"Sure, but while you're dreaming of being Casey Jones, the train might leave the station. Without you."

"Okay, but on the other hand, can't the waiting increase the ultimate satisfaction. I can tell you right now, it was the best thing I ever did. It's better than ..."

She put up a hand to stop me. "Don't say it."

"What?"

"Don't say it's better than sex."

I probably blushed. "I wasn't going to."

"Okay."

"I was going to say it's better than therapy."

"Oh." She picked up another rib and took a bite. "That's okay, then."

When the waitress came back for the fifth or sixth time, she had our bill. Sorry, she told us, no rush. But her shift was about to end and she was getting ready to cash out. I reached for the slip, but Jolie beat me to it and insisted on treating since lunch had been her idea and she'd picked the place. It wasn't fair to stick me with the tab, she said. I told her to stop being foolish. Then I remembered the black belt in karate and stopped calling her names. We compromised. She took care of the bill and I left the tip. Way too big a tip, all things considered.

We didn't say much on the drive back to Summit Street. When I dropped her off in front of our apartment building, she hopped out, then turned and leaned back into the car.

"Wait a second."

"What's up?"

"What did you say was the name of those two steel players?"

"Buddy Cage and Jay Dee Maness. Why?"

She laughed out loud and people on the sidewalk turned to look at her as they walked by. She didn't give any indication of giving a damn.

"You named your cats after a pair of pedal steel guitar players?"

Now I felt like a world class idiot. My face must have gotten pretty red. The skin around my ears felt about a hundred and twelve degrees Fahrenheit. "Not just *any* pedal steel players," I said, feeling quite silly.

"That's beautiful," she said. "Really."

She ran to the front door of the apartment building and pushed her way inside without turning to wave goodbye, or to thank me for a lovely lunch, or even to say *see ya later.* Nothing.

I was still feeling pretty silly when I got to Farmington Avenue and pulled my piece of shit Jetta into the Kinko parking lot on Kenyon Street. I went inside, bought a Dr. Pepper from the soda machine, and waved casually to the long suffering clerk behind the main counter. Then I did my devil's dance across the wide street, dodging east-west traffic -- and drivers bent on turning me into a hood ornament. I survived the ordeal and went up to the rehearsal studio. The guitar needed tuning, strings needed replacement, riffs needed review. I needed to at least pretend I gave a shit about our weekend gig in Bristol. And I had a couple of hours to kill before my meeting with Ernie Newman downtown.

As I entered the building, I began to pray -- literally *to pray* -- complete with the traditional Oh, Remarkably Splendid and Mysterious Creator salutation I'd learned one summer at vacation bible school, that nobody, especially in costume, was lurking in the shadows, waiting to pounce on me and drag me through another lowbrow Elmer J. Shakespeare drama (Elmer being the much disabused younger brother of the celebrated English bard and the inspiration for an animated rabbit hunter who would come along a century or so later). The corridor was empty. I said five Hail Myron Fuller Graces and, lo and behold, the anteroom was also empty. I recited the rosary, or as much of it as I could remember from hanging out with Catholic kids back in elementary school. I slipped the key into the lock of our inner sanctum, swung back the door, and fell to my knees in gratitude. I nominate Patrick, a fig tree, and the spirit of sanity.

The large room was empty, save our beat-up furniture, the abbreviated drum kit, the microphone stands, my guitar, the amps, and a stack of mail collecting dust on the floor. I picked it up, sifted through the junk -- a couple of notices of reminder that we were actually required to pay for the lights and rent -- and opened the important stuff, including my renewal form from The Hockey News and the monthly newsletter from the Pedal Steel Guitar

Association telling me about another wonderful gathering I'd missed. If the Wordstones coughed up some money, I'd be able to cover the THN renewal and pay the other less important bills -- the electricity and rent -- with a few bucks to spare. Artie and the boys would kick in for that. Hopefully. Or I could always try getting blood from a stone.

I was about to drop the rest of the mail in the trash when I came across an envelope I hadn't initially noticed. It bore no stamp and had no return address. I deduced that it must have been dropped off by hand and slipped under the door, just to prove to myself that I had some (if only very limited) skill as an amateur sleuth. My name was written across the front in stylized script. It was about the size of a wedding announcement, or so I guessed, never having been invited to anybody's nuptials, except as a hired hand to provide musical diversion once the serious drinking and regret began to take hold. I rummaged in desk drawers looking for something resembling a letter opener, then remembered we didn't have one. After tearing off one end, I extracted a handwritten note signed by Margaret Waddley-Wordstone, my dear sweet daffy Auntie Peg, requested an audience at my nearest convenience. No need to call ahead. The tone was strangely polite and overly formal. We were family, after all. Had she forgotten the unwritten rule about feeding me a steady diet of insolence and conceit? Or was that *my* unwritten rule? I couldn't remember. This note reflected genuine civility. I was about to discard it as a forgery, someone's idea of a practical joke, and get to work on the Emmons D-10. But I choked back my cynicism and pocketed the note. I locked up the rehearsal hall and headed back to my piece of shit Jetta. There would be time to practice later.

Since she'd asked so nicely, I figured I could give the old broad a few minutes of my time. I might even collect a check out of the deal. Still, I halfhoped the car wouldn't start. God knows, it was way overdue for a bout of untimely engine failure. No such luck.

Ten minutes later I pulled into the circular driveway on Prospect Avenue.

I didn't recognized the antediluvian woman who opened the door when I rang the bell. She was one of those quintessentially medium human beings. Neither tall nor short, neither overweight nor underweight. Her facial features seemed to have been applied with a putty knife and assiduously smoothed over so that none of them stood out from the crowd. I knew I could study her for an hour and forget what she looked like the instant one of us turned away. Only one fact stood out: she had to be a hundred and fifty years old. Credit where it's due, she seemed very well preserved and hearty.

"Yes?" she said, neither rudely nor politely. As if she couldn't care less who I was and only wanted to determine that I had a damn good reason for interrupting whatever it was she'd been doing before coming to the door. And that asking was part of her job and so she must.

I told her who I was. My name clearly meant nothing to her. I held my emotions in check and explained that I had received a note from the matron of the house asking me to stop by. But the old woman made it plain with her mulish hesitancy that I would have to produce the alleged note if I actually hoped to gain entry to the great manse. Hadn't I gone through all this with Rosa once already? I wasn't interested in playing any more games with any more suspicious gatekeepers. I sure as hell wasn't about to jump through hoops for this wannabe ringmaster, particularly if nothing better than a dish of pistachio ice cream awaited me at the other end, just dessert for my heroic efforts. I wasn't even hungry. My stomach had settled a little since lunch, but that could easily change. The nausea had been coming and going for days.

I turned and walked away, leaving the nondescript sentry at the door. I didn't hear the door close behind me. Maybe she was waiting to see if I'd have second thoughts and come back, perhaps to seek her forgiveness or something else equally improbable. At the car, I popped the trunk, and hauled out the heavy box of videotapes I'd taken from Johnny Brashear's garage. The box was plain brown corrugated cardboard, heavy duty stuff with no markings to identify its contents, other than the fraudulent "Sports Videos."

I had sealed it with plastic packing tape and thick twine, knotting it in enough places to insure that anyone who really wanted to open the thing would have to invest about two hours of their time to see what was inside. I'd printed Lillian Buenavista's name on it in black ink, figuring she could dispose of the tapes as she wished. I just didn't care any more. And while she was at it, she could deal with Lita however she saw fit.

The box had some real weight to it, but I carried it steadily to the house under the watchful eye of the prehistoric sentinel, whose identity suddenly came to me. She was Mrs. Rains, and it was her great-grandson, Claude, who had starred in the 1933 movie classic *The Invisible Man*. That's where she got the nondescript traits. Or, rather, where he'd gotten them.

I set the heavy box on the doorjamb, half in the house, half on the stoop. The old lady was going to need some help moving this thing around. I wished her luck finding someone. "Do me a favor, will you? Make sure Mrs. Buenavista gets this."

"Mrs. Buenavista isn't in."

"Thanks for the update."

*The Farce News*

"She's rehearsing for her audition."

"How delightful for her. I'm so glad I asked. Just see that she gets the box. And then make sure you let Mrs. Wordstone know ..."

"Mrs. Waddley-Wordstone."

"... that I was here, as she requested, and that you decided not to let me in? Okay? Great, thanks so much for all your help. It's been delightful. Perhaps we can do it again sometime. Have your people call my people. You do have people, don't you?"

She looked blankly at me. I get that a lot.

I turned on my heels and started back for the car. Behind me I heard the raspy sound of a large, heavy object being moved. No way. I glanced over my shoulder. The old lady had dragged the box in off the stoop and was tilting it over on one end. I stopped to watch. To my utter disbelief, she dropped into a deep knee bend, grabbed the large box around two corners, and deadlifted it off the floor. A regular clean and jerk. If she lifted it over head, I'd personally award her the gold medal -- if it was the last thing I ever did. Although, if she lifted the heavy box over her head, it might well be the last thing *she* ever did.

Last thing I saw was her left foot kicking the door shut as she carried the box into the dark house. I had to remember not to sass her any more, should our paths ever cross again, lest she snap my spine like a dried old twig.

My next stop took me downtown. Ernie Newman had agreed to meet me at the courthouse and act as intermediary for Dee Dee McCool. I wanted Twannie Jefferson's purple *iMac* out of my trunk, out of my possession, out of my life. Slowly but surely, I was divesting myself of all materiel related to the Wordstones and, by association, the hyenas who sniffed around their periphery in the hopes of scoring a piece of meat. A couple of the jackals had already paid the ultimate price for coming too close to the lion's den. But I was done with all the sappy Disney imagery. All I wanted was to put some distance between me and anything that reminded me of these people. Family or not.

Ernie Newman was waiting outside the courthouse when I stopped in front of a street sign that said: No-Parking Tow Away Zone. I almost didn't recognized him. For one thing, he looked rested. And sober. Groomed as well, as if he'd put himself in the care of an actual barber instead of shaving in the darkened centrifuge of half-drunkenness as he usually did. His face was as smooth and free of bristles as I'd ever seen it. His shirt was clean at the collar, his tie bright and tied in a precise Windsor knot. But most shocking was the suit he wore. It was navy blue. I'd never seen him in anything but brown. I didn't even know he had any other colors in his wardrobe.

"Ernie!" I said, giving him a slap on the back. He didn't lurch forward in his usual, off balance way. Instead, he felt solid. This was too much to believe. "Is it really you?"

He beamed at me. "Yeah, George, it's me."

"I hardly recognize ..."

"Yeah, yeah," he said, cutting me off. "You got something for me?"

We walked around to the back of the car. I opened the trunk lid and reached in for desktop computer. There was a plastic grocery bag containing the mouse and all the cords. He put that under his arm, and reached for the keyboard as well. He was scaring me.

"You gonna give this stuff to your friend Dee Dee?" I asked. "Or go into business for yourself?"

"Have a little faith, kid." He smiled. "And it's Miss McCool to you."

I was worried about him. "I'm worried about you," I said.

"Don't be," he said, and said no more.

"Oh, well, that's reassuring. Thanks for the detailed explanation."

He laughed and turned to head for the courthouse. "Stay in touch."

"You shagged her, didn't you?" I said as he was walking away.

"It's a lovely day. Don't ruin it with cheap vulgarity."

He left me standing there, shaking my head.

And that was that.

I was done.

There was nothing left for me to do. I was officially finished with the Wordstones -- except for collecting a paycheck. The old lady would not be forking over any eighty thousand dollars to Twannie Jefferson. Nor would Lillian Buenavista be paying off Johnny Brashear for videotapes featuring her kid sister playing nude volleyball and engaging in assorted acts which arguably fell under the heading of perfectly normal human sexuality, although some might argue it was only normal behavior if you lived in the Land of the Twisted Sisters. In any case, this case was closed.

I should have gone back to Summit Street and walked the dog.

I should have gone back to the rehearsal studio to tune the guitar.

I should have gone home and knocked on Jolie's door to see if she wanted to go get some dinner, even though I still wasn't hungry.

I should have gotten my head examined.

Instead, because I'm stupid and don't know when to leave well enough alone, I jumped in the car and headed northwest out of town, in the general direction of Venus Edwards' tacky dinner theater on Firetown Road in Simsbury. Venus Edwards said she had information about Blackie Buenavista's disappearance, and it seemed that I owed it to someone, somewhere, to find out what she knew, and, perhaps even to find out what had become of Blackie. Because guys like him don't just fall off the face of the earth. Everyone said so.

And yet, that was exactly what he appeared to have done.

To quote the Bard, "Something was rotten in Simsbury," and it wasn't just the food at the Simsbury Dinner Theater. Or maybe that was his brother, Elmer, who said it.

Whatever.

## Chapter 22

If Venus Edwards was happy to see me, she was one of the more accomplished thespians I was destined to encounter at the Simsbury Dinner Theater. She did a masterful job of concealing any sign of delight. In fact, the expression of abject displeasure with which she masked any possible underlying merriment was worthy of serious Oscar consideration. Had the cameras only been rolling.

Call me uncaring, but I didn't waste much time or breath trying to find out what was bothering her. Maybe rehearsals for the upcoming production were going poorly. If that were so, I'm afraid I wasn't going to be able to muster much sympathy. It served her right for staging a musical-comedy adaptation of *Who's Afraid of Virginia Woolf?* What was next? *Cat On a Hot Tin Roof* done in pantomime? *The Pirates of Pinzance* in semaphore? Still, it was as if she'd totally forgotten having extended the invitation to me in the first place. For just a moment I thought maybe I'd dreamed the whole thing up. Our middle-of-the-night colloquy may have qualified as a nightmare, but it was no dream.

She gave me the kind of greeting I'd expect if I were a process server and she were the defendant in yet another law suit involving charges of food poisoning.

Maybe Venus Edwards had contrived, by ardently encouraging me in the first place, to all but guarantee that I would never appear on her doorstep. People like her were apt to try all sorts of trickery, including but not limited to a little reverse psychology, particularly, as in this case, if they were under the erroneous but no less certain impression they were dealing with an adversary of inferior intellect.

I'd show the old cow. To quote the seminal -- and very nearly final -- words of the weak and duplicitous Fredo Corleone: "I'm smart!" (Of course, I was forced to remind myself of this fact at regular intervals, because the more I chased all over the length and breadth of Hartford county in, at best, lukewarm pursuit of the elusive Blackie Buenavista, the dumber I felt.)

It was a little after seven when I got to the Simsbury Dinner Theater. The drive had taken me back through Bloomfield yet again and over Avon Mountain along Route 185. I picked up Hopmeadow Street just past the little bridge spanning the Farmington River where Billie Billie had forced the Monte Carlo driven by Miguel Batista into oncoming traffic, and ultimately over the guard rail into the ravine below. The highway department had already completed repairs.

After briefly wheeling west on Route 167, I made a quick right at the foot of the serpentine Firetown Road, past the Harborside convalescent home bathed in a soft glow of white flood lights, and the Hopmeadow Country Club golf course which sprawled into the darkness on the left. The area was predominantly residential. Tree-lined and well-kept. Modest one- and two-story houses comfortably spaced along either side of the street. A few new dead-end lanes had been carved out, snaking off to the left and right. Sawdust swirled in the gutters where developers had rapidly -- but always with the utmost care and finest possible workmanship -- erected as many chipboard mansions as local zoning ordinances would allow. By the time the glue dried and the sawdust start falling apart and the houses themselves began to crumble, the developers would be long gone -- to some Caribbean beach, no doubt.

Shortly after rolling past a two-story brick elementary school, I came to an intersection in front of a new fire station. Immediately west of the firehouse, the landscape changed markedly. Here only a couple of new homes dotted the terrain, and they dwarfed the houses to the east, some large enough to shelter families numbering in the twenties or thirties. The two-story attached garages alone had more square footage than some of the homes in the neighborhood.

Just west of a sign identifying Barn Door Hills Road, I came upon the Simsbury Dinner Theater about which I had heard so much (so little of it good). It sat by the side of the road on the southern edge of what had apparently once been a large tobacco field. The theater itself was a tall, rectangular building that looked like a remodeled tobacco barn. High side walls and a sharply pitched roof. It was gaudily painted in cherry red and trimmed out in gold. It sparkled with the blinking of a thousand light bulbs. Its only missing feature was a cantilevered marquis hanging off the front. Probably a zoning issue.

On the opposite side of the road sat three more buildings, similar in style to the main structure housing the theater and dining hall, but noticeably smaller. They, too, appeared to be erstwhile tobacco barns. They, too, had been lovingly restored, although in subtler tones. None of them bore any obvious markings to identify the nature of their specific function.

I drove straight past the entertainment oasis and pulled up at the next stop sign, where Firetown intersected Holcomb Street. There I hooked a u-turn and drove slowly back to the theater and rolled into the parking area. I shook off a teenaged boy in black shiny pants and a red satin vest who made a half-hearted pretense of wanting to park my piece of shit Jetta. A quick scan of the large gravel parking lot behind the theater building revealed a fine collection of luxury sedans and high performance European machines, mostly from Germany and Bavaria. One or two from Sweden. I searched for a spot as far from the central flow of traffic as possible, partly because I naturally tend to gravitate toward invisibility and partly because my piece of shit Jetta tended to take the "poor relation" concept to ridiculous extremes in surroundings such as these. However, just to show I have some ego left, I actually locked the car before making my way back to the theater. I could still pretend someone might actually want to steal it.

I was barely into the front lobby when the gruesome and ubiquitous Gomez and Morticia greeted me like a mismatched set of *maitres d'* from the Restaurant at the Center of the Earth. Gomez was dressed in a fresh suit, just as pitch black as the one he'd worn at three o'clock in the morning but considerably less rumpled. Morticia, also bedecked in impeccably drab black, was ready for anything from a shotgun wedding to a mob funeral or an ax murder. Neither of them looked like they'd had much sleep. Ever. The circles under their eyes could have been permanent tattoos.

For a fleeting moment I wondered if they'd just come from the make-up trailer -- assuming such a facility existed here at the Simsbury Dinner Theater. Maybe one of the buildings across the road, next to the infirmary. This musing (for that's all it was) triggered another (musings being a lot like rabbits, but with less fur): what if the whole thing was just a great big charade? A gag. A put-on. Maybe beneath all the grim makeup, Gomez (or Fran, or Sam, or whatever the hell his name was) was just a short, boxy version of Cary Grant, and the tall dead gal, Morticia (or Fran, or Sam, or whatever the hell her name was) was really a modern day Audrey Hepburn in some kind of hellish drag. Maybe Gomez and Morticia were actually a couple of poor students on loan from The Actor's Studio, earning a couple of extra bucks between semesters. Stranger things had probably happened in the world of theater. And I wouldn't even guess at the limits of unconventional behavior possible in the world of higher education.

Then Morticia spoke and my spine tried to curl up and hide in the corner.

"Is there something special we can do for you?" she said, in perfect English, no accent, no stumbling through a bunch of raucously bad translations and misinterpretations.

I looked into her dead eyes. They stared through me and into the empty space directly behind me. If this was an act, she deserved an Oscar.

I took a moment to consider the actual content of her question. I tried on a little smile but it refused to stick. "Honest to God," I said. "I hope it never comes to that. That's partly why I have a living will."

Gomez decided to jump in. "You have some *business* here?" His English was just as good as hers now, although he still bore some trace of an accent. From the Baltics? Somewhere in Middle Europe? It was just too easy to say Transylvania and leave it at that.

"No business," I said. "Tonight it's all pleasure."

I put my hands out to the sides and bowed slightly.

They looked through me. "You have a ticket?" they asked.

"Your boss invited me. Didn't she tell you I was coming?"

The two ghouls looked at each other briefly. Obviously they didn't believe I could possibly be the recipient of any such demonstration of hospitality. Not from Venus Edwards. Not knowing, as they did, how the old crow felt about me in her heart of hearts (a heart which these two ogres must, at some point, have talked lovingly about consuming as part of a romantic candlelit midnight supper). The expression they swapped was remarkably sinister and alarming. Convinced I was lying, they began to display the telltale signs of a couple of rowdy tavern bouncers hoping that before the night was over they'd get to kick ass.

They turned to me and shook their heads back and forth, very slowly, their eyes riveted on me.

"Hey, I've heard the chow here is just awful," I said, to change the subject. "Is that true?"

No answer.

"And I'm told the stage show is even worse. What do you think?"

Blank stares. Their pupils were perfect facsimiles of the ultimate piss holes in snow. They were probably on drugs, too. Anticoagulants to ease the flow of blood through their digestive systems.

"Experience has taught me you can't always believe the gossip. Even the best intentioned rumors can be so misguided. Why, just yesterday, somebody tried to convince me that you two are actually human. I just laughed and said 'nonsense'."

"You think that is funny?" Gomez asked.

I leaned a little closer and spoke in a conspiratorial whisper. "The same person tried to convince me you're alive. Can you believe it?"

"You think we are ghoulish?" Morticia asked.

"Put it this way: I know a corpse when I'm talking to one. Excuse me, Gomez. Two."

Morticia fixed me with a smoldering stare. I could practically smell the smoke. And unless I was imagining it, Gomez was actually vibrating with strangled fury. I thought it might be a good time to take my leave of these beauty pageant dropouts. I hoped like hell they would resist any temptation to forsake decorum and perform a vivisection on me right here in the theater lobby. After all, no matter how mad you get, you can't just go around eviscerating people, particularly in populated venues like the not-quite-legendary Simsbury Dinner Theater.

Still, I vowed to keep Gomez and Morticia on my radar screen at all times, and whenever possible to maintain a distance of three-to-five nautical miles between them and me. I'd keep them in my rear view mirror if I thought they'd cast a reflection, but their ability to do so was yet to be scientifically determined.

"Come with us," Gomez said.

"Where to, fellas?" I didn't budge from my spot. I wasn't convinced Gomez was onto anything but a very bad idea.

"Office," he said. "Madame will receive you in her private office."

His pronunciation of "office" was a little too close to "orifice," and I cringed for a moment.

"Receive me? What, like a gift? Like a burnt offering?"

I could imagine them trying to coerce me down some dark, slimy staircase with rusty chains and the bloody remains of past victims hanging off the walls. Or worse.

Morticia pointed a stunningly bony stick finger at a beige door on the opposite end of the lobby. I studied the finger for a moment. It seemed to be absolutely devoid of flesh. You can't learn that at The Actor's Studio even if you're especially gifted and go quite a while between meals. This was definitely the real thing. I shuddered and followed the projected path of the finger, casting my gaze upon the beige door in question, which blended nicely with the beige walls surrounding it. The door was marked with an eye level plaque in contrasting black letters. It said: PRIVATE. Ah, the private orifice.

I only had to cross fifty feet of beige carpeting to successfully traverse the lobby floor and reach the door. I felt moderately safe and confident about my chances. I could only hope that waiting for me on the other side of the beige door was actually the old bovine matron, Venus Edwards in all her pomp and self-righteous splendor (to say nothing of her cloven hooves), and not some half-starved Bengal tiger with razor sharp claws waiting to do a Siegfried & Roy on my narrow white ass.

"Lead the way, fellas," I said to Gomez and Morticia. Damn if I was going to let them fall in step behind me. I listened for the mournful strains of a bagpiper as we made our funereal death march across the lobby toward the beige office door. No bagpipes could be heard. I did, however, pick up the growling of somebody's stomach. And it wasn't mine. I didn't want to think about whose stomach it was, or what it was growling about. Gomez knocked lightly on the door, then twisted the knob and opened it.

As I left the ghastly duo, I addressed them one last time, or so I hoped. "You know, fellas. I've been thinking. You don't look anything alike. What's the story with that? Were you separated at death?"

"Get in," said Gomez, pointing a sausage finger at the open door.

"Until next time," said Morticia.

I shook my head. "Just like the dead," I said to her, "always trying to have the last word."

I shrugged past them and poked my head into the office which, not surprisingly, was done up in beige, with inordinate black trim. What wasn't beige or black was chrome. All but an antique standing coat rack on which there hung a fur wrap and, inexplicably, a yellow straw cowboy hat. I didn't even try to figure that one out. And there, behind an enormous black lacquered desk, sat my hostess, Venus Edwards, in a beige executive chair that was nearly as thickly padded as its occupant. A scowl was already painted on her rather large and gaudy face. Gold framed reading glasses were perched on the tip of her nose. They reminded me of a swanky but no less despondent bridge jumper contemplating a life-defying leap into the void. And who could blame them?

Whatever Venus Edwards was reading, it was apparently not good news. The reviews of her latest show? The evening menu? The local food critic's most recent lambasting of the cuisine? Had the sheep meat been a bit dry? Perhaps the chef could have basted the lamb more diligently?

Or maybe Venus Edwards was perusing the results of her latest cholesterol test? Was her bad cholesterol still winning the war against her good cholesterol? She eventually looked up at me, after making me wait for what seemed like seconds. Her expression didn't immediately brighten. I didn't take it too personally. Then it darkened as I smiled cheerfully at her.

"Hi, there," I said. "Remember me?"

"Mr. Vaughn," she said. "Terribly delightful to see you."

"Yes," I said, coming forward to shake hands. "Terrible is the word. And after so few hours. Why, we're practically dating. People will talk, you know. Perhaps we should alert the media. The society pages and whatnot. Announce the engagement and start thinking seriously about setting a date for the wedding. What do you think, darling?"

Venus Edwards stared at me as if I had just broken into fluent Urdu.

I doubt she knew what to think.

"Excuse me?" she said.

"Oh, don't go coy on me now."

## The Farce News

She removed her glasses. "Why do you insist on behaving in such a perpetually disrespectful manner? Is there some medical explanation, or are you just happy to be insufferable?"

I snapped my fingers and pointed at her. "I thought you'd never ask!"

She rolled her eyes. "Really?"

"Absolutely. Just between you and me, I blame my parents. They made me what I am today. Not that I believe they intentionally set out to do quite this much damage."

"I couldn't begin to guess what you are talking about."

"It's not very complicated, Venus. May I call you Venus? You see, my parents thought they were doing me a big favor when they decided, early in my childhood, to shelter me from the clutches of organized religion."

"You're an atheist? What an ungodly thought."

"Good one."

"Excuse me?

"Anyway, instead of exposing me to the dubious propaganda of the Christian church, I was introduced to the dazzling cubism of Pablo Picasso, the chaotic choreography of Merce Cunningham, the inscrutable incantations of Alan Ginsberg, the cacophonous musical janglings of John Cage, and, of course, the gregarious comedy of Groucho Marx."

"Ah, yes," she said. "I've heard of Groucho Marx. And Harpo."

I could tell she didn't understand. "You don't understand," I said, just so she knew I knew.

"No, I guess I don't understand."

I hate always being right.

"The point is, while my friends were forced to squirm away their collective youth in the great and gaudy halls of institutionalized worship, I spent Sundays in revival houses all over Manhattan watching Groucho, Chico, Harpo -- and occasionally Zeppo -- wreak havoc right up there on the silver screen. I must have seen every Marx Brothers movie a dozen times before I was ten years old."

She sat back in her heavily padded chair. "Why are you telling me this?"

"My shrink doesn't work Wednesday nights. Wednesdays are bingo nights at the synagogue. And don't interrupt. It's very rude."

"Oh, for goodness sake!"

"Where was I?"

"At the cinema?"

"Oh, yes. Thank you, Venus. You don't mind if I call you that, do you? Good. Anyway, it was a very entertaining way to spend Sundays. But there was a price to pay. There's always a price to pay, isn't there?"

"I'm sure I don't know."

"In my own way, I am scarred for life."

"Yes, that is certainly true."

"You're interrupting again."

"I'm sorry, but is this going to take much longer? I'm exceedingly busy and ..."

"Of course, many of my peers who didn't spend their Sundays in revival houses all over Manhattan Island watching the Marx Brothers, also came away from their experiences scarred. But in a completely different way."

"I must interject at this juncture ..."

"Oh, no you don't!"

"Excuse me?"

"There will be no interjecting," I said. "At this juncture or any other. If you want to interrupt, go right ahead. But for the love of Pete, no interjecting."

"I was only going to say that I thoroughly regret asking you to come here. I don't know what I must have been thinking."

"Then you admit you asked me here?"

"I suppose so. Yes, of course."

"Good. For a minute there I was afraid the whole thing had been a bad dream. God knows we're not in Kansas anymore."

She peered at me. "Are you on any medication?"

I stared at her. "How rude of you to make such a suggestion." Then I smiled. "Anyway, as a result of my misguided youth, I suffer from what appears to be an incurable ailment. What's more, it is both chronic as well as potentially fatal."

"Really," she said, suddenly interested, now that my death had entered the equation. "Is that so?"

"Yes. But don't get your hopes up. Typically, it remains dormant for years. It can be triggered, however, if some great big, fat-assed pompous twit makes the mistake of waving in my face, like a giant flag, the broad cloth of her overblown conceit."

Venus Edwards stood up. "I've heard just about enough."

"Good. Because I've said more than enough."

"Indeed you have."

"Oh, and I think I'm addicted to popcorn."

"What!"

"I take it one day at a time, you know. Forever is a long time. I don't pretend I'll never eat popcorn again. But I'm working at it. It's my problem. I don't need to worry you with it. You're not, are you?"

"Not what?"
"Worried?"
"Heavens no."
"Heavens no?"
"Excuse me?"
"Why not hell no? Why heavens no? What an interesting choice. What does your psychiatrist say about this morbid fascination with heaven and hell?"

"My psychiatrist? Mr. Vaughn, I assure you ..."

"Good," I said, cutting her off. "So, what were we talking about? Oh, yes. Dear old mum and dad. There are times, confidentially speaking, when I think my parents may have gone a little overboard with the whole Groucho thing. Too much of a good thing? What do you think?"

She sighed again. "I think I need a drink."

"I concur," I said. "You do appear a bit thirsty."

"Vodka," she said. "In the freezer. Orange flavored. Will you join me?"

"Join you? I thought we'd gotten past the whole intercourse thing?"

"Will you have a drink?" she said, clearly exasperated. Honestly, I don't know why she didn't pick up the phone and summon Gomez and Morticia to "disappear" me. God knows *I* would have.

I checked my watch. Mickey gave me the thumbs up. I smiled at Venus Edwards and began to like her for the first time. "You know, that's the nicest thing you've said to me all day."

So we sat and drank, she and I. New friends. Don't ask me how it happened. I chalk it up to the restorative effects of alcohol. If Nixon and the North Vietnamese had traded shots of tequila instead of arguing over the shape of the conference room furniture, maybe some lives could have been saved. Who knows? Venus looked at me with a slightly maternal concern and I knew she was convinced I was a deep-ender. Gonzo. Ready for the jacket with the arms that buckle in the back. I liked the feeling. She was easier to take when she was a little on edge. She kept asking me if my drink was okay. I kept telling her it was just fine. It was damn good in fact but I wasn't ready to give her that much satisfaction.

"But, really," I said at last. "People are talking, you know."

She sipped her drink and smiled cautiously. I think she was going for magnanimous. It came out circus clown. Too much rouge. Too much lipstick. I was tempted to sneak a peek under the desk to see if she was wearing size 46 bulb-toed shoes, but she'd probably think I was trying to look up her skirt.

"Really, Mr. Vaughn. Who are *they?* And what could they possibly talk about that would be of any concern to me?"

"Oh, all sorts of interesting things," I said. "Blackie Buenavista. Hubert Edwards. The fact that you look pretty good for maybe pulling the strings on Blackie's disappearing act."

That got her to drop the circus clown smile. I think it actually turned her smile upside down. If only she'd had a great big teardrop painted on her cheek, the picture would have been perfect. "That is patently absurd."

I shrugged and sipped my orange vodka. I felt like an over-the-hill astronaut with a cold glass of high-test *Tang*. "So much of life is patently absurd. If only we knew who held the patent, we could go after her with a chain saw, huh?"

"I had nothing whatsoever to do with his disappearance."

"Which one? Blackie or Hubert?"

"Either one." She sounded pretty sure of herself. Of course, she could have rehearsed the line. It wasn't that long. Even an exceedingly busy woman like her could find the time to learn two words and say them with something approaching real feeling.

"Then what was it you wanted to tell me about it?" I said, putting my glass down on the edge of her desk. It immediately left a small puddle of water. I watched to see if Venus Edwards would get anal and jump up to wipe it away or to shove a coaster under the glass. She looked at the glass, then at me.

"Do you know what September the fifteenth is, Mr. Vaughn?"

I shrugged. Sometimes it's fun to be Fredo Corleone and play the incurable moron in the piece.

"Lemme guess," I said. "Middle of the month?"

"September fifteenth is Independence Day in Nicaragua."

I made a face and nodded. "Sure, I knew that. Everyone knows that. What's your point?"

"It's also the day ..."

"Wait a second."

I reached into my back pocket and took out a piece of folded paper. I unfolded it and found the note I'd written on it. "Yeah, I'll be a dog. Look at that."

"It's the day ..."

"Blackie went bye-bye," I said, finishing her sentence. It was the date Ernie had given me.

Venus Edwards beamed at me. More circus clown, circa 1920. I glanced around the room for any sign of a miniature unicycle. I didn't see one anywhere, but she could easily hide one on her person and I'd never know until she suddenly whipped it out, jumped aboard, and started pedaling madly around the room in tiny circles. I could see it now. I was about to ask if she heard calliope music in her head. But if she said no, all my self doubts would start creeping in again. Besides, we were getting along so well, I didn't want to spoil the mood.

"Yeah," I said. "Funny thing, though. That's also Independence Day in about half the countries in Central America. Maybe more. I found a flyer on that very subject stuck to my windshield this afternoon. Some parade ..."

"Today? On your windshield?"

"Yes," I said. "Today." Then I added: "On my windshield." Just so we were perfectly clear.

That seemed to strike her as rather odd. "That's rather odd," she said. "When is this alleged parade?"

I reached into my other back pocket and took out the folded flyer. It was on dark blue paper with large black letters, some of them in script, with some dancing girls in silhouette. I scanned the information. Now, this was odd. I must have frowned.

"What is it?" Venus Edwards asked.

"The alleged parade was allegedly three weeks ago," I said. "According to this alleged piece of paper, that is. You can't always believe what you read. Allegedly."

"Then why on earth would anyone put a flyer on your windshield? Today of all days."

"Allegedly put a flyer on my windshield, you mean."

Somebody obviously wanted me to arrive at the notion that Blackie Buenavista had skipped town on September 15th specifically because that was the date of Independence Day in Nicaragua and a handful of other Central American countries. Did that same somebody want me to think that perhaps Blackie was a Nicaraguan, a Sandinista even? Far as I could tell, it was all crap. Not even alleged crap, but the honest to God real thing. And I wasn't buying it for a second. I wasn't even renting it. It was a little too convenient, in the same way Venus Edwards was a little too overbearing.

Somebody was jerking me around again. Third straight day of it. And I was getting sore.

I was thinking of changing my name to Antoine Marionette.

"What do you think it means, Mr. Vaughn?"

"Not very much, to tell the truth," I said.

"Oh," she said, disappointed.

"Anyway, let's change the subject."

"Very well," she said, nervous again, her voice betraying her.

"How did you come to know Twannie Jefferson?"

*The Farce News*

Venus Edwards leaned back in her posh leather chair again and adopted a posture she probably thought resembled intellectual circumspection. "As you surely know, I own *many* properties," she said, as if that explained it in as much detail as was necessary. I stared at her until she was forced to go on. "The Jefferson woman was nothing more to me than a small business owner who answered an add from one of my realtors and arranged to lease the Duncaster Road property until she could put together a down payment toward outright purchase. She met all the financial requirements and ..."

"That's a load of bullshit," I said, and picked up my glass, draining it. A couple of these and I'd be an astronaut in full lunar orbit. I put the empty glass back on the desk.

"I beg your pardon?"

"You should beg my pardon. Lying through your teeth like that. You should beg my pardon and you should be ashamed of yourself. I'm sure some of your story has a grain of truth to it, Mrs. Edwards. But certainly not all of it. Why don't you try again and this time leave out the parts that insult my intelligence."

She glared at me. I smiled back and pushed my glass across the desk toward her. She got up and went to the ice box and refilled it. She replaced it, on a coaster this time, very casual about the whole thing, and sat down.

"What makes you think I'm being less than completely honest?"

"For starters, nobody's ever completely honest," I said. "Even under the best circumstances, which these aren't. Secondly, the crap meter is going ding-ding-ding! Don't you hear it?"

"No."

"Well I sure as hell do. Your story's full of holes. Twannie Jefferson was flush. The house on Duncaster is nice enough, but it's no castle. She could have bought it with cash."

A little air went out of Venus Edwards.

"Well, I don't suppose it matters anymore. I suppose I can tell you. She is a ... rather she was an investor."

"In the theater business?" I said, a little sarcastically.

"Yes, as a matter of fact."

"And by any fluke of luck, were you an occasional speculator in the movie industry?" She blanched. "Specifically, were you financing Johnny Brashear's budding career as a filmmaker?"

Venus Edwards blanched some more. If she continued this way, we'd have to get the paint set out and color her back in again, or change her name to Cisco and put to her to work with Sam and Fran, the cartoon ghouls. "I think I've said all I'm going to say about Ms. Jefferson."

*The Farce News*

There was a finality to her tone that was so different from everything else she said, I could only assume it was completely genuine. I could ask ten thousand questions on this subject and several others. I could drill ten thousand holes, and I'd probably harvest a zero sum lode.

"Speaking of the dead," I said, "not counting Gomez and Morticia, are you having me watched?"

"Excuse me, but who are Gomez and Morticia?"

"Sorry, Fran and Sam. Or Sam and Fran."

"Oh." She thought it over for a moment and a smile, a small one, crept onto her face.

"Have you sent any other creepy henchmen out into the world to make my life totally miserable?"

"Henchmen? Really, Mr. Vaughn." She stopped smiling.

"Short, stocky greaseball on a flashy skateboard? Sound familiar?"

She didn't have to answer. Her expression said it all. She had no clue. "I'm at a loss, I'm afraid."

I took the vodka glass off the edge of the desk and sipped it carefully. It was hard not to chugalug the stuff. I put it down again, just to the left of the coaster. She glared at me.

"Something else bothers me."

"Yes, I'm certain it does," she said, reverting back to what she did best: sanctimonious disdain. She just didn't know how to treat a guest.

"I don't know a hell of a lot about the tobacco business, but I know a little. For example, I know it's lucrative as hell. A cash cow, so to speak. So, if you don't mind, would you explain to me why anybody in their right mind would buy a plot of fertile tobacco land in Farmington Valley, which is known, is it not, as some of the best tobacco land in the world, and turn it into, forgive me, a second rate dinner theater where, according to the kindest critics, the food is bad and the stage shows are worse? It makes no sense. Of course I'm not a high powered business person with a loophole savant for a husband. How do you explain it?"

She peered at me at length. Then: "Do I look like a farmer to you, Mr. Vaughn?"

I pretended to think it over for a moment. "No. I guess not."

"No. I guess not," she said.

"Something else, then. Tell me where Hubey the hubby is, will you? The whole world is very curious."

"Why he's ..." She was caught a little off guard.

"Don't do it," I said, putting up a hand. "Don't tell me he's out of town on business. Look, I'm not looking for a confession, I just want some idea of

*The Farce News*

what the hell's going on here. So don't lie to me. Okay? I won't be your puppet. I've met Jim Henson. Believe me, you're no Jim Henson."

She sighed. "Honestly, I believe you need professional help."

"Focus, Venus. Focus. Where is Hubey? Interested people want to know."

"Away."

"But not on business."

"Yes and no."

Clearly she didn't want to talk about it. Was it because Hubert, like LaTwanda Jefferson, was laying dead somewhere? (For his sake, hopefully not watching bowling.) Or was it because she didn't need a husband any more and didn't know how to say so without sounding stringent and cold? Maybe. She was a successful businesswoman who could afford to lose large fistfuls of money on a two-bit dinner theater and not worry about it. If Hubert was such a great pencil pusher and numbers cruncher, he'd probably fixed up all sorts of phony ledgers to cover their action. Maybe he'd simply fulfilled his usefulness, even outlived it.

But even if she didn't need a husband, she still required a decent accountant. Why would she feign indifference to his disappearance? This was an asset she'd want nearby. A phone call away at most. Not off galavanting around in some south-of-the-border boys-will-be-boys adventure with the dubious Blackie Buenavista. That angle just didn't work. She might not need a partner in the sack, but she sure as hell needed a partner in crime. And that meant Hubey the paper genius had to be safe and secure, and accessible.

"You've got him on ice somewhere, don't you? Like a bottle of orange-flavored vodka, for whenever you need him."

She bristled. "The terms of my marriage are no concern of yours."

Another line she'd clearly rehearsed and delivered on more than a few occasions.

I sat up a little straighter. "The problem with that attitude, ma'am, is that it creates a vicious little cycle of suspicion, with you right in the middle. You stick to that particular line of shit, pardon my English, and the heat of public scrutiny will eventually burn your ass but good. Think it over. If Hubey decided to take a walk on the wild side and ran off with Blackie in some mid-life identity crisis thing, which I frankly doubt is the case, then his absence would be easy to explain and nobody would worry another minute about it. But if he didn't run off with Blackie, as you continue to insist, then we have the problem of two guys who, for no logical reason, both disappeared on the same day. And, Mrs. Edwards?"

"Yes?"

*The Farce News*

"That's so far beyond fishy even my cats wouldn't go near it."

Venus Edwards stood up, took my drink away and put it on a glass shelf near the freezer. Someone would be in to clean up later. In the meantime, it appeared that our visit was over. "I'm afraid I find you rather tedious, Mr. Vaughn. When you aren't trying to get my goat, your inquisitiveness is beyond intolerable."

"I have no interest whatsoever in your goat, Mrs. Edwards, or any other farm animals you may be harboring to service your own perverse pleasures."

"And your attempts to be outrageous have grown tiresome."

"Does Mr. Edwards know about this goat of yours?"

She ignored me and moved into professional host mode. "I'm afraid I really don't have any more time to give you. I hope I've been of some help to you."

"You're kidding, right."

"I have much to do."

"You're giving me the bum's rush? Venus, I thought we were pals."

She studied me and went into patronizing mode. "Why not have a little dinner and take in the show? As my personal guest. Everything on the house, of course."

"Thanks, but I'm not much on musical theater."

"Well, perhaps you would like to stay and watch Lillian. She should be arriving soon if she isn't here already. I understand you two are fast becoming friends."

"That's a goddamn lie," I said, with more vitriol than was probably necessary. Just for fun.

"As I mentioned earlier, we're conducting auditions for our new production. In the rehearsal studio. Building B. It's just across the road. We are producing a musical comedy version of ..."

"Yeah, yeah, I know. You told me."

"I'd be happy to have Fran and Sam escort you."

"Don't you dare."

"Are you sure?"

"Thanks, but I'll find it myself. And between you and me, those two shouldn't be allowed out without handlers."

"Very well, then," she said. What she saw in Gomez and Morticia, I'd never know. Venus Edwards came around the big black desk and began to usher me toward the door.

I stopped and turned. "Just out of curiosity, why do you let Lillian Buenavista audition?"

"What do you mean?"

"She doesn't have an ounce of real talent. Or a minute's worth of legitimate theatrical experience."

"If you must know, I do it as a courtesy. Lillian auditions for all of our productions. She's something of a regular around here. God knows she spends so much time in costume anyway. I understand it's part of her ..."

"Yeah, yeah. Her therapy. I heard. Far as I can tell, the whole family should be sequestered on one gigantic couch."

"Well, I wouldn't know about that, Mr. Vaughn. In any event, her audition should be fascinating, to say the least."

Venus Edwards and I hadn't been acquainted very long, but I'd never known her to say the least when extraneous verbiage was an available option.

I let her lead me to the door. The vodka had warmed me. I really wasn't hungry, but the idea of laying eyes on Lillian Buenavista again suddenly sounded pretty good to me.

I should have noticed alarm bells taking the place of calliope music in my head.

"So Venus, what's good on the menu?"

She looked at me and smiled. But for once she had nothing to say.

Now that kind of honesty I could learn to respect.

## Chapter 23

Was there more to this than met the eye? It was a question of the non-rhetorical variety that lingered somewhere between the nebulous parallel dimension of philosophical tomfoolery and the cement, clay and glass domain of harsh reality where it actually hurts when you trip and fall on your face. It was a question I could ponder indefinitely, or permanently ignore. Either way, it would probably nag at me like a spoiled child. Too bad you can't send an irritating question to its room with the threat of no dessert.

I decided to give it some thought, but not too much.

And in the end I concluded that there *had* to be more to the business of Venus Edwards sinking countless thousands of dollars -- countless hundreds of thousands of dollars, no doubt -- into a bunch of half-baked stage productions and overcooked entrees than just her love of the arts or her seeming passion for rubber chicken. Who in her right mind would absorb such a steady monetary loss, or with such evident good cheer, unless there was a hidden upside, a financial back door, a fiscal escape hatch. An incentive. A hidden agenda. In short, a scam.

I had some ideas, but as yet no hard proof. Still, I wasn't worried. Could it be all that hard to uncover tangible evidence of wrongdoing with this crowd? If it's true that familiarity breeds contempt, I suspect that arrogance is just as apt to breed carelessness. Venus Edwards certainly didn't suffer from a shortage of superciliousness (not to be confused with the Wordstone women, who were simply super silly).

As I mulled over the entire concept of a suburban dinner theater, and lost what remained of my appetite, a few ideas pushed their way to the front of the line, raised their hands, and cried, "Oooh, oooh, call on me. Call on me." One was particularly persistent, so I let it give a speech.

The first thing I suspected was that, despite the absence of that caustic bouquet of industrial strength detergent and bleach in the air, nor the presence of rows of coin-operated washing machines and dryers lining the walls, the place gave off the distinct aura of one gigantic laundromat. Just like the tribal casinos which were sprouting up like prairie weeds across the state. Just like the Governor's mansion. And I recalled that, among the several Central American countries whose histories I'd researched, Guatemala had been singularly besieged by a legacy of high level political corruption and was said to be especially infamous for its activity in money laundering. So I had to ask myself, was Venus Edwards throwing Nicaragua in my face to thwart a closer look at her ties to the Guatemalans? Was Blackie Buenavista actually from Guatemala, and not Nicaragua as she would have me believe? And if he was, so what? What the hell difference did it make?

In the long run, did it really matter where Blackie came from? What if he was born in Cleveland? Or Body of Christ, Texas? Or from parts unknown, like all those burly masked Saturday night wrestlers of my childhood. Was all of this just a smoke screen to keep me from catching a glimpse of Blackie's trail and answering the relentless question of where he might have gone? And what if all this conjecture was the same kind of misguided dribble we were handed each year during the president's State of the Union Address? What if the Simsbury Dinner Theater was, instead of a money laundering front, simply a rich woman's play thing? Or, at worst, a very cleverly constructed and effectively monitored tax shelter, guaranteed to lose money hand over fist?

The only thing worse than having so many rambling questions was not having any rambling answers for any of them.

I left the matron of the Simsbury Dinner Theater in her beige office with the black trim and wandered around the place, looking things over. Despite the somewhat debilitating effects of the orange-flavored frozen vodka on my cerebellum, I did my damnedest to think things over and ferret out the facts from the wooly fabric of fiction she was attempting to pull over my eyes.

To its esthetic detriment, the Simsbury Dinner Theater reminded me of every casino I'd ever had the misfortune to visit while playing in road bands hired to provide entertainment for bug-eyed slot machine losers and brain-addled blackjack washouts. The faux-cheerful lighting seemed designed to keep you from checking your watch and discovering it was four o'clock in the morning and long since time you headed home (provided you hadn't lost the deed to your home during the night). The superficial cleanliness managed to disinfect the humanity out of the place without actually getting rid of the thick stench of unhappiness and rank disappointment. The decorators who'd done up the joint for Venus Edwards seemed to have been preoccupied not with an effort to create an appealing environment but by their need to impress and assuage some visiting convention of philistine interior design critics who would be competing to see whose assessment would be most scathing.

The lobby area was an uneasy compromise -- an interior decorator's DMZ -- between "basic Broadway theater," a slow-food mass market restaurant, and a ride at Disney World. Large glass frames on the walls contained posters of past and future productions. Blood red velvet ropes dangled from chrome poles, cordoning off sections which created cattle lanes through which overflow crowds might be herded, should overflow crowds ever become an issue. (There was a certain optimism in it that inspired, if somewhat hesitantly, one's admiration.) Seating areas were arranged to allow patrons to gather in semi-comfort and share their anticipation (or buttress their nerve) over cocktails prior to being seated in the main dining room slash theater.

A matching set of thick bald men in starched white shirts and black bow ties poured drinks at a cash bar just outside the entrance to the eating chamber. Cocktail hour was over and the area was nearly empty. The bartenders cleaned their station and muttered at each other, presumably in preparation for the intermission rush when, if the drama reviews were correct, they'd be doing a *lot* of sudden, urgent business. *Thank You For Not Smoking* signs were posted everywhere. I looked for the *Thank You For Drinking Heavily* signs, but saw none. I'd drop a note in the suggestion box if I could find it. I nodded at the barkeeps and poked my head into the large dining area.

Row upon row of tables, set for either two or four diners, were arranged on ascending risers before a wide proscenium style stage at the far end of the building. Each table had a centerpiece featuring a small electric bulb in the shape of a candle. The light bulb provided just enough illumination to keep customers from sticking themselves in the eye with a salad fork -- at least not by accident. The sound of cutlery clinking on porcelain dinnerware was accompanied by the low murmur of hushed conversation. I wondered if, "Oh, my, this is delicious, don't you think?" was anywhere in there. There was a familiar smell in the air. Not an overly offensive aroma, but not an especially appetizing one either. It was vintage Public School Cafeteria. *Chateau Loaf de Poodle, mille-neuf-cent, souixante-douze.* I wondered if the chef in the kitchen of the Simsbury Dinner Theater was any relation to the large muscular East German woman from way back when. I could still see those thick blond braids, the broad shoulders, those enormous biceps, that strong accent and that short temper. The chief cook at my grade school, the perpetually miserable and overbearing Frau Gretchen von Steigerlitz. If it was Gretchen herself back there, it would go a long way toward explaining the consistently appalling reviews the Simsbury Dinner Theater received for its near-inedible cuisine.

I had no interest in a reunion with Frau Gretchen nor in hanging around for the stage show, so I bade a silent "see ya" to the beleaguered bartenders, who ignored me in return, and made my way quickly toward the nearest exit.

With a little extra attention paid to the mission, I managed to steer clear of Gomez and Morticia. For all I knew, they'd forgotten about me as soon as

*The Farce News*

I left their direct field of vision. They struck me as decidedly task oriented ghouls. Out of sight was no doubt out of mind with them. However, considering the nature of our brief relationship thus far, I'd have to be out of my mind to give them any more opportunities to wreak their special brand of havoc upon me. In the off chance they were actually lurking in wait for me, I was determined to win our unofficial game of hide and seek.

I found an exit door off the lobby. It let me out on the west side of the large theater building, opposite where I'd parked my piece of shit Jetta. It was very dark, and quite a bit cooler. I crunched my way along the gravel (didn't anybody pave anymore?) and crossed to the edge of the roadway. There wasn't much traffic. Tonight's victims had already been led to their eventual intellectual and gustatory slaughter. A quartet of parking valets stood around looking bored. I've no idea if they were bored or not. It could easily have been a function of their being teenagers. Kids their age often appear bored, even when the exact opposite is true. They do it to vex adults, I'm told. Standing by the front doors, they stamped their feet to ward off the chill of the night and tossed barbs back and forth at each other. In the few short moments I remained within earshot of them I learned that one of their mothers was so fat her cereal bowl came with a lifeguard. It just as quickly emerged that another one's mother was so ugly, if she were a scarecrow the corn would run away. Busy with their game, they took no notice of me. In fact, had my clothing been soaked in gasoline and torched with a flame thrower, I doubt they would have taken the time or effort to piss on me to put the fire out. Which might have been just as well.

I crossed Firetown Road and headed for the first of the three buildings directly across from the theater. Tall and dark, its original tarpaper sides had been replaced by wooden siding, the slats freshly painted, although not in the same gaudy red used to decorate the main structure across the way. It was mahogany in hue and had no windows. I circled around to the back and found a new security door with a simple Yale lock. I slipped out my tools and fiddled with the mechanism for a few moments, hoping like hell that it wasn't hooked up to some loud clanging alarm system. It wasn't. If a silent alarm was in place I was screwed. On that happy note, I let myself in to a coldness that rivaled the chill of the fall night outside. Normally, I would have taken a few moments to allow my eyes to adjust to the darkness, but the inky black of this building was so thorough I held out no real hope of discerning its interior without help. I felt along the wall just inside the door and quickly came upon a panel of light switches. I shut the door behind me so no light would escape to alert the sentries of my presence, were any on duty at the moment. For all I knew this was an empty building unworthy of security measures beyond the rudimentary lock I'd already picked.

I should have known better.

The lights flickered overhead as row after row of fluorescent tubes came to life, casting a bluish white light over the expansive room. Unlike the theater building across the street which had been partitioned with walls and offices and stages and, presumably, backstage dressing rooms, this building had been gutted and then refinished as one very large chamber. It was filled with countless rows of steel shelving units, some standing at least fifteen feet high. I started to count them, but quit at thirty-seven, rendering them countless by my methods. Rolling stepladders were placed about the room to enable *whomever* to reach the highest shelves. It was like a Sam's Club for bootleggers, professional thieves and smugglers.

I may not be a licensed detective, but because I'm sharp as a CCM hockey skate, I quickly deduced that I was standing in what amounted to a medium-sized warehouse. After that, the dominos of realization fell like, well, dominos. It wasn't hard to connect the dots and complete the paint-by-numbers picture. The wares housed herein were all too familiar. I'd seen boxes with identical labels in three other locales in the last couple of days: Twannie Jefferson's back storeroom on Park Street, then again in her secret basement room on Duncaster Road, and finally in Johnny Brashear's garage on East Barber Street in Windsor. I didn't see anything that looked like the hundreds of white cardboard boxes of trading cards which had littered the front of Twannie's phony card shop -- boxes which were as likely as not empty. These boxes carried the same kind of foreign language labels I'd seen before. The racks of furs were sleeved in protective plastic.

To my surprise, no obvious proof of a sophisticated security system was in place to protect this valuable cache. No cameras (unless they were hidden). No trip wires (at least none I'd thus far stumbled over). No magnetic tape ( indeed no windows on which to attach said tape). It was arrogance bordering on sheer stupidity to leave such a valuable and illegal stock unprotected. So who was minding the store? Gomez and Morticia? The idea of them lurking somewhere out there in the dark of night made me shudder. The idea of them trapping me in here made my skin crawl and the hair on the back of my neck stand up. I was quite a mess.

I turned off the lights and cautiously let myself out. The night air (and the fact I wasn't immediately pounced upon and torn to pieces in a slashing werewolfian attack) cured me of the heebie jeebies. I screwed up my courage and made a skulking mad dash for the next structure, stopping only briefly to wonder why the hell Peter Sellers had suddenly stumbled into my thoughts, replete with trench coat and bad French accent. Oh, well.

*The Farce News*

The middle building was decorated in beige with black trim, apparently from the same stock of paint used to create the motif in the office of Venus Edwards. I found a door along one side. It was fairly new, made of solid wood. I twisted the brass door knob and found it was unlocked. Somewhat odd? I opened the door. It didn't squeak. It didn't creak. It didn't make any of the standard noises I'd expect from an old tobacco barn or a horror flick. This building had several windows, new ones installed at the time of the renovation. Some of the glow from the theater across the road helped to cut the darkness. I closed the door behind me and stood silently, waiting for my eyes to adjust to the relative gloom. There would be no turning on the lights in here.

After a few moments, I began to make out shapes and realized I was standing in what had been arranged as somebody's living quarters. That somebody was Venus Edwards. There were no interior walls, but areas had been designated to serve specific functions. Over the last quarter of the 20th century, loft dwellers in lower Manhattan and in cities across the country had made an urban art form of creating unique living spaces out of raw square footage in erstwhile warehouse buildings. It looked like Venus Edwards had gone for a similar approach. It was early Tribeca, or late Soho. A living room area had a couple of couches and comfortable chairs arranged around a central low table. A couple of bookcases, end tables, and a pair of matching chrome floor lamps finished the cluster.

The kitchen area featured a large center island, a high counter with four bar stools, an industrial refrigerator, a rack of hanging pots and pans, and all the trappings of a sophisticated resident who must have only the best of everything.

Two separate areas had been designated as bedrooms, with three-panel folding Chinese screens to provide a modicum of privacy. At the far end of the large rectangular space, a loft had been constructed roughly ten feet off the floor with a gently sloping staircase leading up to its large platform. I assumed it was meant as a kind of master bedroom, although it was open in the front, leaving it with little means of achieving any real privacy. Maybe this was a flop for Venus Edwards and intimate guests when she spent late nights at the theater and didn't feel like driving all the way home. Wherever home was. Maybe this was home -- although I doubted that. This had more of a fun house feel to it, but without the warped mirrors and tilting floor boards.

I let myself out, pulled the door shut, and circled around to the third building.

It was the same size and dimension as the first two buildings, but painted in tawdry red to match the theater across the road. It had a sign on the front in block letters. BUILDING B: REHEARSAL HALL. I stood in front of it for a moment and wondered why in hell the third building in a row of three identical structures would be labeled "B" and not "C", or even "A", assuming for a moment that I'd started at the wrong end of the row. It made no sense for it to be Building "B". It was as if some giant hands had been interrupted in the middle of playing the shell game with these three structures, and the original order had been permanently disrupted.

The more I thought about it, the more everything about this place reminded me of some kind of giant shell game.

The rehearsal hall had two large glass doors facing the road. I walked over and pulled the handle on the door to the right. It swung open on pneumatic hinges which hissed quietly as the door closed behind me. I walked into a brightly lit space that was only partially in use. There was a stage against the left wall. It was smaller than the one at the theater across the street but large enough for these purposes. There appeared to be a series of small rooms against the right wall. Cubicles, really. Perhaps dressing rooms for the actors. There was a black grand piano at the side of the stage, brilliantly polished, its lid propped at a 45 degree angle. An array of folding chairs and music stands were scattered to the side of the stage. The chairs were all empty.

The stage, too, was empty.

All except for two straight backed chairs and one person who was sitting on the edge of one of the chairs. It was a woman. Her back was to me, her identity hidden behind the folds of a vibrant crimson hood attached to a flowing red cape. When the door behind me shut, it clicked loudly. The figure on stage jumped up and turned to face me.

"Hello, Lillian," I said. "Long time, no see." I smiled, thinking to myself, Not long enough.

"Oh!" she said, and put a hand to her throat. Very theatrical. Very hokey. A real *Days of Our Lives* moment without the canned organ swell. "You startled me!"

I walked over to the stage, took the other straight backed chair and sat down a few feet from her, straddling it backwards with my forearms on the chair's back. She was in costume, of course. I had never seen Lillian the Vaudevillian out of costume. A thought suddenly crossed my mind without looking both ways to make sure it was safe: Truth be told, I wouldn't half mind seeing Lillian the Vaudevillian out of costume. I just didn't think it was ever going to happen, unless I walked in on her while she was having a bath or a squat over the bidet, but that would be a little lowbrow even for me.

"Sorry," I said. "Venus Edwards told me you might be here."

She carefully pulled the hood back off of her head and laid it gently against her shoulders as if it would break if she wasn't careful. "I was preparing." She put a lot of emphasis on the word, as if she'd said, "I was pulling babies from a burning building."

I nodded, noncommittally. "What for?"

"Why, my audition, of course."

"Of course," I said.

"I'm getting into character."

She sat very straight. Her features looked gaunt in the fluorescent light. She wore too much mascara and it gave her green eyes an iridescent glow -- unless she was on drugs. Her cheeks were artificially radiant. Her lips were highly glossed, bright red. Beneath the crimson cape, which was tied at the throat but fell open as it flowed about her, she wore a baby blue dress with an apron front and lace embroidery around the edges of the hem. Her legs appeared especially long and lean and were sheathed in sheer white stockings. On her feet she wore black Mary Janes. There was something about the divergence between her *innocent little girl* wardrobe and the Times Square hooker make-up job that gave her a slightly pornographic cast. I could easily envision this turning into one of those sleazy, "I've been a very naughty girl" moments. If it did, I would have to wash my hands of this crowd once and for all. And probably shave and get a haircut, too.

"Your audition," I said. "I heard something about that."

"I'm reading for the lead. Rehearsals begin in just a couple of days, you know."

I guess I didn't get the memo. "How exciting for you."

"Yes, it's a musical adaptation of ..."

"I know, I know. *Who's Afraid of Virginia Woolf?* By the way, who's brilliant idea was that?"

She looked a little offended. Maybe Lillian Buenavista herself had dreamed up with this peculiar notion. Maybe I should apologize for hurting her feelings. I decided to hold off on any *mea culpas* until I had a hell of a lot more information.

"Are you familiar with the work?"

She asked in a manner that suggested she enjoyed some intimate relationship with the final product, had made a significant contribution to its greatness.

I was familiar with it, all right, but I didn't say so right away. For one thing, I didn't like her pretentious use of the phrase "the work." It was a play, after all. Mixing work and play just showed what a functional illiterate she truly was. Probably didn't know the difference between some and several either.

Like about a billion other people, I'd seen the movie version with Elizabeth Taylor and Richard Burton. A regular laugh riot. I believe it won an Academy Award in the category of Movie Directly Responsible for the Greatest Number of Deaths By Means of Voluntary Cyanide Ingestion. I'd also read the play in college and even seen a couple of Off-Off-Broadway productions of it, staged in small theaters where the rats outnumbered the audience members by a ratio of about four to one. The play was a relentless campaign of psychological warfare and mental anguish as only an incurably unhappy married couple can wage it, without regard for the enemy, nor any interest in taking prisoners.

"Ah, yes. Good old George and Martha," I said. "Not exactly America's first couple, even if they share the names, huh?"

"America's first couple of what?"

"George and Martha Washington," I said. "Ever hear of them?"

"Oh, them."

Lillian the Vaudevillian probably would have liked the Washingtons better had they been fictional characters. Like her.

"They don't have much in common with Albee's happy couple."

"How do you mean?"

"For one thing, your George -- the fictional one -- has never been president of anything, has he? Not even the local *I Hate Martha Club,* let alone a country. And your Martha is just a miserable middle-aged lush, bored out of her skull, wretched beyond description. Isn't she the daughter of the school headmaster where George teaches?"

"Yes. So what?"

"There's an object lesson here: never marry the boss's daughter."

"Nonsense."

"And what a life they have. Horrible pretty much describes it, don't you agree? No kids. Hopeless alcoholics. They hate each other's guts. They're stunningly vicious and utterly codependent -- although I think the play debuted before shrinks came up with the term 'codependent.'"

Lillian Buenavista looked cross. "Well, George Washington slept around. So there."

There was a childish petulance in her voice. "That's a presidential prerogative," I said.

"Anyway, I'm auditioning for the role of Martha," she said.

"Good thing. You'd be all wrong for George. You're too tall."

She took a moment to decide if I was kidding or not. I don't know what conclusion she drew. It's entirely possible her pencil had no point and her pen was out of ink, rending the question moot. "It's a brilliant piece," she said. "So sweet and funny."

I took a moment now to decided if *she* was kidding or not. I figured if nothing else it was my turn. I don't know what my decision was on the subject. I still needed more information.

"Which aspect of *the work* do you find particularly amusing?"

"Oh, for one thing, the marvelous parlor games they play!"

"The parlor games?"

"You know. *Humiliate the Host.* And *Hump the Hostess.* Oh, and *Get the Guests.* That one especially."

I stared at her. I had forgotten all about the psychotic mind games.

"Those sound like fun to you?"

She cocked an eyebrow at me. "Beats the hell out of *Pictionary.*"

Well, she might have a point there. But I wasn't going to argue too strongly for either side. "I guess it's one's interpretation that makes life so interesting and unpredictable, eh?"

"Oh, and the tightrope walk between reality and make-believe. That poor little boy they have and yet don't have. It's so sad and yet so funny all at the same time. I never know whether to laugh or cry. Either way, I know my mascara will run. And of course there's the other couple, Nick and Honey, and that whole bit they go through with the hysterical pregnancy. That was just, well, hysterical. Yes, hysterical very aptly captures the essence of the piece. Don't you see?"

I waited for her to elaborate. She apparently didn't have any more to add. Maybe she was make-believing this entire conversation and in her head she had already explained her viewpoint sufficiently. Who was I to say she hadn't?

"If you don't mind me asking," I said, "what's up with the red cape?"

"Oh," she said, and her face lit up with what looked like genuine relish, and I don't mean the kind with chopped pickles in it. "This is one of my own little inventions. I'm going to interpret Martha through the eyes of *Little Red Riding Hood.* Isn't it simply magical?"

"No kidding?"

"You know, who's afraid of the big, bad wolf? You get it?"

Unfortunately, I did. I wondered if Lillian got it. Or if she had an incredibly short memory.

"You think Martha really works on that level?"

She frowned slightly at me, then smiled as if she suddenly realized I had asked a trick question, which, of course, I'd had no intention of doing.

"If memory serves," she said. "Martha never worked a day in her life."
I laughed a little. "Okay."
"Would you like to hear my song?" she asked, suddenly standing.
"Your song?"
"Yes, it's the song I'm going to sing for my audition. I wrote it myself. I think it's quite good, actually. Of course, I'm no Andrew Lloyd Webber."

That came as good news. "Who is?" I asked.

"I had to borrow a tune from another song. But I put all the words together myself. I call it *Martha's Song*. It tells the whole story of who she is, her essence, and how she got to this point in her life."

I didn't really want to hear the song, but I also didn't want to miss it. I guess that's the definition of a dilemma. I often have the same conflicted emotions while passing particularly bad highway accidents. I could only hope I wouldn't regret capitulating to my morbid curiosity. After all, there comes a time when you just have to stop staring at crash victims, no matter how much fun it may be. "Go ahead, I guess."

Lillian the Vaudevillian walked dramatically to the piano and made a great flourish with her cape as she sat. She was very good at waving her capes around. Must have spent hours practicing the fine art. She began to play the introductory strains of "Home on the Range."

I wanted to bolt for the door, then bolt it shut once I was safely outside, and then hopefully get hit by a bolt of lightning that would shock this entire incident from my memory. But I stayed put. I was already in for a dime. I might as well get my money's worth. If I knew Lillian Buenavista, I'd have about eight cents in change coming when this ordeal was finally over. I gripped the chair a little tighter.

"It goes a little something like this," she said. Then, in a voice that might not shatter glass but would very definitely annoy the hell out of it, she began to sing, intermittently quavering like some kind of operatic Mel Torme impersonator and screeching like a mother eagle whose nest of hatchlings is being invaded by hawks. It was all I could do not to put my hands over my ears.

*I married a guy six years younger than I*
*But he's such a big flop and a bog*
*He says that my vice of chewing on ice*
*Reminds him of some kind of dog*

> *George isn't as tame*
> *Since we started to play at this game*
> *He's more nasty and cruel*

*Than a turd in the pool*
*There are times when I feel quite ashamed*

*With too much to drink, I might barf in the sink*
*And start smashing the dishes we own*
*I'll cut off your balls and nail them to the walls*
*To remind you of dreams you have blown*

> *George you're not the same*
> *Since we started to play at this game*
> *You're as rotten in bed*
> *As a corpse three months dead*
> *There are times when I think I'm to blame*

*I'm quite vulgar and crude, and outlandishly rude*
*And I'll jump in and out of the sack*
*With any old guest who'll play Hump the Hostess*
*And throw me right down onto my back*

> *George, I'm not the same*
> *Since we started to play at this game*
> *You were once so beguiled*
> *Now you say I'm defiled*
> *There are times when I think you're to blame*

*George has a shotgun, we have one mystery son*
*And between us we're all shooting blanks*
*He's losing his hair, and I don't even care*
*'Cause the only thing I feel is angst*

> *We aren't the same*
> *Since we started to play at this game*
> *We're more nasty and cruel*
> *Than two turds in the pool*
> *I'm quite sure we're both going insane*

By the time she got around to repeating the chorus for the last time, I found myself humming along. I also found myself agreeing wholeheartedly with the sentiment contained in the last line of the chorus, as it related to us: Lillian for composing this peculiar ditty and singing it in public, me for sitting through it instead of dialing 911 on the nearest phone. This was my just reward for indulging the inquisitive streak in my nature. When she asked if I'd like to hear her little opus, I should have said, "No, thanks, save it for the audition,"

She finished playing and looked up at me, an expectant look on her pretty, if rather badly decorated, face. "So? You like?"

I didn't know what to say. I had questions I wanted to pose, such as: (1) Where do you keep the Thorazine?; (2) Are the authorities aware that you've escaped?; (3) Should I call an ambulance?; (4) Do you know what day of the week it is?; and (5) How many fingers am I holding up?

"It was ..." I paused, searching for the right words to describe how I felt at the moment, "... um, very ..." I paused again.

"I'm so glad you think so," Lillian said, clapping her hands quietly in front of her face. "I think so, too. I think this time I really have a good shot."

A good shot. That's exactly what I needed. Venus Edwards and her magic bottle of frozen orange vodka would do the trick. Failing that, maybe George and his shotgun would do. "So, um, when's the big audition?" I asked, checking my watch. It was a lame question, but I didn't think it would be appropriate to ask any of the other ones I had contemplated.

"Oh, any time now. Mrs. Edwards said she'd come once the show got started. So, do you think I should go with *Martha's Song?*"

What did I know? "Go where?"

"I also have some limericks."

"Oh."

"Would you like to hear one?"

"They aren't by any chance filthy limericks, are they? With all sorts of salacious rhymes for places like Dallas and Carolina?"

She stared at me a bit oddly, or, to be more precise, as if I were a bit odd. I could see she was thinking about it, the Dallas/Carolina thing, trying to imagine what in God's name I was talking about. Then a light went on. She blushed hotly and her whole face went as red as the phony rouge she'd smeared on her cheeks.

"No, they're not dirty. They're interpretive. From the text of *Who's?* Now, would you like to hear one, or wouldn't you?"

*Who's?*

Was she kidding? Was this the equivalent of being on a first name basis with a movie star, referring to the play by only the first word? And did I really want to hear an interpretive limerick?

I didn't see how I had a choice. I shrugged and made the kind of face you might make if you were starving hungry and somebody offered you a steaming dish of boiled okra. She immediately took that as an enthusiastic "Yes, oh, please, please, please!" Jim Morrison was right. People *are* strange. Damned strange. I wondered if he would prove to be correct about nobody getting out alive.

Lillian Buenavista was waiting for my answer.

If someone had asked me just how glad I would be the next time I saw Venus Edwards, I'd have probably said, "Not very," (unless she was toting a bottle of orange vodka) but she made a liar out of me by appearing at that very moment and saving me the anticipated agony of listening to any more of Lillian Buenavista's interpretive "work."

"Mr. Vaughn. There you are. We wondered what became of you."

"Who's we?" I asked cheerfully.

"My people and me."

So that let Gomez and Morticia out of the equation.

"I was just wandering around. Enjoying the night air. Quite a spread you've got here."

"Did you find your way around okay?"

I sure as hell didn't know how to take that question. Had she been watching as I committed the crime of breaking and entering? I studied her expression. It was decidedly neutral.

I made a mental note never to play Texas Hold 'Em or any other card game with this broad.

"Well, it is pretty dark out there, but thanks for asking. Actually, I was just leaving. Lillian and I were catching up on old times. Strolling down memory lane, as they say. Shooting the breeze, as it were. Reeling in the years, so to speak. But it's getting late and I should be running along. You ladies have a lot of business to conduct. I'm sure I'd just be in the way."

"Nonsense," Venus Edwards said, very cordial, but without warmth, no hint of a smile on her face. "Have a seat." She didn't say, "Or else," but it was implied.

"Sure," I said. "I'd love to."

A voice in my head was screaming, "Noooooooo!"

An hour later, I was numb from the neck up. An overdose of Novocain administered by the Dentist From the Ninth Ring of Hell could not have been more effective -- or welcome. Against my will and, no doubt, in direct violation of several articles of the Geneva Convention, I was subjected to sixty solid minutes of mental torture which included but was not limited to at least a dozen more helpings of Lillian Buenavista's deranged interpretations of *Martha's Song,* some with piano accompaniment, one with accordion backup to give it a real circus feel, another with xylophone fills, and a couple, worst of all, delivered in the sort of sour, off-key *a cappella* strains only a true amateur can produce. I couldn't honestly say which I preferred, because to do so would infer that I actually preferred one at all, which was simply not plausible.

Lillian also insisted on sharing a handful of extraordinarily bad limericks which, I judged, could not have helped her cause with Venus Edwards very much. The limericks in question would have been entirely more tolerable had they contained at least some passing reference to Dallas and/or Carolina. To say nothing of the old favorite, Nantucket. But, alas, no.

By the time I staggered out of the rehearsal hall and found my car in the back of the parking lot, I felt as if I'd been bludgeoned by a horde of irritated, blue-haired geriatrics wielding Kevlar handbags. Indeed, with the benefit of 20-20 hindsight I wished that, just prior to the beginning of Lillian's audition, I *had* been bludgeoned by a horde of irritated, blue-haired geriatrics wielding Kevlar handbags. Preferably into a state of unconsciousness.

But I just couldn't catch a break.

Equally disturbing was the lingering mystery nagging at me from the cheap seats of my subconscious, heckling me and calling me nasty names and throwing rotten tomatoes.

For the life of me I couldn't figure out why, other than to avail herself of an ideal opportunity to inflict pain and suffering upon me personally, Venus Edwards had endangered her own mental health by subjecting herself to Lillian's grotesque performance. It was, I'm certain, among the worst singing, dancing, and limerick recitation ever seen by human eyes or heard by human ears. Lillian Buenavista had some charm, and sensational green eyes. But when it came to song and dance she was no Jimmy Durante. Or maybe she *was*, and maybe that was the problem.

So, what was the story? Why did Venus put herself -- and me! -- through it? Why suffer so needlessly?

There was definitely more to this than initially met the eye. Things going on that I just couldn't grasp. At the moment, I included my own sanity in this array of illusive entities.

I knew the bottom line, however. I knew I had to get the hell out of Simsbury. Immediately, if not sooner. Only then would I stand even a slim chance to regain some semblance of normalcy. A cup of strong black coffee might also be a good idea.

I said my goodnights and stumbled out to the parking lot, past the valets. On this trip, I learned that one of their mothers was so fat, when she went from room to room, she had to make two trips. Two of the valets responded with laughter while the fourth made a guttural sound and charged. I left them to enjoy their fist fight in peace. I'd suffered enough for one night.

I found my piece of shit Jetta, unlocked it and climbed in behind the wheel. I stuck the key in the ignition and twisted it, freedom and well-being drawing closer with every moment.

Of course, the engine wouldn't start. German engineering. I'll bet somewhere in that stygian chamber the Simsbury Dinner Theater operators roguishly called "the kitchen," Frau Gretchen von Steigerlitz (if that's who it was) was enjoying a good laugh.

*The Farce News*

**Chapter 24**

By the time Triple-A got a wrecker out to me, it was nearly ten o'clock. The mechanic who boosted my battery with jumper cables and wrote up my service ticket was a young guy who wore oil-stained coveralls and a slicked back D.A. with pork chop sideburns. He sported a *Jesus Loves You* tattoo on his muscular right forearm. Looking at him I couldn't help but think of some sort of evangelical Elvis Presley grease monkey. When he finished the paperwork and I signed off on it, I contemplated hitting him with the old baritone Thank You Very Much. But it was late and he looked about as tired as I felt, so I let it go. For all I know he was looking at me and thinking, "You ain't nothin' but a hound dog." And I'd have been hard pressed to argue the point.

Even with my untimely delay, I managed to escape the Simsbury Dinner Theater parking lot a few minutes before the stage show ended. Thus the crowd of well-to-do patrons never had a chance to snicker at my sorry state of affairs from the comfort of their well-appointed luxury automobiles. I was taking small consolations where I could find them.

The teenaged parking valets didn't bother to sneer. They had stopped fighting and insulting each others' mothers and were content simply to ignore me, which they did with a scrupulous attention to detail I wouldn't have thought possible in a group so clearly lacking in basic motivation (parking valets, that is, not teenagers).

Fatigue sat heavily on my shoulders. I tried to shrug it off as I navigated the slow back roads home, but it wouldn't climb down. As a result, a task as mundane as steering the car became a chore. I let my mind drift. It had been another long day. Another exceptionally weird day, one that made me long for the relative normalcy of the smoky bar scene I called home two or three nights a week. Every step forward seemed to leave me three steps to the side, as if I were trapped in a kind of drunken square dance in which only the local hillbillies who live on hootch and homemade fun know how to maintain any real, if perverse, sense of equilibrium. All I needed now was the haunting strains of deep woods banjo music to send me completely over the edge. To sustain any kind of positive morale, I forced myself to look on the bright side: At least I still had all of my teeth, and to date none of them had turned green. And none of my cousins also qualified as siblings.

I hit the Hartford city line around 10:30 and pulled into my street at about quarter to eleven. All ten of my usual parking spaces were taken so I went to the corner and hung a right turn, preparing to circle the block. I found an empty spot pretty quickly and locked up the car for the night, hoping against hope God would strike it with lightning while I slept. The only clause in my insurance policy with any backbone was the Act of God rider, which would enable me to replace the piece of shit Jetta with no out-of-pocket expenses should some uncontrollable force of nature render it thoroughly useless. So far, however, neither flood, nor fire, nor alas even a paltry bolt of lightning had befallen my decrepit automobile.

Jesus may love me, but God had definitely turned a blind eye in my direction, Thank You Very Much.

My own weary footsteps were the only sound along Summit Street as I made my way back to the apartment building. The quiet was almost deafening. If only I'd had something to deafen me a couple of hours ago when Lillian Buenavista was roaring and squeaking and howling and screeching her way through that preposterous burlesque show of hers. Something to both deafen me as well as temporarily blind me. Mushrooms might have done the trick nicely, but where could you score reputable peyote any more? Oh, Mr. Zimmerman, you are so right. The times, they are a-changing.

As I dragged my exhaustion down the street like a large burlap garbage bag ready to burst at the seams, the quiet of the night was broken by the sound of mechanical whirring. I glanced around to locate the offending party. Just ahead of me the passenger window of a car parked in front of my building began to slide down. The vehicle was sickeningly familiar. I knew it like a toothache, intimately and with genuine fear and loathing. Like a toothache, I also knew if I ignored it, it wouldn't go away without surgery. It was the silver Camry with the chrome gangsta rims. My heart sank in my chest and I didn't bother diving in after it.

Lita Wordstone.

Wasn't it past her bedtime?

What could she possibly want with me at this hour of the night?

Did I really think I could get through a whole day without this living, breathing muppet from Hell making her presence felt?

These were all rhetorical questions, so I didn't waste any time trying to answer them.

I strolled over to the Camry and peered in through the open window. Lita Wordstone was dressed for action in black leather pants and a black cashmere sweater that hugged her like an old friend in a time of need. She leaned over and pushed the door open.

"Get in," she said. Not bossy or autocratic like some women in her family. Her invitation was more playful than demanding, more dangerous. Likely more lethal by a multiple of ten or eleven.

I got in. Call me stupid.

The seats were cool to the touch. Same as when I drove Lita Wordstone home in them two nights ago from LaTwanda Jefferson's house of horrors, only on that occasion I hadn't taken the time to appreciate them fully. Lita had been in a near coma. Now she was behind the wheel and I was behind the eight ball. The seats were intoxicatingly comfortable. At the moment, I was suffering from the kind of bone weary lassitude that could easily allow me to put my head back and fall asleep right there in her car. Only the underlying fear that I might never wake up from such a nap kept me at least partially alert.

"If you don't mind me asking, what are you doing here?" This was not intended as a rhetorical question. However, Lita Wordstone treated it as one and didn't waste time forming a response. She had her own agenda and was ready to address the first item on her list.

"So, did you miss me?"

I have no idea what kind of question that was. It wasn't rhetorical. It was delusional.

"How could I miss you?" I said. "I didn't even shoot at you yet."

"Come on, answer the question. Did you miss me?" Apparently she was not satisfied by my first adroit remark. Maybe she didn't know adroit when she heard it. "Tell the truth. Say you did."

"You'll have to pick one or the other. I can't do both."

"Poo-poo head."

I started to open the door to get out. I was pretty much out of gas and my brain tends to work even more slowly than usual when I'm exhausted, but I was realizing what a mistake it had been to get into this woman's car in the first place. By contrast, getting out seemed like a very good idea.

"Goodnight," I said. "Drive safely."

"No, wait!"

I stopped. "What is it, Lita?"

"I have something for you."

I couldn't wait to see what it was. Wait, that's not entirely accurate. In fact it's completely inaccurate. I could wait to see what it was. Given the chance, I was prepared to wait forever. I was just too tired to sort out the Sarcasm cards from the Truth cards in my mental deck.

Lita Wordstone took a roomy black leather carryall bag from the back seat and arranged it on her lap. She reached into it while I looked on with growing trepidation.

Once again, fatigue started to play games with my psyche. For just a moment I couldn't decide if I hoped it wasn't a gun in there and that she wasn't about to shoot me, or if I hoped it was a gun in the bag and that she *was* about to fill me full of lead, thus putting an end to my evening of torment. Just my luck, it wasn't a gun. Instead her fleshless hand emerged clutching a yellow one-pound bag of peanut M&M's. She tore it open with those lovely, expensive, sharp little teeth and spilled out a handful in her palm and offered them to me. I looked down at the colorful array of candies, then up at Lita Wordstone. She was bleached white and virtually devoid of color.

"No, thanks," I said. It would be a bad day in the life of Robby Vaughn when somebody like Lita Wordstone had me eating out of the palm of her hand. There was such a thing as self-respect, and I liked to pretend I still had some.

"Oh, go ahead," she said. "They're yummy."

I didn't move.

She shrugged and poured the M&M's back into the yellow bag, replaced it in the leather handbag and pulled out something else.

"How 'bout some Twizzlers?" she said, with an eerie enthusiasm I didn't share. I watched her rip open the fresh pack of cherry-red licorice twists. She deftly unwound one of the sticks and made a long string out of it. It was like watching a jungle dweller strip bark off a tree and fashion rope out of it, only in reverse. "Watch this," she said. She took the single strand of red licorice, put it between her lips and sucked it into her mouth the way a child might slurp a strand of spaghetti from a dinner bowl.

I did my best to remain expressionless. It was my hope that by maintaining a neutral countenance I might discourage any further zaniness from this certifiable fruitcake. I should have known better.

With her lips clenched together, she worked the licorice string in her mouth. I wondered if this was going to be the old tie-the-cherry-stem-into-a-knot trick. It wasn't very unique or original and it would certainly represent another disappointment in a long day of them if it was the best Lita Wordstone could come up with at this late hour. Again, I should have known better. In a matter of moments, she opened her lips and extracted the licorice string. It was tied in a perfect miniature hangman's noose.

My skin crawled into the back seat and tried to hide.

I was very impressed and I said so. "I'm very impressed."

I was also horrified. But I kept that fact to myself.

"Oh, that's nothing. Want me to teach you how? It's all in the tongue." I shook my head. She tossed the noose out the window and replaced the package of licorice in her leather handbag, then pulled out a clear plastic bag of Snickers bars, which she proceeded to offer me. "You like?"

I shook my head again. "Nothing for me, thanks."

"Oh, come on. Live a little. Be a man. How about a Chunky?" she said. "I'll bet you haven't seen one of these in years."

It was true. I hadn't seen a Chunky in years. I also hadn't seen any of my high school classmates in years. I hadn't worried too much about the countless missed reunions with them, so why should I fret over some candy bar? (Rhetorical question.)

Lita winked at me conspiratorially. "I know where to get them," she said and produced a handful of small, silver bars. I recognized their distinctive thick, trapezoidal shape. "Did you know they're made with rich, creamy Nestle Milk Chocolate, roasted peanuts and plump California raisins. This will bring back fond memories!"

"You sound just like a commercial."

"Thanks," she said.

"It wasn't a compliment."

"I have all the commercials memorized."

"Really? Usually, I leave the room when the commercials come on."

"Oh, don't go."

I wasn't going anywhere. Lita Wordstone was the kind of freak show one just couldn't tear oneself away from, no matter how much one knew one should. She held out her hand.

"It's generous of you to offer, but ..."

Not a girl to take no for an answer, Lita Wordstone dropped the Chunky bars back into the black leather bag and pulled out something else.

"How about a Clark Bar?" she said, holding up several red and yellow candy bars. "Do you know they were originally produced by the D.L. Clark Company? They've been a Pittsburgh favorite for over a hundred years. They have a rich chocolatey taste and a peanut butter crunch. Try one and see if you don't agree. Their homemade peanut butter makes all the difference. Enjoy one today!"

How could I refuse?

Easily.

"No, really," I said. "I'm on a diet."

She dropped the Clark Bars back into the bag and rummaged for a moment before pulling out another treat, this time in a small rectangular flat box. "You can't say no to Goobers," she said, shaking the box so it rattled like a snake under a rock. "Goobers are roasted whole peanuts covered with Nestle Milk Chocolate. In case you didn't know, Goober is actually a southern word for peanut. Isn't that fascinating? Oh, those southerners! So quaint."

It occurred to me that "Goober" is also a useful synonym for schmuck, hayseed, jackass, yokel, hick, bumpkin, and/or rube. The list, like the proverbial road, goes on forever. I wondered if the party would ever end. At the moment, I felt like a bit of a goober myself, allowing this mental patient to hold me hostage so effortlessly. "You're not an easy girl to refuse," I said. "But I'm gonna keep trying 'til I get it right. Or until you learn to accept rejection a little better. Listen carefully to the words, Lita. No thank you. No candy for me."

Without showing her disappointment, if in fact she was disappointed, Lita Wordstone sighed and dropped the box of Goobers into the black leather bag. But that was hardly the end of it. No, indeed. This party was just getting started. I half expected Sammy Davis Jr. to return from the dead and serenade us with, "Who can take the sunrise and sprinkle it with dew ..."

Lita Wordstone had a new idea.

"I'll bet you're just dying to taste my Cherry Heads," she said.

"Say again?" I was pretty sure I hadn't heard correctly.

She pulled out a small box which, like the Goobers, rattled ominously when she shook it. "These are a midwest favorite from my childhood! They have a sour cherry center and a hard panned candy coating. Make memories today!"

That was precisely what I was trying to avoid. "You should try reading a book now and then, and stop getting all your information from advertising copy."

"How about Jujy Fruits?" she said, undaunted by my reprimand. "And Thin Mints. If those are too small I have York Peppermint Patties. And Hershey Kisses. Wouldn't you like some kisses?"

"You're kidding, right?"

"Or Reese's Bites? Or Boston Beans?"

"Are you by any chance an industrial spy working a counter espionage angle for the American Dental Association?"

She replaced the Cherry Heads and produced another bag of M&M's. A brown bag this time. The regular, non-peanut variety. "You don't like nuts, do you?"

I thought of mentioning that I liked her well enough, but I held my tongue. After all, my tongue was clearly no match for Lita Wordstone's tongue.

"I understand completely," she said. "Here, have some of these ..."

She tore open the M&M's. Again I shook my head. "No, thanks. Really."

She looked a little miffed, but by no means defeated. "Watch this."

Oh, great. More tricks.

Lita Wordstone held a single M&M between her left thumb and index finger, showing me the object like a magician setting up a gag. It was a red M&M. My favorite. How did she know? She placed it on her tongue, sticking her tongue out just a little farther than Miss Manners would probably deem appropriate. It was a very lovely tongue, but still I wished she would be a good girl and put it away.

I tried to look bored. It took some effort.

Lita retracted her lovely tongue, closed her mouth and did something that looked half like swallowing and half like choking. Then she pressed her right index finger against the side of her right nostril and blew hard. A cyclist friend of mine who would never consider pulling to the side of the road for such a mundane chore as blowing his nose, once described this action as "launching a snot rocket." Always the little lady, Lita Wordstone shot a small object out of her left nostril into the palm of her left hand. I doubt I still wore the bored expression anymore. Something in the way of shock and horror must have replaced it by this point.

"Look!" she said, holding out her left hand so I could see for myself what was in it.

It was the old highway wreck scenario again. I didn't want to look, but I didn't want to miss it either. In her palm was an M&M all right. But it wasn't red any more. It was blue.

"That's an interesting trick," I said. "Did you go to a special academy to learn it?"

She ignored my question and asked one of her own. "Want to know where the red one went?"

Actually, that was the last thing in the world I wanted to know, next to where the remains of Jimmy Hoffa were buried.

She smiled and stuck her lovely tongue out at me. Sitting on the middle of it was another M&M. A green one this time. Still no sign of the original red M&M.

"Look," I said. "This is all very..."

"She chewed the green M&M. "I bet I know what you'd like."

She stuffed the package of M&M's back into her black leather handbag and took out a very large rectangular bar of Hershey's chocolate, the kind with almonds. She tore the paper from one corner of the bar, stripped back the silver foil as if she were peeling a banana, and took an extremely large bite out of it. As she chewed she held the chocolate bar out for me to take a bite of my own. I smiled politely and held up my right hand in the internationally recognized symbol for *please stop this insanity.* She chewed vigorously. I couldn't believe she hadn't gagged yet. I was about to gag just watching. Soon a coating of brownish saliva began to leak from the corners of her mouth. She gave me a frown to show her growing disappointment and frustration at my refusal to partake. I ignored the theatrics. This was a game for her. I could only hope she'd taken her anti-allergy medication this time.

"It's late," I said. "I think I'll just be running along."

I reached for the door handle and was about to climb out of the Camry when the power door locks all snapped shut in perfect unison. "Don't go," she said, swallowing hard and licking her lips. "I have All-Sorts, too. And Good & Plenty. If you don't like licorice, I have Milk Duds, and KitKat bars. And dark chocolate, and semisweet chocolate. You know, sometimes, I even like to nibble on baking chocolate, except it's so bitter."

"What about your allergies?"

"Oh, poo! That's just hooey. Nobody's really allergic to chocolate. That's just quack doctors talking, running up their bills."

"Yeah, well, I don't want any of your chocolate. And I also don't feel like rushing you off to the emergency room if you go into anaphylactic shock."

"Who's Anna?"

"A girl who's very shocking. You'd like her."

"Oh, you. Stop changing the subject. Want a piece of Bazooka bubble gum? Everybody loves Bazooka bubble gum. Even nuns."

"What?"

"And, of course, if all else fails there's always taffy."

"Of course," I said. "There's always taffy." Why was I suddenly thinking about Scarlet O'Hara? Just plain tired I guess.

"So, what can I give you? How about a Blow Pop?"

"A what?"

"A Blow Pop. Candy on the outside, bubble gum on the inside."

"Nothing, Lita." I looked around for the button to unlock the door. I couldn't find it.

"Oh, don't be a party pooper. I'll bet I know what you like."

"What's that?" I said, fumbling around for the lock release.

"Loose candy."

I didn't bother to respond to this accusation.

"Admit it," she said. "You like it loose. A little piece here, a little piece there. Something different every time. Some people can't commit to one flavor. I understand. But, hey, noski problemski. I've got it all." She rummaged around in her bag as she yammered on. "I have Mary Janes and Bit-O-Honey and peppermints and Silvermints and Honey Sweets and Tootsie Rolls and butterscotch and chocolate mint Starlights ..."

"Stop," I said. "Enough all ready."

She stared at me. Her eyes were wide.

*The Farce News*

"Why won't you share my candy with me?" she said. She was working me over like a Tupperware salesman in a room full of persnickety suburban housewives.

I looked at her squarely and studied her face. It was too dark in the car to see whether her pupils were completely dilated. If she was loaded on anything, it was probably nothing stronger than pure cane sugar. "I'm a diabetic when it comes to you."

She giggled. "That sounds like a song title."

I let her giggle alone. I certainly wasn't going to join her. As far as I was concerned, none of this was a laughing matter. "Release the locks, Lita." Somewhere, in a parallel universe, the hounds had just been turned loose, I was sure of it. So, why, sitting there in Lita Wordstone's car, did I envy the target of the vicious hunting dogs?

"If you offered me some of your candy, I'd take it," she said.

"Open the door, Lita."

"If you offered me a Blow Pop, I wouldn't refuse."

"Yeah, well that's just the kind of girl you are," I said.

"What's that supposed to mean?"

"Fun, fun, fun 'til your daddy takes the T-bird away."

"Huh?"

"Forget it." I needed to find the lock. The air was getting thick in the comfy Camry.

"My daddy's dead." She was very serious all at once.

"It's the Beach Boys," I said.

"I don't even remember my daddy."

"I'm sorry, Lita."

"Don't you say anything mean about my daddy."

At least she wasn't going on about candy anymore. "I promise."

My fingers found the button to release the lock on my side. The mechanism clicked and I pulled the handle before she could lock me in again. The door swung silently open and I began to climb out.

"Anyway it was nice seeing you again," I said. I hated to lie to her, but the truth was she scared the crap out of me. However, I wasn't about to admit that particular weakness without a court order compelling me to do so.

"You're no fun," she said, the perfect spoiled brat. "No fun at all."

I looked in at her through the open door. "Sorry, Lita, but it's been a long day. I'm pretty beat."

"Before you go, I brought you something. A present. Don't you want me to give it to you?"

Back to the candy thing. "I really don't have much of a sweet tooth."

"It isn't candy, silly."

I stopped. "Oh?"

She twisted lithely in her seat and reached into the passenger bench behind her and retrieved a medium sized package, gift wrapped in silver foil with a glittery gold ribbon tied around it.

"Here," she said, handing it to me. "You don't have to open it now if you don't want to."

It was roughly the size and shape of a large bottle of champagne. Not quite a magnum. And not nearly as heavy. There was a small decorative envelope tied to it with a purple string, presumably containing a note of some kind.

I didn't really know what to say. If it would speed the process of getting free of Lita Wordstone, I'd gladly accept the gift, much as I hated to be beholden to her. But to argue the point would be to prolong the agony.

"Thank you," I said. "This is a bit unusual. I don't usually ..."

"Forget it," she said. "It's just a way to say thanks. For all you've done for me and my family."

Before I could respond, she fired the Camry to life, jerked it into gear and peeled out, with the passenger door still hanging open. The centrifugal force of the car turning at the corner slammed the door shut. I stood there, the bottle-shaped gift in my hand, watching her tear off into the night on what I hoped was only a sugar high. I could only pray the cops nabbed her before she did any real damage to herself or somebody else.

The street grew quiet once more. I caught my breath and let myself into the apartment building. I checked my mailbox. It was empty, just the way I like it. I went upstairs and let myself into my dark apartment. Accept for J.D., Buddy and Rufus, it was empty, too. Just the way I like it.

A note on the kitchen table from Jolie confirmed that the cats had been fed, the dog had been both fed and walked.

I put Lita Wordstone's gift on the table and pulled off the ribbon and the foil wrapping paper. It wasn't champagne after all, which under normal circumstances would have been just fine because I don't like the stuff much.

In this case, however, I'd have preferred a nice big bottle of bubbly. I'd have opened it, poured several glasses, and drunk myself into oblivion. Hell, I deserved it.

But Lita Wordstone hadn't given me a magnum of the best bubbly in the house, nor even a bottle of the worst. Instead, she had presented me with a bowling pin. And not just any bowling pin. At a glance, it looked worrisomely like the one she'd used the night before in Windsor to attack Johnny Brashear and his girlfriend, Jennifer.

Well, this sure made a hell of a lot of sense.

I opened the small envelope, hoping Lita Wordstone had included a note that would provide some coherent explanation, although why I suddenly thought she could be capable of anything approaching coherency, I'll never know. Alas, there was no such offer of justification or rationale, just a small round object that stained my fingers when I held it.

It was the missing red M&M.

And it was still wet.

Given the choices, I could only hope it had melted in her mouth like it was supposed to.

## Chapter 25

Thursday morning arrived on a brisk northerly breeze, the hint of impending winter about as subtle as a nearsighted proctologist with a refrigerated probe. I struggled out of bed around eight, set up the coffee pot, and treated myself to a long hot shower. My muscles were sore, my lower back ached, my throat was scratchy, and my mood was sour. I wondered if someone had broken into my place during the night and given me a sound beating, but when I checked the locks on my front door I found no sign of tampering. If I was lucky it was just the flu. If I was especially fortunate, the worst of it would hold off until after my weekend gig with Artie and the fellas in Bristol.

Jolie hadn't seen fit to stop by with breakfast. It probably shouldn't have bothered me, but for some reason it did. Her absence from the scene made me down right cranky. And the more I thought about it, the more I realized that quite a few things which wouldn't ordinarily have irritated me had, in the last few days, been lining up like the Monday morning crowd at the unemployment office, hellbent on annoying the bejesus out of just about everyone, most of all me.

For example, where the hell was this Blackie Buenavista character, and why was I supposed to give a damn? Nobody else seemed to. Oh, sure, everyone was plenty concerned about the possibility of me looking for him, but was anyone stepping up to help me actually locate the elusive sonofabitch? No. It wasn't as if I'd gotten a whole lot of cooperation on this ad hoc manhunt. It wasn't as if I'd received any help, come to think of it.

I needed air. A walk. A change of scenery.

I threw some clothes on and hooked the leash to Rufus' collar. The front end of this particular double-play was comparatively effortless. As a rule, I don't tend to jump up and down like a spastic mental patient with an organic brain disorder or hop around like a jackrabbit on crystal meth when I'm getting dressed. However, the backside of the double-play, the relay to first base was another story. Rufus becomes nearly apoplectic at the mere sight of his leash coming down off the hook by the door and, in fact, begins to jump up and down exactly like a spastic mental patient with an organic brain disorder and hop around exactly like a jackrabbit on crystal meth. Thus, connecting him to his lead tends to be a somewhat labor intensive process comprised of one-half cajoling, one-half Greco-Roman wrestling, and one-half pure willpower, the kind of sheer determination that inspired man to conquer the wild beast in the first place. In other words, futile willpower.

But I felt a little bad for Rufus, so I didn't put the usual Half Nelson on him during our Greco Roman wrestling match. I'd neglected him pretty thoroughly over the last few days. Of course, I'd been busy tending to The Lunatics, so my excuse was pretty solid. Still, he'd been the one to pay the price with endless lonely hours curled up on his mat. I wondered if he was aware of any of this, or if his memory banks were more or less devoid of interest-bearing deposits (and contained only calcium deposits) and was otherwise uncluttered by useless chaff. For his sake, I hoped the latter was the case. The notion of a dog haunted by sad memories of forced solitude was more than I cared to contemplate at the moment.

For his part, Rufus was so happy to get out in the world, he stopped to piss about thirty times before we'd gone half a block. After a while, he was reduced to raising a leg and aiming his urine at various objects without any measurable results, his tank having run dry. He didn't seem to notice or care and I wasn't about to spoil his fun with a long, tedious explanation of the futility of the exercise, a lecture which in all likelihood would have gone over his head anyway.

As we strolled along, I had plenty of time to think. It occurred to me, as I reviewed events of the week, that I was fairly hacked off at Jolie. And not just because she didn't bring me breakfast. Hell, she wasn't my personal valet. I had no right to attach my own random expectations to her peculiar patterns of behavior. She was free to come and go as she pleased, just as I was. It was a little easier for her because she had keys to my flat, but that's another story. Meanwhile there were other issues in need of immediate attention. In the last couple of days, she'd managed to ruin some of my favorite practices and procedures, traditions I'd held sacred. Worst of all, I hadn't seen it coming. Hadn't noticed the obvious warning signs. Some detective I was turning out to be. Brought new meaning to *amateur* (for I sure as hell didn't love the work itself). Mulling it over, I could not deny the presence of subtle but significant changes, and not just the seasonal shift carried on the wind.

It crystalized for me as Rufus and I neared the campus of Trinity College. The problem was simple. Jolie was ruining my life. Proof was right in front of me. Here we were, Rufus and I, in the very heart of our prime bird watching territory, where coeds of all shape and size, color and age scurried from class to class, or sat reading and talking on benches, or lay in the grass catching a few morning rays before catching their Ethics in Politics class at 11:00 o'clock. It was a smorgasbord of lovelies. The very reason we came here, the pooch and I, to admire God's work in the spirited setting of academia, to do a little offshore fishing for females, with Rufus as the unwitting bait. Now I realized, much to my dismay, that I didn't give a damn about any of these fine young women. They were just as lovely as ever. The problem lay with me. I barely noticed them. And I had Jolie to thank.

Of course, the Trinity coeds knew nothing of my state of befuddlement. Therefore it was fitting that on such a fine morning as this they should approach in record numbers and literally queue up for the chance to pet the cute doggie, pull his ears a bit and idly pass the time of day chitchatting about nothing at all with the tall, half-a-hippie in the two-tone cowboy boots. Days when I showed up ready for intramural extragender interaction, they seemed to sense my intentions and dash for cover behind every tree, bush, bench, and/or building. Ah, life on the veldt.

After fifteen minutes of shamelessly soaking up adoration, Rufus gave me his "get me outa here" expression, the one that told me he'd had enough for one day, that his ears were now suitably sore from massaging, and that his ego had been properly stroked. Since he'd been neutered at six months, he really had no way to deal with all the conflicted sexual feelings he was experiencing. *So could we please just go home?*

I knew exactly how he felt, and I hadn't even been neutered.

We said our good-byes and turned for home. As we were leaving the Common, my peripheral vision picked up the incongruous motion of someone traveling quickly against the general flow of pedestrian traffic. I looked over and observed a short, stocky kid on a flashy skateboard. Not just any kid and not just any skateboard. It was the kid from yesterday morning. I did a double take and quickly stopped to examine him, and by default to examine my own basically suspicious nature. Was he really following us? What if it turned out he was a college student, or just some kid from the neighborhood? Was I being unduly paranoid to view him as a possible threat? Is there such a thing as being unduly paranoid?

The kid on the skateboard answered the question with his clumsy behavior. He was neither deft enough to stalk us discreetly, nor quick enough to look away when I spotted him. There was something ridiculously furtive about the way he averted his gaze when we made eye contact, a gesture which announced that he was up to no good, and that I was in fact the object of sinister pursuit. Unless he was plotting some dastardly scheme to steal my dog. I discounted this ludicrous notion. Who in his right mind would snatch Rufus?

I looked down at the mutt. He smiled up me. His expression seemed to say, "What's up, Chief?"

I stood still for a moment, staring at the kid on the skateboard.

Rufus tugged on his lead, then quit and sat down when he realized we weren't going anywhere.

The kid on the skateboard rolled along a few yards, neither in any big hurry nor exactly dawdling. He had the rhythm of an aircraft in a holding pattern. It was definitely the same kid. I wasn't imagining things that weren't actually there. He had the same long black hair. Same baggy jeans. Same black shirt and denim jacket with the sleeves torn off. Same enormous sneakers.

He looked over my way a couple of times, covertly, like he wasn't really interested, like he was just enjoying the morning. But I stood my ground and stared right at him and he flinched each time our eyes met. I kept watching until he disappeared around a corner. I gave the dog a gentle tug and he leapt to his feet.

"Come on, Roof."

He smiled at me again and we headed for home in lock step.

I'd really had my fill of all these stupid cat and mouse games. My life was turning into a dog and pony show. All that was missing was an elephant balancing on a big red ball. If this grease ball kid wanted something with me, I planned to give him every chance to test his nerve. My back was up and I could actually feel my usual passive-aggressive nature giving way to a far more confrontational bravado. My common sense was apparently out to lunch at the moment, for arguably this was exactly the kind of attitudinal shift that could land a person -- me, for instance -- in the hospital, should the confrontation end up being with the wrong dude on the wrong day down the wrong alley.

But I didn't really care. I wasn't thinking straight. And this was something else for which I felt I had Jolie to thank, or perhaps to blame. I don't usually go around feeling invincible. In fact I've always been quite comfortable with my vincibility. When you've been vinced a couple of times, either emotionally or physically, you tend to accrue a healthy respect for your own vincibility. I hold no illusions on the subject. If you stab me I'll bleed. If you shoot me I might take permanent action and do something everlasting, like die. If you mug me on the street and steal my wallet I'll probably call the cops and waste a whole lot of time filling out paperwork and looking pointlessly through thick books of mug shots, studying pictures of guys who look as much like cops as they do like hoodlums.

But if you follow me around the neighborhood on a skateboard and try to intimidate me, I'll just get pissed. No matter how nice your skateboard might be.

I'm no black belt in karate, but I was spoiling for a fight.

We walked home purposefully, Rufus and I, man and mutt. Or, vice versa, respectively. He was beyond pretending he needed to mark everything in sight. His priorities had clearly shifted. He was anxiously anticipating a long drink of water, a hearty snack and a few hours at the dream works. With these goals in mind, he kept a steady pace all the way back to Summit Street.

A couple of blocks from the apartment, I heard the wheels of the skateboard. I glanced quickly over my shoulder. The stocky kid in the huge sneakers was about fifty feet back, coming our way. My adrenaline was flowing like a mighty river, carrying me to God knows what kind of stupid encounter. My luck, I'd survive the rapids and go over a waterfall that made Niagara Falls look like a leaky faucet. I turned right at the corner and stepped into the first doorway we came to. Rufus immediately lay down, his chin on his crossed paws, his tongue hanging out of his mouth, panting. So much for him watching my back.

About thirty seconds later, the sound of skateboard wheels heralded the arrival of my pursuer.

I stepped out of the doorway and he nearly ran me down. But I was ready for the showdown and perhaps he wasn't. I shifted my weight, planted my back foot, and stuck my right hand in the center of his chest. Standing on the skateboard, he was only a couple of inches shorter than me. With the help of my stiff arm to his solar plexus, he stopped short and hopped off the board. It rolled on down the sidewalk. Rufus barked at it, then put his head back down again. Standing on the pavement, the stocky kid was considerably shorter than I, well under six feet. But he had girth to him and felt solid against the pressure of my hand on his shirtfront.

"Dude!" he shouted. Genuine surprise lit up his dark eyes. "You scared the shit out of me."

"Hold it right there!" I said. "Don't fucking move!"

He looked up at me, waiting, out of breath. "Whoa! Chill out!"

"Who the hell are you and why have you been following me?"

He didn't answer right away, but he didn't look away either. He certainly didn't shy away from my laser beam stare, which discouraged me somewhat. Clearly I'd have to spend some time working on my laser beam stare for future use.

"Dude, take it easy. I don't even know, like, what you're talking about."

"Right," I said. "What were you gonna do, steal my dog?"

He frowned, then his face went neutral. He looked at Rufus, then back at me. "You crazy, man?"

He had a point, even it was left unspoken. "Just checking."

"Dude, why would I want to steal your freakin' dog?"

I liked it better when the point had been left unspoken. Now he'd spoiled it and I'd have to fight for the honor of my beloved comrade. I grabbed a handful of the kid's shirt front.

"Where do you get off calling him a 'freakin' dog'? There's nothing freakish about him. He's a perfectly normal dog in every respect. In fact, he's an excellent dog. You could do a lot worse."

The stocky greaseball kid was beginning to look a little worried. Not scared. Worried. He probably thought I was nuts, and, of course, you can never predict what a crazy person might do. But credit where it's due, he took a deep breath and screwed up whatever courage was lurking in his round belly.

"Dude, you're the dick, right?"

I released his shirt front from my fist and studied him for a minute. He had a broad pale face in stark contrast to his jet black hair, which was combed straight back. He might have weighed a couple of hundred pounds but he didn't look fat, just well constructed in a pointlessly thick fashion. Too short for football or he'd have made a good lineman. I didn't see him as a surfer, although he was giving it the full Southern California treatment. And he did travel by urban surfboard, so maybe he was a transplanted Malibu beach bum. His jeans hung low on his hips. His enormous sneakers were not *Adidas*. I recognized the brand name and wondered briefly about the Third World child laborer who'd probably earned all of four cents to stitch the things together prior to this guy spending a C-note for them at the mall. What was the industry term for it? Out-sourcing? Oh, no. Slavery. That's it.

"You don't know me well enough to call me a dick," I said.

He looked a little confused. But also a little less worried.

"Dude," he said, as if imploring me to persevere, and to remain calm as well. "You're the private eye." As if he had to convince me of the fact.

"Unofficially," I said. "But the question of the moment is who the hell are you?"

"Dude, I'm nobody," he said. "Just a guy with something to sell."

"You have a name?"

"Yeah, of course. Everybody has a name."

"Okay," I said. "So, what is it?"

"They call me Stick."

"Why? Don't they like you?"

"Hey!"

I thought about it for a minute. I'd heard of guys seven feet tall being tagged with stupid nicknames like Shorty and Stumpy, and guys who weighed eighty-three pounds with moronic pet names like Fats or Stumpy, and guys the size of a house with ridiculous nicknames like Tiny or Stumpy. Maybe that was the idea here. Maybe he'd been going for ironic and his only real crime was falling so far short of his goal. On the other hand, maybe this was all the rage in Malibu.

"I assume that's a nickname."

"No way, dude. At least I don't think so."

I waited for the punch line, but he didn't say anymore.

"So, what's your story, Slick?"

"Stick, dude. Not Slick."

"Okay, Stick. So, why you following me? And don't say you aren't following me because that'll just make the dog angry."

I glanced down at Rufus. He was asleep. Stick shrugged at me, perhaps in sympathy. "He sure doesn't look too angry."

"Okay, then what do you have to sell?" I said, quickly changing the subject. "And what makes you think I'd want to buy it, whatever it is?"

The kid wavered. "Dude, you always ask so many questions?" He was clearly flustered.

"What's the matter, junior? You need me to write it down so you can keep track?"

He looked hurt. "That isn't funny, dude."

"Sorry, I flunked out of comedy college. So sue me."

"You got a real attitude, problem. You know that, dude?"

"Let's hear your story. I think I smell winter in the air."

He just gaped at me. I couldn't decide if he was losing his nerve or maybe he thought I was the wrong guy to do business with after all. I was fine either way. "Dude, you're confusing me."

I paused and let a silence grow between us. Confusing this kid was not the proudest achievement of my adult life, or even of my morning. I decided to give him a break. You can just take browbeating so far and then it stops being fun.

"Look, here's the thing, Stick," I said. "I'm heading home right now. As you can plainly see, my freakin' dog here is a little tuckered out. Too much flirting with the honeys. I assume you already know where I live. In case you've forgotten, it's the apartment building on Summit Street. After I drop the hound, I'm heading over to my rehearsal studio. It's on Farmington Avenue. You want me to write down the address? It's right across the street from Kinko's. That's the copy shop, not the S&M parlor, in case you're still confused. I'll be there for a while. The studio, that is, not the S & M parlor. If you want to chat, by all means drop in. Should you decide you don't want to chat, then feel free not to drop in. I won't hold my breath waiting either way. If you come by, we can have tea and crumpets. But only if you bring them. Otherwise, piss off. You dig me, dude? I don't want to see you in my rear view mirror anymore. Are we at least clear on that point?"

He took his time composing a suitable answer. He eventually came up with one. "You're from New York, aren't you?"

I smirked at him. "You didn't answer my question."

He thought it over, scratched his head, then nodded. "No problem," he said, then scanned the sidewalk for his errant skateboard.

"Good," I said. "I'm so glad." I started to walk away.

He called after me and I turned. "Dude, be cool," he said, waving.

I laughed and turned my back on him.

When I locked up the apartment twenty minutes later, Rufus was sound asleep again, this time on his mat. I passed Jolie's apartment and stopped briefly to listen at her door. I heard nothing. If she was home, she wasn't listening to loud music, or running the vacuum cleaner, or singing at the top of her lungs, or screaming bloody murder about the invading cossacks. I wanted to knock, but I didn't know exactly what I'd say if she was home and actually opened the door. "Where was my breakfast?" That wasn't going to work. And what if she was just playing games with me again? What if I rang the bell and there was no answer? Would that mean she genuinely wasn't home? Or would it suggest she was in there but was taking the opportunity to teach me another lesson in moral virtue, hurt feelings, disappointment, or any of a hundred other emotional responses?

Did I always ask so many questions?

That's what Stick wanted to know. Maybe the greasy little bastard was on to something.

There had been no thunderstorms during the night and my piece of shit Jetta had, yet again, failed to be struck by the dreamed-for bolt of lightning. It had also failed to be stolen or even irreparably vandalized by common street thugs. To my surprise, the charge had failed to leak out of the battery and the engine started the first time I turned the key. I jammed the stick shift into first gear and released the clutch.

And the engine stalled.

Now that was more like it.

I went through the ignition process once more, got the motor running and moments later was on my way to the studio on Farmington Avenue. Just for the hell of it, I kept an eye on the rear view mirror. I didn't expect to find Stick back there, but it wouldn't have surprised me, either. Stranger things

*The Farce News*

had been happening to me lately, at a rate of about three per hour.

After wedging my car into a slot between a Chevy Suburban and a UPS truck parked in the rear lot behind Kinko's, I popped into the copy shop, slid a wrinkled dollar bill into the soda machine by the door and punched one of the buttons. Several seconds elapsed before the dwarf who lives inside the machine processed my request and sent a plastic 20-ounce bottle of Dr. Pepper careening down the delivery chute. If I ever bothered to twist the cap off and open it, the contents would no doubt explode in a spray. This was precisely why I never opened the bottles of soda I bought at the copy shop. My purchases were only meant as a gesture of good faith, a small way to support local business.

No, not really.

There was a brown-suited UPS guy kneeling at the FedEx drop box by the counter. He was jamming what looked like a wad of gum and chewing tobacco into the lock on the side of the box. One of the Kinko counter clerks was watching, a fairly evil grin on his face.

I was delighted to find nobody waiting for me in the alcove outside the studio. I was marginally less delighted to find a pile of mail waiting for me just inside the door. I bent over to pick it up. It was the usual junk. Flyers from the *Big Y* supermarket chain and the sale sheets from the Brooks drugstore conglomerate. I sat at the desk and browsed through it quickly. One item caught me eye. Chap Stick -- buy one get three free. Who could turn down such a killer deal, particularly with winter in the air? I crumpled the flyer and tossed it in the trash. I didn't even bother looking through the stack of third class crap. The fact that it represented millions of uselessly murdered trees and billions of gallons of carcinogenic printing ink just made me mad.

My spirits were improved by the discovery of a business-size envelope on which my name and the studio's address had been meticulously handwritten in elaborate feminine script. I opened it and pulled out a bank check in the amount of two thousand dollars. In the upper left-hand corner was printed the name and address of my client and distant relation, Margaret Waddley-Wordstone. If it was Auntie Peg who'd actually filled out and signed the check, I'd never be able to prove it in a court of law without the assistance of a professional handwriting analyst. The penmanship was beyond the limits of excessive stylization. The capital M's and W's were virtually interchangeable, the lowercase g's and y's so similar as to be all but identical. It wasn't so much a signature as a fine example of modern hieroglyphics. The handwriting lacked anything in common with the note that had been delivered by hand earlier in the week. This was curlicue central, way over the top. But the numbers were legible and dazzling.

## The Farce News

Two grand for a couple of days of work didn't go down too badly at all. It was roughly seven times the pay I would earn for two night's worth of picking tunes with Artie and the fellas down in Bristol this coming weekend. However, notwithstanding the drudgery of tending to The Lunatics and risking prosecution for a spate of petty offenses committed along the way, I could live like a king with a job a week at the Wordstone rate of pay. If only I could fashion a way to make it happen, which I doubted was possible.

I made a mental note to call the old lady and say thanks. Hopefully, I'd get in and out of the conversation before she had a chance to invite me over for ice cream in her frozen lair, or, worse, to ask me if I had learned anything about the whereabouts of Blackie Buenavista. We still hadn't had the meeting she'd requested yesterday. Oh, well. It wasn't as if I didn't try.

I was still daydreaming about the tax bracket I'd temporarily joined when there came an overly polite tapping on the office door. I put the check away. "It's open."

To say I was surprised to see Stick appear in the doorway would be a lie. I assumed he'd come knocking, after taking a little time to get his sales pitch right. If he was looking to seal the deal on some transaction regarding the Wordstones, *et al.*, he'd want to get it right the first time around. Might also want to figure out to his own satisfaction if I was dangerous or just crazy. And perhaps to come to convince himself he could approach me without slinking around like a comic book character in search of a decent dialogue balloon.

"Dude," he said, by way of greeting. "How's it going, man?" As if we were old pals, reunited after too long a separation.

"Come on in, Stick," I said. I didn't get up. I wasn't feeling *that* hospitable. I pointed to the various pieces of furniture in the room. "Go ahead, take a load off. Anywhere you like."

He had recovered his skateboard and now carried it under his left arm. He came around to the chair in front of the desk where I was seated, and planted himself, the skateboard across his lap. He looked around the room. I watched his face and quickly concluded that he was no better an actor than Lillian Buenavista or any of the other hacks at the Simsbury Dinner Theater. His opinion of our rehearsal hall was clearly displayed in his expression.

"Some dump, huh?" I said, needling him.

He was embarrassed now. "No, dude. Not at all. You play the drums?"

"Steel guitar."

"Oh," he said, nodding. "Cowboy stuff, huh?"

"I'd offer you something to drink, but all we have is warm Dr. Pepper."

"That's okay, dude. I'm not thirsty."

*The Farce News*

"So, what's your story, Stick? You said you had something to sell."

"Yeah, that's right."

"I assume it isn't a used car, since you don't appear to own one."

"No, dude. It isn't a car. It isn't anything you can carry around on you. Except maybe in your head. Y'know, up here." He tapped one temple, in case I was confused about where his head was. It was a helpful tip. I'd been under the impression his head was up his ass, but now I could see I'd been wrong about that.

"So that means whatever it is, you don't have it on you, right?"

"Right," he said, grinning. Then the smile slid away as it dawned on him that I might have just called him stupid.

"This is very intriguing," I said, and yawned. "By the way, when did you get to town?"

He paused before answering. "I've been around a little while," he said, perhaps offended by my implication that he wasn't much of a city slicker. "I pretty much know how shit works, though. I got friends, dude. I know how to make a dime when I need one. I know the score."

He knew the score. That was good. So why did I have the feeling he didn't know the names of the players or which team was currently on the field?

I smiled at him. "You miss it much?"

He frowned. "Miss what?"

"Malibu Beach," I said. "Or wherever you come from."

He stared at me for a minute. His eyes were dark brown, and quite shifty, as if he were afraid to leave his gaze on any one object for too long for fear that some unseen object would leap out at him from behind and whack him upside the head. Maybe he had a history of letting just that sort of thing happen to him.

"I'm from La Jolla, dude. Not Malibu, get it?"

He said it like I owed him an apology. I made a face, one of those really useful "Who cares?" faces, and stopped just short of sticking my tongue out at him. It wasn't as if I'd accused him of being from Passaic, New Jersey. While he took his time getting over it, I picked up a piece of mail and gave it a cursory glance. It was a signed photograph of the president of the United States, an eight-by-ten color glossy, smiling monkey kind of thing, with a caption thanking me for my support. Now, *that* was funny. I crumpled it into a tight ball and fired it across the room at the circular trash can in the corner where it could keep company with the Brooks drugstore sale flyer.

"Nothing but net," I said.

Stick cleared his throat. But then he didn't say anything. I considered

*The Farce News*

pointing out that he was the guest at this surprise party, he could cry if he wanted to or just sit there. It was his dime. He could start talking any time the fancy struck him or just watch me go through the mail. In a few minutes, I'd be changing the strings on my guitar. He might find that interesting. Probably not. Instead I remained silent and let him work out the particulars for himself. He was a big boy, after all. Figuratively as well as literally.

He finally got around to it.

"Dude, we heard maybe you're looking for someone."

"What, you mean like a girlfriend? Someone to watch over me?"

"No, dude. Not a girlfriend. A guy."

I leaned back and put my feet up on the desk. "You got your information wrong, pal. Last time I checked, I don't swing that way."

"Dude, that isn't what I'm talking about."

"Sorry," I said. "Go on with your -- excuse me -- fairy tale."

"My what?"

I took a deep breath and let it out slowly. This wasn't going very well. He was like a quadruple amputee who just doesn't know when his leg is being pulled. I could hear the clock ticking away the seconds of my life. "Let's skip the song and dance, Stick. Who sent you to talk to me?"

"Nobody sent me." He was offended again.

"Really? Because I'm having a hard time believing any of this was your original idea."

"Nobody sent me, dude."

"Yeah, yeah. You keep saying that. But it doesn't have that ring of truth. Tell me something. Who do you hang with when you're not cruising the neighborhood on your skateboard? Not the Wordstone women, surely. You're not quite loopy enough to run with that crowd of clowns. And I have it directly from the horse's mouth that you're not a flunky for Venus Edwards. She likes her minions fresh from the crypt and you appear to have some life left in you. So, who are your pals, Stick? Maybe Johnny Brashear? He's dead, you know."

Stick got up and stood over me. At least he would have stood over me had the desk not separated us. I was ready to jump into action if he came at me with the skateboard. There was plenty of room under the desk. I could hide down there indefinitely. "Johnny was, like, a super excellent dude."

"Relax, Stick," I said. "Take a seat."

Surprisingly, he did. There was no anger in him, just sadness. "Dude, Johnny B. was practically like a friend to me."

"Yeah, well, I'm very sorry for your loss. It's awful when we lose practically friends."

"They didn't have to kill him. That was truly a cold gesture."

I had never before heard the act of premeditated murder referred to as a "gesture," cold or otherwise. I wondered what was in the drinking water in La Jolla.

"It wasn't they," I said. "It was her."

"Same difference."

I wasn't going to argue the point, particularly as I didn't understand what the phrase "same difference" meant, if it meant anything at all. "So, what exactly is it that brings you here, Stick? Why have you been lurking ominously in my periphery?" I hoped he knew what the word "lurking" meant. I had some serious doubts about him getting the "ominously" bit, and chances were next to nil he'd grasp the concept of a "periphery" without the help of a dictionary and someone to show him how to operate it. But you can't always talk down to people. "You and Jennifer in cahoots now?"

His jaw dropped. He picked it up and put it back on. "Dude, you been followin' *me* around?"

"Just a guess," I said. "Besides which I don't own a skateboard."

"Jenny's like a super excellent girl."

"Great," I said. "Johnny was super excellent, and now he's dead. Jennifer's super excellent, and she's, well, dead from the neck up. Super excellent, isn't all it's cracked up to be, is it? So, talk to me, Stick. In complete sentences. The day is getting, like, super long."

Stick put his skateboard down and organized his thoughts.

"Dude, it's like this. I need some dough so's we can beat it out of town and get a new start somewheres else. Maybe So-Cal. Maybe Maui. Anyway, we gotta get the heck outa Hartford. I'm tellin' ya, this place is like deadsville."

"Who's us, Stick?"

"Me and Jenny," he said, as if it should have been obvious.

"What's the problem? The cops after you?"

He looked hurt. "No way, dude. I'm no criminal."

That was debatable, but I wasn't inspired to take sides one way or the other. "Just a surfer in search of a little piece of the ocean?"

"Dude, you are, like, so correct."

"And whoever is after you is, I presume, a bigger threat to you than the police?"

He didn't want to answer. I didn't press the issue. "We need to leave. Super soon."

"And to do this you need money."

"Yeah, but we don't want a handout or nothing like that. That's not our thing. We got something to sell, me and Jenny. Information. About that guy you're supposed to be looking for."

"Oh, so we're back to that again."

"Dude, a thousand bucks and we can hit the road. Me and Jenny. Once and for all."

"A thousand dollars? That's a lot of money, kid. You must have me mistaken for someone else. What are you selling that's worth a thousand dollars, anyway?"

I was thinking about the check Auntie Peg had sent, and how this guy already had his hooks into half of it.

"It's about that guy," he said. "Booneyvister."

"Blackie Buenavista."

"That's the guy."

"What about him?"

"Dude, we heard some stuff."

"That's terrific news. You heard some stuff. Why don't you let me hear some of it, too?"

Stick shifted nervously in his seat. I thought he was about to look around the room to make sure we were alone. He didn't. "We heard Venus Edwards had him done."

"Done?"

"Y'know. Capped. Snuffed. Bumped. Iced. Rubbed. Canceled."

"I get it. I get it. You have quite the vocabulary when you want to."

"Thanks."

"It wasn't a compliment."

"Oh."

"Why would Venus Edwards do such a nasty thing?"

"Dude, 'cause of the thing with her old man."

"You mean Hubert?"

"Yeah. That's the guy. Hubert"

"And what is the thing to which you refer?"

Stick took a deep breath. "The way we heard it, this Buenavista dude was like some kind of big revolutionary, right?"

"From where?"

"Dude, who knows? Nicaragua? Honduras? El Salvador? What difference does it make?"

He had a point. "Keep talking."

"So the old man, Hubert, right? He gets to be like excellent pals with Blackie, and Blackie sees dollar signs and like plays him for money. You know, for *la causa.* You follow me?"

*The Farce News*

Did I follow him? Was that the question? I shook my head, only to myself. Should there ever come a time when I was unable to follow Stick's simplistic narrative, at least I'd always have enough pride not to admit to such a humiliating mental defect. "Keep going, Stink. So far, I've heard all of this before."

"Yeah, dude. I'm so sure. And it's Stick, not Stink."

"My bad."

"Anyway, so, you've probably heard about Hubert and Blackie disappearing together. Or at least how they both like went bye-bye on the same day. Right?"

"Right, just like a couple of high school love birds."

"No way, dude. It wasn't like that at all."

"How would you know that?"

He didn't answer right away. But I could tell he was thinking about how many beans he'd have to spill to get the money he was after. "Okay," he said. "I knew Blackie. A little bit, not a lot."

"Then what the hell was this 'Booneyvister' crap you handed me?"

Stick looked down at his feet for a moment. "I don't know, dude."

"How many more lies have you got buried in the folds of this epic tale of woe?"

"Whoa, I'm not lying to you, dude."

"No, but you're not telling me anything I don't already know, either. This is all last week's news. And so far your rendition is pretty lame. I wouldn't give you ten bucks for effort."

"That's super cold, dude."

"Yeah, and it's only October. Hang around a couple of months and you'll find yourself up to your ass in snow, just like right now I'm up to my ass in your bullshit."

"Dude!"

"Oh, I forgot. You want to blow town. You don't want to hang around."

"That's like totally correct, dude. We definitely don't want to hang around."

"Then tell me something worth paying for."

Stick looked like a kid who'd successfully climbed to the top of the jungle gym and was just feeling good about himself when some wise ass dared him to jump off. It was a heavyweight contest between pride and common sense, and common sense didn't have a jab, a hook, or any kind knockout punch on which to pin its hopes. He's on top of the world, but he knows he's gonna hit the ground all wrong and break something. Hopefully it will only be an ankle or an arm and not his neck.

*The Farce News*

"Hubert and Blackie weren't fags," he said.

"You already said that."

"I heard Hubert was bored and wanted to go live a little, have some excitement in his life. Dude, you can understand that, right? I mean, the guy's like a super pencil pusher. Has loads of dough, sure. But he's still a white collar geek all the same, isn't he? And, dude, here's this guy, Blackie Buenavista, with adventure written all over him."

"In crayon?"

"Compared to Edwards, he's a real go-get-'em kind of hombre. Scared of nothing and scared of nobody."

"Sometimes fearless is the same as stupid, you know."

If Stick knew, he wasn't letting on. "And he had this trophy wife and like millions of dollars just waiting, but he didn't feel like hanging around. Doesn't that seem strange?"

"What seems strange is you referring to Lillian Buenavista as a trophy wife."

"Why?" he said, afraid I was taking offense.

"Last time I looked they don't hand out prizes for finishing last."

Stick made a face, but he didn't take the bait. He was learning. "Anyway, dude, the old lady, Venus Edwards, she sees the writing on the wall, sees how Blackie's gonna take her old man away. And she freaks, dude. I mean, here's her bookkeeping genius husband, a bookworm with a knack for turning shit into gold and hiding the profits so everybody thinks the shit is still shit."

I was thinking about that shitty little dinner theater.

Stick was still talking. "And suddenly he's getting ready to climb on a horse and ride out of town. You can understand how maybe she'd like freak out and whatnot."

If I were Venus Edwards, I'd freak out and whatnot every time I saw myself in a mirror, but I didn't say so to Stick. He had a lot on his mind already. There were so many holes in his story, I could see Valhalla on the other side. This fairy tale was a no-sale so far.

"Go on," I said, curious to see how far afield he was willing to go.

"Well, think about it for a second, dude. If it's true, if her old man did run off with Blackie, you know, for the mountains of Central American, right, to fight for freedom or whatever, then how come she's going around happy as a freakin' clam all the time?"

"Is that a rhetorical question, Stick? Or have you constructed some sort of clever answer that will remove any vestiges of mystery?"

"You have some cash, dude?"

## The Farce News

I shook my head. "I still haven't heard anything that isn't mere speculation or hearsay?"

"Yeah, dude? Well I got a news flash for you."

"What's that, Mr. Cronkite?"

"We know where Hubert really is. And it ain't Costa Fucking Rica, or El Fucking Salvador, or Guate-fucking-mala. So, what do you think of them apples?"

"Don't you mean 'them fucking apples'?"

He smiled, clearly feeling a little too smug.

I pulled my feet down off the desk and sat up a little straighter. I looked the urban surfer bum in the eye. It was time to try some Hollywood bullshit on him, see how he reacted. Besides, I had never had the chance to play out one of these scenes. Hell, on stage with Artie and the boys, I don't even have a mike half the time. I have to yell all my best quips at him, and then he repeats them and gets the laughs. I turned to Stick and gave him the full dose. "On the level, kid. Don't even think about shaking me down with some bullshit line of science fiction. Okay? You could never get away with it. I would hunt you down like an animal. And if that didn't work, I'd call some people I know in the law enforcement racket who'd happily slap cuffs on you and make sure you spent the rest of your misguided youth and half of your misguided adulthood behind bars. Far from the beach. Far from the thundering surf. Far from the endless summer and the eternal pursuit of babes in joyland. Think it over before you say another word."

I sat back, feeling pretty good.

Stick, meanwhile, looked truly offended. Again. "Dude!"

Clearly he needed another dose. At least he wasn't like my cats, who have to be held down and have their medicine forced down their throats. Stick took it pretty well, comparatively speaking. "Here's the deal, sunshine. I'm making you a one-time offer. Take it or leave it. Your part is simple. Tell me where I can find Hubert Edwards. No tricks. No riddles. No secret codes. No scavenger hunt. You give me a legitimate address. One I can find without hiring a sherpa or an Indian scout. You do that and I'll give you two hundred bucks. If I find Hubie where you say he is, you'll get another three bills. That's five hundred, in case you're wondering. Total. Now, that's the good news. Here's the flip side. If I don't find him, or it's a bogus lead, or any other kind of bullshit, then I'm gonna drop a fistful of dimes and sic the Rottweilers on you and your pretty girlfriend. Are we clear?"

"Yeah, dude. We're clear." He clearly didn't like the deal.

"Just remember: time cools, time clarifies; no mood can be maintained quite unaltered through the course of hours."

"Huh?"

I think Artie would have been proud of my performance. It was a little bit of George Raft, a little bit of Humphrey Bogart, and a little Thomas Mann just for chuckles.

"Forget it, kid. First things first. What's the address? Where do I find Hubert?"

Unfortunately Stick wasn't as impressed with my performance. Just confused. He shook his head. "Dude, I can't tell you."

I sat back again. "Somehow I didn't think you could."

Then he smiled at me. "But Jenny can."

*The Farce News*

## Chapter 26

I had roughly thirty dollars in my wallet and damn few illusions about Stick's claim that he could put me in touch with Hubert Edwards or, with only two degrees of separation, with Blackie Buenavista. I thought the thirty bucks and my dearth of hopes would probably get me through the day. I'd gotten through longer days with less money and even fewer dreams.

What I wanted most at the moment wasn't some half-assed hot tip from a surefire scam artist trying to finance his great escape from the bad guys. What I wanted was a sense of forward progress, some evidence that my life wasn't a perpetual fourth-and-long struggle. I was tired of punting from my own end zone. Much as I wished for it, I couldn't shake the hillbilly square dance music that played in my head. The cross-eyed, sideways-slipping doe-see-doe was in full swing and I was stuck the middle, looking for a two-stepping ladykiller called Blackie Buenavista. For all I knew maybe the guy just wanted to be left the hell alone. But instead of finding him and concluding my business with the Wordstones and my many peculiar relations, I was sitting around the dingy rehearsal studio waiting for a meeting with dead Johnny Brashear's pretty but dense girlfriend, Jennifer.

I should do something productive. Change strings. Tune the guitar. Play some scales.

Unfortunately, ennui had me by the scruff of the neck.

If Stick was to be taken at his word, Jennifer was prepared to trade hard cash for the whereabouts of Hubert Edwards, and maybe that would shed light on Blackie Buenavista's locale. A lot of maybes and a hell of a long way to go for at best a dubious payoff. Worst of all was the increasing number of "middle men" wedging themselves into the action. Was I pursuing a missing persons case or had I somehow gotten mixed up in the middle of some reinsurance swindle. Either way, I wished I could take a shower and wash the feeling off me, the feeling of being handled. But I doubted there was a detergent strong enough or a brush with bristles stiff enough for the job.

While I waited for Stick to make arrangements for an early evening *tête-à-tête* with Jennifer, I spent an hour clipping my nails and filing the edges smooth, a necessary evil if I want my finger picks to sit right. Along with alcoholism, bleeding hangnails are considered the chief occupational hazard for any steel player worth his salt, lime and Tequila. I must go through about a gallon of Skin Shield and Nu Skin every year. Don't know how many gallons

*The Farce News*

of Tequila I go through. My rough estimate is somewhere between two and too many.

The gig in Bristol was only a day away now, and I hadn't touched the guitar since Sunday. These damn Wordstones had become a major distraction, not unlike a giant hangnail. Pity I couldn't clip them or drown them in Nu Skin.

Around four o'clock the phone rang. It was Stick, sounding a little out of breath and nervous. He asked me if I remembered the house on East Barber Street in Windsor.

"Sure," I said. "Johnny Brashear's place."

"Yeah," he said, "but now it's our place. Me and Jenny's."

"But it's in roughly the same location, isn't it? I mean, you didn't have it moved?"

He said it was in the same spot and I told him how terrific that was. There was a short silence on the line. Then: "So, dude, how soon can you get here?"

"Is Jennifer there with you now?"

"Do you have that money we talked about?"

"Does she know where I can find Hubert Edwards at the moment?"

"Dude, isn't that what we've been talking about?"

"You know, fifteen more questions and one of us will have to make a guess," I said. "That's the rule. You're aware of that, aren't you?"

"What?"

"Make that fourteen."

"Dude, are you making fun of me again?"

"Thirteen," I said, impressed that he was aware of my having abused him for sport.

"Hey, are you interested in this information or not?"

I should have said, "Not," and hung up. Instead, I continued busting his balls. "Twelve."

"Dude, can't you be serious?"

"Eleven," I said, then: "I'll see you in forty minutes -- give or take an hour for traffic."

I hung up the phone and stared at it, silently cursing it for ringing in the first place. The more I considered it, the less I wanted to make the drive back out to Windsor, the less I wanted to revisit the scene of Johnny Brashear's not very dramatic death by lawn darts, the less I wanted to renew not-so-old acquaintances with the pretty but vapid Jennifer, and the less I wanted to continue my budding dudeship with Stick.

On the same subject, I was rapidly losing the last traces of interest in Hubert Edwards and Blackie Buenavista. As the minutes grew into hours and the hours stretched into days, the less I truly cared what had become of either of them. If they'd run off together, so what? If they'd run off separately, what difference did it make? If they had taken up residence together, or indeed had never even laid eyes on one another, who cared?

In twenty-four hours, Stick and Jenny would be gone and I would be expected to show up at the gig in Bristol, ready to rock and roll. Artie was adding three new songs to the set list. Some old Gene Clark number called "Lonely Saturday," a Burrito Brother's classic called "High Fashion Queen," and "Eight Days A Week," just because we all still loved the Beatles and that was a pretty obscure selection from that vast library of gold. I'd have to fake my way through them if I didn't carve out some serious practice time in the next few hours.

I was still thinking about the Bristol Road House and delaying my departure for Windsor when there came a knock on my office door. Now what? Or rather, now who? Lillian Buenavista perhaps, back for a curtain call? Lita Wordstone with more sweets? The landlord looking for rent?

Before I could shout, "Go away," the door opened and a very tall, very wide, and very solid looking man entered. He smiled demurely at me, then turned and closed the door quietly behind him. Gently, as if he were afraid he might break the doorknob off in his fist. He was well over six feet tall and probably weighed close to three hundred pounds. He had the meaty presence of an ex-NFL lineman who hasn't yet gone to fat and maybe never will. He was dressed in a Wall Street suit that looked a little too expensive for the body wearing it. There was a little Arnold Schwarznegger in him. The roughhewn exterior in highly cultivated duds. It was, if nothing else, amusing. He had a starched white shirt and a blood red necktie. On his large square head there sat an incongruous yellow straw cowboy hat which completely disrupted the flow of his ensemble and provided what could only be characterized as sartorial comic relief. Whether it was intentional or accidental, I know not. Before he spoke, I stood and said, "Can I help you? I was just leaving."

He pointed a very thick finger at my chair and said: "Sit."

I don't even speak to Rufus this way.

We stared at each other for a moment. I didn't detect a particular accent. Certainly not Austrian. But then again, perhaps I failed to detect an accent because my unexpected visitor had thus far offered only the single monosyllabic utterance. I did, however, recognize a distinct tone of authority. This was a guy who, when he said, "Sit," expected you to cop a squat regardless of whether you were dog tired or you were bursting at the seams

*The Farce News*

with nervous energy.

I remained standing.

"Do you have an appointment?" I said, knowing full well he didn't.

"Sit," he said, still quiet in his manner, again pointing the same thick finger at the chair from which I had only just arisen. The finger seemed even thicker the second time he pointed it.

"I prefer to stand," I said. "But maybe you'd like to take a seat." If he sat and I stood, at least he couldn't tower over me. I didn't think he'd go for the idea, and I was right.

"Please, sir, don't make me say it again."

Great, I thought. A solicitous bully. Please, sir, don't make me beat the shit out of you. As if he were afraid he'd wrinkle his suit in the process -- or worse, offend me.

"No, really, after you," I said, gesturing with a freshly manicured hand at another chair. My counter offer seemed to give him pause for thought. I took the moment to catalog his features. Should I ever see him again, I'd remember to run the other way. Fast.

He was exceedingly well coifed. His posture was erect and almost perfectly symmetrical. His face had the gleam of the freshly barbered. Whatever brand of after shave he wore, it sure wasn't the kind one purchased at the local *CVS* or *Rite-Aid*. His eyes were light brown and clear and bright. His nose was thick and appeared to have been broken once or twice, maybe more. At the same time, however, he didn't have the mashed potato face of a former prize fighter. His bone structure was chiseled without the cro magnon exaggeration of some thugs you meet. This was an Ivy League heavyweight wrestling champion, not a washed up club brawler. A blue blood with hams for hands and, hopefully, enough brainpower to exercise a little restraint in case I managed to piss him off, which I seemed well on my way to doing simply by declining his polite if comically terse invitations to be seated.

We locked stares for a couple of long moments, then slowly lowered ourselves into our respective chairs, keeping the desk between us. A look of patient satisfaction came over him. It was a draw and that seemed fine with him. I leaned back and smiled. For me, it was a spectacular moral victory, worthy of a ticker-tape parade down Broadway.

"I don't believe we've met," I said. "Who might you be?"

"Please," he said, waving one of his large hands as if to brush away the very notion that he was personally worthy of discussion. "I'm not important. I'm nobody." Stick had tried the same angle. But with this gigantor, the claim seemed ridiculous. My initial instinct was to disbelieve him. On the other hand maybe he was nobody. A large, strangely attired figment of my imagination, in which case I needed therapy in a very big way. Or maybe I'd finally stumbled across somebody who could really act. "I'm simply a messenger," he added, no doubt to fill the void he had created with his false modesty, and to attach some notable purpose to his unscheduled visit. "No more, no less."

"That's some suit. You must be the best paid messenger in the history of lackeys."

"Oh, indeed," he said, smiling. "I am."

I didn't like the smile. It was a smile that made the room grow cold. It was a smile that chased away the banjo music that had been haunting me all day and replaced it with the eerie strains of a solitary oboe. It was the smile of a hungry omnivore. His teeth were white enough for commercial work and, unless I was imagining things, they looked sharpened at the edges. They were the teeth of a very large *Carcharodon carcharias*. For just a moment, I wondered if, by any chance he had more than just the single row of each, top and bottom. I didn't think it would be prudent to ask.

Comfortably seated, he pinched the crown of his yellow straw cowboy hat and removed it from his head, revealing a shock of equally yellow hair. He placed the hat on the edge of my desk and sat back. It was a casual gesture, but it carried a very specific air of command. Had he pounded a heavy wooden gavel, the meaning would have been just as clear. This impromptu conference was now in session. And it was his meeting to run.

Of course, that didn't stop me from grabbing the floor.

"I'm probably wondering why you called me here," I said, hoping a little levity might help to levitate the mood in the room, which had depreciated significantly since the unveiling of the man-eating smirk.

"I'm told you were recently hired by Margaret Waddley-Wordstone to carry out an assignment."

"Were that true," I said, "it would be between Mrs. Wordstone and me. For the record, she's my aunt. So I'll thank you to be careful how you talk about her."

"Oh. Are you very close?"

"Nah, I barely know her."

"But you *are* in her employ."

"Worse, I'm in her family."

"But you don't deny that you're working for her?"

"Sorry, pal. No sale. I'm not gonna discuss it one way or the other. It's none of your business, no matter how many ways you ask."

I don't know if he liked my answer, or if my response fit in with what he thought he knew about me. I didn't fret over it much.

"Be that as it may, I'm informed that you have fulfilled your assignment, if in a not completely unsatisfactory manner. That is, to forestall any further advances by a Miss LaTwanda Jefferson."

"Nice try, but that's confidential. Assuming it's true."

"In other words, you don't deny it?"

"In other words, I'm trying to think of a polite way to convince you it's none of your goddamn business. But you seem impervious to subtlety. No offense."

He smiled a bit. "Be just as rude and ill-mannered as you like. You won't hurt my feelings."

"Good to know."

"But we're getting off the track."

"To say nothing of going far afield."

"It is also my understanding that as regards your employment by Mrs. Wordstone, you have been handsomely compensated for the completion of said assignment."

"*Said assignment?* Where do you people learn to speak? The University of Pompous Assholes? Or did you get complimentary diction lessons when you bought that funky hat?"

He ignored my insults. I suppose that was better than him slamming me into next week with one of those big fists. Then I'd miss the gig in Bristol. "As I said ..."

"So far, the only one who's said anything about any assignment is you, big guy. And I've already said that I have nothing to tell you, one way or the other. It's just not up for conversation."

"In other words, you don't deny being paid?"

I thought about the check sitting in my pocket and wondered if this guy knew about it. Was he intercepting my mail? Was he the one who'd sent it. Neither of those choices made any sense. "That would be between me and my aunt and the I.R.S. and the Postal Service. Is that who you work for? You do kind of look like a government employee. Maybe it's your unnaturally large forehead."

He smiled. It was a warning. I had to stop baiting him, otherwise he'd murder me with that smirk.

"The point is this," he said. "You may now cease and desist. You are officially released from any further investigation of any persons or incidents relating to any persons or incidents you may have encountered as a result of your former employment by Mrs. Waddley-Wordstone."

"You mean dear old Auntie Peg?"

"A rose by any other name ..."

"Wow," I said. "Do you memorize this stuff, or are you using cheat sheets?"

"The point is ..."

"You already said what the point is. And I'm damn glad you did, because I was just sitting here wondering what the point of all this could possibly be. I don't mind telling you I'm a bit disappointed, even though your little speech was very impressive."

"What I'm pointing out to you, Mr. Vaughn, is that your work here is done."

I smiled a little. "Like the Lone Ranger?"

"Do we have an understanding?"

"Hi-oh, Silver. Away! If I had a horse, I might saddle up and ride off into the sunset."

"That would be a very good idea. Now you're starting to get it."

"There's just one problem," I said.

"Yes? What's that?"

"No horse."

"No horse?"

"Or a good hat."

"A hat?"

"You have a hat. Maybe I could borrow it. That would only leave the problem of the horse."

"You could use your imagination. Ride a metaphorical horse into a metaphorical sunset."

"Wearing a metaphorical hat?"

"Exactly."

"Do I feed this horse metaphorical oats and sleep under the metaphorical stars? Frankly, that would start to feel a little foolish after the first week or two."

"Metaphorically speaking ..."

I shook my head, made a face to show my displeasure. "Metaphorically speaking, that's quite a load of crap. And were I to do as you suggest, I might never get a chance to satisfy my curiosity."

The smile crept off his face and hid in the shadows while a much darker expression spread quickly across his broad features. "Mr. Vaughn, I assure you the satisfaction of your curiosity could prove to be an extremely expensive proposition. To say nothing of ill-advised."

He stared blankly at me. Maybe he was waiting for me to blink, or flinch, or cry uncle, or crawl under the desk and whimper like a child with a bad nightmare. I didn't give him the satisfaction. After a moment, I tore myself away from his bland glare and let my eyes fall on the yellow straw cowboy hat that sat on the edge of my desk. It was a real piece of junk, the rim bent this way and that, the straw mottled and pocked with small holes that looked like mice had been snacking on it. I wouldn't put the thing on my head without first getting a tetanus shot. Although, oddly enough, there was something familiar about it that I couldn't immediately identify.

I looked back at my large, uninvited visitor. He, too, had shifted his gaze to the hat. He was looking rather fondly at it, which, as far as I was concerned, didn't say much of him or for the caricature Stetson. As we stared at the hat together, he reached over and lifted it gingerly to a height of approximately six inches off the desktop.

I don't think my jaw actually dropped, but it felt like it should.

In the space beneath the hat where previously only empty space had existed there now sat a neat stack of hundred dollar bills held together by a thick rubber band. Unless I was seeing things, that was the somber portrait of Ben Franklin clearly in view. I wondered for a moment if the bills under the top one were part of the same family, or if this was just another cheap scam.

"Why, Beelzebub, in the name of everything unholy, how did you manage that nifty trick?"

"This is a mere token," he said. "In the event you felt you deserved greater compensation."

"Bullshit. I know a token when I see one. I grew up riding the subways in New York City. That's no token. That's a bribe. If we're going be whores, let's at least be honest about it."

He didn't smile, he didn't frown. He didn't tell me to grow up. He simply let the comment pass harmlessly into the sub-ether along with every other inane comment I'd made in a lifetime of taking things either too seriously or not seriously enough.

"Let's call it a kill fee. Shall we?"

I grunted. I hardly knew what do say. First came the check from Mrs. Wordstone for two thousand dollars, and now this. There had to be five grand in that pile of Benjamins. My ship was really coming in today. I just wished it didn't feel so much like the *Lusitania.*

"A kill fee, huh? That's a good one."

He smiled again. He didn't offer me an apple, but I had the distinct feeling he had offered other people other kinds of apples at other times in his career as Satan's lackey.

He put the hat back down over the money as the original smile settled in, refreshed from its hiatus, rested and ready to finish the job on me. His overall expression brightened. He seemed almost happy. All I got out of it was some more of that *Lusitania* sinking feeling.

"You're not nearly as stupid as you would have people believe," he said.

"Thanks, I think."

"It wasn't a compliment."

I brushed him off. "It never is."

"So, then, are we clear?"

I looked over my fingernails for a minute. I'd done a hell of a good job on them. I could think of half-a-dozen Korean manicurists on Park Street who would be envious. Then I looked at my visitor.

"Not entirely, no."

His smile faded and he looked disappointed. He also looked at his watch. Maybe he had a previous engagement, too. "What aspect of this arrangement do you fail to comprehend?"

I sat back again and put my feet up on the desk. If the time came when this gigantic thug was going to come around to my side and pound me into a pile of bruises, I was at least going to go out with a little self-respect. I suppose I could have gone out with a little self-preservation, but every time I called, self-preservation was washing her hair or had other plans. That was the story of my life. I would have to be content to go out with self-respect.

"For one thing, I'm dying to know whose step'n'fetchit monkey you are exactly?"

"Find a way to quell your curiosity, for your own good."

"C'mon, cowboy, don't leave me in the dark."

A hint of impatience stirred in him. "You can figure out that much, can't you? And you call yourself a detective."

"Oh, no I don't. I call myself a starving musician. That's all."

"Well, think it over. Solve the problem for yourself."

"What if I don't want to? Suppose, for the sake of argument, that I want you to tell me precisely who sent you on this mission, and what exactly this stack of money is supposed to buy? My silence? In that case, my silence about what? Or maybe it's my acquiescence you're after. Fine, but to what? Or maybe it's all about getting me to agree to drop whatever I'm doing. You've certainly made that overture in a none-too-subtle way. But you refuse to define exactly what it is I'm supposed to be doing -- or, conversely, what it is I'm supposed to stop doing. You see my problem? The whole thing is so vague. So understated. And, if you don't mind me saying so, pretty cheesy and ridiculous."

The large square-headed man stared at me. "Excuse me. Did you say cheesy?"

*The Farce News*

"I sure did. I mean, take a look at yourself. Sure, you've got the nice suit, the whole clean-cut-appearance thing going on. Very impressive. The polish. The manners. The quiet undertone of menace. It's all very cultivated, I'd almost say rehearsed. Bottom line, however, it comes off totally phony. Another big stage show, an act, a routine, a bit of schtick. Excuse me for saying so, but in spite of your best efforts, you end up coming off like some store-bought vaudeville hoodlum. From the generic aisle, no less. Except for the hat. I'll give you credit for the hat. It's quite a unique lid. A little corn ball for my taste, a little too much Arkansas and not quite enough Amarillo, but who am I to criticize? Where'd you get it, anyway? Snatch it off some drunken hay farmer at the state fair?"

The reptilian smile my visitor had been wearing suddenly slid off his face and grabbed the first bus leaving town. I didn't expect to see it again. In its place, my nameless guest slipped into something a little more comfortable, an expression of patient serenity bordering on tranquility. Maybe he just needed an excuse to drop the pseudo urbane affectation and make his transition to the violent portion of the show. I certainly hoped not. I also wondered, although only fleetingly, why I was so hellbent on pushing every button I could find on this guy.

"My father presented me with this hat. As a graduation present."

"Graduation? From what?"

"High school."

"So, your old man finally finishes twelfth grade and he gives *you* the present? I thought ..."

My visitor suddenly stood and put the rest of the room into a state of total eclipse. Stick had done this, too. This time I was a little more concerned. It seemed I had officially gone too far. All that remained to be determined was how nasty a price I'd pay for my insolence. "It's true what they say. You are indeed a feckless and tedious human being." He leaned over me, his large hands flat on the desk. He stared down. I waited for the classic threat of physical violence that would be my comeuppance if I didn't stop being such a nuisance to him and to whomever had sent him.

"There's a kit in the corner," I said, hooking a thumb at Tony's drums. "I'm not very good, but I could probably manage a little drum roll for you, if you think the moment warrants it."

He didn't say yes or no. He didn't look over to see if there was drum kit or not. He just stared at me and didn't say another word. It was as if his condemnation of me as a feckless and tedious human being was commentary enough. It almost hurt my feelings.

I laughed a little. "That isn't quite the threat I was expecting."

*The Farce News*

He nodded solemnly at me. "I don't make threats." Then he reached over and picked up his hat. The stack of hundred dollar bills was gone.

"Hey," I said, pointing at the empty spot on the desk.

"You had your chance."

Does everybody but me know magic tricks? I shook m head. "You people don't play fair."

He didn't bother to defend his honor, nor demand to know exactly what I meant by "you people." It's been my experience that most people bristle at their inclusion in the genus *you people,* regardless of who these people might actually be. But this large gentleman with the square head and the silly hat had no such soft spot in his ego.

"I've said what I came to say."

"Yes, bravo, you've delivered your message like an obedient errand boy, haven't you?"

"And now I will say goodbye. In parting, let me just say that I sincerely wish you a long and fruitful life. I can only hope you won't do anything foolish to foreshorten it."

There it was! The not-so-veiled threat! I knew he had it in him.

"You mean like smoke and drink and stay out all night long? Thanks, but I already got that advice from my guidance counselor back in fifth grade. Sadly, it didn't seem to take."

He put the yellowish straw cowboy hat on his large square head, turned for the door, opened it gingerly, and left, pulling the door quietly shut behind him. No theatrics, no histrionics, no gratuitous shattering of furniture or knee caps.

A minute passed before I started to tremble.

Then I got mad.

Just when I was ready to quit waltzing around town half-looking for Blackie Buenavista (and by doing so completely pissing off everyone connected with him) this nameless merchant of mild-mannered menace had to barge into my office in his understated way and dare me to step off the dance floor, the metaphorical dance floor, that is.

No way.

I locked up the studio and paid a late visit to my bank's 24-hour ATM. I deposited Auntie Peg's check and withdrew two hundred dollars. I hated to carry that kind of money around, but I doubted if Jenny and Stick took Visa -- credit or debit.

I found my piece of shit Jetta where I'd parked it, once again not so much surprised as a little disheartened that nobody had taken the opportunity to steal it. I got in and cranked the engine. How the car knew I didn't really want to go to Windsor, I couldn't say. But it started on the first attempt. Maybe the car felt about me the way I felt about it.

Even the traffic conspired against me. There wasn't any. I made every light between Farmington Avenue and the Windsor town line and arrived on East Barber Street in record time. Thank God I wasn't in a hurry or it would have taken hours.

I walked up the sidewalk in front of the house, noticing the windswept coil of yellow police tape swirling in the front yard. The cops had come and gone, and nobody had apparently mentioned my name. That was a good sign. I wondered, in passing, if Jennifer had simply forgotten I'd been there at the moment of Johnny Brashear's demise and thus had failed to mention it to the investigators. Or if she was more clever and calculating than she let on, and had intentionally withheld the fact. I voted for option (a).

I rang the doorbell and studied the peeling paint around the door frame as I waited for somebody to let me in. I saw a lot of peeling paint in the time it took for nobody answer the bell. When I knocked on the door, it fell open several inches, which is almost never a good sign. I listened for activity inside but could detect none. I pushed the door open a few more inches. It didn't creak or anything, which was more encouraging. I stepped inside and called out. There was no reply.

The living room hadn't changed much since the other night. Somebody, probably the crime scene cops, had drawn chalk marks here and there. Not those caricature cartoon forms outlining dead bodies. These were small circles and arrows. More like the marks used to record the placement of specific evidence. Blood spatters, perhaps. Maybe cookie crumbs. Or the approximate trajectories of the lawn darts Billie Billie had thwacked into Johnny Brashear's chest.

I checked out the downstairs and discovered nothing helpful or enlightening. The kitchen was clean but empty, the stove top cool. There were no dishes in the sink. The bathroom hadn't been used recently either. The sink was dry. The hand towels weren't damp to the touch. The toilet was running. I jiggled the handle and it stopped. At the foot of the stairs leading to the second story, I spotted Stick's trusty skateboard. It was laying on it's back, so to speak. Wheels up. Like a stranded turtle (a bad thing) or a dead cockroach (a good thing). I didn't like the look of it.

With a growing sense of foreboding, I climbed the stairs to check the upper bedrooms. I was right back on Duncaster Road poking my nose into other people's business -- something I'd just been warned against -- and finding corpses I didn't want to find, and failing to learn anything very useful from them. More and more I thought it was a mistake to agree to help out

Auntie Peg in the first place, even if she'd paid off rather generously for very little actual work. I just didn't like where this adventure was taking me. It made me think of the lyrics to one of the songs we covered in our set. "It's a good news, bad news situation, depending largely on your state of mind. I believe we're on the road to rack and ruin. The good news is we're making damn good time."

The front bedroom was empty, its only single bed neatly made.

In the second bedroom, the one facing the back of the house, I found them. Jennifer and Stick, that is.

In the bed, or rather, on it. They were fully dressed, Stick in his customary street garb complete with enormous sneakers, and Jennifer in her usual snug fitting jeans-and-sweater ensemble. They lay side by side. As if someone had arranged them neatly. A shapely Barbi doll and her 3XL Ken.

They looked serene. Almost as if they were asleep. So this was what was meant by the hackneyed phrase *rest in peace*. I felt a genuine wave of sadness wash over me. All the wrong people were turning up dead. I looked around for the phone, figuring I'd call it in, anonymously, and get the hell out of there. This was it, after all. The last straw. I was done. My career as an amateur sleuth was officially over, and not a minute too soon. Probably several minutes too late, in fact.

Of course, my gloom was quickly replaced by near-blind fury when Stick, who looked so peaceful in death, suddenly burst out of what seemed to be a rather serious state of sleep apnea, and snorted. Just like a pig.

Oh, for Christ's sake.

"Hey," I shouted. "Wake up, goddamn it! Both of you!"

I walked over and kicked the side of the bed. Hard. It rocked. I kicked it again, then began to push down on the mattress with both hands to get the trampoline effect going.

Stick came out of his slumber in an explosion of energy, as if somebody had shocked him with an electric cattle prod. I only wished I had.

"Dude!" he said, grabbing the edge of the mattress to keep from falling off the bed.

Jennifer was a bit slower to recover from her afternoon nap. She rolled onto her side and stretched, then sat up and rubbed her eyes. The hair at the back of her head was tussled from laying on the pillow. Otherwise she was just as pretty as ever.

"Jesus Christ!" I said. "You guys ... I thought ..."

"Dude," said Stick, his hands out in pitiful surrender. "We were tired."

"Mr. Vaughn?" Jennifer said. "Is that you? What're you doing here?" Sleep still clogged the works, but she was working her way out of it.

*The Farce News*

I gave Stick a dirty look. He responded with a sheepish shrug. I turned to leave.

"I'm going down to the kitchen and make some coffee. You two have five minutes to get your story straight and join me. If I don't like what I hear, I'm gonna take a walk and I won't be back. And you won't get a dime. You understand? Do you need it in writing?"

It was a rhetorical question and I didn't wait around for them to answer.

They didn't take the entire five minutes. I was just pouring out a cup of fresh coffee when they quietly entered the kitchen and came to the table. They took seats opposite each other and stared down at their hands, like a couple of high school lovers caught screwing.

"Okay, kids," I said, feeling extremely foolish and old. "This isn't summer camp. You're both in over your heads and you know it. So what are we going to do about it? You want to skip town? I think that's a great idea. I understand completely. The thought has crossed my mind a thousand times -- several hundred times this week alone. The question is, how are you going to pull it off? You don't know, do you? Of course not. You think you have something to sell and you think I might want to buy it. So, tell you what, why don't we skip all the pointless window shopping and start trying some shit on, huh? What do you say?"

"Dude," Stick said, as if to rebuke me for resorting to profanity in the presence of a lady.

"I'll start," I said, not because I wanted to tip my hand but because I wanted all of this to be over. "For reasons I can't yet explain, the whereabouts of Benizio Buenavista is an ongoing concern, which is not to say that anybody particularly wants to know where he is. Rather, everybody seems to be sure I should be looking for him, even though I don't want the job. Just this afternoon, a large man with a sinister smile and a battered yellow straw cowboy hat more or less offered to end my miserable existence if I didn't lose interest. At least I think that's what he was hinting at. I'm afraid I couldn't get him to talk in anything but modified riddles."

I stopped talking because Jenny and Stick were suddenly sharing a look of abject horror.

"Now what is it?" I asked.

Neither of them said anything. I guess it was a case of too many rhetorical questions. This question actually required an answer, yet neither of them was immediately forthcoming with a suitable one. Or even an unsuitable one.

They made eye gestures at each other, twitching their eyebrows and contorting their faces. They nodded back and forth, as if taking turns relinquishing responsibility for addressing this latest twist in the melodrama. It was

*The Farce News*

the silliest form of sign language I'd ever seen, and it didn't surprise me at all that these two were perfectly fluent.

"Somebody say something," I said. My coffee was growing tepid, but not nearly as tepid as this one-way conversation I was having with the Incredible Gesticulating Mutes of Hartford County.

"Did you say a battered yellow straw cowboy hat?" Jenny said.

I turned to her. She looked truly frightened. "Yeah, so what?"

She glanced at Stick. I glanced at Stick. Stick glanced at me.

"Big guy? Built like a houseboat?"

"Yeah, but without the rudder and all the deck furniture. Why, you know him?"

Stick looked at Jenny. I looked at Jenny. Jenny looked at me.

"Dressed like a stock broker?"

"Look, I'm getting dizzy. What do you know about him? He wouldn't even tell me his name."

"It's Canary Carswell," they said in unison, which left me wondering which of them to look at. I looked at her, then at him. Then back at her. She was infinitely easier on the eyes. And, after all, despite my behavior at times, I'm not a total schmuck.

"Canary?" I said. "As in the bird?"

"As in the color of that hat he wears," Jennifer said.

"Yeah, well, I didn't think he got if for singing."

Stick jumped in. "Dude, that isn't his only rep. If you know what I mean."

I turned to him. "How in the world would I possibly know what you mean?"

"He's a button man," said Stick.

"Bullshit."

"A hired gun," said Jennifer.

"No way."

"A hit man," said Stick.

"Total crap."

"A doer," said Jennifer.

"Stop it," I said. "I get the picture." Why did everybody feel compelled to say the same thing fifty different ways? Did they take me for a complete idiot? Okay, now *that's* a rhetorical question. "Assuming you're right -- which I highly doubt -- who does he work for?"

Jenny and Stick looked at each other, then spoke again in perfect unison. "No clue."

I don't know the Funk & Wagnall's definition of a rhetorical lie, but I know one when I hear one. I took my coffee cup to the sink.

"Well, it's almost been nice knowing you," I said. "I can see we're not gonna get anywhere with this song and dance. Pretty soon the curtains will come down and this pathetic show will officially be over. Thank God. Anyway, I'd hate to get stuck in traffic, so I think I'll get a move on and try to beat the rush. You can't help me and I can't help you. So, really, what's the point in dragging out the irritation, right? We can say we tried. It just wasn't meant to be. Let's quit now and savor the happy memories, shall we? I hate a long goodbye, don't you? Since this one's already well into sudden death overtime, I'll just say adios. So long. Farewell. *Ciao! Arriverderci! Adieu.* Oh, and good luck. From what I can see, you're gonna need it."

"No, wait," Jenny said. "Don't go."

After all that, she still wanted to drag things out? Why wasn't I surprised? "We're done."

"Dude," said Stick. He gave me a look, as if words failed him. Why wasn't I surprised?

"Yeah, what?"

"We heard he's connected to Venus Edwards."

"As a gunman?"

Now they shrugged in unison. Then nodded, tentatively but still in perfect unison. I had to give them credit for sharing what appeared to be a genuinely symbiotic relationship, twisted though it may be. "Yeah," they muttered. I thought about it. I didn't believe it for minute. I'd never heard of a hired assassin coming around to warn a subject that trouble was coming his way. Not even in really bad *noir* fiction. That seemed like a fairly significant blunder for any self-respecting professional to commit. Unless Jenny and Stick had their facts mixed up -- and what were the chances of that?

Another possibility was that I wasn't actually Canary Carswell's target -- if he was, in fact, a "doer." In which case his warning could be construed as a calculated ploy to get me out of the way, off the metaphorical playing field, out of his cross hairs. Or perhaps he *was* a hired gun but this time his orders were to buy me off. He could be a Ph.D. triggerman with a master's in bribery and bag-manning. After all, you don't always have to kill everyone, do you? Real life isn't a Quentin Tarintino flick, is it?

"Okay," I said, sitting down again. "Let's change the subject. Let's forget about Venus Edwards and Canary Carswell for the time being. Instead, let's talk about Hubert Edwards. He's the reason we're all here, right?"

"What do you want to know?" Jenny asked.

I looked at Stick. "Does she even know you came to see me?"

"Yeah, dude. Of course." He looked offended. I wasn't buying the act.

"You went to *see* him?" Jennifer said to Stick. She looked offended, too. I thought she pulled it off a little better. But in a high school play, I'd still cast them both as trees.

I turned my full attention to Jennifer. "Slick, here, says you know where Hubert Edwards is."

"It's Stick," he said. "Not Slick."

I glance at him. I sure wasn't. I turned back to Jennifer. "He says you have reason to think Hubert didn't go off with Blackie Buenavista after all. That he's gone to ground, letting everyone think he ran off so nobody will look too hard for Blackie. Any of this sound familiar?"

Jenny blushed. She was even prettier with a little blush on her pale cheeks. I could see why Stick was doing this chaotic whirling dervish routine to impress her and, ultimately, perhaps to win her heart. I could only hope he got what he wanted, and not simply what he had coming.

"Tell him, Jen."

"Yeah, Jen," I said, smiling. "Tell him."

She looked at me, puzzled, and pointed at Stick. "Tell *him*?"

"No," I said. "Sorry. Tell me."

"Oh. Okay."

It took a few minutes to get the story out of her. But once she began to let the proverbial cat out of the metaphorical bag it was an allegorical claws-to-the-wall fur fight and she proved to be more than ready to abdicate the analogous throne of secrecy. Thankfully it wasn't a very complicated story or it's unlikely she'd have been able to get past the "once upon a time."

As it turned out, Jennifer and the late Johnny Brashear had shared, among other things, a love of horses. Jennifer said she'd grown up on a cattle ranch out west and had always been around horses. Conversely, Johnny was a city boy who'd grown up on the streets of Hartford, spending as much time as he could at the movies, wishing he was Butch Cassidy or the Sundance Kid. He didn't care which. Sure, they both ended up dead, but who doesn't? And what fun they had on the road to Hell and damnation. In any event, Jenny and Johnny spent every possible weekend roaming the surrounding countryside in search of equestrian stables. And they spent every extra dime they could scrounge up to pay for horseback riding, and basically getting away from everything that reminded them of the two-bit hustle their lives in Hartford had become.

On a Saturday afternoon not three weeks ago, they'd been in Granby, a town of roughly 10,000 situated more or less halfway between Hartford and Springfield, Massachusetts. They were at one of the many horse farms dotting the Farmington Valley, saddled up, and walking along a small road just off Route 189 when they spotted Venus Edwards at the wheel of a red Mer-

*The Farce News*

cedes convertible. Not a battered antique red Merc like Johnny's, but a shiny new one. It was the car she used on weekends when Gomez and Morticia weren't escorting her around Hartford in the funereal black town car.

Of course, they recognized her right away. Had there been any doubt, the vanity plates reading VENUS-1 confirmed her identity. In the passenger seat beside her, with the breeze ruffling what little hair he had left over each of his large ears, sat Hubert, his chin tilted slightly up, like a dog with his nose in the wind. They were laughing about something. And then they were gone.

"We only saw them for a second," Jenny said. "But it was definitely them. The trail guide who was leading our group was very upset. She's part of some local group called the Horse Brigade, or the Horse Commission. Something like that."

"The Horse Council," Stick said.

"Yeah, that's it. Nice enough people, really, a little on the eccentric side. A bit out of touch, if you ask me. They think everyone should walk or ride a horse. Like it's the seventeen hundreds."

"Maybe they're on to something," I said.

"Or *on* something," Stick said, and snickered at his own joke. We stared him into silence.

"Anyway, they hate cars, and motorcycles, even bicycles. But they especially hate cars. When Venus and Hubert went by in the Mercedes, they had to be doing seventy. I think that road is posted for, like, forty-five at the most. Our ride leader said something like, 'Oh, that awful woman is back in town.' And Johnny started asking questions about it. Never letting on we knew Venus, of course. That was Johnny. Always looking for an edge. Some tidbit that could get him ahead."

"Or get him killed," I said.

"Dude," said Stick, reprimanding me again with but a single word, this time perhaps for the negative vibe I brought to the room with my talk of death and destruction. Or something like that. Who knows?

"Anyway, Johnny found out that Venus and Hubert had a house in North Granby. We looked on a map. There's regular Granby, there's East Granby, and there's West Granby. Apparently there's no South Granby. Weird, huh?"

"And the house itself?"

"It's on a cul-de-sac off a road called something like Silver Road. I forget. Something like that. Maybe it's Silver Lane. You can look it up. It's near that weird little notch where a little square of Massachusetts juts down into Connecticut. She told Johnny that Venus only came up on weekends, but that Hubert lived there pretty much all the time. Drives a brown Volvo into town once or twice a week and shops at a supermarket called Geissler's. Keeps to himself, mostly. Not rude or anything, but he doesn't go out of his way to make friends, either.

"Johnny went to the post office the next Monday morning and asked how he could get a letter to Hubert Edwards in North Granby, but they told him there was no record of any family called Edwards living in North Granby. He tried to get a phone number, but there wasn't one."

I looked at Stick for a moment. He was smiling now. He had dollar signs in his eyes. I could hear him yelling, "Surf's up," and hitting the waves off some southern California beach. This kid had no business living in a land-locked state like Connecticut. Too many walls. He needed wide open spaces and salt air in his face. I hoped the story Jennifer was telling me was on the level, because I had decided to give them some getaway money and, more than anything, I hated the idea of them pulling one over on me.

"So, let's see if I have this straight. A month or so ago, Blackie Buenavista and Hubert Edwards disappeared off the face of the earth. On the same day, no less. And everyone is content to pretend they ran off together. But now you're saying that just three weeks ago, you and Johnny spotted Hubert and Venus happily cruising the back roads of northern Connecticut in a red sports car with the top down. And with a little nosing around, you were able to find out they have a place up there. It's all very convenient. Tell me something. Why did you sit on the information?"

Jennifer looked at me with a searching expression. "What could I do with it before now?"

It was a decent question. One I couldn't answer. Hell, it was damn near a rhetorical question.

I reached into my jacket and took out an envelope. "Here's two hundred bucks."

"Dude," said Stick, obviously moved that I'd brought cash.

"It's the best I can do at the moment. You have my number at the studio," I said, taking out a pen and writing my home phone and address on the envelope. "When you get where you're going, send me a post card and I'll send you another three hundred. But you need to leave town immediately. Tonight would be best. Buy a couple of bus tickets. Go to Cleveland. Somewhere big where you won't stand out. Then change to a different bus line and keep heading west. Change a couple of times along the way so nobody can track you without working real hard at it. You understand what I'm saying? Keep a low profile. It won't be first class travel, but it should keep you relatively safe. If this guy, Canary Carswell, is hooked up with Venus and they find out about our little conversation here, you two could be next in line for a visit from him. And that might not be a good thing for either of you. If he is what you say he is."

"Dude," said Stick, putting out his hand to shake. I took it. The next thing I new the greasy little urban surfer had me locked in a bear hug.

"Okay, dude," I said. "That's nice. Please let go now."

He turned me loose. My ribs ached. You could drive a Trailways bus through the grin on his face, but you might knock out a few of his teeth.

Jennifer said, demurely: "How can we ever thank you?"

The only thing I could think of to say was "By not bullshitting me." But I didn't say it. I decided it would bring a negative vibe to the room, and that would only get Stick on my case again. And I'd had my fill of being called "Dude," for one day. Although it was a improvement over "Be-yotch."

"Pack a couple of bags and get on a bus. Do it tonight."

Stick was still wearing that smile when I left them a few minutes later. I hoped he'd still be wearing it when they got where they were going, wherever that was. I don't know how many breaks Jennifer and Stick had received in the course of their lives, but I wasn't philosophically opposed to the idea of banking a little positive karma by giving them one myself.

Still, as I drove away from Windsor, one thought nagged at me: Please don't be lying to me.

## Chapter 27

I stopped in at the first drug store I could find and dropped $16.95 plus tax for the latest edition of the Arrow Street Atlas for Central and Eastern Connecticut. Sitting in the car, I flipped through the book and found the map for Granby spread across pages sixty-two and sixty-three. It was a sprawling rural area with a handful of thoroughfares and about a million miles of back roads. There was nothing called Silver Road, but I did locate a long north-south artery called Silver Street near the notch where Massachusetts sticks its nose into the northern border of Connecticut. Right where Jennifer said it would be. So far, so good.

I'd practically been in Granby on Wednesday night when I visited Venus Edwards at the Simsbury Dinner Theater and burgled her outbuildings. Little did I know she had yet another secret hideaway just a few miles farther north. And what if I had known, would it have made any difference? Would it make any difference now?

I jumped on I-91 and followed the signs for Springfield. Traffic was light and twenty-five minutes later I veered off the highway at Exit 42 and swung the car west onto Route 20, passing directly under one of the final approach patterns at Bradley International Airport. I fell into a line of local westbound traffic and roller coastered my way through the hills of East Granby until I came to a mildly chaotic intersection where Route 20, Routes 10 & 202, and Route 189 all converged. I spotted the Geissler's supermarket where Hubert Edwards was said to shop for groceries. It shared a parking lot with a laundromat, a video store, a sandwich shop, a fast-food burger joint, a Mexican restaurant, a phone store, and, somewhat incongruously, a tile and carpet shop. Across the street was a small brick post office, a bank with a drive-through window, a drug store with a drive-through window and a dark wood tavern. I wondered if it, too, had a drive-through window. I'd heard of such things in Texas, but I'd never seen one for myself.

I made a wide right-hand turn on Route 189 and continued north. Four miles later I passed under a flashing yellow light with another post office and a flower shop on the left, and a small country library on the right.

Half a mile further on, I came to a small green bridge on the right side of the road. I slowed and made the sharp turn, crossed the narrow bridge over a strip of bubbling water called Salmon Brook, and began the long steady climb up the winding road known as Silver Street. It was entirely residential, woody in sections and heavily shaded as the light of day faded. Every once in a while, a view opened up to the west, overlooking the valley I was leaving behind and below me.

My review of the atlas had prepared me for the many turnoffs I would encounter. The first was a horseshoe street called Stone Hedge Way. It was followed by a larger horseshoe: Silver Brook Lane, then a road cutting back to Route 189 called Northwoods Road. I expected to find a dead-end street on the right called Dara Lane. After that came the Massachusetts border. With the exception of Dara Lane, all of the other roads sprouted smaller offshoot streets of their own. I was ready to take a look at every one of them if I had to, but it seemed logical to start at the northern most point and work back south. If Venus and Hubert Edwards were using this place as a hideout, they'd no doubt want maximum seclusion for their money.

Silver Street climbed and dropped and wound its way around several sharp turns before I came to the south entrance to Stone Hedge Way. I marked it for future reference and continued north, soon passing the north entrance of Stone Hedge. Within moments I came around a right-hand turn, the road dipped, and I saw the sign announcing the Silver Brook Estates. I slowed the car. From a distance the development looked fairly new and economically high end. It also seemed a little congested, with houses placed in much closer proximity than you might expect considering how far they were from town and how hefty their price tags probably were.

I had to shift gears constantly as my piece of shit Jetta struggled up the hills and then wanted to race down the slopes on the far side. My clutch was probably not too happy, but I was loving it. This was the kind of road that made driving fun. I was no doubt going too fast, but who's counting? I didn't see any cops anywhere. I took a *no harm no foul* attitude as I sped along.

The left turn onto Northwoods Road came on suddenly. I hoped Venus and Hubert Edwards had eschewed this heavily built-up stretch of houses. By itself, it featured no fewer than four dead end side streets, two to the south and two to the north. Calling them dead end streets was perhaps a little old fashion, if not outright politically incorrect, considering the ambient tax bracket. From a sociological perspective, it could be argued they were indeed dead end streets, but who had the time to engage in such philosophical silliness?

I slowed as I came to a white signpost on the right with vertically stacked letters reading DARA LANE. It was the shortest of the side streets on my target sheet, not counting the two cul-de-sacs off the eastern arc of Stone Hedge -- Sutton Drive and Gloucester Lane, just in case anyone forgot we were deep in the heart of New England. If Dara Lane didn't pan out, I'd head back south and give them a look.

I was way overdue to catch a break. Maybe today would be the day.

I hit my right turn indicator and applied the brakes as I cranked the steering wheel hard to the right. Then, as I slowed to a crawl, the road dropped off in front of me, giving me a full view of the cul-de-sac ahead. The area was heavily wooded and the houses were spaced out a bit more casually and set back away the road. Thankfully the driveways weren't especially long and only one or two were the kind of crooked, winding paths that disappeared back into the forest. I could see most of the garages from the road as I idled by.

A red house on the right was, I thought, a little too close to the road to meet the Edwards' need for seclusion. A brown clapboard two-story house on the left had a large double garage with the doors up. Inside I could see a white BMW sedan and a red Jeep Wrangler with a vinyl top. The next house was a white two-story cottage with front dormers, but it had no garage in sight. I'd have to double back and take a look from the other side. The fourth house featured a gravel driveway that disappeared completely into the woods, and for the first time I began to feel the pangs of frustration dancing around in my stomach and raising a small sweat on my back.

This wasn't going nearly as well as I had hoped it would. I should have known my blind-man's search could easily turn into a major aerobic exercise in futility, with scant few calories burned.

On the bright side, at least it was a lovely evening to be out in the country, a welcome change from the dirt and dinge of Hartford. The leaves had begun to turn; in a month sightseers would arrive from miles around to enjoy the fall colors. Some trees were already shedding their foliage.

On the left, I spied another home planted in among the trees. A brown split-level structure with a second-floor deck. The garage doors were open, but the owners had made it even easier for me by leaving their cars parked in the driveway. Both were mud-spattered sport utility vehicles. Neither was a brown Volvo or a red Mercedes convertible.

The end of the street suddenly bubbled out, forming the "sac" part of the cul-de-sac. Three roads branched off from the turnaround. The first road tried to sneak around through the trees, but too many leaves were already down, and I could just see through to a dark brown house that blended very nicely with the foliage surrounding it. I could also see a doublewide garage with one door open, as if it were winking at me.

I stopped short.

A brown sedan sat in plain view. A Volvo four-door, a 240 DL model unless I missed my guess. But I couldn't make out the license plate from this distance. I parked my piece of shit Jetta back up the lane, pointed toward Silver Street in the event I needed to make a quick getaway. I hoped it wouldn't attract too much attention, or arouse any suspicion (or fail to start when next I turned the key). I walked back toward the driveway leading to the brown house in the woods. More gravel crunched under my feet. How rustic, I thought. What a drag, I thought, preferring stealth to charm at the moment.

I was still fifty feet from the house when the vanity license plate on the Volvo 240 DL came into focus: HFE-2. Signifying what? Perhaps the fact that this was Hubert F. Edwards' second car? Brilliant! I looked for the bumper sticker claiming that his other vehicle was a Massarati. That one, of course, would carry the vanity plate: HFE-1.

I stopped by a large elm tree to think things over. From here I could not see the house, and presumably could not be seen from it. I had to give Hubert and Venus credit for finding a very quiet and charming spot. Amazing what could be accomplished with enough ready cash.

There was nothing else for me to do at the moment but finish the reconnaissance by taking a look inside the other half of the garage. The license plate on the brown Volvo was a nice piece of confirmation, but a red Mercedes convertible trumps a dull old Volvo any day of the week. From what little I'd seen of it, Granby struck me as the kind of town where you might see quite a number of Volvo sedans. A sensible, conservative car in a sensible, conservative town.

I peeked around the tree and looked up at the back windows of the brown house. There were curtains in most of them, no doubt to keep the glare of the setting sun from blinding its inhabitants. I didn't see any movement, but that didn't mean a damn thing. If both cars were here, didn't that suggest someone was home?

With careful steps I tried to cover the last fifty feet between my elm tree and the Edwards' country home in silence. And I thought I managed pretty well. At least nobody took a shot at me.

And there in the garage beside the brown Volvo, not collecting very much dust at all, sat the car I was looking for, the red Mercedes. It wasn't just any old run of the mill red Mercedes, however. This was somebody's very expensive play thing. A late model SL-500 Roadster, which I estimated to carry a minimum price tag of around a hundred thousand dollars, depending on whether she'd gone for all the extras, like a combination AM-FM cassette player, or a cigarette lighter. Or a global positioning system.

This *had* to be the hideaway. Which meant Jenny and Stick hadn't lied to me. Which meant that maybe -- just maybe -- my luck was about to change.

Then it changed, all right. For the worse.

"Mr. Vaughn!" someone said, rather sharply, from a few feet behind me. "What a ... surprise."

I knew the voice. And it sure as hell wasn't one I had been looking forward to hearing again any time soon. It wasn't music to my years, but I turned to face it anyway. Standing in the middle of the driveway in his fancy duds and stupid yellow straw cowboy hat, was Canary Carswell, effectively blocking my only means of egress with his wide stance and wider girth. Unless I wanted to make a boar-like charge through the woods, I was trapped.

"You were about to say, 'What a *pleasant* surprise'."

"Yes, but I reconsidered."

I shrugged. "Story of my life."

"Mr. Vaughn, I must ask. What on earth are you doing here? I thought I was perfectly clear this afternoon at your office."

"Well, it's like this, Canary ..." I stopped. His expression changed rather significantly in rather short order. "You don't mind if I call you that, do you?"

He didn't answer. Some people become pensive and reserved when they suddenly realize they don't hold all the high cards in the deck. I wondered if Canary Carswell lacked the sort of confidence necessary to fly by the seat of his pants. Without crashing and burning, that is, and getting a rather painful rash on his ass. I could give him a lesson or two. I considered myself something of an expert in the discipline of low-altitude stunt aviation.

"This is private property," he said. "You are trespassing. I could have you arrested."

"That's true," I said. "But, by the same token, you are standing in the way of me and public property. That is, the road behind you there. Unless you step aside and allow me to pass, you're committing what's tantamount to kidnapping."

"Tantamount?" He grinned at me.

"Yes," I said. "If you don't know what it means, look it up."

"Oh, I know what it means," he said. "I'm just surprised to hear *you* use it in a sentence."

"The point is, kidnapping is a federal offense. That's a major no-no. You'll turn twenty-one in prison, doing life without parole."

"*Mamma Tried*," he said. "Merle Haggard."

"Exactly."

"What if I were to invite you in," he said, gesturing up to the house. "Then there'd be no crime, now would there?"

"The only crime would be if I accepted the invitation."

"What if I were to insist?"

"What if I were to refuse?"

Canary Carswell reached into his finely tailored jacket and brought out a medium-sized pistol. I'm guessing it was an automatic, although I don't know a whole lot about handguns. It was matte black and his big hand dwarfed it. He pointed it at me and suddenly I didn't feel very well. "Mr. Vaughn, you are a difficult man to figure out."

I stared at the hole in the barrel of the gun in Canary Carswell's meaty hand. There was no light at the end of this particular tunnel, save the light you see just before you go to Jesus, or perhaps when you're having one of those out-of-body experiences. I wouldn't have minded an out-of-body experience right about then. My own body was right in the line of fire and I was pretty sure it was going to hurt like hell if anyone, especially Canary Carswell, struck a match.

"That's an ugly little toy," I said. "Why don't you put it away before someone gets hurt?" My voice may not have had quite the bravado I'd wished for it, but I did my best under the circumstances. And the front of my pants was still dry. That was something.

Canary Carswell walked slowly toward me. I watched the pistol in his hand. Suddenly it did a nose dive, with the barrel flipping forward, looping around upside down on the fulcrum of his thick trigger finger. He gracefully took the gun by the barrel and thrust it at me, handle first. More sleight of hand.

"Go on," he said calmly. "Take it." It was the same voice he'd used to tell me to sit when he'd stopped by to boss me around the rehearsal studio, as if I were some kind of disobedient dog. I thought of Rufus. I'd sure miss him if this encounter ended badly. I was pretty sure he'd miss me, too, provided it ever occurred to him that I didn't come back. Maybe Jolie would take him in. Lucky dog.

Jolie.

I hadn't thought about her for a while. Funny how she managed to creep into my head at this particular moment. I reached out a hand, tentatively, thinking that as soon as I went for the pistol, he'd spin it back around and start pulling the trigger. "This another gag?"

"No, sir. Merely an attempt to establish a basis of mutual trust."

"Really." It sounded far fetched. I was tempted to say so, but on the off chance he meant it, I'd hate to spoil the moment with another demonstration of my rank pessimism.

"You're making me work awfully hard at it," he said. "My patience is not boundless, you know."

"You want me to take the gun?"

"That's the general idea. Yes."

I took the heavy handgun and wrapped my fingers around the grip. "Woah," I said, hefting it. I felt stupid and a little thrilled. Carswell's expression made me feel even more foolish.

"Ever hold a gun before?" he asked. If I was the giddy novice, he was the campus slut.

"Of course," I said. "Once or twice."

"Good. In case you're curious, that's a fully loaded Smith & Wesson nine-millimeter automatic. The safety currently *on*. If it's all the same to you, I'd prefer you leave it that way."

He turned away and made for the house. He had a long stride and quickly closed the gap to the residence. This was my chance to take action: either to tear ass up the driveway and run for my piece of shit Jetta, or shoot the bastard Carswell in the back. However, while I had a gun in my hand and a pretty large target, I had no idea how to get it to work and no particular desire to enter the fraternity of homicidal maniacs either behind bars or walking the streets undetected.

I had received a relatively benign invitation from Canary Carswell to come on in and set a spell. I struggled momentarily with this dilemma and ultimately let my inquisitiveness win out again. After all, what the hell had I driven all the way out here for, if not to find Hubert Edwards and perhaps even get a line on the elusive Blackie Buenavista? It seemed I'd at least found where the missing CPA was hanging out. Maybe he was in there and I could chat with him a while and wrap this up.

Or maybe it was going to be that bastard Bengal tiger lurking hungrily behind door number three.

A small flight of wooden stairs led to a cantilevered deck and a set of sliding patio doors. I trotted after Canary Carswell, the Smith & Wesson surprisingly heavy in my hand, and caught up to him at the top of the stairs. He slid a glass panel door to the side and gestured for me to go ahead. He was by far the most ingratiating assassin I'd every met. If, in fact, he was a hired killer. I hoped Jenny and Stick had at least been wrong on that particular score.

The interior of the house was dimly lit and very cozy, straight out of the pages of an L.L. BEAN catalog. The furniture looked comfortable and expensive, crafted for serious lounging. All the fabrics had that well-worn plaid feel to them, as if you could hardly go wrong no matter where you sat. A stack of firewood and old newspapers were organized beside a stone fireplace, with a nice set of blackened andirons in a brass rack to one side. The pictures on the walls were all of woodland scenes, which I thought was fairly stupid, since you could look out any window and get the real thing. Then

*The Farce News*

again, what would one put on the walls of a country home, portraits of city skyscrapers and industrial machinery? Hardly.

"Sit," Canary Carswell said, indicating one of the heavily padded chairs opposite the fireplace. He was very comfortable doling out the monosyllabic directives.

I noticed I was getting better at heeding them. I didn't particularly like this development, but it wasn't the right time to worry about it. I dropped into one of the chairs, holding the gun loosely on one knee.

"Where are the owners?" I asked.

He stood by a waist-high counter that separated the living room part of the large space from the kitchen area behind him. He smiled at me. It was that smile. The one that made me wish I knew how to turn the safety on this heavy SW9 to the off position.

"The owners?"

"Venus and Hubert Edwards," I said. "Surely you've heard of them. I'm told you work for them. I'd like to talk with Hubert. Is he around?"

"I don't know where you get your information, but I'm afraid you've been misled."

"Meaning?"

"For one thing, I don't work for anybody."

"No?"

"And for another, I own this house."

"You own it?"

"Yes."

"Bullshit," I said.

"I can assure you it's not bullshit, Mr. Vaughn. Would you care to see a copy of the deed?"

"No," I said. "What I would like to see, however, is a copy of Hubert Edwards. Unless I'm mistaken, that's his brown Volvo in the garage."

"You are absolutely right," he said. "It *is* his brown Volvo in the garage. That much is true."

"Good. Now we're getting somewhere."

"May I offer you something to drink, Mr. Vaughn? A vodka gimlet, perhaps? Or a tequila sunrise? How about a sloe gin fizz?"

"Nothing, thanks," I said. I wouldn't have minded a stiff belt, but I didn't like the choices.

"You don't mind if I have something ..."

"Hey, it's your house."

"Yes," he said. "It is."

"But I'm told this is where Hubert Edwards has been hiding out for the

*The Farce News*

last month or so. And you haven't denied it. So, I'm guessing that part is true, too. I'd really like to speak with him if you don't mind, find out what the hell is going on. You think that would be possible?"

Canary Carswell made himself busy in the kitchen, cracking ice, pouring from a bottle he had taken from the freezer, and shaking a silver cocktail mixer over his shoulder like a Broadway bartender working the tourist crowd for tips. He carefully poured clear liquid into two martini glasses and brought them over, ignoring my question.

"You must try this," he said, delicately handing me one of the glasses by the stem. "It's orange-flavored Stolichnya."

I took the glass. "I've had this before," I said. "Just last night, as a matter of fact."

"Really?" he said, sitting down opposite me on an overly stuffed couch. "And where might that have been, Mr. Vaughn?"

"In the office of Venus Edwards. Over at the Simsbury Dinner Theater. Some coincidence, huh?"

"Oh," he said, somewhat dismissively, sipping gingerly from the edge of his glass. "She got it from me, you know."

"She got what from you?"

"The taste for this," he said, holding up the glass. "She's been copying me our whole lives."

I was about to take a sip, but I checked myself and put the glass down on a small table beside the chair. I felt as if someone had just slapped me in the back of the head, like they used to do back in sixth grade when we were waiting on the lunch line. Suddenly I remembered where I'd seen that stupid yellow straw cowboy hat before. Hanging on the coat rack in the office Venus Edwards.

"Excuse me? What does that mean? Your whole lives."

Canary Carswell put his drink down and got up. Without any sense of urgency whatsoever he went about the room turning on small lamps and arranging throw pillows. Pockets of soft light colluded to give the room a very warm and comfortable feel. I could understand why someone might want to hole up for a while in such a well cushioned environment, even without a Smith & Wesson nine-mil in lieu of a lap dog for company. Carswell came back carrying a picture in a dark wood frame, roughly eight-by-ten. He handed it to me. The photograph was a black-and-white print showing a small girl, maybe ten years old, in a white t-shirt and shorts, bobby socks and sneakers. There was a boy about twelve on her left, dressed in jeans, sneakers and a light polo shirt. Another boy, maybe eleven or twelve, on her right, in a white short sleeved shirt with a bow tie and dark pants and dark shoes.

The girl in the middle was instantly recognizable, even in this unexpected form.

"Hey, this is Venus Edwards," I said, tapping the glass with the barrel of the Smith & Wesson. "How'd you get this?"

"No, actually, it isn't."

"Yes, it is. I'd know this face anywhere. I'm sure ..."

"It's Vicky Carswell," he said. "And please don't break the glass."

That stopped me in my argumentative tracks. "Vicky Carswell?" I looked at the picture some more. It was Venus Edwards, no matter what this guy said. The boy on her left, in the jeans, had a big blond head and large hands. His left hand was clamped on his left hip, the thumb forward. His right hand was clamped firmly on the girl's shoulder. I looked up at Canary. He was giving me the weirdest smile. "I heard a funny story about your hat today," I said.

"Oh, yes? What's that?"

"I was told it's the basis of your peculiar monicker. I have to say, I have my doubts."

He smiled some more. "You don't say."

"You were called Canary as a kid because of your yellow hair, weren't you?"

He didn't answer. He didn't give me the creepy smile. He just sipped his frozen vodka. "You see," he said. "You really aren't as stupid as you like people to think."

I ignored the compliment. I assumed it was a compliment this time. I also had the slightly edgy feeling all at once that Carswell was coming on to me. I'd let it go for the time being. Hell, I had the gun if I needed it. If I could figure out how to get it to fire.

"So, you're saying this is you in the picture?"

He nodded, although he had said no such thing.

"You and Venus, huh? A brother and sister act? That's pretty weird."

"There's nothing weird about it, Mr. Vaughn. And it's not an act. It's simply a fact of life."

I stared at the picture some more. The other boy in the photo, in the more formal clothing, looked shy and sharp at the same time, as if the expression of timidity on his face was just a mask he wore for the benefit of others. *Let the world think I'm a schmuck. I'll show them.* Not immediately obvious, but there nonetheless, was the inescapable fact that in his left hand he was gripping the right hand of the little girl. She wasn't fighting it, but she was definitely trying to conceal the fact by keeping her right hand almost, but not quite completely, hidden from view just behind her. She also had a somewhat mischievous look on her face that seemed to say, "Guess what we're doing?"

I looked up at Canary, who was already finishing his drink.

"You're saying the boy in the jeans is you and the kid in the bow tie holding hands with your sister is Hubert Edwards?"

"The picture was taken a very long time ago," he said. "I admit it's not a particularly good photograph, but it does evoke some rather fond memories. Beyond which I think you'll have to admit that you made the proper identifications without any direct help from me."

I put the picture down and picked up my martini glass. I took a big sip. Carswell knew how to chill it. "You magician types never do anything directly," I said. I still had the Smith & Wesson in my right hand, but I was feeling increasingly foolish about it. However, I wasn't ready to crawl into the spider's web and surrender my only implement of self-preservation just because the spider was behaving in a rather urbane and solicitous manner. Seduction by any other name is just as humiliating for those who unwillingly fall prey. And it's even worse for those who capitulate without a fight. At least that's what I've heard.

I put the martini glass down beside the eight-by-ten black-and-white photograph. I looked down at the pistol in my lap. I found what looked like the only tab on it that could be the safety catch. I pressed it with my thumb and it slid silently a quarter of an inch to the left. Then I looked up at my host, Canary Carswell. He either had failed to notice me flicking the safety to the off position, or he simply didn't care.

"So, why'd they call you Canary? Other than the blond hair? You do much singing as a child?"

"Virtually none."

"So?"

"A nickname seemed like a good alternative."

"To what?"

"Our mother came from a long line of Welsh coal miners and she thought it appropriate to have me christened Llewellyn. She may have been reading *How Green Was My Valley* at the time of my arrival. Anyway, I don't blame her. Pregnant women are prone to somewhat irrational behavior, if I might be permitted a somewhat gross generalization. But where was my father at the moment of truth? Why didn't he talk her out of it? She was very strong willed, I admit, but I'm sure she would have listened to reason if only my father had seen fit to offer some. Sadly he didn't."

"I see."

"Do you?"

I thought about what it was like to go through life with the same name as that obnoxious personal injury shill on those nauseating dial-a-lawyer television commercials. It hadn't been so bad when my namesake was Napoleon Solo and he went all over the world knocking off bad guys, but when he himself became a harping, lock-jawed villain in all the good dramas, it became a source of genuine embarrassment. "Yes, albeit from a slightly different perspective."

"I see."

Llewellyn Carswell had a way of being extremely dismissive. It made me feel about ten years old. He would have made a good fifth grade teacher.

"So, when do I get to meet Hubert?"

Carswell sighed. "I'm afraid you don't." He sounded genuinely sorry. I very much doubt he was genuinely sorry.

"Well, that sucks," I said, behaving as if I were about ten years old.

My host got up. For such a large guy, he was fairly graceful as he climbed from his place on the couch and made his way back to the kitchen for refills. I guess he'd had a fair amount of practice. "Don't take it too hard."

"It's pretty disappointing," I said, hefting the pistol in my hand. No way to tell if there were actually any live rounds in the clip, or if one had been chambered. He said it was fully loaded, but I didn't know if I should take a guy like Carswell at his word. It wasn't so much that he was cold-blooded, but there was a certain *sangfroid* about him that kept me a little unnerved.

"Life is full of disappointments," he said. "You'll find that out as you get older."

"Oh, I'm old enough to know *that* much."

"Good. Then you can accept the many limitations life may present."

"Where is he?"

"Who? You mean Hubert?" Carswell checked his wrist watch. "At the moment, airborne."

"Like pollen?"

Carswell laughed and shook the silver mixer over his shoulder. "He's on a commercial jetliner with briefcase full of money, traveling under an alias with forged documents no government official could hope to detect, and an itinerary that will keep him busy for, oh, several weeks I should think. Perhaps even longer."

"An impromptu European vacation?"

Canary Carswell poured himself another heaping helping of frozen vodka without offering me any more. Just as well. I needed my wits about me, if only to figure out how to use the pistol. Just in case.

*The Farce News*

"Europe is an increasingly uninteresting and unprofitable place for us to do business. Although, I do miss Madrid in the fall."

"Okay," I said. "This is all very interesting. To someone, that is. Just not to me. For the record, I'm not really very interested in Hubert. No offense. I'm not all that interested in his business, either. Whatever it may be, or wherever it may take him, or however profitable it may be, or not be. I was hoping to talk to him about a guy named Blackie Buenavista."

"Benizio!" Carswell raised his glass and drank, as if the name was some kind of a toast.

"You know him, then?"

"But, of course."

"Then you probably know how he dropped out of sight about a month back."

"Did he, indeed?"

"Yes. And I'm told Hubert mysteriously did the same. At virtually the same moment."

"You've apparently been told a great many things," Carswell said. "Your challenge will be to decide what to believe and what to discard as mere tripe."

I ignored his editorializing. "A lot of people think tripe is quite delicious. Or so I'm told. But you're right. Quite a number of theories have been proffered lately about the meaning of these coordinated disappearances."

"Coincidental," he said. "Not coordinated."

"To tell the truth, while there are some interesting details in each fable, none of them ring particularly true. But you've probably heard them all yourself, since it turns out you're all family. Jesus! You and Venus, brother and sister. I can hardly believe it. She never even mentioned you."

He gave me a long look. "How long have you known my sister?"

"Couple of days."

"And in that time, how many topics would you say she has brought up that were not directly related to herself or her own interests?"

I thought it over. "Good point," I said.

"She tends to be rather ... egocentric," he said.

"No comment," I said. I was beginning to think it ran in the family.

"Me, I prefer to keep a somewhat lower profile," he said. "I had been hoping, for example, that you and I would not have to meet. Not once, let alone twice. No offense."

"None taken."

"And yet, here we are."

"Yes, here we are."

*The Farce News*

"So, you see. Life is full of surprises and disappointments."

"For the record, I'm not gunning for Hubert," I said, and waved the pistol at him, just for comic relief. He didn't laugh or even crack a smile, for which I was somehow grateful. There wasn't much humor in his grin. Instead, he merely sipped his cold vodka and studied me. Not exactly like an item on a dinner menu; more like a single cell organism on a slide under an electron microscope.

"Forget Hubert," he said. "That's my best advice to you."

"Gladly," I said. "But, you see, he's my only link to Blackie."

"In that case, I'm afraid you don't have a link."

That could be construed as either good news or bad news. I simply had to decide which road to rack and ruin I was going to take. I thought it over while he sipped his vodka. I took a sip of my own. It was quickly losing its chill, but I didn't feel like asking him to freshen it up. "That's bad news."

"I suggest you go forget about Blackie Buenavista as well."

Forget about Blackie? This was the same message he'd given me in not so many words earlier this afternoon. Now the pretense was gone, along with the menace, the physical threat, the underlying violence. Of course, now I was holding the loaded gun.

"I'd like nothing better," I said. "And if I knew where he was, believe me, forgetting it would be the very first thing I'd do."

"You don't seem to understand," Carswell said. "I'm not suggesting you stop looking for Blackie Buenavista. Rather, I'm encouraging you to stop caring about him one way or the other. He was nothing. Don't you see? He was an insignificant grifter. A cheap Lothario."

"Lothario?" I was impressed. You don't hear that word much any more.

Carswell sipped his drink. "A gigolo. A skirt chaser. A womanizer. A cunt-hound."

Oh, here we go again, I thought. "Yeah, I get it, I get it."

"Blackie Buenavista was unworthy of concern on the part of anyone with a shred of self-respect. Why do you think Lilly kicked him out on the sidewalk?"

"Lilly?"

"Lillian Wordstone. I thought you knew her."

"Know her? We're related."

"How fascinating."

"Talk about life's little disappointments."

"Yes, I suppose so."

"But I didn't know you were in with that crowd. Of course, with your sister being Venus ..."

"Oh, certainly."

I took a long sip of the cool vodka and now my glass was empty. "Okay, so talk to me, Llew. Tell me something useful so I can put this thing to rest and get back to my life. I'm supposed to be in Bristol in twenty-four hours and right now Bristol feels million miles and a hundred years away."

Carswell navigated the room like a large ocean dweller, deftly avoiding knocking things over as he swept through. He retrieved my glass, unbidden, and returned to the kitchen to refill it. I didn't object. I was thinking about this unexpected brother-sister thing with him and Venus. The thought stumbled clumsily through my brain that, between them, Vicky and Llewellyn sure knew how to mix a cocktail.

"Hubert and I have been friends for forty-five years," Carswell said, pouring my second drink. "And business partners for nearly as long. We are extremely successful because we make careful investments, pick our associates with the utmost caution, and protect our investments and partnerships with what some people might characterize as inordinate vigilance. Part of that is making sure nobody gets hurt. Violence tends to attract a crowd, you know. All the wrong kind of people. Mostly law enforcement types. We operate at a level of legitimacy which ensures our anonymity in the eyes of law enforcement agencies. At the moment, Hubert has become a concern. I tell you this in extreme confidence, knowing full well you won't repeat it. You won't repeat what I say, now will you?"

"Since 'No, Mr. Canary,' is the right answer, let's just pretend I said it."

Carswell raised an eyebrow but refrained from scolding me for my bad manners. It was one of the only things about Carswell which made me prefer him -- if only by the slimmest margin -- to his sister, who was constantly harping on this bad habit or that lapse in etiquette.

"Hubert made one or two independent business decisions, choices which were ill-advised and which, ultimately, did not work out very well for him or for the parties with whom he was conducting these affairs. As a result, there are some people, not just you, Mr. Vaughn, who would like the proverbial word with my brother-in-law. Suffice it to say we're attempting to negotiate a peace and hoping reconstructive facial surgery won't be required. More than that I really can't say, in the name of self-protection. I'm sure you understand."

Maybe I did, and maybe I didn't. In this world, sometimes it's better just to go along and pretend. Hell, that's what everyone around me seemed to be doing.

"Exactly what line of business are you in?" I asked. It seemed like a stupid enough question but I hadn't asked a really stupid question in a while.

He smiled the reptilian smile and brought me my drink. "Imports and exports. I thought you knew. All your snooping around, all your breaking and entering. Honestly, you're quite fortunate not to have charges filed against you, Mr. Vaughn."

"Bullshit," I said, taking the glass. "If you had me busted, you'd have a fair amount of explaining of your own to do. And you don't want any part of that, I'm sure."

"We can agree it would be better all around for each of us to remain out of the spotlight."

"So, it's you guys," I said. "You and Hubert. Is Venus just the front? Is she the money launderer? All this time I thought it was the Guatemalans."

"Which Guatemalans?"

"Exactly."

"Blackie Buenavista isn't Guatemalan, if that's what you mean."

"I was just going to say that. I'll bet he isn't from anywhere south of the border."

"You mean the Connecticut border?"

"You and Hubert cooked up the whole thing, didn't you? As one of your masterful paper shuffles. You run the business from the shadows while Venus, or Vicky, or whatever the hell her name is, plays the part of public entrepreneur. It's brilliant. Not as good as the whole six-pack of Guinness thing, but damn good."

"Actually, the original concept was Vicky's. Hubert and I simply put it into motion."

"No! You saying she's the brains and you guys are just the mechanics? Hard to believe."

"Well, credit where it's due. She's a very bright girl."

Ouch. That one stung. Calling Venus Edwards a girl was like calling the Queen Mary a row boat.

"You're really just a pack of scam artists, aren't you? Gilded grifters. Modern day camel traders. Smash and grab thieves in silk suits. You probably vote Republican, am I right? Was it Hubey's job to find all the tax loopholes?"

Carswell shrugged. "Everything we do is perfectly legal."

"Sure it is," I said. "Like the Norwegian seal furs?"

"I don't know what you're talking about, and what's more, neither do you."

"And the goods from Iran? Don't we have a trade embargo with them?"

"You're out of your depth here."

"Oh, you're slick. But you're not that slick."

"We have paperwork to support every transaction."

"Sure you do."

"We even pay taxes. City, state, and federal."

"Sure you do. Devil only knows what kind of preferred rate you get. How much did you give to the committee to re-elect? I'll bet it was a shitload."

"Only what the law allows, Mr. Vaughn. Only what the law allows."

"Thieves."

"You should tone down your rhetoric a little. Remember, a guy's gotta make a living."

"Right. Next you'll be telling me how nobody ever gets hurt."

I was thinking about Johnny Brashear with a couple of lawn darts in his chest, and LaTwanda Jefferson with a couple of bullet holes in her, and Miguel Batista at the bottom of a gully in a casket of twisted metal, and I started to get sick to my stomach. None of them, with the exception of Big Jeff and, to a lesser degree, Johnny, had a direct link to the Carswell-Edwards cartel, but they were victims nonetheless, thanks to the kind of bad blood that bubbles up when you dabble in their brand of financial hooliganism. Carswell and his crew had applied their assiduous methods of preservation and a couple of people who didn't have to be dead were dead just the same. Or maybe that was just the Stoli talking.

"We all take risks," said Canary Carswell. "It's part of the game."

I sipped my vodka and wished it were stronger. "So, where does that leave me with Blackie? I've got an old woman who misses her ice cream eating gigolo. And I've got an ex-wife who isn't nearly good enough an actress to pull off the disinterested ingenue routine."

He laughed a little, not making fun so much as enjoying a small irony. "I wouldn't worry very much about Lilly. She's a big girl. She can take care of herself."

"Okay, but that still leaves Mrs. Wordstone. She's my aunt, you know. That makes it family."

"I'm afraid I can't help you there."

"You can't help me or you won't?"

He sipped his drink and studied me. "It amounts to the same thing, doesn't it?"

"I was hoping for a little cooperation."

Canary Carswell thought for a moment before speaking again.

"I think I've been very cooperative. I've told you everything you need to know. I've offered hospitality. What more can I do? You should forget Blackie Buenavista. That's my best advice. Frankly, he always struck me as the kind of man who's bound to let his libido get him into serious trouble. If he hasn't already done so, he no doubt will in the very near future."

"That's as weak a summary as I've heard since *L.A. Law* was mercifully cancelled."

I put down my glass and carefully placed the pistol beside it. With a little help from the arms of the chair, I climbed to my feet. That was one damn comfortable chair and in a way I hated to leave it. But I'd had my fill of Canary Carswell and his phony refinement. And I'd had my fill of this going-nowhere conversation. It was traveling in bigger and lazier circles and the fact that it kept coming around to the same question (a question nobody wanted to answer, or help me answer) didn't seem to bother anyone but me.

Where was Blackie Buenavista?

That was the question. So long as he remained missing, everyone seemed quite content to pretend they only sort of cared in the most nonchalant terms. The status quo was maintained. Equilibrium was preserved. It was only when I began thrashing around, poking my nose into everybody's business, that the relative anxiety quotient of the circle I was running in became more pronounced. Maybe the smart thing to do was simply to walk away. Throw up my hands and say, "Fine, be that way," and give it up. After all, what the hell did I care? I'd never even met the guy. What was Blackie to me? Just another player in a drama even the Simsbury Dinner Theater wouldn't stage. He was a ghost and I felt increasingly foolish for chasing after him.

"Okay, you win," I said. I put my hands out to my sides. "I give up."

"Don't beat yourself up over it," Carswell said, a little too smugly.

"No, no," I said. "That's just it. Maybe it's the booze, but I just realized I don't give a shit. Not about Blackie Buenavista. Not about you or your lunatic sister, whatever the hell she calls herself. Not about Lillian the Vaudevillian or her sociopathic kid sister. Hell, I don't even care that much about Mrs. Wordstone."

Llewellyn Carswell put his glass down. "You did the best you could," he said as he approached me. I wasn't afraid. I was sick and tired. On top of which I suddenly realized I missed my dog, who was a whole lot better company than any of the selfish creeps I'd run into the last few days. "Come, Mr. Vaughn, I'll show you out."

I let him take me by the arm and lead me to the front door. He wasn't aggressive or pushy. In fact there was something altogether too gentiled in his manner, as if we were old chums looking back on our Princeton days, reminiscing on our time as crew mates on some mist covered river, pulling our oars in a single, unified effort. More bullshit that made me feel like I needed a shower and a shave.

*The Farce News*

"I probably won't bother you anymore," I said, as we stood at the front door. He offered his large hand and I shook it.

"Don't feel bad, Mr. Vaughn."

"Oh, I don't. I just don't get why you didn't tell me all this earlier."

"Frankly," he said, smiling, "I was just trying to find a polite way to tell you it's none of your goddamn business."

"Right," I said. "Touché."

"Sometimes, things work out as they're meant to even when the contrary appears to be the case."

"Mmm," I said. "Very pithy. You get that out of a book?"

He chuckled. "I'm neither a poor winner nor a poor loser. Neither an optimist nor a pessimist. I'm simply a realist."

"Do yourself and everyone else a favor, get rid of the book."

I walked down the wooden staircase to the driveway. In the growing darkness of early evening, I found my way back up to the wide cul-de-sac. My piece of shit Jetta was waiting for me like a trusty, if somewhat rusty steed. Perhaps out of sympathy it started the first time I tried the ignition. Maybe it just wanted to get the hell out of there as badly as I did.

With my luck, today would be the day I'd be pulled over by some twenty-year-old jarhead country cop with nothing better to do than harass motorists and throw them in jail for driving under influence. I didn't even have a stick of gum to fool myself with. Fuck it. I rolled down the window to let in the breeze. At the top of the lane, I flipped on my headlights, signaled left, and made my turn onto Silver Street, heading south, away from Massachusetts, away from Carswell's house in the woods, back toward Granby, and eventually Hartford.

It had finally dawned on me why everyone was so uptight about me finding Blackie.

*The Farce News*

**Chapter 28**

I headed back to Farmington Avenue to kill some time -- and some more brain cells, if the Surgeon General had it right. The frozen vodka administered by Canary Carswell had mostly worn off, like the underdose of novocain my sadistic, cheapskate dentist always dispenses, leaving me not-quite numb enough, sore to the touch, and a little like I'd been in a street fight and placed first among the losers. I was stone cold sober by the time I hit the Hartford city limit sign. I was also stone cold depressed, rock hard disgusted and generally speaking, feeling rather like a pebble that's been kicked down about three miles of bad road. In this condition, I was in no mood to go home to my empty apartment. And I'm sure the animals would appreciate me sparing them my sour mood.

After parking in the lot behind Kinko's and collecting the bottle of Dr. Pepper, I went up to the studio. Something about the empty studio held marginally more appeal than the empty flat with only Rufus and the cats, J.D. and Buddy, to keep me company. I found an empty Fred Flintstone grape jelly jar and a half-empty pint bottle of Jim Beam in the bottom drawer of the file cabinet where we keep the booze, and settled in at the desk. Feet up. Spirits low.

The Emmons D-10 still needed new strings but I was in a serious Fuck It All frame of mind.

I poured bourbon and pondered the peculiar parade of community theater wannabes who'd made cameo appearances here during the week, how they'd attempted to entertain me with their miserable melodramas. Lillian Buenavista, the gorgeous but hopelessly incompetent quick-change artist. Stick, the helpless stranger in the strange land. Llewellyn Carswell, the heartless predatory prestidigitator. They were like Hell's own traveling salesmen, each one hawking a different version of the same bad juju. In their case, it was lies and threats and more lies. How much of it had I bought? And had I kept the receipts so I could return them for a full refund?

I tried to put them out of my mind, but it wasn't easy and Jim Beam wasn't doing as good a job as he should have to help the process along, considering what I was paying in hourly wages.

Around ten o'clock I called Sully. He answered on the third ring and, surprisingly, sounded happy to hear from me. Sully wasn't the kind to stay mad long, and if by some chance you got pissed at him for any one of his many idiosyncrasies, his perpetually cheerful outlook made it damn hard to stay hacked off.

"Do you have a story for me?" he said.

"Maybe."

"Does it start with 'Two Rabbis walk into a bar ...'?"

"No."

"Good," he said. "'Cause I've heard 'em all."

I recapped the last four days, since my first meeting with Lita Wordstone and her grandmother on Monday afternoon through my back-to-back tête-à-têtes with Canary Carswell. I did my best to piece it together in a coherent manner. I had to pour a couple of refills into my Fred Flintstone jar along the way to keep my mouth from going dry. It's entirely likely some of the details got lost or jangled. I might have ranted a bit. It's been known to happen. I may even have raved a time or two. Sully didn't interrupt. He let me tell the tale in my own clumsy fashion, complete with stops and starts and probably a repetition or three.

"What an adventure," he said, when I finished the part about pouring a double shot of bourbon and calling him up. "What's your next move?"

I'd been asking myself the same thing. "Hell if I know." It wasn't much of a response. But it was honest and I thought honesty should count for something after the week I'd had. "I'm tired of stumbling along like a drunken spaz."

"But you're so good at it."

"Thanks, Sully. Thanks a million."

I hung up on Sully, stashed the Jim Beam, and locked up the studio. It was about eleven-thirty when I retrieved my car from Kinko's. The night manager, still in his blue apron, was shutting down for the night, wrapping up bins of paper garbage, sweeping the floors. I gave him a casual wave. He gave me a nasty look. My piece of shit Jetta was the only car left in the lot, a dirty neglected hors d'ouevre left to rot on an abandoned concrete snack tray. Maybe I'd worn out my welcome.

A few minutes later, I pulled into Summit Street and parked about a block from the apartment building. A couple of college kids smoking a joint walked by without noticing me, but otherwise the street was empty. No Camry with gangsta rims parked out front. No lurking hulks on skateboards. No hoodlums in yellow cowboy hats and Brooks Brothers suits. Thank God.

Things continued to go well until I opened the door to my flat and found no lights on. This was a strange. Jolie never leaves the animals in the dark. She insists they don't like it. I don't know how she procured this beguiling kernel of information about cats and dogs. For all I know, she asked them.

For all I know, they told her so. I always leave a light on for them, and I know she does too. When I flipped the light switch, I discovered that someone had cleaned up.

The dishes were put away. The counters were wiped clean. The floors were swept. Even the newspapers were piled in the recycling bin. A note and a cassette tape recorder sat on the kitchen table.

The note was from Jolie. I put the paper to my nose. It carried her scent.

*Rufus and the kitties have moved in with me. I have a bigger apartment than you. This just makes more sense. Also, take a listen if you get a chance. The song speaks to me.*

As usual, she managed to be short and sweet without being overly sweet. That was one of the things I liked best about her. There were a number of things I liked best about her.

I put the note down and went to the fridge. There was a six-pack in there. I didn't remember it being there. I took out two bottles. In the pantry closet, Rufus' 25-pound bag of kibble was gone, but there *was* a bag of ranch flavored Doritos. I didn't remember buying it. I grabbed it. Then I noticed the cat food cans were missing from their usual spot on the third shelf. I took the beer and chips through the apartment with me, turning on lights as I went, then shutting them right back off. The mat Rufus used as his private sanctuary was nowhere to be found. The cats' litter box was gone from the bathroom. The floor looked like it had been mopped. Even the air was fresh. No stink of stale cat piss.

I took the cassette recorder into the living room and collapsed on the couch. My mind wandered around aimlessly for a while without me. I occupied myself with the beer and chips. I flipped the TV on and ran through all 95 channels, three times, before giving up and shutting it off.

The joy of procrastination wore off and I started to feel downright ashamed of myself. The clucking of a barnyard chicken played in my head and I heard myself yell, "Shut the fuck up," before I remembered I was alone. I pressed the PLAY button and waited to see what Jolie had in store for me.

After a moment of audio hiss, music came up; country music. A snappy steel guitar riff. She was obviously playing to my good side. The eight-bar intro ended and the vocal kicked in. It was the raspy voice of Buddy Miller. Her hero and uncrowned king of Nashville.

I sat back and listened to the song.

*I don't need nobody to call me on the phone,*
*I don't need no company I'd rather be alone*

*I'm just happy by myself here being blue,*
*I'm not lonely I'm just lonesome for you*
*When my friends come I don't care if they stay,*
*When they talk to me I don't care what they say*
*You're still gone so darling there ain't nothing new,*
*I'm not lonely I'm just lonesome for you*

*I'll just be lonesome without you here,*
*'Cause there ain't no one I'll love like you, dear*
*Thinking of you is all I want to do,*
*I'm not lonely I'm just lonesome for you*
*Any comfort I get these days is small,*
*Everybody tries but nothing helps at all*
*They'd just give up before they started if they knew,*
*I'm not lonely I'm just lonesome for you*

*I'll just be lonesome without you here,*
*'Cause there ain't no one I'll love like you, dear*
*I'm just better off alone here being blue,*
*I'm not lonely I'm just lonesome for you*

It occurred to me as I listened to Miller croon on that there is a significant difference between lonely and lonesome, and it wasn't geographical or linguistic or idiomatic. It was somewhere in the head and in the heart. I couldn't quite decide which I felt at the moment.

Then it occurred to me that the song probably wasn't intended to initiate an outbreak of runaway intellectualization, which is what I was doing because I was basically terrified, and intellectualizing was easier than facing the cold, hard -- or warm, soft -- truth.

Then it occurred to me, because I'm pretty slow on the uptake, what Jolie was getting at. Then it dawned on me why I was terrified and my stomach did a back flip. I sank deeper into the couch and let the darkness embrace me. I drank the second beer without tasting it.

Had I but a shred of energy left to my name, or perhaps an ounce of courage, I'd have marched down the hall to Jolie's place to fight for my parental rights, to demand the immediate return of my house mates, and of course to wrap my arms around Jolie and never let her go. If I had a moral leg to stand on, I would in fact have stood. But I was physically whipped and mentally thrashed and emotionally paralyzed. On top of which there was no escaping the embarrassing fact that I'd been guilty of fairly gross negligence these last few days. I could easily see how the boys -- Rufus and J.D. and Buddy -- might prefer to hang with Jolie than with their absentee lord and master.

I was shackled by indecision. I tried the TV again for a while, but the images went right past me, the sound gradually melting into a gurgling wash of meaningless noise. Or maybe that's what it started out as. I couldn't be sure. My central nervous system was a little fuzzy at the moment, what with the vodka, the bourbon and the beer still swirling through my blood stream looking for a way out. And the girl down the hall with the killer smile, messing with my heart, looking for a way in.

I don't remember falling asleep. Maybe I just lost consciousness. It happens all the time.

Sometime in the middle of the night, there was a thump outside my apartment door and I awoke with a start. Only then did I realize I'd even been asleep, sitting up fully clothed on the couch with an empty beer bottle still clutched in my hand.

Where was Rufus to growl threateningly at the potential intruder? Oh, yeah, down the hall, bivouacking with Jolie. Where I should be. Ungrateful sonofabitch.

I waited for another noise, hoping for some indication of what was going on. Was I being burgled? How ironic would that have been after my week of profligate breaking and entering? Or had I imagined the noise altogether? Was my guilty conscience doing a telltale heart number on me? Maybe I should just crawl off to bed and pretend it was nothing.

Instead, I kicked off my *Adidas* runners and padded silently to the door, listening for any sound. There were no further bumps or thuds of any kind. I put my face to the fisheye peep hole and peered out into the distorted picture of the illuminated hallway outside my door. And saw nothing. No unwanted visitors. No cartoon ghouls. No cops. I put the chain on -- feeling awfully damn stupid as I did it. After all, how many times had I seen, in one bad movie or another, some half-wit victim-to-be slide the chain into place only to have the door, the door frame, and the chain itself all shatter in an explosion of wanton violence as the crazed ax-wielding assassin in the goalie mask kicked it in?

Nice thoughts for three o'clock in the morning.

But this was the hour when Venus Edwards liked to come calling.

I opened the door a few inches and saw nothing in the hallway. No sign of life. Or death, for that matter. I glanced down at my welcome mat and my heart sank. Oh, no, not again, I thought. There on the mat sat a folded copy of *The Farce News,* fresh off the press. I reached through the partial opening

-- too lazy to close the door, remove the chain and reopen it. When I picked up the paper, it was warm to the touch. Just like last time. Great. I closed the door and went directly to the kitchen phone. I dialed Sully's number. He picked up right away.

"It's me," I said.

"I recognized your voice instantly." He sounded very alert.

"How come you're not sleeping?"

"I'll sleep when I'm dead."

"How'd your paper get on my doorstep?"

"Delivery service. Thought you'd be interested."

I hung up and went back into the living room and turned off the television, which was now showing what appeared to be a rerun of the earlier airing of the *Tonight Show*, just in case there were any insomniac masochists out there for whom one viewing simply didn't induce enough pain and suffering. I went to the bathroom and splashed cold water on my face.

Then I sat down on the couch to read whatever it was Sully had composed that was so important he had to have it hand-delivered to my apartment at -- I checked the wall clock in the kitchen -- three-twenty in the morning. The headline gave me a start.

### OH, BROTHER! OH, SISTER! OH, PLEASE!

I didn't want to read it, knowing how mad I'd probably get. But this was one highway wreck I simply couldn't ignore.

*Corruption in the absence of arrogance may be mistaken for primordial greed. However, when mixed with a healthy dose of disdain for everything right and fair in society, corruption becomes not just another art form pursued to its extremes by the elite and privileged, but indeed a bawdy and unforgiving blood sport in which the bodies of the innocent and guileless are apt to pile up like so many neoprene sacks containing yesterday's detritus.*

*Among the cloistered elitists populating this category is none other than Hartford County's own Llewellyn Carswell, wealthy dealmaker and shadier-than-the-underside-of-a-beach-blanket trafficker in all things suspect and illegal. That "Canary" has not been caged in the slammer and forced to sing for his supper is an outrage, and proof positive that crime does pay (if only in the form of bribes). Of course, Carswell's kid sister, the real estate robber baroness Venus Edwards, the mistress-mind behind the felonious family operation, also roams free despite her many questionable covenants. As does her humble hubby Hubert F. (for Fugitive) Edwards,* the eminent local tax accountant, whose thievery of the U.S. Government via tax fraud makes Jesse James look like Robin Hood.

Clearly these three should be in prison stamping out license plates, and yet they are not. Why? Because wealth equals power, and power brokers are permitted to operate outside the parameters of legality and decency which the rest of us are required to observe.

The editorial board of *The Farce News* thus challenges state prosecutors to haul this unholy trinity onto the judicial carpet and to hold their collective feet to the proverbial fire. An ever-growing landfill of evidence supports the convening a grand jury which would no doubt result in a barrel of indictments and thus initiate the overdue process of shipping this mob of mischievous monkeys, i.e., Carswell and the Edwards pair, to extended stays at the nearest state correctional facility.

A close inspection of the Carswell-Edwards import/export business might be the perfect place for a probe to begin. No doubt the Internal Revenue Service would find a bountiful harvest of wrong doing were they to jump in and run their combine through this fertile field of flagrant financial flimflams. Let us not forget the fate of that legendary mob boss Al Capone, who, in Harry Houdini style, escaped all but the stickiest of charges: income tax evasion. What was good enough for Scarface should be good enough for these modern-day bootleggers.

The U.S. Department of State may be interested in a series of business transactions said to have taken place between the Carswell-Edwards cartel and certain Middle East countries with whom the U.S. does not currently extend a formal trade agreement.

According to the latest update, Hubert Edwards, the pencil-pushing Zorro, fled the country sometime Thursday night on what was characterized as "an extended business trip." It would be interesting to know if any of the countries on Hubert's itinerary share extradition agreements with the U.S.

In addition to the rash of RICO statutes violated by this triple threat of smugglers, money launderers and shakedown artists, there are a couple of homicides with their figurative (if not actual) fingerprints all over them.

Local law enforcement should take a long look at the link between the Carswell-Edwards consortium and a phony trading card shop on Park Street in Hartford. The shop was owned and operated (or was it merely fronted?) by LaTwanda Jefferson, *who was found dead in her Bloomfield home earlier this week. Investigators believe the woman, AKA Big Jeff, was shot to death by an associate, Johnny Brashear. But we know different. West Hartford resident Miguel Batista, who died the same night in a suspicious car accident, was the man behind the trigger. The shooting is alternately being characterized as an act of revenge and a crime of passion, depending on whom you ask. H.P.D. and Bloomfield authorities decline to offer further details and refuse to confirm or deny a connection between Jefferson and a West Hartford heiress who was the target of a recent extortion-blackmail scheme.*

*Ms. Jefferson also dabbled in the world of videography, allegedly furnishing the financial foundation for low-budget soft-core gay and lesbian sports-related porno. Go figure. C'est la vie. Big Jeff was purportedly a patron of petty player Johnny Brashear, who was killed in his Windsor home earlier this week.*

*Hartford police early Wednesday morning arrested Willemina Williams, a.k.a. Billie Billie, in connection with Mr. Brashear's death. Prosecutors expect to file first degree murder charges within days. Ms. Williams was the personal aide to Ms. Jefferson. Her motive has not yet been divulged by state attorneys. Unconfirmed rumors suggest Ms. Williams is angling for a plea bargain in exchange for her testimony. Against whom she intends to spill the beans remains to be seen. Llewellyn Carswell, perhaps? Venus Edwards? Hubert Edwards? All of the above?*

*Mrs. Edwards, nee Victoria Carswell is renown for her zealous passion for real estate — acquiring it, that is. It's been said she never met a For Sale sign she didn't like. She is also famous (although perhaps infamous would be more appropriate) for her "championship of the arts," as she has been said to describe it. Mrs. Edwards owns and operates the outrageously appalling Simsbury Dinner Theater, whose next favorable review will be its first.*

*Husband Hubert, who's known for keeping a lower profile than road paint, is alleged to be in deep marinara with The Mob. Precise details are scant, but there are hints he's up to his pince nez in gambling debts -- apparently he's soft on ponies, greyhounds, and the Indiana Pacers. Others say he's been skimming swag and cooking phony books, an offense punishable (according to mob law) by a sentence of life without life. Thus did Hubert skip town, not to avoid arraignment, but to duck the assassin's garrote.*

I put the paper down. I couldn't read any more. I didn't want to wake up in the morning and find this, too, was nothing more than a pathetic nightmare. I appreciated what Sully was attempting, but I hardly believe his weekly paper would significantly impact events. Llewellyn Carswell and his ilk were the professional snake charmers in this flying carpet circus. They knew how to barge into trouble and how to barge audaciously back out of it. Freedom from culpability at all cost.

As far as I knew, no other paper had plans to pay any attention to Llewellyn Carswell and the Edwards couple. The *Courant* wouldn't say a word until the *New York Times* or the *Washington Post* already covered it. Then they might reprint a day-old story with a "Special to ..." byline. Just as the Hartford Whalers had done, Llewellyn Carswell, Venus Carswell Edwards and Hubert Edwards were gonna skate.

I put down *The Farce News* and staggered off to bed. It was nearly four o'clock in the morning. I brushed my teeth but put off flossing for the seventh straight year. I didn't bother with pajamas, but I was at least civilized enough to crawl out of my jeans before flopping on the bed. The sheets were cool. The pillow caressed me. I missed Rufus not jumping on the bed and breathing his steamy dog-breath in my face. I knew I would miss J.D. and Buddy kneading my back and purring in my ears when I fell asleep. Tomorrow I'd have to figure out a way to get them back.

Too bad Jolie was a black belt in karate. What if I tried to kiss her and she broke my back?

*The Farce News*

## Chapter 29

When I woke up Friday morning, my first conscious thought was, "Oh, shit, I gotta walk the dog before he explodes." With that image in my head, my second thought was, "Yecccch."

Then the centerfield scoreboard flashed a news update: "Hey, Einstein, your dog's been kidnapped."

Oh, yeah.

Being fair-minded and reluctant to jump to conclusions before I have at least 10% of the available facts, I quickly modified this to, "Easy now, he's only moved down the hall. No problem."

And yet, with each revelation, I became not more relaxed but more agitated. Anticipation of my impending confrontation with Jolie weighed heavily on my mind. By the the time my addled brain worked its way through this morass of fractious, one-man-in-a-padded-cell conversation, it was too late to roll over and go back to sleep. A shower and a pot of coffee did little to put Jolie out of my mind, but at last I gathered the attention surplus necessary to sort out the week's chaotic stream of events.

But first I had to get even.

Show I could play her game, too. Maybe not as well, only time would tell. But I had to at least give it the old junior high school try. From my CD shelf, I selected a Jim Lauderdale disc, found the song I wanted, and shoved Jolie's cassette into the appropriate slot on the CD player. I hit the PLAY button on the CD side and the RECORD button the cassette side. The song came up. A snappy shuffle with a fiddle and steel guitar intro. Then Lauderdale sang:

*Hey girl, we've been friends for so long,*
*I've always been your shoulder when you cried*
*Now you're asking how to end your heartache,*
*I'm telling you right now, take my advice*

*If I were you then I'd love me forever,*
*I'd be here in these arms where you belong*
*And I'd spend my life being happy,*
*If I were you I'd hold me from now on*

*There's no point in taking chances,*

*You want someone you know will always stay*
*I've always been here when you needed someone*
*To help you make it through your darkest day*

*If I were you then I'd love me forever*
*I'd be here in these arms where you belong*
*And I'd spend my life being happy,*
*If I were you I'd hold me from now on*

When it was finished, I ejected the cassette and wrapped it in a piece of paper on which I wrote: "You have something of mine. I'll be by later to collect." There. To say I was very proud of myself would be a mild understatement. If Jolie wanted to play it cryptic, I could do that. Or at least I thought I could.

In twelve hours, come hell or high water or both, I'd pack my gear in the Jetta and be on my way to the gig in Bristol. This left only a few hours to wrap up what felt like an inordinate number of nagging loose ends.

I sat down with coffee and a pad and pen and began to make notes. The first one: "Jolie, leave me alone and go to your room." Then I considered the Wordstone tribe and the case at hand.

Certain truths I recognized as being incontrovertible. A handful of blatant lies I strongly suspected of untwistability. Several riddles I didn't think I could solve without a team of MIT professors at my disposal. And an injustice or two (or five) existed, but where I was flush with righteous indignation, I lacked the authority -- or the right gavel -- to make a difference.

(I knew Sully's piece in *The Farce News* might stir the pot a little, but I wasn't holding my breath that the soup would go very far toward feeding the hungry or ending the epidemic of social inequity.)

I made two columns. What I Know and What I Don't. I was sure now that Miguel Batista had killed LaTwanda Jefferson over his perception of Twannie's role in coercing Lita Wordstone to participate in "Volley-Ball!" Blinded by love, Miguel had missed a signal or two. To my mind, Lita was a more willing participant than he could have guessed.

I felt certain that Billie Billie, who either was or wasn't Twannie Jefferson's lover (ultimately it didn't make a damn bit of difference either way), had used the purple Lexus to run Miguel off the road to his death. I attributed this act of hot-blooded retribution to temper, if only because Billie Billie didn't strike me as a naturally cold-blooded killer type, although, like Canary Carswell, she had a certain *sangfroid*. But she was no assassin. She had brokenhearted avenging angel in black leather written all over her. Sadly, she was going to serve a lot of time, maybe the rest of the time she had left, behind bars unless some lawyer sold the idea that Miguel's murder was just a lamentable traffic accident. To make this contention successfully, the lawyer would require that both the judge and the 12-member jury be certifiable retards. Billie Billie also had to answer for the lawn darts she stuck in Johnny Brashear. I could only guess on this one, but I guessed that Billie Billie, already distraught over Twannie's demise, fingered Johnny for moving just a bit too quickly on the Park Street materiel, suggesting perhaps he'd had some role in Big Jeff's termination -- and thus deserved payback. And to paraphrase Billie Billie, payback was a be-yotch.

The other column was where the Carswell/Edwards Trio lived.

How nice it would be to tie them in somehow, as Sully had attempted to do in print, to all the death and destruction. To link them to the killings and drop the weight of the law on their heads like a cartoon bank safe from a third floor window. Sure, that would be nice. But I didn't think it would happen.

Llewellyn and Vicky were sharks, complete with thick, tough skins and sharp, nasty teeth. They were predatory carnivores to be handled with extreme caution (Sully's audacious frontal assault notwithstanding). God knows what childhood experiences had transformed Llewellyn, Vicky and Hubert into The Three Stooges of well-dressed grifters they'd become, what chain of events had set them on their path of pinstriped larceny. These weren't petty thugs who knocked down little old ladies and stole their pension checks. They were worse. This unholy trinity was into Byzantine felony -- thumbing their collective nose at society at-large -- and they had the genius of Hubert Edwards to cover their backs with a seamless wallpaper of documentation guaranteed to keep the authorities, to say nothing of some nosy parker without even a legitimate P.I. license, from taking them down.

The tough question I had to ask myself, and for which I continued to wrestle for a definitive answer, was this: How much culpability can be attached to the Carswell-Edwards conspirators vis-à-vis the deaths of Big Jeff, Miguelito Batista and Johnny-Boy Brashear? Were they complicit in this trail of violence, or was their role only implied?

And what possible role had they in the strange disappearance of Blackie Buenavista, whom Canary had dismissed as less worthy of concern than a housefly. While I rode the gut feeling that Blackie was dead, I couldn't see Llewellyn, Vicky or Hubert getting blood on their hands, not when they could contract that kind of help if needed. I certainly didn't buy Jenny and Stick's assertion that Carswell was a button-man, "doer" or any of their other preposterous names for it.

There was a tinge of cheap and tawdry greed -- like a cancerous tumor -- that poisoned everything the Carswell/Edwards consortium touched. They were dispassionate feeders. Theirs was a row boat built for three floating down Love Canal, with Chernobyl-like fallout.

Johnny and Twannie, on the other hand, had died for their dreams. Seedy, lowbrow dreams, perhaps, but dreams nonetheless. It seemed Miguel and Billie Billie had murdered out of love. Questionable, misguided love, perhaps, but love. This was not an unprecedented (if oxymoronic) way to go through life. Hadn't Richard Shithouse Nixon condemned countless thousands of American troops to early death in Southeast Asia in a benighted policy of "fighting for peace"?

Love could certainly be just as dangerous as organized crime. Mobsters who screwed the pooch invariably ended up with one or two in the back of the head. As a rule they never saw it coming -- just like losers in the game of love.

A quick scan of my scribbled notes revealed that I was nowhere. Paddling a left-handed canoe with a right-handed oar. Circling like a seagull who can't remember if he's hungry enough to bother diving for that elusive mackerel. I added one last question, one that had been bothering me all week.

Why did LaTwanda Jefferson hit up Margaret Waddley-Wordstone for eighty thousand dollars in the first place?

Eighty large wasn't very large in this world. It was chump change for this crowd. It was an odd and perplexing figure. Eighty grand. Why not an even hundred thou?

There was one person who could probably tell me, but the thought of another visit was almost more than I could bear to contemplate. But I could think of no better solution, and unlike all its rhetorical cousins, this question was begging and pleading on bent knee for an answer, lest my business with this family remain forever incomplete.

So it was, against my own better judgment (which is how I do most things), I dressed and locked up the apartment. Down the hall, I listened at Jolie's door for any sounds of life, be they human, feline or canine in nature. I stood there for a moment, listening to my own breathing. I thought I heard breathing coming from the other side.

"Roof?" I said quietly. "That you, boy?"

I made out the sound of a dog whimpering, but not necessarily unhappily, followed the jingle-jangle-jingled of his tags as he retreated into the recesses of Jolie's apartment. I knocked on the door. There was no human response. I gave up after a couple of minutes and slid the cassette tape and note through the old-fashion mail slot. Hopefully Rufus wouldn't eat them.

I hit the street, ready for action. This time I managed the feat without tripping and landing face-first on the pavement.

As a rule my piece of shit Jetta always starts on the first try when I'm (a) in no hurry, or worse, (b) have no desire whatsoever to get where I'm going. This morning was no exception. As the cold engine whined spitefully and the leaky muffler growled mockingly, I cranked down the window, not a little surprised when the handle failed to snap off in my hand. The cool fall air washed over me as I pulled into morning traffic, giving me an all-too-brief sense of well-being and good cheer. Heading west for Prospect Avenue and the Wordstone mansion, the sensation steadily drained away and was replaced by a knot in the pit of my stomach. It might have been all the coffee but I don't think so.

Twenty minutes later I parked in the circular gravel driveway and grabbed the package from the trunk of the car. I crunched my way to the heavy front door and pushed the brass doorbell and listened to the chimes sound inside. To my surprise, it was Rosa who opened the door moments later. She looked equally surprised to see me.

"Meester Phone," she said, approximately. "What a sooprice!"

"Rosa," I said, shifting to grim solemnity. "I'm very sorry for your loss."

Vintage Andy Sipowicz.

She waved a hand in front of her face, as if I were a bumblebee hovering too close to her nose. "Oh, no, no, no. Than' choo." Then she crossed herself. "Miguelito with he father, now." She didn't clarify which father she specifically meant, his biological progenitor or Good God Almighty, Himself. I couldn't think of a way to ask without risking embarrassment all around, so I let it go. "Anyway, don't nobody can't hurt hing no more," she said. Then she stepped away from the door. "Come in, come in. I hope choo not here to see the old lady."

"Actually ..." I followed her into the grand foyer. She stopped abruptly and turned.

"Because chee not here."

"Mrs. Wordstone?"

"Chee go away."

I was, of course, unaware of the travel plans of dear old Auntie Peg, close as we had recently become. "Actually," I began again. I didn't get any further this time before Rosa jumped in.

"Chee go to Alaska."

"Alaska?"

"For the winter."

I studied Rosa's face to see if she was joking. There was no way to tell.

Her expression was blank, her eyes wide. She was either a world class Straight Man, or was dabbling in narcotics, which considering her recent loss would not be hard to believe or accept.

"Alaska," I said, to confirm that I had heard correctly.

"Chee go for the climate."

"Of course." Perpetually in search of the frostiest milieu. I knew that. Why not Fairbanks, or Kodiak Island, or Yakutat, or Moose Pass? Or wherever the frozen hell she went. More power to her. The fewer Wordstone women for me to deal with, the better.

"Chee leave last night. First chee fly to Wancoober. In Canada."

She pronounced it "Can-*yada*." I didn't bother to correct her.

"Then chee take a cruise."

This was quickly getting into the area of more information than I needed or wanted. But how to steer this doomed ship of conversation smoothly away? Too bad Edward J. Smith wasn't there to offer some pointers. I held up the package in front of me.

An almost sickening girlish smile came over Rosa's face. "For me, Meester Phone? Oh, choo chudding hab."

Super. Another awkward misunderstanding. "Er," I said, instantly regretting my tactics. Real smooth, ace. "Actually, I came to return this to Miss Wordstone."

The smile slid from Rosa's face like a tangle of spaghetti down the kitchen wall and was immediately replaced by a mask of sheer disgust, as if the noodles had turned to pig intestines. I thought I heard her mumble something on the order of *"Maldita puta"* under her breath.

"Is she home?"

Rosa held the dirty look, clearly judging me guilty by association for mentioning the name of her least favorite Wordstone family member. Or it could have disappointment that the package was not a gift for her. I'll never know. (I sure as hell wasn't going to ask.)

*"Mierda pequena!* Chee never home."

"She's out, then?"

"No. Chee here. *Chupaverga.*"

I don't speak a whole lot of Spanish. But I didn't think I'd find Rosa's choice of expletives in a conventional English-Spanish book of phrases. There was a heartfelt belligerence about the way she spit them out that suggested profanity in its purest form.

"Would you mind telling her I'm here."

Apparently, Rosa did mind, for she turned on her heels and walked away, saying "Fin' her jorsel'. What do I look like to choo?"

*The Farce News*

I would have said, "The housekeeper," but she turned a corner and disappeared from view down one of the long hallways that snaked through this labyrinthine manse. I didn't see much point in yelling after her, lest she unleash her animus in my direction.

Though this was a somewhat unexpected development, I didn't let it shake my resolve. Perhaps I should have.

For the next few minutes, I wandered around the place. Eventually I found myself in the sitting room with the Van Gogh and the Elvis-on-black-velvet paintings. There was a new addition hanging in an ornate frame between two windows. I stopped in my tracks. It was a brilliant reproduction of Leonardo da Vinci's *Mona Lisa,* spectacularly recreated with only a couple of subtle modifications. For instance, in addition to the impish smirk that made the subject so famous, the girl now wore a green plastic eyeshade and black garters on her sleeves. And she was sitting at a round table dealing Blackjack to a quartet of cigar-smoking animals, including a German Shepherd in a bowler hat, two chimpanzees in matching red satin vests, and a dandy leopard with an ivory cigarette holder in his mouth. The leopard, whom I suspect, spoke in an English accent, had the lion's share of chips. I didn't see the lion anywhere. Maybe he was the game's big loser.

I found the French doors leading to the flagstone patio where I'd first met Lita Wordstone not a week ago. I didn't expect to find her outside, but I went out anyway, if only to get some fresh air. A couple of minutes in this madhouse left me short of breath. Of all my dumb-ass ideas, this was quickly lining up for a spot on the top step of the medal stand. What was that thing we were supposed to leave alone? Oh, yeah. *Well enough.* Only problem, nobody in this house qualified as *well enough.* Still, I should have more carefully weighed the cost-effectiveness of taking time to come over, considering I was more or less off the case and, thus, off the clock. And after concluding my cost-analysis, I should have stayed home.

So what was I thinking, venturing across town just to return a stupid present that held no meaning to me whatsoever? I could have shipped the damn thing and saved the aggravation. But there was the burning question I needed to ask and I didn't imagine the middle management yeggs at Fed Ex would allow one of their drivers to serve as an ad hoc interrogator. So, here I was.

I stepped through the doors and out onto the deck.

And there, just to make me a liar, sitting back in a reclining lawn chair slung in blue and white striped canvas and which appeared to have a rocking mechanism built into it, was Lita Wordstone. She was dressed in faded blue jeans and a gray sweatshirt with the name of some Ivy League college stenciled in red letters across the front -- unless it was a toothpaste company sweatshirt. She wore tattered sneakers and a pink terry cloth band in her blond hair. On a small cast-iron table beside her was a large crystal bowl filled with small pieces of hard candy. She was seated with her back to me, staring off at the tall trees in the enormous back yard. Or maybe she was staring at the empty space beyond the trees, beyond the clouds, beyond the edge of earth's atmosphere, dreaming of home. She didn't take immediate notice of me. I took a couple of steps across the stone deck and let my boot heels clack out the unmistakable fact of my arrival. She turned suddenly and leapt from the chair.

"I didn't do anything!" she yelled, then caught herself. "Oh, Mr. Vaughn. You surprised me."

"Who were you expecting?" I asked. The gestapo?

"Nobody," she said.

"Just your guilty little conscience at work, huh?" I said, smiling to show I was only kidding. (I wasn't kidding at all.)

She sat down gingerly on the edge of the reclining lawn chair. It rocked a little under her weight but she didn't lose her balance. "That's funny, Mr. Vaughn. Not ha-ha. But in a weird way." She tried to smile but failed and could only manage to look somewhat queazy. "Just like you." Maybe the candy disagreed with her like my pot of black coffee had disagreed with me. Maybe something entirely different was making her sick. Maybe she'd been into the Egyptian cocoa again. Maybe it wasn't the coffee that was making me queasy, either.

"Here," I said, walking toward her and holding the package in front of me. "I brought this back."

She shifted effortlessly from nausea to disappointment. "What's wrong? Don't you like it?"

It wasn't that I didn't like it. I just didn't have much use -- or any, in fact -- for a bowling pin. Particularly one with a big dent in it. I didn't bother trying to explain. "Sorry," I said with a shrug.

She took it pretty well, didn't pout any more than usual. However, she did launch into a little whiny reminiscence. "Miggy loved bowling."

"Yes, I believe you might have mentioned that."

It occurred to me that it probably *was* Miguel who'd situated Twannie Jefferson -- post-mortem -- in the basement rocking-chair to watch the TV with the eternal bowling championship. It stood to some brand of distorted reason that he would have doubled back to the Duncaster Road house to retrieve Lita. Finding her gone (thanks to me) and with the house empty, had he taken the chance to have the last laugh before heading back south, where Billie Billie chased him all the way to Simsbury before she ran him off the road? If so, I could only hope he enjoyed his last laugh.

"We have our own, you know?"

Actually I didn't know. I couldn't even guess. "Your own *what?*"

"Our own bowling alley, silly."

Yes, of course. She was right. It was silly of me not to have known. Or at least to have *guessed.* If we hadn't been standing outside, I would have suggested that someone immediately check the house for a carbon monoxide leak. Everyone in the place seemed to be halfway to complete dementia and I was beginning to wonder if it was something in the air. But here we were, standing in the great outdoors and the only thing in the air was the chilly portent of winter and the faint echo of past lunatics howling at the vast empty sky whilst waiting for the return of the nocturnal moon.

"Your own bowling alley?" I said. "That's pretty unusual."

"Yes, it is."

"There's one in the basement of the White House," I said. "In Washington, D.C.," I added, for clarity's sake. For all I knew there could be a white house right across the street or up the block and then Lita Wordstone would be totally confounded. "At least there used to be. Some people say the only thing in the basement of the White House is the skeletons of the people who crossed the president."

"Really? They say that?"

"Or, in some cases, the First Lady."

"Oooh."

"Depending on the particular First Lady."

"Well, we have one in the basement," she said. "And this isn't even the White House."

"No."

"Or Washington, D.C."

"No," I said. "This certainly isn't Washington, D.C."

"It's Connecticut," she said. "The Nutmeg State."

"Yes," I said, "with emphasis on the nut."

She giggled. I hated when she giggled. It made my fingernails ache.

"Of course, we're *very, very* rich," she said.

"Yes, how nice for you,"

"Yes. It is."

"Me, personally? I wouldn't know what to do with a bowling alley if I were unfortunate enough to find one in my basement. Maybe I'd turn it into a recording studio or a one-lane lap pool. I'm not much on bowling. As a matter of fact, under normal circumstances you wouldn't catch me dead in a bowling alley unless I've had an awful lot to drink first."

I found myself thinking about Twannie Jefferson again, sitting in front of the television set in the basement, dead, her eyes wired open, watching a bowling tape that wouldn't stop. Talk about Hell.

"You want a piece of candy?" Lita said, suddenly changing tones, holding out the large crystal bowl.

"No, thank you. It's a little early in the day for me."

"Oh, poo. It's never too early."

She put down the heavy bowl and rummaged around in it for a moment before picking out a red-and-white striped peppermint disk from which she meticulously removed the cellophane wrapper, which she then dropped on the patio. She popped the mint into her mouth and let out a sound that was just a little too satisfied to be made in mixed company, or for that matter, in public.

"Is that peppermint particularly delicious, or are you just showing off in front of the help again?"

"Oh, they're all yummy," she said. "Each in their own way. Just like little children."

I didn't doubt it, but I did pause to wonder, using her imagery as my guide, why the hell she was consuming them by the handful. "Mind if I change the subject for a second?"

She shrugged. "As long as we don't talk about Lilly."

Lilly? Her big sister? "Why don't you want to talk about Lilly?"

"Because she's a fucking cunt," she said, cheerfully, with a great big smile, as if she were talking about her favorite teddy bear.

"Oh?"

"She tried to steal my candy."

For the first time in a long time, I wished I'd stayed in school and gotten that doctorate in abnormal psychology instead of heading out west to play music. "Oh, now I get it," I said, having not a single clue what she was rambling on about.

"I had these Lifesavers?" she said. "And I was saving the red ones? They're the best. Cherry. Anyway, she tried to take them? But I caught her. Then she tried to deny it. Ha!"

"Oh."

Lita moved the peppermint to the other side of her mouth. "So, what did you want to ask me?"

I had to think about it for a moment. "Oh, yeah," I said. "About the money."

"What money?"

"The eighty grand Big Jeff wanted from your grandmother."

"What about it?"

"Why that number?"

"What do you mean?"

"It's too specific. Why not a hundred thousand? It's a pretty odd blackmail request."

"Blackmail? Don't be silly. It wasn't blackmail."

"Excuse me?"

"Who in the world ever told you it was blackmail?"

I peered at Lita. "Your grandmother, for starters."

She waved it off. "Oh, well, that's just plain silly."

This must be Silly Friday at Lita's playhouse. I took a deep breath but the dizziness didn't immediately subside. "Okay, then what was it?"

Lita shrugged. "What do you mean?"

I frowned at her. "If it wasn't blackmail."

She shrugged some more. It wasn't an *I Don't Know* kind of shrug. It was a *No Big Deal* shrug. I stared at her and waited for the beans to spill. "Expenses," she said, finally. "You know."

"Expenses? No, I don't know."

"To cover costs. Expenses."

I smiled. "That's a good one, Lita."

"Thanks."

"What for?"

"For complimenting me, silly."

"I wasn't complimenting you. What were the expenses for?" It was like talking to a orangutan, only not as much fun. Or as productive.

She switched the peppermint back to the other side of her mouth. "Production and distribution, silly."

"Production and distribution of what? And stop calling me that."

"Calling you what?"

"Don't make this so difficult. I feel like I'm pulling teeth."

"Ouch, I hope you're using loads and loads of novocain."

"I wish."

"I absolutely hate dentists, don't you?"

"If you don't lay off the sweets you'll be seeing one soon."

"Oh, poo," she said and crunched hard on the candy, chewing it vigorously. "Watch this."

I didn't want to. But I did. She swallowed the candy, then reached into her mouth and removed her teeth, pulling out a complete set of sparkling white dentures, uppers and lowers. Then she licked her lips and smiled at me, the quintessential toothless grin. She looked like an old-time hockey player. My stomach lurched. She giggled and replaced the choppers. "It was for production and distribution of my film."

"Your film?"

"You know," she said. "The one ..."

Of course. "Oh." The historic landmark in off-the-wall adult video entertainment, "Volley-Ball!"

"I assumed Big Jeff wanted your grandmother to pay her to keep it quiet? Are you saying ..."

"Keep it quiet? Oh, no, don't be silly. The money was to pay for having it made and then reproduced for distributioners."

"You mean distributors."

"That's what I said."

"Whatever."

"Anyway, like I already said, it was for production and distribution."

I mulled it over. "She expected your grandmother to foot the bill?"

Lita nodded and looked a little sheepish. "I promised."

"What do you mean, you promised? You promised whom?"

"I promised Twannie and J.B. That was the deal if they let me be in it."

"Who's J.B.?" I asked, although I knew it could be only one person.

"Johnny, of course," she said, then she started to giggle again and I wanted very much to hit her. My right fist was telling me to go for it, but my left-wing, middle-class conscience insisted it was morally and ethically wrong to pick on the handicapped.

"Johnny Brashear?"

"Who else?"

"You people are truly unbelievable." My right fist was saying, "Told you, told you." My left-wing middle-class conscience was shrugging sheepishly in the corner. "I thought Jenny recruited you."

"She did. In the beginning. Then I wanted to, but they said only ..."

"I get it. You're some world-class sucker, Lita."

"Thank you."

"It wasn't a ... Oh, forget it."

"But then they wouldn't give me any copies. They're greedy and mean. I plan to tell them so."

"Who?"

"Johnny and Big Jeff."

"Really?" Could she have forgotten they were dead? Was this a record-breaking case of consummate denial? Or worse? What the hell. If she didn't know or remember, I sure as hell wasn't going to be the one to break the news. "So that's why you attacked Johnny with the bowling pin?"

*The Farce News*

She shrugged impishly. "It seemed like a good idea at the time. You had to be there."

"Um, Lita. I was."

Lita Wordstone shrugged and turned away, reaching into the crystal bowl for another piece of candy. This time she selected a tubular brown and white candy. A root beer barrel. At least that's what they called them when I was a kid. She unwrapped it and popped it into her mouth and looked up at me. "So, you wanna see it?"

There wasn't the slightest hint of shame in this girl. It was as if every vestige of modesty had been surgically removed, or perhaps even genetically precluded from her makeup prior to birth.

"No, thanks," I said. "Amateur skin flicks aren't really my thing. No matter how ridiculous and amusing the concept."

"Oh, not that, silly. I mean the bowling alley. In the basement."

Didn't I feel like a schmuck? "Thanks," I said. "I think I'll pass. And stop calling me that. It's starting to give me a rash."

"Oh, come on," she said. She got up and took the candy bowl in one arm, the wrapped bowling pin in the other. "I have to put this back anyway. Help me, won't you? I can't carry the candy bowl, too. It's awfully heavy. Pretty please?"

I counted slowly to three. If she added, "With a cherry on top," I would let my right fist have its way with her. My left-wing middle-class conscience could go straight to Hell. One day it would meet up with Lita Wordstone and they could have a laugh over old memories and kid themselves that these had been "good times."

Thankfully, she didn't utter the fateful phrase.

"It won't take long," she said. "I promise. Come on."

I did as I was told. It was just too much work to argue with her.

*The Farce News*

## Chapter 30

I took the crystal candy bowl from Lita Wordstone. It was surprisingly heavy. She gazed at it, cradled in my arms, with a look of trepidation. Perhaps she'd have been happier had I taken the bowling pin and left her to contend with the safekeeping of her precious candy bowl -- and its cherished contents.

"Lead the way," I said.

Putting aside her concerns, she did as I suggested. I followed her back through the house, down a long hallway away from the front door, opposite the long hallway down which Rosa had earlier escaped the demands of her domestic duties We turned left, we turned right, we turned left again, and eventually arrived at a kitchen about the size of my apartment -- if you tripled the size of my apartment. I took the opportunity to unload the crystal bowl, depositing it on one of the many marble-topped counters. Lita frowned at me. I sighed and picked up the bowl again. She smiled giddily and we continued on our journey. Across the large kitchen, we skirted islands with butcher block tops and came to a door on which there hung a large monthly calendar with a Hartford Habitat for the Humanities logo.

"This way," she said, twisting the doorknob.

She pulled the door open and a swoosh of frigid air slammed us. Every basement in my life seemed to be cold and dank. I peered down into the darkness. The staircase was long and wide, and plushly carpeted. And it seemed to go on forever. Lita flipped a light switch at the top of the stairs and we started down.

And then the smell hit me. A truly vile aroma. Strawberry mixed with vanilla, mixed with pine, mixed with lemon and a heavy dose of roadkill. Musk mixed with month-old trash. Somebody had gone absolutely hog wild with the air freshener, a fact which struck me as weird on several levels. One would think a family with these means would address the issue of mildew and other basement-related stench with a more rudimentary focus on cause and effect. One would think they'd make a greater effort to get at the root of the problem instead of simply trying to drown out the effect with an ocean of chemically scented backwash. And one would be wrong.

There were more light switches as we went, and Lita flipped each one as we came to it. Each time, as more lights came on, each new set seemed brighter than one before it. We reached the bottom of the stairs and the room opened out before us. By comparison to the rest of the house, it had a fairly low ceiling, but I still couldn't reach up and touch the finished plaster without standing on a fairly tall chair. Inset panels of fluorescent ceiling light were everywhere. The room was a large and long, as if a tunnel had been specially excavated to accommodate the long bowling alley that comprised the central focus of the space.

I wanted to be a polite guest, but eventually I'd have to say *something* about the nauseating odor. Pretending not to notice was an insult to our collective intelligence, to say nothing of our olfactory systems. I decided not to wait. These people were family after all. Surely they could stand a little constructive criticism from one of the clan. (Right.)

"That's an interesting scent you've chosen," I said.

"I'm not wearing perfume," Lita said.

And I hoped (again) to learn that I'd actually been adopted.

"The air freshener," I said.

"Oh."

"What do you call it, *Au de Dumpster Juice?* Or maybe *Essence of Low Tide on Garbage Bay?*"

She stared at me as if were nuts. Maybe she didn't smell it. Maybe she knew something I didn't.

I shrugged and looked the place over. Someone had gone to extraordinary expense to recreate what appeared to be a perfect facsimile of a commercial bowling alley, complete with a shoe rental counter and its rack of about fifty pairs of red and yellow bowling shoes in cubby holes. A full wet bar was arranged against one wall, with a wide array of liquor bottles situated before a large oval mirror. None of the bottles appeared to have been opened. Three draft beer handles bore seals of a domestic light beer, an English pub standard and a dark Irish stout. I had no doubt they were fully charged and ready to be pulled. But I wondered if anyone ever did. Against another wall there stood a large red *Coca-Cola* machine that seemed to be humming. I wondered what it was so happy about. Perhaps its own lack of an olfactory system. I tried to breathe through my mouth, but it only made me want to spit.

An enormous jukebox with a gigantic glass dome squatted against another wall. It looked to be stocked with about a thousand miniature records, forty-fives from a bygone era. Beside it stood a row of three arcade-style pinball machines. In the corner was one of those racing car games you sit in, with a steering wheel, foot pedals and a large video screen displaying road and track courses from Formula-1 and the Indy series.

While I was at it, I decided to ask another stupid question. "Does it have to be this cold?" My fingertips were beginning to grow numb.

She ignored me some more. Maybe she didn't feel it. Soon I wouldn't either. What was it with these Wordstone woman and cold climates? I'll bet their heating bill was lower than mine.

In addition to the bright fluorescent lights overhead, neon lights glowed everywhere. Red and blue and orange and green.

The bowling alley itself featured a standard scoring table with a plastic molded chair on a swiveling post and a pair of thickly padded wraparound benches for the players. The ball-return chute fed a circular rack large enough for a dozen balls. Behind the benches stood a rack of bowling balls, four shelves high, with two dozen balls in total.

"Would you like to hear some music?" Lita Wordstone asked.

I walked over to the mock shoe rental counter and put the crystal candy bowl down. It was a relief to unburden myself. "No, thanks."

"How about a soda?" she said, pointing to the Coke machine. "It takes quarters."

"I'm fresh out of change," I said with a shrug.

"I could lend you the fifty cents."

"That's okay, Lita."

"I know how to get 'em out for nothing."

"I'm not thirsty."

"I know. I'm just saying ..."

"Right."

"So, you wanna play a frame or two?"

I have to admit I was impressed with the setup, but I wasn't that impressed. I was never going to be that impressed. "Another time," I said. Like when I die and I'm reincarnated as a schmuck with no apparent life ... oh, hang on a minute. Been there. Doing that.

"Miggie and I used to come down here all the time."

"That's nice," I said. I couldn't imagine it.

"Sometimes we even bowled, you know, *au natural.*"

"Volleyball *and* bowling," I said. "Interesting."

"Come on. It's easy. Watch."

I wondered if she was about to disrobe.

She ran over to the scoring table and sat in the plastic chair. She pressed one of the several buttons on the electronics panel. A cranking, clanging noise began at the far end of the alley. The automatic pinsetter descended, in preparation no doubt for placing a fresh set of pins in their triangular formation. Predictably, ten new pins appeared and were placed neatly on their spots. Then the pinsetter ascended and disappeared from view. Lita got up and selected a ball from the rack. It was pink with shiny silver and gold sparkles. She kicked off her sneakers and prepared to throw the ball. She kept her jeans and sweatshirt on. Holding the heavy orb in front of her face she appeared to be studying the pin placement. Why, I couldn't say. It wasn't as if they were ever, in a million years, going to be arranged any differently than they were right now. Lita took a deep breath, swung her right arm back, and began her approach.

And in the flash of an eye, as I stood and watched, the grace and youthful athleticism left her body like a vegan ditching the company pig roast.

She approached the foul line awkwardly, like a person whose legs are of different lengths. Her hips swung unevenly. I wondered if the ball was way too heavy for her, or if, in the final analysis, she was just a dork. She'd been pretty good at gymnastics, but this was almost too sad to be funny. She reached the foul line, slid way over it in her socks, and released the ball. It left her hand on a forty-five degree angle to the alley, slammed into the polished wood, bounced twice and ricocheted into the gutter.

"Oh, poo!" she said. We watched the ball wobble slightly, then run to the end of the alley and disappear. "So close!"

She walked back to the ball return chute, smirking shyly.

I remained anchored to the shoe rental counter. No way in hell was I was going to be dragged into this freak show.

"Um, nice try?" I said.

"Yeah," she said, as if she thought I meant it. "I'm really showing improvement. Throw me a Tootsie Roll, would you?"

I looked in the candy bowl and poked around with a half-frozen finger. But didn't see any Tootsie Rolls. "Sorry."

She shrugged and turned her back on me. She stood with her left hand on her hip, her right hand extended over a small fan that blew cool air on her fingers. In case it wasn't already cold enough. I tried to stop imagining her bowling naked. Without much success, I'm afraid. I wondered, too, what Jolie thought of bowling, regardless of the attire involved. Or what Jolie would think of me if she knew I was working up a vision of Lita bowling in the nude. She'd say, "Grow up." That's what she'd say, and she'd be right. Not that it would do much good to say it. I'm very likely hopeless in that regard.

The pinsetter raised all ten pins as the mechanical arm swept away the nothingness which so fittingly represented Lita's nonexistent bowling prowess. The ball rumbled down the chute. Lita grabbed it and adjusted her grip. Then she repeated, with frightening exactness, the clumsy approach and release of her first ball. Only this time the ball went directly from her fingertips

*The Farce News*

to the gutter with just once bounce before it rolled pathetically the length of the lane, leaving the undisturbed bowling pins standing in perfect parade format, no doubt laughing at her under their collective breath.

"Oh!" she said. "So close!"

"Oh, well." I said. "Better luck next time. Listen, this has been fun, but I should be going."

"Aren't you going to try?"

"Um, no." I said.

And then I notice something odd.

At the far end of the alley, the pinsetter's arm had come down again to sweep away the ten untouched pins. In a mechanically perfect world the pins would be automatically collected, recycled to the setter and replaced in their original spots for the next bowler. But there was a problem. I could still see the pins. They had been swept back, but not swept away. They were still laying in plain sight. And now the pinsetter was going up and down, empty, straining against some unseen obstruction, like a psychotic garage door trying to crush a tricycle, only to be stymied by a fully-functional anti-catastrophe sensor.

Lita Wordstone noticed it, too. Or, rather, she noticed me noticing it. But she was apparently bent on pretending to ignore it, just as she ignored everything she didn't like.

"Stupid machine," she said and went over to the scorer's table where she started punching buttons. One of them must have been the OFF switch, because the pinsetter suddenly stopped in midair, still empty. The grinding noise ceased, the pins remained in sight. "Well, thanks for coming," she said. "Sorry you didn't like the present."

"Hang on," I said. "Don't turn off the lights just yet."

"You said you don't want to bowl. You don't want a soda. You don't want my candy ..."

"I'd like to have a look down there."

"There's nothing there. Trust me."

"Fine, I'll just ..."

"There's nothing there! Trust me!"

"I trust you," I said. Call me a liar, I can take it.

"So stay away!"

"Take it easy, Lita."

"You have to go now. You're trespassing."

"You invited me, Lita. I'll just be a second."

"I didn't do anything!" she yelled, then suddenly collapsed onto one of the padded benches, sobbing uncontrollably. Big close-up. Organ swell. Fade to black. Cue the detergent commercial.

I ignored her -- hell, it was my turn anyway -- and strode the length of the bowling alley, my boots leaving black scuff marks on the finely polished hardwood floorboards. The closer I got to the end of the alley, the less I wanted to arrive. I had all kinds of bad feelings about this scenario, part of which was fueled by it taking place here at the Wordstone asylum where the patients had the run of the place, and the sane, if they wished to remain so, would be well-advised to run from the place just as fast as their feet would take them. Among the present population of the house, I alone fit the mental health criteria for sanity. So why didn't I run? Not smart enough, I guess.

In order to fit myself under the overhanging pinsetter, I had to get down on my hands and knees. It crossed my mind that Lita could easily punch the button to start this thing up again and I'd be stuck in here like a caged animal. Or crushed like a mislaid tricycle. I hoped she wasn't that far gone.

I crawled under the pinsetter and back a couple feet to where the ten bowling pins lay in a small pile. One at a time, I pushed them aside. I'd only moved four or five when I saw the hand. It was black. Not black as in African. Not black as in the color of the tuxedo I don't own or the ebony keys on the piano at Venus Edwards' rehearsal hall in Simsbury. Black as in decomposed, rotten.

Black as in Blackie Buenavista.

As quickly as my hands and knees would take me, I crawled out backwards, all ass and wiggles for anyone watching from outside, still breathing through my mouth, panting like a dog. Trying not to retch.

It was deathly quiet in the basement bowling alley. Lita had quit her sobbing, if she'd ever really started. I sat on my ass, my forearms resting on my knees, trying to catch my breath without gagging, trying to think it through without losing my hold on reality. Last thing I wanted was to go back under there to make a positive identification of the body attached to the black hand. I had a good idea about knew who it was. Far as I was concerned, the cops on the forensic squad could do the dirty work of hauling out and processing the corpse. That's what they got paid the big bucks for, wasn't it? Yeah, sure.

"Oh, Rob," a voice said. It was a small, girlish voice. Like a really bad impression of Laura Petrie whining at her beleaguered clown of a husband.

I turned. Lita was standing over me. She had a lollypop in her mouth and the dented bowling pin in her hand.

"What is it?" I asked. I didn't believe for a minute that she'd take a swing at me.

"Are you terribly, terribly mad at me?"

I ignored the question. "You know who's back there, don't you?"

She looked past me in the direction of the pinsetter. She put the lollypop in her mouth, then took it out again. "He was a bad man."

I climbed to my feet and took Lita Wordstone by the elbow. "Come on," I said and led her back to the padded bench. "Sit." She didn't fuss or resist. In fact, I thought she'd made a fairly remarkable recovery. I'm sure the lollypop was partly to thank. Or to blame. Unless the whole thing was an act. What were the chances?

"Want to tell me about it?" I said.

She looked up at me, sucking her lollypop. "Tell you about what?"

"Tell me about how Blackie Buenavista ended up dead in a heap in the back of your bowling alley."

"I dunno?" she said, shrugging.

"Come on, Lita. The time for games is over."

"She doesn't have to say another word," said a another voice, coming from the direction of the staircase. I turned around. It was Lillian the Vaudevillian. Lillian the ex-wife. Lillian the widow. She was dressed in a sexy black dress, black stockings, black high heels, and a sheer black veil over her face, connected to a Jackie Kennedy pillbox hat done in black satin. Very elegant.

She approached us serenely.

If Lita noticed her sister's arrival, she made no sign of it. She had slipped into some sort of daze. Or she was putting it on. Playacting was always a possibility with this crowd. Or it could have been another sugar coma. Or a psychotic condition. I'm no doctor. Not even a veterinarian. Anyway, I was just as happy to have her quiet, if only for a couple of minutes.

This was my first experience dealing with both sisters in the same room. It was a daunting and intimidating challenge. I bolstered myself by imagining them both in their underwear. It helped a little, but was also very distracting. In Lita's case, it was a step in the right direction which actually required mentally putting clothes back *on* her.

I hadn't seen Lillian since her audition at the Simsbury Dinner Theater two days ago. It seemed like only yesterday. I guess time flies when you hope to God you'll never see someone again. "Lillian," I said. "We have to stop meeting like this. In fact, we have to stop meeting, period."

"My sister did nothing wrong," she said. "You understand?"

"Sure," I said, blandly. "I guess that pretty much wraps things up, then, doesn't it?"

She lifted the veil from her face. She wore black lipstick that gave her a punk rock bearing that was very nearly funny, but not quite. It ended up only making her look harrowed. "My sister is innocent."

*The Farce News*

"Yes, she certainly *seems* innocent. But I'm going to write it down so I don't forget it. Got a crayon? No? Oh, well. In the meantime, how about I just call the police so we can get a little professional help down here? What do you say, Lilly? Sound good to you?"

"Go ahead. I'm not afraid of the police. I've done nothing. I have nothing to hide. I'm a grieving widow. Don't you see my outfit?"

"I though the clothes defined the man, not the woman."

"It's a new era."

"Yes, of course. Post-apocalyptic, right? And where'd you say the phone was?"

She stared at me. There was no playfulness in her. The actress was out in the trailer fretting over her green tea -- was it hot enough, or too hot, and who she should blame? "Don't you want to know what happened?"

"Sure I do," I said. "Who shall I ask?"

"Ask me."

"I mean somebody I can actually believe."

She cocked one eyebrow slightly. "Believe *me*."

"Could I please have a second choice?"

"No."

"And that is because ..."

"Nobody but Miguel and my sister know what happened."

"And Miguel's dead, isn't he?"

"Tragically, yes."

"And Lita's in no condition to talk about it?"

"As you can see for yourself."

I glanced down at Lita. She was either catatonic or "doing" catatonic. My system of beliefs had been shattered. I no longer believed my ears or my eyes. I believed my nostrils, of course, but that only took me so far. I was ready for a new source of reliable information. Perhaps I could believe my adam's apple? Nah. My chin? Hmm.

Lita worked the lollypop like an autopilot flying a jumbo jet plane. She was there but her heart wasn't in it. She wasn't looking out the window and enjoying the view from thirty thousand feet. Poor kid. I hoped she was equipped with some kind of psychological parachute in case all the engines suddenly failed. Unless, of course, it was an act, in which case a crash landing would serve her right.

"Okay, let's have it," I said, turning back to Lillian, completely prepared to believe absolutely nothing. "Talk to the chin."

Lillian Buenavista took a breath. "My husband was a philanderer. Do you know what that is?"

"Yes." Did she think I'd mistake a philanderer for a philanthropist?

"It's a womanizer," she said.

"Somehow I knew you were going to tell me anyway."

"Not a person who gives generously to various charities."

"Maybe with a little plastic surgery, I wouldn't look so stupid, huh? You think?"

"Benny was a shallow hedonist who didn't care about anything or anybody but himself."

"You mean he *wasn't* a Nicaraguan freedom fighter? I'm shocked."

"A freedom fighter! My God! What a ridiculous lie! He was no hero. He was a dishwasher from Watertown. A hustler. A con man. A fast living, fast talking Casanova who wanted nothing more out of life than for cocktail hour to arrive on time every day and for women to lay down before him every night."

I thought about that. Sadly, Blackie Buenavista sounded pretty typical. "In other words, your basic garden variety rat bastard."

"Exactly. I divorced him because of his countless infidelities. But he wouldn't go away. He had wormed his way into Nana's good graces, and she insisted he continue his visits. Not all the time, mind you, but often enough."

"To do a little bowling?" I asked, hooking a thumb down at the far end of the lane where even now there lay the grifter's rotting remains.

"To do a little hunting," she said, a new hardness in her voice.

"Hunting?"

"He was after Nana's money, which is why he told her all those ridiculous stories about rebellions and guerilla warfare. It was a soap opera to keep Nana entertained. And a way to the money tree."

"And Auntie Peg was the sap."

"Exactly."

Blackie Buenavista sounded less unique by the minute. As well as less interesting and less likable.

"He was also stalking my little sister. He wanted her. He wanted her as a conquest. That was his style. His *modus operandi.* Not to love them and leave them, but to fuck them and dump them."

"Nice. Ever think of writing poetry? Or maybe Hallmark cards?"

"But Lita didn't get it. She's just a kid, really. Innocent, in her own way. My God, her generation doesn't even think a blow job counts as sex."

"Wait a minute," I said. "You're only three or four years older, right? What do you mean *her generation?*"

She stopped and thought it over. Then moved on without offering further explanation. "Benny wanted Lita. He wanted it all."

"So he kept coming around to work his inconsiderable charms."

"She was here, in this very room, waiting for Miguel. Benny was trying to get money from Nana. He came down, found Lita alone and tried to put the moves on her. He was smooth, but when she didn't play along he got rough with her. It isn't very complicated, Robby."

"It never is."

"Benny tried to force himself on her. And she fought him off."

"With a bowling pin?"

"No. She didn't do that."

"So says you. I've seen her swing a bowling pin."

"She didn't do anything like that."

"Okay, then who did?"

Lillian paused. Then, in a small voice: "It was Miguel."

I smiled at her, though I wasn't very amused by her story.

"That's awful damned convenient, isn't it? For you and your sister."

"I resent that."

"Sue me."

"Miguel came down and interrupted Benny's assault on Lita. Miguel pulled him off, and they fought. Benny was small and wiry, but tough and strong. And he was accustomed to fighting. He didn't mind at all. I think he rather enjoyed it. But Miguel was young and in love. It was a vicious encounter. Miguel eventually got the upper hand. Suddenly the bowling pin was within reach. It was the heat of the battle, Robby. You don't mind if I call you that, do you?"

"Go ahead," I said. "After all, we're related, right? Unless by some chance *you* were adopted."

"He didn't mean to do it, but he was so mad."

"And ..."

"He used the bowling pin to finish Benny off."

I counted to five. She had no more to say. "You've practiced this soliloquy, haven't you? Like a scene out of one of your melodramas."

Her eyes widened. "That's very unkind of you."

"Where'd you got the story? From Miguel and Lita?"

"Yes, why?"

"You didn't see it yourself."

"No. Why? Is that a problem?"

"Oh, no, Lillian. Not at all."

"Good."

"Except there's nobody to corroborate the facts."

"Meaning?"
"Everyone's either dead or certifiable."
"I resent that."
"You resent a lot of things."
"You're just mean."
"Sorry if I hurt your feelings."
"No you're not."
"Can we agree to disagree?"
She took a step toward me. "Can't you try to see things my way?"
"I don't think so. For starters, I'd have to spin around like a top for five minutes. And then I'd probably puke. Who'd clean it up? You? I don't think so. And besides, doesn't it smell bad enough already?"
"But why would I lie?"
"Seriously? I can think of about a thousand reasons. Want to hear a few? I guarantee you won't like them. Some of them even include you. Let's start with the possibility that you killed Benny yourself. Out of jealousy because he was getting it on with your little sister. That works, don't you think?"
She paused. "Robby, you're entirely too cynical."
"Go ahead," I said. "Call me Robby."
"There comes a time when you have to show some faith in your fellow human beings."
"And by your cosmic calendar, today is that day?"
"Wouldn't this would be as good a time as any to give it a try."
I thought about it for a minute. "You know something, Lillian?"
"What?" she said, hopefully.
"It's a good thing you're such a genuinely lousy actress."
"Really!" she said.
I believe she was sincerely offended.
"Makes it just a little easier to tell when you're actually being honest. If you could act worth a shit, I wouldn't know which of your stories to believe and which of them to reject on face value."
She relaxed, apparently willing to bear a scathing review of her artistry in exchange for a vote of confidence as regards her basic good nature.
"So you believe me?"
I shrugged. "It doesn't matter if I believe you or not."
"Oh, but it does."
"No, believe me. It *doesn't.*"
"I can sleep easier if I know you believe me."
"If you're having trouble sleeping, try pills. Or booze."
"You can be cruel when you want to be."

"I can also be cruel when I don't want to be. I won't argue the point. But, tell me something, Lillian. Just out of curiosity, why'd you cover this up? Why in the world did you keep the body down here? Why didn't you go to the police immediately?"

"Do you always ask so many questions?"

"Apparently."

"Look, it's really very simple. Lita was in love with Miguel. She didn't want to see him to go to jail. He had a checkered past, you know."

"And checks don't go with prison stripes?"

"As for myself, I simply hated Benny's guts."

"Enough to go through all this?"

"I didn't mind one little bit seeing him dead."

Her honesty was actually refreshing, albeit a little scary.

"Okay, but you don't mind him rotting in your basement?"

"I don't care one way or the other. I never bowl."

"Well, I hate to be the one to give you bad news," I said, "but you have to call the police. You can't leave that stinking corpse down here indefinitely. It must violate about a hundred civic health codes."

"What will I do if the police get involved? I don't want to go to jail."

"I doubt you will. I suggest you hire a couple of damn good lawyers ..."

I stopped short, choking on my words. Holy mother of God. I had actually done it. I had finally become the mirror image of my celebrity namesake, shamelessly hawking legal advice to people in a jam.

"What's the matter," Lillian asked.

"Nothing," I said, wondering where I could get a quick Listerine gargle. "Look, suck it up and make the call. Get an attorney. If the family has one on retainer, call him or her. Ask for a reference. You'll want a good criminal lawyer. Once you find one, call the cops. Tell them everything. Tell it straight. Don't leave anything out. Don't get cute. Your lawyer will help you weasel out of the squirelly parts. That's what they do. Then you can sit back and hope like hell the authorities buy your story. With your money and obvious charms, I think you stand a good chance of skating. Anyway, the only alternative is to go on living here with Blackie rotting in the basement. How long do you think you can do that? How long can you keep the secret, Lillian, before you end up crazy, paranoid, and totally alone. Don't let that happen. That's my best advice to you. It's your play. I'm just an impoverished pedal steel guitar player living paycheck to paycheck."

I damn near said *Johnny Paycheck to Johnny Paycheck*, but didn't. I was very proud of my restraint.

"Oh, Robby, you have such a wisdom about you."

"Stop it, Lillian. The house lights are up. Everybody's gone home. The show is over. It's just you and me and the dead guy."

She dropped her head and nodded. "Okay, you win."

Then I thought of something else. "How much does Venus Edwards know about all of this?"

Lillian Buenavista laughed a little. "Venus Edwards? Believe it or not, she actually thinks Benny ran off, as advertised."

"Obviously not with Hubert."

"No."

"Then with whom?"

"Oh, some bimbo or another. It was his nature, after all."

"I see."

"It would hardly be the first time."

"Present company excluded," I said.

"Venus isn't quite as bright as she likes everyone to believe. Benny made the moves on her, too, you know. Which goes to show he'd have fucked a pile of rocks if he thought there was a snake hiding in it. Pardon my French. The little shit. *Mierda pequena.* Pardon my Spanish. It was bound to catch up with him."

This was an opinion shared by Llewellyn "Canary" Carswell.

"So it seems."

Lillian suddenly looked very worried and I suspected we were about to relapse into Community Theater 101. "What will happen to Lita?"

"Lita? She's the one who brought me the dented bowling pin," I said. "I'm no shrink, but I'd guess she wants out from under this thing, whether she realizes it consciously or doesn't."

"Do you really, really think so?"

"No, Lillian, I'm just yankin' your chain." I shook my head at her. "Jesus Christ, will you knock off the theatrics for ten seconds?"

"Sorry," she said.

"Look, Lillian. Lita keeps insisting she didn't do anything. Maybe with a little help -- and a change of diet -- she can start believing it."

"And maybe a change of scenery, too. We could travel. See the world. I've always wanted to see the world. I just don't know where to start. I suppose at the airport?"

"After you deal with the law."

"Oh, yes, of course."

"If you don't mind me saying so, I think you should replace Rosa."

"Rosa? The housekeeper?"

"Unless you have somebody else named Rosa floating around?"

"No."

"I think she's carrying a bit of a grudge against your sister."

Lillian laughed again. This time bitterly. "She thought Miguel was in it for the money. Or at least she hoped he was."

"Well, there's your out. Pay her off. Send her packing with a wad of cash. Let her get on with her life. You can afford it. There's no good reason to keep her on. For you or for her."

"Nana loves her."

"Bullshit. Your grandmother thinks Rosa is an idiot."

Lillian looked beaten. The starch was gone. "I'm so tired. It hasn't been easy, you know."

I didn't know anything about how easy it had been, but I *did* share a general feeling of fatigue. Mostly I was tired of this family, tired of wishing I wasn't related to them. And now Lillian the Vaudevillian was initiating a conversation that didn't appeal to me on any level. If she wanted to feel sorry for herself, she could do it on her time, not mine. If she wanted my approval, she'd have to wait in a very long line with everybody else. If she wanted absolution, she could see a priest.

"We did the best we could, you know."

She was persistent. I had to hand it to her.

"People solve problems in various ways," I said. "Sometimes the methods are even intelligent and creative. Most of the time, the quick fix gets the nod and people behave selfishly, destructively, with little or no regard for long term consequences or the effects of their actions on those around them. Or am I just a bitter, sanctimonious prick?"

"I'd rather not answer," Lillian said.

"Fair enough."

"I'm just not sure."

"You accused me of being too cynical. I think I'm just cynical enough. It's the world at large that dictates my level of cynicism."

"Well, at least nobody got hurt," she said with a dramatic sigh. She was either doing a very weak Edith Bunker impression, or was insane.

"Except for, well, just about everyone," I said.

"I'm so terribly sorry you had to get involved," she said.

"Yes, well, me, too."

In the midst of this going-nowhere conversation, Lita snapped out of her trance and looked up at us. Her hands were out, palms up. In each hand she held a single red M&M. I don't know if she was offering them to us or showing us they were all she had left.

I bade farewell to Lillian and Lita, the twisted sisters and climbed out of the freezing chamber, back to natural daylight. I didn't even smell the stench of the basement anymore, and I only noticed the fact when I reentered the kitchen and inhaled the comparatively lovely smell of lemon-scented floor wax. I wound my way through the house, down several long hallways. On my way to the main foyer, I stopped in to say so long to Elvis and Mona Lisa. He thanked me very much for all my trouble. She just smirked. I let myself out the front door and out into the fresh fall air. I never did see Rosa again.

The sound of my footfalls on the gravel driveway was the music of a sledgehammer shattering the locks on a set of metaphorical leg irons. With every step that drew me closer to my piece of shit Jetta, I felt the weight of the Wordstones and their misery falling away from me. I was checking out of the Hotel California. It *could* be done.

It occurred to me, not for the first time nor probably the last, that you can't pick your family. Like it or not, your family picks you. That's the team you play for, win or lose.

It was a beautiful autumn day and I had a gig in a few hours. Two nights of debauchery with Artie and the boys. I couldn't wait to get a little high and pick a few tunes. Trade a few licks and crack a few jokes. Make fun of a few drunks and sing some harmonies. Forget what it was to work for a living. Feel like a twenty-year-old kid again. If only for a couple of nights.

But first I had to get back to Summit Street, to face my showdown with my beautiful, sweet-smelling neighbor, Jolie, and fight for the custody of Rufus, J.D., and Buddy. And negotiate the annexation of my heart.

Ah, Jolie. What manner of trouble lurked in my future? What was it going to take to get her into these arms where, as the song so nicely put it, she belonged?

I climbed into my piece of shit Jetta, rolled down the window, took a deep breath and twisted the ignition key.

Of course, it wouldn't start.

ISBN 141207975-6